WHEN MAN HAS FALLEN

BOOK ONE: *RENEGADE*

A NOVEL

BY

PRESTON K. BULLARD

Bullard

Bullard

This series is dedicated to Crystal Barr and Hunter Bullard – My two personal saviors, who brought me back from the edge of a life not worth living. You two are my world, and while I know I haven't shown it much – Here's to hoping this will rectify that.

This book is dedicated to everyone who had the audacity to tell me that I couldn't follow my dreams. Thank you kindly for the extra boost of determination.

CHAPTER 1 – REMEMBRANCE

JAN. 7, 2014

Silas stared deep into the well, down, down into the darkness, reminiscing about the past few years. How it all went to hell.

He pulled slowly on the rope, attempting to keep quiet. Leaning a little, he tilted his head back, looking up at the night sky, choking slightly on the dust-filled air. He stared at the glistening stars and all their coldness as they sparkled and shone in the cold crystalline atmosphere, taunting him and his sorrows. He cursed them in return, silently asking them why they had brought this down upon humanity.

He had admired their frail light as a young child, reaching for them, wondering what it was like out there amongst the twinkling lights. But even now, as he begrudgingly admitted their beauty to himself, he remembered the night that the stars and their unmerciful cold had come to them.

It was the year two thousand and twelve, and everyone had been living in fear, waiting for that fateful day in December when the world was going to end. Silas had scoffed at the idea – then. In a way, he still justified himself, thinking everyone and all their theories were just a bunch of bullshit.

Because they had been. All that stupidity about a solar flare, comet strikes, global warming, it was all pointless conjecture. On those grounds, it turned out that nobody had anything to worry about for December twenty first two thousand and twelve. Nobody had come close to predicting what occurred that fateful day. He sighed, thinking to himself.

<How could they? They attacked our military bases within the first ten hours. Our world seats of power were the first to go. They knew us. They were ready. We were, we are, nothing compared to them. All our might, our coveted power, destroyed in less than two weeks, reduced to nothing. We were dead from the start.>

Bullard

A small voice flashed through his mind in response to his thought.

<We had over four thousand years of study on you. What do you expect? We knew your society inside and out. Even if we hadn't had advance scouts, you broadcast the very fabric of your society into space where anyone can pick it up.>

A twig snapped off to his left and he froze, his train of thought vanishing. He turned his head ever so slightly, keeping movement to a minimum, glaring out his peripheral vision the best he could. There was one off about fifty paces. From the angle where he stood, Silas was unable to determine what subspecies it was. From its size and posture, he was assuming it was a *Snapper*.

Hunched over, fingertips grazing the frosty pavement, its gray skin glistened in the moonlight. It stiffened suddenly, sniffing, drooling, its many eyes glowing soft yellow in the dark. Silas' eyes widened in anticipation of being seen, but it was for naught; he was too well hidden in the dark and the wind was in front of him.

He tried to reach out through the Hive Mind and touch it, sense what it was, what it was doing here. Nothing. He couldn't sense it from this distance; it had been cut off from the main Hive Mind. He raised an eyebrow. Another *Renegade?* They were becoming more and more frequent lately. He sniffed, catching a scent: the bitterly pungent aroma of the *Viral* mixed with that of clay and bark. This beast had been on its own for some time. It was indeed a Renegade.

It turned, looking his way, breathing heavily. His guess at the subspecies had been correct. It was a *Snapper*. Standing at just over eight feet tall, it was a grotesque evolution of a human being, taken by *Infection*. Five yellow and purple eyes sat in two rows across the upper half of the face, wrapping around the head, which was nearly split in half by a tooth filled maw, giving the creature its namesake. It was naked but for a few denim rags covering its lower extremities, muscles bulged against the skin in a manner which any champion body builder would be proud to have.

Silas kept quiet, not moving, resisting an urge to rush out and kill it with his bare hands. As his fingers flexed, the voice echoed in his head once more.

<The enemy of my enemy is my friend, Silas. You'd do well to remember that. It may one day serve you kindly. You may be wont to disagree, but we're not all monsters.>

Gritting his teeth, Silas acknowledged the statement as he turned his attention back to the well.

Continuing to slowly pull on the rope, his thoughts turning again, back to that fateful week; the last week of mankind's rule over Earth.

DEC. 15, 2012

Silas strolled down the Miami street, avoiding passerby, his hair blowing slightly in the cool breeze, Silent Asylum blasting in his ears from his Selenidi Infinity. He stopped in front of a store featuring the newest Selenidi Entertainment Surround Sound Laser Systems, nicknamed SEXSELLS. He had to hand it to the big corporations. At least they didn't get caught up in all the end of the world shit; they kept right on churning out their products. It was all just another Y2K in Silas' opinion. He'd told people they were morons then, too, at the age of seven.

Glancing downward, he whistled at the price tag. On second thought, maybe they did. The price was set 150 Ameros, which was a bit outside his price range and more than just a little outrageous. He only had 6 Euros in his pocket. If nothing else, they were certainly trying get a profit out of all this. He chuckled.

<But who buys stuff at the end of the world?> he asked himself. A moment passed before he answered his own question, looking down at his new Selenidi and chuckling. <People like me, of course.>

Looking around the display, a man on television caught his eye. It seemed to be another raving idiot at some pulpit or another. Everyone had seen plenty of those recently. The military telling people to remain calm or else they would have to enforce martial law within the week. Religious pastors calling people to congregation, calling them to repentance.

Silas himself was mildly religious, but he still didn't buy into the Mayan calendar crap, and found it kind of insulting that many people belonging to any self proclaimed 'Christian' religions would worry about something from a people whose highest god ate his denizens. Let the Scientologists believe what they will, Christians subscribed to one God, god damnit.

Leaning into the glass, he took a closer look at the television. It actually seemed to be something from NASA rather than a religious leader. Still, just some raving idiot at a pulpit. Silas caught the words; "Coming our way," and "Within the week."

<Yeah, yeah, whatever,> Silas thought to himself.

He walked away from the glass-paned store front, avoiding a beggar coming out of the alley, eyes squinted, hands outstretched. Disgusting filth; why should Silas do anything for them? He hoped he would never end up like that.

He strolled on, head moving in time to the music, singing softly under his breath.

> **The end is nigh,**
> **We don't matter**
> **But we'll try and we'll try,**
> **To soothe the mad hatter.**

Silent Asylum – Finding Alice - 2012

JAN. 7, 2014

Silas pulled the bucket from the well, icy water spilling slightly onto his hands. He untied the rope from it and set it down carefully, a few feet from six similar buckets. After picking up a curious looking notched stick that was leaning up against the well, he stood between the buckets, sliding the stick underneath the bucket handles, which fit neatly into the small, hacked grooves along its length.

Heaving silently in the dark, Silas lifted the stick above his head and lowered it gently down onto his shoulders. It was lighter than usual, which was bad, as it meant the well was running dry, but it was also a bit of a relief for Silas.

The trek home was far from easy. Not only did he have to navigate the treacherously icy footing and pitfalls that led down into the old sewer system, but he also had to avoid the nocturnal creatures which mankind had come to fear and loathe. He was less worried about the first than he was the second.

As one of the group's most seasoned members, he had been chosen as a gatherer; one who kept the people provided for. There were other reasons besides, but those were known only to a very select few. If anyone else were to find out, a riot was sure to be started and Silas murdered, along with the heads of the town.

He trudged slowly through the thin, dirty layer of snow, wending his way back to the fort. His heightened senses lay the moonlit landscape bare before him and he hopped easily from rock to rock, traveling along the worn path he knew by heart.

As he approached the towering walls of the fort, his mind again turned back to the day it all began, as it often did.

DEC 21, 2012 11:32 a.m.

Silas awoke with a grin firmly upon his face, glancing over at the clock. It was nearly noon. His grin widened. Nearly twelve hours into the end of the world and the world was still here. Let the "I told you so's" begin.

He bounded down his dorm stairs after breakfast, proclaiming, "OH, SAVE ME, GOD, FOR THE END IS HERE!"

Several people that were huddled in the corner of the room crossed themselves in fear and several others who shared Silas' mindset snickered at the action.

Silas went over to the latter group and exchanged high fives, winking at the women, playing up his arrogance in the matter. He chatted for a few moments before getting up and wandering outside.

It was a beautiful day out with blue skies and few clouds. The temperature was around 70 degrees, with low humidity for the day. A perfect day in Miami. Certainly not a day for fear and panic. He sighed contentedly.

He'd been standing there for some time admiring the view when his best friend Luke, who was currently stressing out over the date, came up behind him, tapping him on the shoulder.

"Uh – hey man, you might wanna come and check out the television..."

Silas waved his hand in dismissal.

"What interest could a T.V. possibly hold for me on a day like this? I'm gonna go hit the surf, man. Sure, I'll probably freeze my balls off, but with surf like that –" He pointed, trailing off, admiring the view.

Luke pleaded with him, ignoring his comment. His voice was shaky and distraught. "Dude, seriously, come look. Please."

Silas sighed. "Fine..."

He turned, finally looking at Luke, who was pale and trembling, beads of sweat popping out all over his face.

"Luke, dude, chillax. You look like shit, man."

Luke looked Silas in the eyes and said very calmly: "Silas, we are all going to die."

The words sent a silent chill through Silas' soul, even as he scoffed and patted his friend on the back. It was a chill that never quite left him; one that had reverberated through his core as he leaned over Lucas later that evening, their faces twisted in agony and ever onward into the years.

JAN. 7, 2014

As he approached the massive concrete and log walls of the fort, Silas touched the small short range transmitter in his ear, activating his com-link with the guards.

"Alpha. Piotus. Caesar. Lycan. Pi."

He really didn't see the point of the pass-code, as an *Infected* would still know the words, being able to look through its host's memories. It was foolish, but he supposed that it helped the people sleep easier at night, somehow.

For not wanting to die, a lot of the people overlooked things that could prove deadly to them, or implemented safety measures that didn't do anything to keep them safe at all.

The gate slowly came down in front of him, crossing the moat. The gate itself was composed of old billboards, welded together and covered in massive amounts of duct tape. A weak point for a gate in the midst of nigh impenetrable walls. Silas huffed, thinking to himself.

<How far we have fallen – And how stupid we have become.>

He crossed the gate quickly, passing through the green energy field just inside the city wall. A tingle washed over him and stung at the base of his skull, causing him to scowl in discomfort. Glancing at a nearby guard, he gave a nod. The guard nodded back and then turned to the wall and switched off the alarm that was getting ready to sound. Its automatic function had been disabled specifically for Silas and had instead been given a five second kill switch.

Turning his eyes back to look ahead, Silas felt sorry for the man standing there, who was probably going against everything in his moral code by hitting that switch.

Bullard

It was probably more in the man's moral fiber to whip out his pistol and put a few bullets in Silas' skull.

Still, Silas couldn't blame the man. The people had been exposed to such horrors committed by The Viral, or *Mayans,* as they were sometimes called, that they were not willing to ever witness them again while it was in their power. Letting one of those creatures into the city was punishable by death, even if done by mistake. Especially those still in the *Zombie* stage.

He laughed silently to himself. It was punishable by death for everyone else, at least. He was rather hard to kill. He doubted even a few bullets to the skull would kill him. He wasn't in a rush to try it out any time soon though, so he usually just did as he was told.

He reflected on the term *Zombie.* Growing up, *Zombie* had been a reference to a fictional, slow moving, dead creature that could only be killed if its nervous system were destroyed. Today's fell creatures were far worse; and while easier to physically kill, they also were, in the same sense, far harder to kill.

In the movies, zombies were pale and rotting heaps of flesh, easy to look at as dead, inconsequential, even if a threat. Easy to laugh at, you were gleeful when the main character made a kill. The living demons of this world were not.

For a time, a few hours at least, they were your friends. Your family. They could talk to you. Appeal to you. Bring up old memories of being together, only to kill you as soon as you let your guard down – or worse, make you one of them. Only the merciless in this world could survive. The only reason the early stages were referred to as *Zombie* was their secondary transmission of the *Mayan Infection* – Biting. Once someone was bitten, once they were infected, they were done for. They could fight it for a day or two, but soon the call of *The Hive* would drive them insane and they would do what it wanted them to do. Follow it to their doom. To the *Drillers.* To *Infection,* for which the only cure was death. If you were not given over to the *Drillers* immediately and then you became a true Zombie, a mindless slave, doing only the bidding of the Hive Mind. A *Drone;* half-human, half-alien, despised by both.

Silas himself had killed his mother and younger sister with tears in his eyes; one with a bullet to the heart, the other; the throat. Most any other method, except for a bullet to the head, and they healed too quickly, sometimes within minutes. Too far along, the hosts developed a second heart. Some people speculated even a third, considering the size to which some of the creatures grew. In such cases, shooting them in the heart wasn't much of a safe bet at all.

Frequently, it usually rang true to be better safe than sorry, but Silas just hadn't been able to bring himself to shoot his family members in the face.

He closed his eyes momentarily, remembering the incident; and a single tear leaked out from the corner of one of them, trailing down his face. "Alicia," he whispered. "I hope you've forgiven me…"

The voice entered his head once more. It just wouldn't shut up lately. It had been dormant for about two months after their last power struggle, sulking, but now it seemed determined to make friends. Silas found it irritating to no end. He had absolutely no interest in being friends with the blasted thing. They'd made their agreements; there needed to be no further discussion between them.

<If it counts for anything – though I do not understand the love for family – I see how painful it is for you in your mind. And I am sorry for your loss, Silas.>

He ignored it, focusing on his own thoughts.

He'd heard speculations of late, from scientists speaking of being able to possibly surgically remove the alien parasite from the brain of the host, if they could capture the infected person in time. It was a well known fact that the parasite did not kill off the host, rather suppressing them inside their own mind, taking control of motor functions and major thought processes, rendering them helpless.

They had proven this very early on with brain monitoring technology in newly infected individuals. *Infected* persons had two very distinct brain waves. The creatures referred to as *Zombies* had an entirely different brain wave sequence than either of the other two. Their brain essentially turned to gook. There was no intelligence there. Only madness and loyalty to the Hive.

Silas had no hope for this procedure. and had said as such, telling them that removing the parasite from the brain almost always kills the host. He knew all too intimately the details of such a death.

Crouching down, he relinquished the buckets and then straightened up with a slight stretch and walked toward the sleep shelter, feeling sorry for himself for a moment.

These people treated him like dirt, even though they regarded him as immensely dangerous.

The only authority he had was as a battle commander: all soldiers had to obey him without question, unless directed otherwise by the town council. He had no respect beyond that, and he had been made out by the council to be a pariah in the town, with them saying that he was psychotic and dangerous and that his only merit was battle command.

They also told the people that this was also the reason he was sent out daily on supply forages, that he was able to keep himself safe and that he was a danger to the town. In truth, the people who knew what he was just didn't want him in town and could care less if he was dangerous to the people or not.

They made him sleep with the homeless when he needed shelter, and dine at the soup kitchen on the remains of the dead when he was hungry. Humans had long since turned to cannibalism as a way to fight decreasing food stores. They served the flesh of the deceased to the people who could not afford their own food.

Silas was given nothing but a wide berth. All Silas owned was in a single backpack buried in a small hole he had dug under the inner wall that lined the city.

He sighed, thinking to himself. *<But what else can I do? Go over to the other side?>*

His eternal companion answered his unspoken question, with an odd note of sympathy in its voice.

<Sadly, Silas, I do not think that is an option; they would kill you. You would be loose cannon, and the Judges do not tolerate such individuals. Hence the Renegades. They have to cut themselves off from the Hive so as to be individuals at all. To have their own thoughts and secrets.>

Silas hung his head as he replied. *<Yeah. I know man. I know.>*

DECEMBER 21, 2012, 11:54 a.m.

Silas hurriedly followed Luke inside, where a group had gathered around the dorm television. It appeared to be a news station. The image behind the anchorman appeared to be some sort of massive floating object, floating over the ocean. Instinctively, Silas threw a glance out the window at the water. Nothing.

He looked back and it had gone to a new scene, with a reporter broadcasting from a city in fully-fledged panic.

"NEWS! At Noon on FOX."

"Hello, this is Nathan Croswell reporting from Tampa Bay, Florida! As you can see, there is widespread panic through the city oof! Sorry Chuck, people are everywhere! Just got a little side swiped! But as you see here, there seems to be some sort of stationary object floating over the water, about a mile or so offshore! It has been here about 45 minutes and we have seen absolutely no activity from the object since its sudden appearance!"

"Any idea what it is, Nathan?"

"No idea, Chuck." The reporter pointed, squinting. <If you look closely, this thing seems really to be a giant rock! It's irregular in shape, dark and mottled looking; full of craters really. Wasn't NASA saying something about space anomalies earlier this week, Chuck?"

"Why, yes, I think so, Nathan, but I can't quite remember the particulars – well, folks, this is simply astounding! You say it's just floating there, Nathan?"

"Well, that's the way it appears Chuck – just a giant floating rock."

"Hold on Nathan. We've –"

"Ok."

"We've just received report of one over Miami! And another! D.C.! Phoenix! Niagara! Salt Lake City! Minsk! We have one over Poland, Hollywood, Melbourne – oh my God, they're coming in too fast for me to name! What the hell is going on here?"

"I don't mean to cast a bad light on this, but considering the day, this seems a bit coincidental; don't you think?"

The reporter stood, peering at the small screen provided him.

"Somewhat, yes – did it just move?"

The reporter on scene turned around and stared for a moment as the rock trembled in mid air.

"I think so, Chuck!"

And with those weak words signaling the end of mankind, the rocks fell from the sky and the world would never be the same.

JAN. 8 2014

Silas awoke, bleary eyed. He stood up shakily, dusting off his old and worn clothing, trying to at least look like he somewhat cared about his appearance. He stretched his arms, reaching for the ceiling and then retched at the smell emanating from his underarms. Deodorant had disappeared probably six months or so ago. It was something nobody ever really got used to. He desperately needed a shower.

<Or you could just change. You know that it does the same thing. And it's so much more enjoyable, don't you think?>

The thought entering his mind was tempting, but something he knew he couldn't succumb to. The damn thing must be lonely. Silas gave in and replied to it.

<Only when I need too. We've gone over this.>

Warmth emanated through him at his words and he momentarily felt like a jerk.

Shaking the feeling off, he stumbled to the washbasin, careful to avoid others sleeping in their bags and cots. Splashing water carefully on his face, he attempted to wash away some of the bleariness and dirt, to no avail. Maybe he would have to go for a run and transformation. Do some hunting. He was sick of eating fried finger fingers, as they not-so-humorously called them down at the soup kitchen.

He turned and picked his way through the room to the door, walked down the hall and then proceeded to fall down the stairs. He picked himself up at the bottom, cursing and wincing. The guards at the doorway rushed in and several people ran out of the sleeping room in a panic, weapons raised, faces alarmed; then, realizing what had occurred, they began to laugh uproariously at him.

"Yeah, go fuck yourselves," he muttered and then stomped out the door, pushing between them, which only made them all laugh harder.

Really, he couldn't be angry at them for laughing. He was glad he could make them do so. There just wasn't much around for humor these days.

Suddenly, red lights flashed and an ear splitting screech sounded throughout the city.

"ATTACK. WE'RE UNDER ATTACK. WE HAVE MULTIPLE MOVEMENTS COMING FROM OUTSIDE THE GATE. ALL SOLDIERS, READY YOUR WEAPONS, ALL CIVILIANS ARM YOURSELVES AND STAY INDOORS."

Pandemonium erupted all around the fort as Silas flung himself in the direction of the gate.

Bullard

A man ran past yelling, eyes crazed. "THEY'RE HERE!"

Silas' eyes flashed with a glimmer of gold and he grinned with pointed teeth.

<Finally.>

CHAPTER 2 – BURN

DEC 21 2012, 12:45 p.m.

Silas stumbled through campus in shock. He vaguely recognized shops and some faces as they flowed past him, terrified, tears streaming down their faces through a coating of dust.

Names were being screamed, wails of pain resounding from groaning buildings, sound came from every direction; filling his ears, searing his mind.

The blast had been huge. As they all held their breath, watching the rock fall from the sky on screen, something in the back of Silas' mind kept repeating, *<One was reported here. One was reported here. One was reported here.>*

It had begun with a rush of air, followed by something like a giant sucking noise, some void being filled. It was the noise that signaled the beginning of the end.

Silas later learned that this was the sound made by the quarter mile wide irregular mass, which had appeared slightly south of the beach he regularly visited, falling from the sky and then plunging straight into the ocean, displacing massive amounts of water.

He often later wished that it had been the last sound that he had ever heard. That he had lived no longer than that moment. The terror that followed over the next few months was burned into the mind of every single surviving soul and the pain endured by millions would echo through the halls of infinity.

Silence still filled the room, though slowly filled by a soft, static like noise, which quickly grew in volume, becoming a powerful roar. No one moved, no one spoke, until suddenly from the back of the room suddenly whispered, saying; "The window."

As one, they all turned to look out the window, the ground beginning to shake. The light fixtures swayed and then flickered and went out. As the shaking continued, those few of them that hadn't yet fallen to the ground in awe and fear were thrown to the ground, colliding with bookshelves and desks.

Peering through the city buildings, they could see a massive wall of water was coming straight for shore, maybe a hundred feet out to sea and building in height and power.

Two hundred and fifty feet high, the Miami wave was one of the largest recorded waves in human history, owing to the fact that the Miami Vessel was the one of the closest to shore, landing just off the shelf; plunging to a depth of about 300 feet within a single second, displacing almost a square mile of water. In addition to flattening most of the city of Miami, the Miami wave took out Cuba and Florida Keys. Not a soul was spared on those islands.

The single largest wave ever was attributed to the New Zealand/Australia Vessel, which fell to the ocean floor between the two landmasses, creating a wave almost a mile high; traveling across all of New Zealand, flattening the bottom half of Australia and then wrapping about the continent, continued on towards India and Asia, killing nearly six hundred and thirty two million persons total by the time it had subsided. Many people later would say that New Zealand was "The Luckiest Damn Country ever. Besides Cuba, of course."

The Miami wave reached shore within twenty seconds, growing to its full height less than ten. It crashed into the shoreline, obliterating all that stood in its way, tearing buildings apart, uprooting hundred year old trees in mere milliseconds. It was raw, devastating power and it would not stop until its appetite had been sated.

The wave was unstoppable, traveling through the city, flooding the streets; it pounded violently into skyscrapers and lower lying buildings, washing cars and people away in a horrific flood of death. Later, survivors would tell how the Vessel Waves all flowed red at their edges, as the wave came to its end; their waters tainted with the blood of millions, gushing from the bodies as they pulped against the buildings.

JAN 8, 2014

Running full speed for the gate, Silas felt the adrenaline coursing through his veins, the Infection taking effect. Stopping before the guard tower, he yelled up at the guard.

"What happened?"

"They followed the latest hunting party! A few *Tankers* and a slew of *Stalkers*! Donovan is the only survivor, the rest were slaughtered! They've been throwing the heads over the walls!"

<Damnit.> Silas paled. <Tankers and Stalkers? They mean business this time.>

Tankers, or *Titans*, as they were sometimes known, were literally the tanks of the *Viral* army. Standing fifteen feet tall at the shoulder, with a massive, hulking frame, it truly lived up to its namesake. They were nigh invulnerable, taking out entire squadrons of soldiers in the early months; they could take a thousand rounds and keep going. Though, later on in the war, it was discovered that they had a weakness to fire. Burn them and they stopped dead in their tracks, sometimes even turning tail, causing havoc among their own ranks.

In direct contrast to the *Tankers*, *Stalkers* were the black ops of the *Infection* ranks and seemed to be one of the *Mayan's* most recent developments, only having been seen in action within the last six months or so. *Stalkers* were given the best the Infection had to offer, armor, tools, weaponry; but what made them truly terrifying was that they didn't even need it. *Stalkers* were the perfect predator; with chameleon like skin, perfect night vision and long retractable claws they utilized to scale walls and trees.

Rage filled Silas as he stared up at the guard.

"Why didn't you send me out there? Why the *bloody hell* were they sent out alone?"

He knew it wasn't the guards fault, but he felt like yelling at someone.

The guard suddenly looked fearful and began stuttering. Silas ignored him, waving for him to shut up.

Dec. 21, 2012, 12:57 p.m.

Safe and away back on the slightly raised campus, the wave barely reached them, swirling around violently, the foam tinted red as it washed through the campus grounds. It flowed gently about the feet of the people who'd not managed to run for shelter before being tossed to the ground like the insignificant specks that they were in the face of the fury of nature.

Silas peered around through the settling dust. Nothing looked particularly familiar, it was all the same shade of grey, all coated in the same dull grey color. Though, he was sure he knew some of the places that he was looking at, but he just couldn't remember from where. Something told him it didn't really matter.

He heard a coughing off to his side. He wasn't sure which. He glanced to his... left? He wasn't sure. He saw a familiar face there, about level with his. He couldn't think of the name. He thought they might be friends with him. He didn't really care.

"Silas! Silas!" Someone was yelling something at somebody. It sounded in Silas' already ringing ears, making his head hurt.

"SILAS!" It was the guy off to his side. Silas had no idea who the guy was yelling at. He waved his hand at him, waving him away.

"Silas! It's Luke man! You're hurt! Your head man! It's bleeding all over!"

Absentmindedly, Silas reached up to feel his own head, checking to see if it was alright. Feeling around tenderly, his fingers roved into a sticky, gritty substance. Slightly alarmed, he pulled his hand down to examine it. It was covered in filthy, nasty blood, filled with dirt and debris. His eyes widened in alarm as his stomach turned. Suddenly, the memory of the past few minutes hit him and he recognized Luke and his surroundings.

Gasping, he turned to Luke. Grabbing him by the arms, he began to shake him violently. "*Shit*! Ohhh, god, I'm bleeding."

"Silas bro, you have to calm down."

Calm down? There was no calming down. He hated blood! The world had just ended! The stupid doomsayers were right.

Reaching up to feel his head once more, he felt something pull away and a sudden warmth began running down his face. As it trickled across his lips, his tongue darted out to taste it. It was salty and metallic. Grimacing, knowing what it was, he pulled his hand away from his skull and immediately saw that it was covered in fresh, clean blood.

Feeling the world beginning to spin around him, his knees gave out and he crumpled to the ground, unconscious.

There's a monster in me,
Feeding on my heart.

Fill the Void – No Better Than You – 2014

JAN 8, 2014

"Lower the gate!"

The guard paled. "S-s-sir? L-l-lower the g-gate?"

"That's what I said, isn't it?" Silas snapped at the man.

"But we are sending more troops as soon as we can!" The guard looked unsure of what to do, torn between doing what his commander ordered him and what seemed like common sense.

Silas snorted. "JUST DO IT!"

"Ye-Yes Sir!"The guard snapped off a sloppy salute and stumbled over the crankshaft and yanked on it.

Silas tensed, listening to each individual ratchet click, resounding in the air like notes of death. Glancing up, he saw a *Stalker*, stripped of all its equipment, fully camouflaged; attempting to squeeze in through the tiny space created by the lowering of the gate. He snarled at it, baring his teeth.

At eight clicks he yelled at the guard to stop and then ran full speed at the gate, launching himself through the air from about ten feet away.

Slamming into the gate, he pounded his fingertips into the hard material, digging the tips into the softer bits of duct tape, finding purchase, his diamond hard fingernails digging into the rough material of the billboards; he propelled himself up the nearly vertical walls. The guard gaped on in amazement.

He barreled towards the *Stalker,* which paused, surprise registering in its multiple eyes.

The emotion quickly passed and it bared its teeth; drooling in anticipation, pulling itself fully through the opening, lightly moving towards him, wary of his movements.

He snarled at the beast as his eyes flashed yellow once more and his teeth grew past his lip. Gathering his strength, he threw himself at it.

Surprised by this new enemy and its abilities, the *Stalker* was thrown off, unknowing of how to handle the situation. It paused, making a fatal mistake.

Silas collided with the creature, claws extended; he tore into its flesh. It roared, its camouflage flickering through various colors.

Bullard

Swinging himself up onto its back, his claws penetrated its skin and muscle. Bellowing with an inhuman cry, he tasted blood in his throat as it was torn by the sheer force and volume of the sound escaping it.

Screaming, the *Stalker* was losing its grip on the tenuous material to which it clung. With a creature on its back weighing not much less than itself, which was quickly gaining in size and weight; it could not hold its position on the wall much longer. With a quick motion of his arm, Silas tore into the bicep muscle of the creature. Screaming again, it fell, Silas still hanging onto it, both of them thudding to the ground.

Hopping lightly to his feet, Silas backed away from the *Stalker*, watching it, waiting for the moment to kill it. Struggling to all fours, the *Stalker* looked at him, snarling; drool hanging from its oversized torso fangs, which were located in its main feeder mouth.

Silas studied its stature, examining, searching for weak points.

Scientists hadn't quite figured out the *Stalker* evolution, as it almost seemed to be a completely different creature than most other *Infected*. All other *Mayan* sub species had almost 80 percent Human DNA, along with what was obvious alien DNA, containing six chemical compounds, whereas all other life on earth had four. All life on Earth was governed by four very small chemicals. GTAC. *Mayan* life was governed by six. GTACND.

Stalker DNA not only had human DNA, but also traces of Reptile and Fish DNA, as well as some Insectile DNA. But, what made it most intriguing is that its Genetic Makeup was almost 68 percent Extraterrestrial DNA. Some scientists were beginning to think that maybe they were a higher caste in the *Mayan* command and control.

Needless to say, being composed of mostly alien DNA, *Stalkers* were as radically different from other *Infected* as regular *Infected* were to humans.

Some had even speculated that they were made in a manner similar to Tankers, which were created by cocooning several young *Infected* together (before they reached their *Snapper* phase) and allowing them to create a singular being, but it was thought that perhaps they were made by combining older, mature *Infected* whose human DNA had burned out. The speculations on as to how the animal DNA was in their system ranged far and wide, but it was a commonly held thought that perhaps the *Mayans* had begun animal farms, harvesting DNA from various Earth creatures and injecting it into growth cocoons to see what sort of soldier could be created.

Stalkers, even without genetic examination, were as alien as they came. Standing at over just nine feet tall, they walked on their primary hands, located on their arms, or front legs.

The arms were grotesquely large in comparison the rest of their body, which was relatively slim, both arms having twelve joints a piece and making up the majority of its height, being eight feet tall each. Each hand was the size of a small sedan's tires, with five jointed clawed fingers the length and width of a grown man's forearms. Their legs were extremely small in proportion to their body, with small clawed hands that could be used for grasping weaponry and defensive measures. The body was maybe half the width of a man's, with a spine that had over three hundred vertebrae which, being combined with the many joints in the arms and legs allowed them unlimited flexibility.

The head had been determined as its weakest point, being somewhat of an odd thing itself. Unlike most creatures, the *Stalker's* heads did not contain their nervous system; rather it was a house of nothing but eyeballs. Housing twenty yellow hued balls of jelly, they stared in every single direction, even downward, allowing the *Stalker* unlimited twelve hundred degree vision. Having virtually no blind spots, they were absolutely impossible to sneak up on, even from behind while they crouched on all fours.

However, the eyes were extremely vulnerable and the head had no bones, only dense muscle and ocular tissues. Blinding a *Stalker* was relatively easy, once you had a lock on its head. Though, even blinded, they were still a formidable enemy.

Extending his claws further and allowing them to secrete their venom, he decided on his target and leapt while his enemy was still disoriented. Landing lightly on the ground immediately in front of the *Stalker*, Silas flung his clawed hands out, feeling himself grow and his muscles wax in size with each swing of his hands, with each snarl that escaped his throat. He was vaguely aware of a silent crowd gathering around them and the sound of gunshots slowly fading into echoed memory.

His hands connected with flesh, ripping, tearing into the ocular tissues. A reverberating, ear splitting shriek emitted from the center of the beast, as Silas danced around the creature as it lashed its arms out, attempting to kill its enemy. Silas danced easily out of its way, fury gripping him; he lunged forward and snapped his jaws at it. It jumped back from his teeth and then swiped at him once more. This time its claws caught his flesh and blue tinged blood spattered across its body. The *Stalker* lost its balance and toppled to the ground, screaming and Silas leapt, landing atop it.

Swinging his arms in growing hatred, Silas' claws dug into the flesh again and again, the screams getting lesser and lesser. Even as he knew that it lay dead, the fury grew stronger. He screamed in rage, falling to his knees, plunging his massive hands into the innards of his fallen enemy, greedily coming up to his mouth, cramming the hot, steaming blue flesh into his now gaping maw, reveling in the flavor of his enemy's defeat.

A gunshot was fired and slammed into his shoulder with a dull thud. He stopped, staring, blue filling his vision, seeing men in uniform in front of him, guns pointed. The urge to hunt swept over him, the urge to run free as he'd never before done. But at the same time, something else surfaced as well, something cold and resilient, fighting the hot blood coursing through his veins. A voice of reason, a voice of memory, calling up thoughts of a young woman bleeding before him, mouthing the words 'thank you...' Luke's still face, bathed in blood and the cold pale moonlight, countless tears of pain running down his face over the past years, leaving their permanent marks on his soul.

Struggling against the primeval rage threatening to consume him, he threw his head back and let out a scream. Startled, the men backed away, some falling over, others running for cover. As they broke rank, others filled in their place, keeping the circle about Silas complete.

<I will not let you take me.> Silas growled in his mind. <I will not allow you to control me through my anger. You know I will take control again eventually. We had a deal!>

With a final burst of pent up, angry energy, the Parasite relented.

Eyes widening as he regained control, Silas' arms fell to his sides, fingers clenched tight and claws melding back into his fingernails. His vision dimmed as he shrank down, his fangs retracting, the extra eyes sinking back into his skull, skin stretching tight over the sockets in which they sat.

Standing fully human, he stared into the ashen faces of the

men and women of the fort.

The parasite in his head remarked nonchalantly.

<Looks like we're in trouble...>

Laughing out loud, Silas replied sarcastically to the empty winter air.

"No shit."

CHAPTER 3 – SILVER VIGIL

Two men approached him, hand guns aimed at his head. Cocking an eyebrow at them, Silas spoke nonchalantly.

"Hey guys... It's me. You know me... I ain't gonna do nothin'."

Their faces didn't change; showed no recognition of him saying anything.

"Shut up freak. Hands where we can see 'em."

Silas slowly raised his blood covered hands and the men each jabbed a single hand into his armpits, yanking him to his feet.

"Hands on your head, freak."

Silas lowered his hands to his head and they slapped a pair of handcuffs on him.

He laughed, tilting his head back slightly, turning it to look at them.

"If I wanted to get free, you really think these would stop me? Or those?" He motioned towards the guns, still aimed at his head. "After I just ripped a *Stalker* shreds with *my bare hands?*" He made sure to put careful emphasis on the fact that he hadn't used a weapon.

At the mention of this, their faces twitched in what might have been fear.

"Besides... You're aiming at the back of my head... Where my hands are. You gonna shoot through my hand bones first? Dumbfucks."

They stared at him blankly for a moment and then readjusted their aim to the back of his neck.

"There ya go... Hope for you two yet!" He grinned at them with still pointed teeth. At the sight, their eyes widened and they took a step back.

Turning his head back to look forward, Silas grimaced, thinking to himself.

<Shitttttah. Caught. Again... Now what? I really hope I don't

have to fight my way out of here.>

They marched him down the street, towards a decrepit building which, unknown to most, was a hidden entrance the real power bunker here in the fortress. Fifty feet underground and protected by shield tech, it could withstand a bombing and sustain anyone contained within for almost a full six months. The 'Town Hall' a was actually nothing more than a symbolic front to give people strength; and indeed, had absolutely no access to this bunker.

<God damnit. I'd really rather not kill anyone.>

An alternate thought raced through his brain. *<Why not? Could always let me out and I'll do it.>*

His jaw clenched in silence.

Stepping into the building, one of the men held a hand out and placed it on a slightly discolored, water damaged patch of wall. A buzzer sounded and the fireplace grated, the back sinking slowly into the ground, revealing a passageway.

Halfway down the passageway, they passed a single guard, Joshua, one of Silas' very few friends. Josh threw a curious look at who their prisoner was and then turned to the wall and flicked a switch, which shone an ultraviolet light across the soldiers.

Turning back, he stared at Silas. Silas shrugged.

The two men escorting Silas let go of him for a moment, rolling up their left sleeves to show the invisible tattoo of authority which was inscribed across the inside of their wrists. It was a major mistake on their part.

Clenching his hands together, Silas lifted them up over his head and spun quickly in a circle, his double fist slamming into the head of one of the guards, who crumpled immediately, slamming into the floor. The second guard swung quickly, rapidly squeezing off two shots, but not quickly enough: Silas had already dodged out of the way.   Dropping to one knee, Silas quickly swept the legs out from underneath the second guard and catching the gun as it fell, stood and pointed between his friend's eyes.

Fear engulfed Joshua's eyes, as Silas stared coldly at him.

"Unlock these damned handcuffs."

Joshua's countenance hardened; his sense of self-preservation instincts taken over by his love of his friends and family.

"No."

Silas groaned inwardly. He hated having to act like this.

"Unlock them, or I'll kill you, Joshua. And then, I'll go to your house. How old is your daughter now? Four?" Even as he said the words, he hated himself.

The guard was silent for a moment.

"... She just turned four, yeah – Silas... I heard things, over the radio, freaky shit; I don't know what to think – I just saw you take out two of our best men – I can't. I can't let you hurt anyone."

"If I wanted to hurt anyone, Joshua, you wouldn't be breathing right now and neither would Dmitri or Red. Yeah you heard some freaky shit. Big deal. We live in a freaky world these days, in case you hadn't noticed yet."

Joshua stared at him in fear and distrust. "What are you, man? Are you one of those, enhanced soldiers they tried making a few years back?"

"Josh... I can't explain. I don't know myself. Just – give me the keys and you can say I knocked you out along with them... You can go home to your daughter, your dog, your fireplace. You have a good life here and that's not something many people can say."

Joshua stared at him, not speaking.

Silas cocked the gun.

"Or... I can kill you, if that's what you want. Hit you over the head, smash your skull... It would be quieter. Don't wanna take any shots in here; it'll blow my ears out."

Silas wished for nothing more than to take the gun and shoot himself as the next words left his mouth.

"Your little girl will grow up without a father. No provider. Her mom's dead, right? Where will she go? Oh. Right. She'll go to the soup kitchen within a month, the homeless will be eating the withered scraps of her starved flesh soon enough."

The look on Josh's face made Silas' gut cringe in guilt.

"What? You think that babysitter whore you hired will take her in? Maybe... It's a long shot. Probably not. The bitch can barely feed herself, that's why she's fucking you, isn't it? I guarantee your daughter will end up in the banquet hall. All because you wouldn't give me the god damned keys!"

Joshua paled. Then, slowly, reaching behind him, pulled out a small set of keys and taking a step to the side, began to unlock the shackles upon Silas' wrists.

As they snapped and fell to the floor, Silas caught a look on

Josh's face. "Shit. Josh! Don't!"

Joshua swung his hand up to his back, reaching for the sawed off shotgun strapped there, while at the same time, snapping his hand gun up to fire from his hip, he fired three quick bullets into Silas' leg, ripping through the flesh and into the floor. Silas staggered a moment, falling into the wall, leaning, before regaining his balance.

Josh screamed at him. "You piece of shit! How dare you threaten my family?! I don't give a shit what you are, I'll kill you!"

Bringing the shotgun to bear, Josh dropped the hand gun, swung the shot gun to his hip and took a shot at Silas.

The sound was deafening in the twenty yard stone corridor. The buckshot missed by a fraction of an inch.

Silas dropped to the ground and rolled to the side before jumping up again. As he landed on his feet, he deftly leaped to the side, pushing off the other wall, jumping towards Josh; he threw one leg in the air, catching Josh in the stomach, who doubled over in pain, coughing.

Turning quickly, Silas brought the butt of his hand gun down on the back of Joshua's skull. Josh hit the floor, face first. Blood pooled out from his nose, spreading across the stone floor. He groaned, sputtering in the blood, still coughing.

Silas got down on one knee and rolled Josh over, lifting him slightly and then propped him up against the wall.

He held a hand in front of Josh's face.

"How many fingers am I holdin' up?"

Josh wavered, his nose pouring. He reached a hand up to feel it and then lay it back on the floor, squinting at Silas. "... Three? Two? No, no. Three."

He was correct. No concussion at least.

"Josh... you idiot. I wasn't going to hurt you or your family. Shit man. I might have a monster inside me. But that doesn't mean I am one..."

His voice trailed off in doubt.

Picking up on this, his inner plague took the time to taunt him. <You're not? Since when? You are a monster. I gave you that, remember? Isn't that what you always tell me? I made you a monster?> It sounded bitter.

He ignored the voice, continued talking.

"I didn't wanna hurt you, but damn. I just wanted to leave."

Joshua stared at him through dazed eyes.

"You… you threatened my daughter."

"Just wanted the keys, bro."

"… Oh. You weren't really…?"

"Just tell them I knocked you out and took the keys from you, ok? Tell them there was a skirmish and you don't remember what happened. All right?"

"Alright. Sure thing… Where am I?"

Silas didn't think that Josh had any idea what was going on anymore, or what had happened. He was losing blood fast.

He patted Josh on the shoulder, sighing in relief. Tearing a piece of cloth from Joshua's sleeve, he made two small plugs and shoved them in his friend's nose.

Satisfied with his work, Silas stood quickly, slapping a small symbol on the wall that signaled an emergency situation. Someone would be up from the bunker soon.

A small blessing, as Lucas would have said. Touching the cross around his neck, Silas set about collecting the guns off the guards, strapping them onto his legs and back.

Heading back towards the door, Silas again reached up to touch the small silver cross which adorned the simple rope necklace which he wore, rubbing it between his forefinger and thumb.

Dec. 21, 2012 4:17 p.m.

Silas came too groggily, staring up at a whitewashed ceiling. The smell of antiseptic filled his nostrils. A hospital? He could hear the noises of the injured all around, the groans of the confused, the agonized scream of the dying.

"We have another Driller! I need a surgeon, NOW!"

A yelling male nurse ran past, pulling a woman on a stretcher, writhing in pain, face down in the pillow, screaming in absolute agony.

Silas stared at her… There was something clamped onto her back. It appeared to be an organic contraption of some sort, it looked almost like a squid… it was about 6-7 inches long, jet black, with four long splaying legs that had been riveted into the woman's flesh. Standing up slightly, its mouthpiece, if that's what you could call it, was perhaps two inches away from the skin on her spine. It was eating away at the center of her spine with what looked to be six giant hooks.

Bullard

They were stabbing into her flesh, yanking out pieces of skin and muscle tissue on the barbed ends, which it then pulled up into the innards of the creature with a hideous squelching noise. It was drilling a hole in her, about an inch wide.

They stopped wheeling the stretcher, almost immediately in front of the table on which Silas had been tossed, as the surgeon ran up, a miniaturized rotating saw in hand, already whirring. Two men grabbed the conical structure that made up the body of the Driller, another four ran up and held down the struggling woman, keeping her tightly pressed against the stretcher, while a female nurse came up and turned the woman's head to the side and spoke soothing words to her.

Making sure not to move too quickly, the surgeon pressed the saw blade up to the joints of the legs on the Driller. With a sound like a circular saw cutting through a steel screw, he began to work through the finger-width leg of the creature. It took about thirty seconds... Thirty seconds with a saw that could cut through a femur in twenty two.

The Driller made no pause, gave no indication that it was hurt, disabled, anything. It continued ripping away, even as a thick, iridescent blue liquid poured all over the place, across the woman, down the stretcher legs and pooling on the floor. Silas couldn't believe that much had come out of such a small creature.

Another nurse ran up, nodding to the four who were holding the woman down, who pressed even harder down upon her. Biting his lip, new nurse grabbed a hold of the now severed leg and yanked. The woman screamed in renewed agony as the leg tore from her flesh. The nurse tossed the leg on the table next to Silas.

Silas glanced down at it in numbed horror. It looked like a giant cockroach leg, having three segments; the first portion and the last portion were covered in iron hard bristles; to which flesh still clung. Silas assumed this was for gripping the victim while it tore into them, kept them from getting away.

Another leg clattered down, landing in the last one's goop, splashing some up onto Silas' face. He grimaced. It burned slightly and had a sickly sweet odor similar to antifreeze. He wiped it off with the back of his hand and then wiped it on his shorts, looking back up at the screaming scene taking place before his eyes.

The two male nurses holding onto the main body of the Driller began to pull and yank on the creature, but it had no effect, in the slightest. Even with only two legs, it was holding fast and with two grown men pulling on it, not budging at all.

The hooks seemed to be plunging deeper, with cracking noises now among the tearing, pieces of bloodied bone coming up among the red flesh falling and skittering across the floor. The woman was no longer screaming. Rather, her breath was coming as short gasps and her back was arching, even under the pressure being exerted from the men. Staring, Silas found himself wondering why her spine hadn't snapped yet from the angle she was curving her body.

Suddenly, the hooks stopped and all of them pulled up into the belly of the creature. The woman let out a small gasp and her eyes widened and then closed.

Taking a step back, one of the male nurses asked a tentative question. "What's happening?"

"I don't know," Remarked the surgeon. "We've always managed to remove them before they got too far into the drilling process. I guess it's... full." A shudder ran through the people standing witness. The surgeon reached forward with the saw, carefully placing the blade against one of the two remaining legs.

As the metal touched its leg, a clicking noise emanated from the main body of the creature, followed by a soft slurp. Alarmed, the doctor pulled away.

Everyone turned their head slowly to look at the creature. It appeared to vibrating, rocking back and forth slightly.

Suddenly, the maw on its underside, from which the hooks came, opened wider. A feeling of dread filled the room, as all of them stood frozen, knowing they should do something to prevent whatever horror was about to occur – but dying to know what was going to happen.

All six hooks rushed downwards, something dark and covered in long waving tentacles contained in their middle, cradled by them; they plowed into the woman's spine, delivering their hideous package with an audible crunch.

The woman exploded in agonized screaming. She screamed so loudly that everyone in the room shrank and turned away, dug their ears into their shoulders, clapped their hands to their temples, ignoring the blood smearing across their faces. As she screamed, the tower on her back slowly toppled, the legs releasing, falling to the floor with a hollow and metallic sounding thud.

The woman convulsed so strongly that all four men holding onto her were thrown back and she toppled from the stretcher, throwing herself about, foaming at the mouth, screaming, her mouth forming half intelligible words, blood leaking from her back. One of her convulsions brought her into the table Silas was sitting on.   She rolled into the table legs, arms flailing and knocking it sideways, causing Silas to fall. He landed on his left hip, looking directly into the face of the tortured woman.

Looking into her eyes, he saw that they were rolled back into her head. Later, thinking on the situation, he swore that he'd seen her optic nerve pressing up against her lower lids.

A rattle escaped her lips, a beg to kill her and then, she shuddered – a deep breath and then nothing. Her body fell slack.

Unable to take anymore, Silas scrambled to his feet yelling, running for the door, knocking over equipment and nurses alike.

The images were burned into his mind, he kept playing it over and over in his head, and he could see nothing else. He tripped several times, each time landing on his knees and each time jumping up once more and pushing people aside in a desperate search for an exit.

Suddenly, someone stepped out in front of him, hands outstretched and he ran straight into them, losing his balance, falling back, landing flat on his hind side.

Reaching down a hand, Lucas stood over him, his face grave. "You OK?"

Silas stared at his friend for several moments, wild eyed before taking a deep breath, calming himself. "Yeah. I think so. Fuck, what am I talking about, no, I'm not."

Taking the proffered hand, Silas leapt to his feet, questions leaving his mouth even before he landed.

"What the bloody hell is going on? How the hell did I get here?"

Lucas stared at him silently, biting his lower lip, not answering right away. His bright blue eyes bored into Silas' tawny brown ones. Silas suddenly had an image of a man giving a last confession, weighing the worth of his next words against the worth of his life.

"... I don't know, Silas. The world outside those doors is in chaos. There's rioting in the streets, shops being looted, people killing one another over canned goods in the stores... The police have their hands full, the national guard is overwhelmed and the army is here trying to keep things under control. This is one of the only buildings left with power, everywhere else is dark and a lot of places are burning. A lot of people are dead."

He ran a hand through his hair, exhaling forcefully.

"A lot doesn't even begin to cover it. Millions are dead. The rats got forced up into the streets by the flood. Gators got washed into the city. All the animals are suddenly gone insane with fear, dogs attacking people, cats shredding passing children. If you aren't killed by one of your friends, you're likely to get attacked by something else."

Silas stared at Lucas, trying to process what he'd just been told. Finding himself unable too, he asked his next question.

"How did I end up here?"

"You fainted. You hit your head after the..." He trailed off, obviously not wanting to discuss what had happened, or what was happening. His face was drawn and tight. "Well you know... But yeah, you hit your head on something and when you saw the blood, you passed out." He grinned suddenly. "Never knew you were so squeamish, tough guy!"

Silas scowled at him. "It's not funny, asshole." Glaring a moment, he cracked a small grin himself. "Ok, well maybe it is a little." He gazed around the room, at all the injured and bleeding, and the smile disappeared. "However... It looks like I may have to get over that pretty quickly, eh?"

"Yeah, I guess."

They stood awkwardly in silence, looking around the room.

"Well... I wanna step out and take a look around..."   Silas began to push his way past Lucas, who again, put an arm out in front of him, blocking his way.

"No. You don't. "

Silas glared at him angrily. "I have every right to go out there if I want too!"

Luke didn't budge. "...yeah. I guess so. But dude – there are these other things. They look like a cross between a cockroach and a squid. They're fuckin' creepy. They ju-"

Silas held up a hand, silencing him.

"I know what they do. I just saw what they did to a woman back there. Drillers they called them, I think."

Bullard

At his words, Luke's face grew even paler. Silas stared at him, dread building in his gut. "Luke? What's wrong?"

Luke chewed his lip even harder, blood leaking down, and his eyebrows knitting together. Silas stared at it, his stomach turning, unable to look away. He was fascinated by the way the light gleamed so cleanly off the single drop. Lucas opened his mouth and the moment passed.

"One got Emily."

Silas stared at him a long moment before looking down to stare Luke's shoes, bringing a hand up to his head, running it up through the front of his hair before sliding it down to rest on his cheek.

"Oh... Shit. Luke... Oh man. Oh... Man. I am so sorry... Oh, shit. Oh God. How?"

Lucas replied in an empty voice. "I left her at the apartment, when I brought you here, she was too scared to leave... and you needed medical attention. After signing you in, I then when get back to get her... It took a while, but I finally coaxed her out of the apartment, told her she needed to come here too, I was afraid she was in shock. We'd gotten about halfway, we were down by the Maple Street bus station, when a group of them came out of that alleyway there... You know the one," Silas nodded, "But yeah, a group of like ten just came flying out of there... One jumped, hit her in the back, took her down... I tried to help her up, but she couldn't and the others were coming... And I ran. I ran Silas. Like a coward. I left the woman I love to die, because I was scared."

Silas didn't know what to say, so he remained silent.

Anguish for his friend bubbled ferociously in his stomach. "I went back about twenty minutes later, but she was gone... there was no sign of her. Just a lot of blood. So much blood..." Luke's voice trailed off.

Silas still couldn't find words to utter aloud. Nothing seemed real for him anymore.

Lucas misinterpreted the silence and grabbed Silas by the shoulders, shaking him.

"There was nothing I could do, do you hear me? Nothing! Nothing at all, nothing nothing nothing! We were walking along and then bam, these things and then bam, she goes down, I didn't know what to do, I was so scared... You don't, you can't, even begin to understand."

He began to cry and Silas felt him go weak in the knees as his weight slid down a bit and reaching out, embraced his friend in a hug. Lucas broke down, sobbing into his shoulder.

"So scared... So scared... And now she's gone. Gone, gone... Gone forever. Gone gone... Gone gone... Gone. Forever."

Silas held him tight, running a hand through his friend's hair, comforting him and thinking about what he should say.

"I don't really know what to say, man... That's not the kind of pain that will ever go away. Trust me, I know-w." Her face flashed through his mind and his voice caught. "But, I knew Emily... And knowing her, I know that she forgives you, Luke. She loved you, with all she had and you made her happier than she ever dreamed, coming from where she did. She understands and she loves you still."

Lucas choked a little, tears streaming down onto Silas shoulder and then wrapped his arms about him.

They stood a moment and then pulled apart.

Lucas heaved another sob and then inhaled sharply, holding the air, stifling the tears.

After about seven or eight seconds, he exhaled, sighing. Reaching up, he put his hands behind his neck and began untying the woven hemp necklace which he always wore, the one that carried the silver cross he always worried at with his fingers.

He held it a moment out at arm's length, dangling it, looking at it. Then he turned, speaking softly.

"Emily gave this to me, about four years ago... Around the time we met. I told her I wouldn't take it off, till the day I die... And I just died with her. I want you to have it, Silas."

Silas stared at him, worried. "Are you sure?"

Luke nodded. "Yes... I'm sure. It felt like an iron weight tied about my neck, the whole way back here without her and while I sat here, waiting for you to wake up."

Silently, Silas reached out a hand and Lucas dropped it. It shone slightly, as it fell the short distance.

Taking it in both hands, he reached up and tied it in a simple knot behind his neck. Lowering his hands once more, he paused, one hand resting on the small silver cross, rubbing the worn metal softly between his forefinger and his thumb. Sitting softly in the chairs that lined the walls, he looked up at Luke. "Thanks."

CHAPTER 4 – INHERITANCE

He sighed, slamming his head into the wall. "Shit. Shit shit shit shit shit – Shit."

He was so sick of running. He couldn't deal with it anymore. Moving from one fort to another, never laying down roots, keeping himself isolated, never having anyone to rely on, to confide in... Except the damn bug in the base of his skull, but he wasn't good company at all. Bitter son of a bitch, more like.

Keeping all this weight to himself, these dirty secrets, this forbidden knowledge – It was tiring. Exhausting, even.

He'd explained to the council elders of this fortress whom he was, when he'd been scanned and found as *Infected*. But even then, everyone involved that night was sworn to secrecy under penalty of death. Silas was classified as a class one weapon. And exempt from having any knowledge of his existence in the case of his discovery. He was, for all intents and purposes, alone. How he wished for a friend, a companion. It seemed like an eternity since Lucas had died.

Almost absent-mindedly, his hand flew up to his necklace.

He sighed again, turning to look further down the alley, hearing voices. A gang of troops was running down the main way, shouting. Probably wondering why his guard hadn't come back yet. The people in charge weren't stupid; they'd know that he'd run.

Something wet plopped against the top of his head. Then his shoulder. Then his head again. He looked up.

It was beginning to rain; the snow was finally going to stop falling. He smiled. About time... Would help better with the harvest... His smile dissipated. Another harvest he was never going to see, or partake in. Another few weeks of struggling to find enough food to feed his ravenous appetite loomed before him. His stomach gurgled in protest at his line of thinking.

He was fond of venison; he might hunt some deer this time...

Bullard

He enjoyed the hunt, though every once in a while it was hard to return back to his regular form... Like this last battle. It was almost like he was back in the beginning... He had killed so many people. He'd never failed to return, but sometimes he lost the fight, simply blacking out, awakening mostly naked upon the ground, surrounded by half eaten bodies. He grimaced in distaste and guilt.

Since the decline of humankind, wildlife abounded. For the most part, the *Mayan* left animals alone... Except for those that could prove useful. They had had a field day with Zoos and monstrous creatures came forth from them. Aside from that though, nobody had really been able to determine what they ate. Some thought that perhaps they had taken our cattle as a mainstay, as cattle were the one thing you never found roaming the fields. There were certainly no bovine-esque nightmares traveling the wastes.

Still staring at the sky, he noticed a small tear in the eternal cloud cover... Fascinated, he stared... He could see the blue sky. It had been months since he'd last seen the atmosphere. The nuclear attacks that had ravaged the world in the first year had destroyed the sky, covering it in a constant gray cloud cover, with an occasional green or yellow cloud. Also, as a result, it was almost always cold, as the sun's rays could no longer reach the surface of the earth.

He sat back, leaning against the wall, thinking. He wished it could all go back to how it was. Reaching into his pocket he pulled out an old cracked digital wristwatch.

12:23 p.m. on... He rubbed the watch face. *Tuesday, Jan 8, 2014.*

He laughed slightly. It was his birthday. He was 21 years old. He mused to himself cynically.

"Maybe I'll walk down and buy myself a nice six pack." He laughed.

He looked down at himself... He hadn't aged a day. At least not by human standards. Not since he was *Infected*. But even though he hadn't changed since then, so much else had.

Dec. 21, 2012 5:22 p.m.

He sighed, slamming his head into the wall.

"Shit. Shit shit shit shit shit – Shit."

He stared at the ceiling. Lucas, off to his left, shifted slightly to look at him, a questioning look on his face.

"We've been sitting here twenty minutes bro, I'm sick of seeing dying people come through here."

Lucas stared at him, eyes slightly glazed... Like he wasn't all there. It chilled Silas to the bone. He'd never seen Lucas like this before... He couldn't blame him, but still... This was not the time to lose one's self.

When he spoke, it sounded hollow. "Well... What exactly do you propose that we do, bro?"

The way he said that last word, that <Bro', it sounded almost sarcastic, venomous even.

Silas felt a lump rise in his throat and anger bubble up from somewhere around his navel. He jumped up, words escaping his mouth before he could think about what he was about to say.

"Hey, screw you man. I'm sorry what happened, did, but it's not my fucking fault, you hear me? Shit! You left her all on your own, I didn't make you do a damn thing!" He immediately regretted it. He stared at the floor, expecting a blow to land any second.

Lucas didn't even flinch... Just sat and stared.

"Shit. I'm sorry man. Ah God Damnit. Damnit it all to hell. I just don't know what to do! I don't even know what it looks like outside!" Lucas had been quite diligent in keeping him away from windows... It was the only time he moved, when Silas made a motion to go towards a window.

"No... You're right. It was wrong of me to be rude towards you."

Lucas heaved a heavy sigh and stared at the floor. A single tear drop leaked from his eyes.

Silas watched in silence as it rolled down his nose and dangled from the tip a moment, before it fell, twinkling in the harsh fluorescent lights as it made its way downward. He couldn't begin to imagine the pain his friend was in.

He sighed again.

"We should go. We can't stay here forever."

They'd already been reprimanded twice by a stern African American orderly, who wasn't taking any more shit.

Lucas replied softly, not looking up from the floor, his lips barely moving.

"I know."

He stood, his eyes locking with Silas. They were empty. His normally sparkling blue eyes were completely devoid of life. Lucas was already dead... His body just hadn't realized it yet.

"Let's go."

Turning slightly, Silas nodded and then began to walk towards the far door.

Jan. 8, 2014

Silas rolled his neck, popping the vertebrae.

<*You know how uncomfortable it is for me when you do that?*>

<*Yes, I do, asshole, it's why I do it.*>

<*Why can't you just be civil? I leave you alone for the most part, don't I? Raknir...*>

Reaching out a hand, he grimaced slightly as he concentrated on his fingertips, willing them to grow.

Tilting his hand back slightly, he watched in his never ending fascination.

The wrist cracked as the tendon rolled over and expanded with the width of his hands. His fingers grew, elongating, becoming thicker, as thick, pointed, diamond hard fingernails moved outward, releasing from their dormant state and pushing out with a slight "schick." Two extra knuckles appeared upon on all the fingers and the hair on the outside of his hand sucked back in, as the skin turned gray. He felt his arms begin to lengthen and cut off the energy flow.

He held his hands out before him, examining the changes, as he often did. They were now about the size of frying pans, smooth, pale grey and each finger with a black, diamond hard talon attached to the end of them, about four inches in length.

Killing tools.

He flexed them momentarily, then, leaping a good ten feet in the air, slammed them into the stone and mortar wall of the alley way, clinging on. Ripping one hand free of the stone, he threw it up and forward, slamming it again into the stone, chips and flakes breaking off, falling to the ground below. Hand over hand; he continued the process until he reached the lip of the building.

Grabbing a hold the lip, he launched himself up and over, landing on the rooftop with the grace and sinew of a cat.

Standing from the slight crouch in which he had landed, he

brushed some remaining wall debris from his shoulders and then cracked his neck once more.

    <Stop it you schlackna!>

He did it again. A stony coldness rolled through his mind and he laughed. Willing his hands to return to normal, he began to stroll along the rooftop, avoiding any sags. He didn't want to go crashing through into someone's home. That would just be rude.

Hopping from rooftop to rooftop, he nimbly made his way towards the far wall of the city, opposite of the gate. Happening upon an alleyway between the buildings, he prepared to jump, but a sudden noise caught his attention. Peering over the lip of the alleyway, he saw, far beneath him, a young girl, crying.

It seemed that she had probably been playing atop the trash pile in the alley, but had fallen off. She seemed to be badly hurt, he could smell blood. His mouth twisted off to one side. He wanted to help her, but he really needed to get out of here, before he got shot again. He laughed.

"Shit. I forgot."

He examined his leg quickly. The three bullet wounds were barely visible now, his body having the regenerative powers that it did. Dried blue blood surrounded the rapidly vanishing scars. He peered closer, noticing that the healing process had even pushed out the rounds while the flesh grew. One round had remained lodged in the upper layer of his skin. He plucked it out, staring at the smashed surface, chuckling to himself.

"Always did like that part of this deal. Eternal Life and no ugly scars... Well, besides the one..."

He rubbed his middle back.

    <Not exactly. By my calculations, you will live to be about five hundred thousand seven hundred and twenty six of your Earth years... If my people don't kill you by then. I've been doing some calculations about your genetics and metabolic functions... Raknir knows I have nothing better to do...>

    <Really? That long? Holy shit. That's cool.>

The girl whimpered from the bottom of the alley once more, catching again his attention. The smell of blood was getting stronger.

He sighed, calculated the distance to the ground and then taking a slight step back, leaped from the rooftop, dropping down to the alley floor and landing softly in front of the young girl.

Bullard

He turned to look at her, catching a glimpse of a small scared face, a lot of red and more white than he cared to see showing through. He muttered softly at the sight.

"Shit."

She'd broken a leg; he could see that without even examining her. Her bone had busted clean through the skin. It looked like it was her femur that had been broken.

"Poor kid."

He crouched down, attempting to get a better look and she flinched away from him.

The sudden movement caused her to cry out softly, grabbing at her leg in pain.

Raising a hand, he indicated he wasn't going to hurt her. Trying to examine her again, he once again moved closer and this time, instead of flinching, she simply sat and stared at him. Glancing up at her, he saw that her big solemn brown eyes flowing with tears. She couldn't have been more than 4 or 5 years old.

He spoke softly, hoping to calm her down a little and to earn her trust.

"It's okay sweetheart. I'm not going to hurt you. Looks like you hurt yourself pretty bad. May I help you?"

She stared at him a moment longer and then nodded.

"Alright... I'm going to have to pick you up. It's going to hurt... Really bad. But if I leave you here, you could get sick and die, baby. Need to get you some help right now, okay? Can you be a brave little girl for me? What's your name?"

She whimpered slightly and then whispered, "Natalie..."

"Ok Natalie, can you be a brave girl?"

Another whimper.

"Natalie?"

"I guess so..." She answered.

Moving quickly to spare her as much pain as he could, he grabbed the foot of her broken leg and gave it a slight pull and twist, straightening it. She made a strangling noise in her throat, doing her best not to scream. Children were taught from a very young age to be as quiet as possible, especially when in pain. Nobody wanted to attract predators.

As the bone moved, blood ran from the open wound like water from a well spring. Silas grimaced, staring. She needed attention, fast.

"Ok baby, I'm going to pick you up and when I do, I need you to put a hand here," He placed a hand on the back of her knee, "and here," He laid a hand above the wound on the front of her thigh. "And hold it still! Don't let it bend, ok? Alright, here we go." As he laid his hand across her, he let a single claw stab into the flesh of the wound, allowing a slight amount of venom to drip into it. She took no heed, gave no signal that it gave her any pain. With any luck, it would cause her leg to go numb within ten minutes.

Still in his crouch, he slid a hand and forearm underneath her butt and laid the other across her shoulders and then straightened his knees.

She made another strangled noise of pain, a scream caught in a throat... It made him sad. In his time, a young girl would be and have every right to be screaming at the top of her lungs. How times change...

Turning, looking down the alley, he listened for a moment, trying to locate people.

"Where's your mommy and daddy Natalie?"

Silently, she pointed back towards the garbage pile where she'd just been sitting. Silas hadn't noticed because of where she was, but sticking out from the bottom of the trash heap was a desiccated, rotting human foot. He stared in disbelief.

"You've got to be shittin' me. Ugh. I have the worst luck..."

<No such thing as luck.>

<Oh, shut up. I'm busy.>

He needed to find someone for her, quickly, or she'd be taken to the soup kitchen. Especially since with the condition she was in, they would probably just kill her. Might as well do it himself – save her the suffering.

He thought a moment. He could snap her neck right now, leave her dead in the alley with her folks, nobody would ever know, or probably ever care. It was certainly better than being eaten. He looked down at her, weighing his heart against the thought and she looked back up at him, her eyes shining with hope.

He groaned. No, he needed to find another option, quickly. Still thinking, he ran through his extremely limited options.

Margaret had just lost her child to the pox, she might take her in. But she was on the other side of town.

<Better to just throw her on the mercy of the town, I guess... I suppose I'll just take her to the med camp.>

The Parasite laughed in his head at his thought.

<You know far better than I do what the "Mercy of the Town" is.>

<Yeah, well I've got to try, don't I? She's going to die.>

<True. Make haste my friend.>

Having made up his mind, Silas half jogged down the alleyway, making sure to not let her leg move too much, gripping it tightly in his hand.

Upon exiting the alleyway, he found himself coming off on the main 'street' as the town called it. In reality, it was little more than a dirt path strewn with brick and gravel. A few people stood in over hangs, avoiding the rain, but not many. Silas assumed that most people were probably still near the front gates, or cowering in their homes after the attack. The few people who were standing in their doorways stared at him. He ignored them, walking down the street at a hurried pace.

Taking in his surroundings, he realized that he was in a bit of luck – the med camp was only about 2 miles from where he was.

Dec. 21, 2012 6:00 p.m.

They walked through the streets avoiding bodies and puddles of red tinted water. Silas still couldn't believe his eyes. Just this morning, this city had been bustling along, the people concerned with work for the day and what they were going to eat for dinner that night.

Now, they lay dead in pools of their own watered down blood, mouths agape, eyes staring eternally into the sky. Silas' mind was on overload mode, barely able to take in anything he was seeing. He had never known such destruction was even possible. He'd been present in New York at the time of the Nine Eleven attacks. It was nothing compared to this. There was blood absolutely everywhere. Splashed on walls, street signs –everywhere.

He struggled not to lose his stomach contents as they passed a bent and ragged stop sign... With half an arm hanging from it, the sign sliced into the arm and stuck in the bone. Water, tinted red, dripped from the fingertips as blood ran from the top of the severed shoulder, down through the sopping wet remains of what was once an expensive suit.

Lucas seemed to take nothing in, walking forward, eyes dead set in determination. Silas hurriedly caught up to him and waved a hand in front of his face, only to have Lucas' hand fly up and crush it in a vice like grip. Silas' eyes widened in pain and he cried out.

"Ow ow ow ow ow ow DAMN, LET GO!"

Lucas released him suddenly, realizing his error. He stared at Silas, eyes still empty. He was beginning to scare him.

"I'm sorry."

Luke turned away again, as Silas stood rubbing his hand. Silas watched him silently as he walked away, wondering what he could possibly do to make this all go away. Sitting in the waiting room, he'd watched as the realizations of what had happened slowly sink into his friend – and it was killing him. Both of them. Lucas, literally, Silas in the instance that he didn't know what to do. Looking around him, he came to the very somber realization that he couldn't do anything. Nothing at all.

Heaving a sigh, he stood and hurried after his friend, leaping and jumping over the bodies, doing his best to not stare.

JAN 8, 2014

Blood was leaking from Natalie's wound profusely; he could feel her pulse getting weaker. He had to hurry.

Looking up, he saw he was still about a mile from the camp.

"Screw it," he muttered under his breath. "She's going to lose the leg anyway."

Reaching forward, he focused a moment and then stabbed her in the leg with a single claw. She didn't react, except to place her thumb in her mouth and stare at him with those big eyes. The venom appeared to have done its job. He closed his hand around her leg, holding it in place firmly. Looking down at her, he nodded and then spoke firmly. "Ok. Hold on baby."

She nodded, still sucking on her thumb.

He opened up into a run, needing to get her to the med camp as soon as possible.

Suddenly, she gasped a little, her head going limp against his arm.

Bullard

"God damnit."

He drew on his amino acid reserves, feeling the copper based acids flowing through his veins, giving his muscles an inhuman boost.

Letting himself go into a sprint, he darted forward, moving at speeds impossible for any human. Onlookers gasped as this seemingly average man suddenly began to fly down the street, moving at speeds upwards of forty miles per hour. Several of them pointed and shouted. He gave them no heed, focusing only on his goal.

One minute and ten seconds later, he threw on the brakes, slowing into a regular run so as not to startle the meddies. This girl needed treated and quickly. That wouldn't happen if the meddies were all in a panic.

Approaching the first mud flap, he threw it back, trying to avoid hitting her head with it. As he passed through the inner double doors, he called out; "I need assistance!"

Several meddies poked their heads out of various doorways, saw what he was holding and then called out in reply:

"Take her to the chopping block! We don't want her!"

This upset Silas a great deal.

He cried out, enraged, "I need assistance *NOW*!!!"

His voice rang through the air, a battle cry of desperation.

Aggravated and a little scared, some of the meddies stepped out of the various rooms, examining the beast of a man who stood before them.

One of them, a short, burly, hairy looking man stepped out, grumbling in a thick Russian accent.

"What do you want?"

"This girl, I found her in the alley... She needs help."

"Ugh. Let me see her. Come, lay her on my table." The short fat man turned and went back into the doorway he'd come out of.

Following him, Silas took the room in with a glance. It was disgusting – blood dripped on the floor and rusty, unkempt tools lay everywhere. A few *Bugs* were suspended in fluid in jars along the walls, appendages missing, stumps torn and ragged.

A cold wave of anger rolled through him, emanating from the base of his skull. He struggled not to smile.

<Friends of yours?>

More frosty feelings from within.

<We do what we do because it is our nature. Our leaders may

have taken an evil agenda, but is that truly our fault?>

For the second time that day, Silas felt like an ass. He turned his attention back to his immediate surroundings.

The meddy eyed him. "Don't like it? Too bad, it's all we have."

He turned, eyeing the meddy. "It will have to do. What can you do for her?"

Reaching into his pocket, the meddy pulled out a pair of grubby glasses and a handkerchief, using the latter to clean the former. After rubbing them a few times, the meddy placed the glasses upon the bridge of his nose. Silas was amazed they fit without causing the man's nose to turn blue. The man leaned in, examining Natalie's leg, shaking his head slowly, grumbling.

"Are you this child's father? We could remove the leg. For a fee of course. 30 rations."

Silas stared at him, his cold feelings beginning to match those of his symbiotic partner.

"No. I'm not."

Sighing, the man took off his glasses.

"Well, does she have a legal guardian?"

Pursing his lips, Silas turned to Natalie, staring down at her. "No."

"Well, in that case – I'm afraid there's nothing I can do. I'll just euthanize her and call the butcher. He will pay handsomely for such young meat."

Silas' face twitched, his upper hackles rising and suppressing a snarl.

<Stupid fat man. Kill him.> The parasite sounded in his thoughts.

The fat man had turned to his desk and was rummaging through the vast amounts of rusty tools and bloodstained paper which was strewn across it.

Silas couldn't believe this little fat man was just going to consign a little girl to death. "Nothing? You're absolutely sure? There must be something."

"Ah – Here we are – And no, nothing. In all honestly, if you were her father, I would charge you to remove the leg; then tell you that you were screwed anyway! Ha-ha!" He laughed. "That's how business works around here."

The fat man turned once again, this time holding a large rusty needle.

He pointed to Natalie's leg, gesturing at the pale flesh. "You see how her skin has gone white and it's stopped bleeding around the edges of the wound? She's practically out of blood. There is really almost nothing we could do for this girl. If we left her alive, she would be nothing more than a cripple, a liability, feeding off the rest of us. Survival of the fittest... Oh, look, she's awake. How pleasant."

A soft moan had just escaped Natalie's lips and her eyes cracked open, staring around the room.

They both glanced up, the doctor in indifference, Silas in horror.

She looked at them each in turn, a look of confusion upon her face.

Silas grabbed the man's arm and led him off to the side, gesturing to the needle.

"Is this going to hurt her?"

"Oh yes – Quite a bit in fact. It's a concentrated dose of rattlesnake venom – well, actually, it's really just any venom we can get a hold of. We inject it directly into the brain, through the ear canal. They scream a lot before the end – hallucinate – That sort of thing. Can't breathe, heart stops, convulsions. You know; the usual. This way, the rest of the meat is still usable. Nobody eats the brain nowadays, the squeamish bastards. Nifty, right?" He laughed.

Silas' eyes widened and he could feel the rage within him rising. Keeping his tone level, he answered softly.

"Yeah, nifty."

The doctor chuckled once more.

Reaching out, Silas grabbed the doctor's arm, speaking softly.

"Just – just one thing, doctor."

"Oh yes? What's that?"

"I'd like to do it myself."

"Really now? A man after my own heart!" The doctor laughed heartily, handing Silas the needle. "Here you are son!"

Turning away, struggling to contain himself, he willed his fangs to extend some; just enough to grow past his lower lip. He walked over to Natalie, the needle gripped tightly in his hand

Leaning over her, he looked her in the eyes, tears forming in his own.

"Don't worry baby – It will be ok. It's all over now. You're safe.

47

Nothing can hurt you anymore."

He then kissed her on the forehead, his fangs piercing the flesh, pumping venom into her body. She gasped softly and then closed her eyes, slipping away into a peaceful death, her tiny heart and mind shut down immediately by Silas poisonous' bite.

Standing up straight once more, Silas raised his hand, positioning the needle by her ear, poised to enter.

He took a deep breath, trembling, playing the moment.

The doctor stood idly by, wringing his hands greedily, licking at his lips, watching the scene before him intently.

Silas sighed, pulling his hand away from her rapidly whitening temple.

"I – I can't do it. She's just a little girl. There must be something we can do. Does she really have to die?"

The doctor snorted and shuffled towards him.

"You weak son of a bitch. You bastards can face monsters ten times your size, but not off a little girl? Give me the needle."

Turning his head slightly to the doctor, Silas grinned, light glinting off his rapidly lengthening teeth. The doctor caught sight of the changes and gasped, moving backwards.

Silas roared, spinning around, hand outstretched, arms and hands growing rapidly already and slammed the needle into the side of the doctor's temple. The force of impact forced the plunger down and injected the contents of the vial directly into the fat meddy's frontal lobe. His eyes widened and he began to shake. As Silas released the syringe, the doctor crumpled to the floor, a scream building in the back of his throat, foam forming at the corners of his lips.

Silas now stood at ten feet tall, with his claws and fangs fully extended.

He cracked his neck.

<You just had too, didn't you?>

Bending over, Silas reached down and picked the fat doctor up by his neck, bringing him up to his face. Terror filled the man's eyes and an unintelligible scream was emanating from his throat – but Silas didn't care. Not this time. He may have been in the form of a monster, but this man was a true monster. Disgust filled his soul and shame for his species coated his tongue.

He hauled the doctor around over his head and slammed him

into the desk, atop his own tools of torture, where they embedded into his flabby back. The screams intensified, rising and falling in pitch.

Smiling, Silas hauled the meddy into the air once more, holding him before his face. He roared at the man, his maw gaping open, spittle flying everywhere –lunged forward and bit down, separating the man's head from his shoulders. The screams stopped abruptly.

Spitting the foul tasting, greasy object across the room, Silas took the body and hurled it through the nearest wall. Several terrified meddies peeked in the door, curious about the roar – The screams were heard all the time – the roar was not. Several others peered in through the hole left by the fat doctor's body. He roared at them all, making a move towards the door. The meddies all scampered, tripping over one another, screaming for mercy.

Silas' chest heaved, still infuriated. Whipping around, he lashed out at the vile room which he was in, flinging jars and tools into the walls. Upon request from his partner, he smashed all the jars containing the *Bugs* and then, much to the Parasite's satisfaction; picked up the Doctor's head and stuffed it into one of the empty jars which lined the room.

When his rage subsided, Silas returned his attention back to the still, small form lying in the center of the room. Natalie.

Tears burned his many eyes as they overflowed and ran down his face. Natalie.

Standing over her limp form, he reached down gently, taking her in his multiply jointed arms, cradling her soft human body to his hard, muscular alien self. He lowered his head, shielding her body and jumped once, two, three times against the roof before busting through.

With a final push of his legs, he jumped up through the hole in the ceiling to the top of the compound. He was in luck once more – the med camp was right beside the back wall.

Getting a running start, he made his way towards the building ledge and launched himself through the air, easily making the twenty feet to the ledge of the wall. He landed atop the wall between two guards, quite possibly leaving them with nightmares for the rest of their lives, before leaping once more, out across the moat, landing upon his feet and rolling.

Freedom.

CHAPTER 5 – CROSSROADS

Silas bounded across the open, rock strewn plain, making great leaps and strides, her limp body cradled to his.

The fort walls slowly faded into the distance, shrinking, becoming a small speck in the distance. Signs of civilization quickly petered out, vanishing altogether within five minutes.

He was alone in the cold Missouri plains. Crossing a road, he remembered the time he and his family had driven through here, heading back from Vegas, taking a detour through towards Chicago to meet up with some of his father's old army buddies.

It had looked far different then, covered by flowing grass that waved softly in the breeze and streams that laughed softly as they bubbled along – Dotted with farmland, it was once a wild and free land.

Now it was desolate, covered in rubble. Several weeds struggled to survive in the nooks of the rocks, but not much else could survive. Out here, there was little protection from the elements.

Silas heaved a sigh in mourning for his once beautiful earth. He had once dreamed of traveling the world; see its various wonders. He wanted to see the Colorado mountains, hike them to their towering peaks.

No chance of that now. They had been leveled, turned into massive mining complexes by the U.S. government during the first six months of the Invasion. Last year, he'd stood on top of the now tallest peak of the American Rocky Mountain chain –A boulder, a bare 3000 feet high, jutting up out of the ground, at the base of the once proud Mt. Elbert: 14,500 feet. The government had left Mt. Elbert alone – It had been destroyed when Yellowstone National Park had gone off, due to the seismic activity which had been triggered by the many nuclear strikes around the world. It wasn't as big a bang as they'd all been predicting, but the explosion had been heard on the other side of the world. Millions had died.

He had wanted to see Yellowstone one day too.

New Zealand had been destroyed by Tsunami the first day of the Invasion. It had been stripped bare. It was nothing more than a rocky wasteland, the soil poisoned by the salt deposits left by the ocean water. He had always wanted to see some of the areas where they had filmed Lord of the Rings – Little chance of that now.

Every beautiful thing on the planet had been destroyed. Human culture was reduced to near that of an animal. The Louvre in France had been washed away. The Smithsonian lay in ruins, having been used as an Alamo of sorts. The Hanging Gardens of Babylon had been burned down. The Great Pyramids of Giza had been torn apart, their stone used in fortifications, the gold found within hoarded by all those that found it, smelted down to use in alloys, for weaponry. The Taj Mahal, too, had been used as a final stand. Two years – To destroy the progress of five thousand.

He slowed his pace and strode lightly across the barren landscape. The ground was still too hard, but it was getting softer. He probably wouldn't have to go much further to find a decent area.

Her body was growing cold in his arms, the fingers and nose beginning to turn blue. Small as she was, her body heat had vanished quickly out in the cold.

A sudden noise reached his ears. Soft and slight, barely carried on the wind, it reverberated in his enhanced ears like a gunshot.

It sounded like a soft growl, from fairly nearby. Probably within fifty yards. It sounded like that of a dog – but that was unlikely. No dog would growl within the presence of a *Mayan*.

His face twitched. He hated thinking of himself as one of them.

Standing, he pulled himself up to his full height. From ten feet up in the air, he could see quite the distance. He gazed about, surveying the darkening horizon.

...Nothing. How strange. He sniffed, his nostrils flaring. Still nothing.

Grunting in derision, he resumed walking.

****

Crouching behind the rocks, she stared at the *Mayan*, strolling across the plains. He was a beast of a creature, at least ten feet tall. He carried a small body in his arms. Possibly that of a child. He was cradling it to his chest, almost like he was protecting it. He was about seventy five feet away – too far to tell exactly what he might be carrying, but she had a hunch that it was a small child.

She tilted her head sideways, curious. She'd never observed this behavior in a *Mayan* before. She sniffed, searching the air for the scent of the burning scent of a *Renegade*. Nothing. No scents at all.

A scout perhaps? But even then, what was he doing out here alone? And why was he carrying the body of a human child?

Whatever it was, it appeared to be looking for something.

Sitting by her side, Ragger suddenly could no longer control himself and let out a low growl.

Eyes widening, she threw a furious glance at the Jackal, reaching out through her Hive link.

<Shut up Ragger! We can't take him! Look at him!>

<Says you. May I remind you that I have hunted and killed elephants?>

<Yes says I, you're going to get us killed. Just look at the size of him.>

It was still strange when she was speaking to Ragger. They hadn't been travel companions very long and she wasn't yet used to having an animal speak back to her.

Animals weren't capable of much thought-speech and while they understood most of what was being said, they weren't capable of thinking in whole sentences – let alone replying.

The Hive mind allowed her the capability of linking into the mental processes any living creature, which as far as she or Ragger knew, was a unique ability. Normally, the Hive Mind only allowed access to *Mayans* and limited control to *Infected* beings; *Infected* being a mind that had been touched by the viral form of the *Mayan* race, but not yet injected with a *Squid.*

Simple infected beings were humans or animals which had escaped from an attack by a *Mayan*, if the *Mayan* had managed to get their claws or teeth in them, at least. Every infected creature carried a form of retrovirus in their claws and teeth – upon biting or scratching another creature, this virus entered the bloodstream, if the creature so chose.

If the creature under attack managed to escape, this virus would slowly act on their systems, making them sluggish and confused at first. Later, within six hours or so, it caused them to take on traits like heightened aggression and sensory perception.

At that point, they too would begin to produce the virus, along with copious amounts of pheromones, which would draw *Drillers* to them, which allowed the Infection process to be completed. It was also a tactical advantage of flushing out resistance packets. In the early days, many a safe haven had been overrun because of a single individual.

If the creature had not been happened upon by a *Driller* within 48 hours, the virus would have changed the molecular structure of the host brain enough to be literally taken over by the Hive Mind – And so it drew them to itself, where the Infection process could be completed.

The *Mayans* as a race were a perfectly oiled killing machine.

Fully infected hosts could not be taken over, as an embedded *Squid* could just switch off the link to the connection. The ones that chose to permanently do so, who chose to permanently destroy that part of the host's brain and their own, were known as *Renegade's*. However, they still maintained the ability to communicate mind to mind – The Hive Mind itself was the only thing incapable of touching them. Nobody was really sure how it all worked.

Ragger was a *Renegade Hellhound.* The bug in his brain was perfectly capable of speech.

He was also capable of changing between his typical dog form and his more fearsome Hellhound form.

He was currently in his common dog form. It was how Roach preferred him. She had been chased by *Hellhounds* some time back, an event which had ended badly for her. She still had nightmares about the ordeal.

They'd come across each other about six weeks prior and after a vicious, bloody battle, they'd recognized the other for what it was and nursed one another back to health in a cave not far from where they sat.

In tandem with his ability to shift between his two forms, he still seemed to take on dog like tendencies from time to time as well. Reckless behavior, undying loyalty, vicious attacks against those who would harm his territory.

He was a good friend.

Glancing back up, Roach saw that the *Mayan* had stopped and pulled himself up to survey his surroundings. Standing at his full height, she could see that she'd been right about his size. He was about twelve feet tall. Beyond that, she'd been wrong.

This was no scout.

She'd never seen anything like this *Mayan* before. She propped herself up a little to get a better look.

Ten to twelve feet tall, he was covered in rippling muscle. What appeared to be a pair of loose jeans hung around his hips, torn and tattered, massive muscles protruding from underneath. Running down his spinal column were large spikes, each one about eight inches long and an inch thick. Each shoulder sported two large bony growths, which jutted outward, curving at the ends.

His legs were positioned like that of the hind legs of a horse, only unimaginably thick, covered in knots of muscle. Near the bottom, a second knee formed, reversing position. Each thigh was probably the width of a full grown man. His feet were clawed and each one about the size of Ragger himself, were he to lie on his side.

She couldn't see his hands, but his arms were each about the size of his legs, though considerably shorter. He had the typical boxy head of a *Snappers*, square-like with a slightly elongated skull.

He was sniffing the air, searching for the source of the noise.

She wasn't worried – He wasn't going to smell anything. Ragger had seen to that for them.

Still, she threw another angry glance at Ragger, who curled his tail between his legs.

The *Mayan* had apparently decided he'd been hearing things. He gave a snort then hunched down and resumed his previous pace, casting looks back and forth across the plains, digging his feet into the ground, searching – Ever searching.

But for what?

****

Walking along slowly, he felt the soft earth begin to give way beneath his weight, indicating that the ground had finally softened up. He clenched his toes, digging his claws deep into the earth.

Kneeling, he laid Natalie's body upon the ground and then sniffed around for a moment, searching for an area to begin to digging. Somewhere preferably dry, he didn't want to be working through mud.

Finding a place that smelled good, he leaned down and slammed a hand into the dirt, feeling its consistency.

<Oh yes,> he thought to himself. <Here is good. This shall do.>

He dug his claws deep into the soil, pulling up a huge handful of dirt and tossed it to the side and then slammed his other hand into the hole he had just made, pulling up yet another clod.

As he dug, he reminisced.

Dec 21, 2012 9:03 p.m.

Luke sat silently in his armchair, staring at Silas sleeping on the couch. He was kicking in his sleep, whimpering at unseen phantoms.

"What a mess," Luke muttered under his breath.

Standing sullenly, Lucas walked over to his apartment window, peering out. Fires were still burning on the campus grounds. It was all that illuminated the night, save for a few flickering street lamps here and there. Several buildings still had power and floodlights had been turned on full blast in all areas of refuge. Lucas thought this was rather foolish. It would be like moths to a flame.

The city had perished by water and the college by fire – He heard a religious or political pun in there somewhere, but he was too numb to care.

He raised his hand to his cross, going to rub it, before remembering that he no longer had it.

He glanced at Silas once more, focusing on the glistening silver piece about his neck. Silas snorted and then rolled over, pressing his face into the couch, hiding the cross from view.

A sudden wave of sorrow swept over Luke and as his eyes filled with tears, he turned back to the window, staring.

"Emily..." He whispered.

After today, he wasn't even sure if he believed in any kind God anymore. How could any God let this happen?

...She would be ashamed of him.

He felt as though his heart had burst – Into a billion tiny pieces, which had been caught by the winds of this living hell and burned to ash. There was nothing left of it. There was nothing left of him.

He was a shell, a shadow of a man. He had let everyone down

in his lifetime. His parents, himself, Silas, God – Emily.

"Oh Emily. You were the only one who believed in me – And how did I repay you?"

A tear slid down his cheek. He reached up and wiped it away. Holding his hand in front of his face, he watched the tear roll towards his fingertip.

He didn't even feel like himself anymore. He watched his own movements in a detached, fascinated sort of way. It was like watching someone else move his body for him. He lowered his hand.

Still staring out the window, he saw a sudden movement. A solitary figure was walking down the street, limping. A young woman, it looked like.

As he watched, she turned and looked over her shoulder and then broke into a run, screaming. He peered closer. Three or four small spidery shadows emerged from the flames of a burning building. It seemed several of those Driller things were following her.

Luke stared at the floor, feeling a twinge of sympathy for the girl. What horror she was about to endure – It was simply unspeakable.

Her screams carried on the wind, in through the broken window, the screams of the woman he'd thought he'd never see again, let alone hear. Her screams. The same words she's screamed at his fleeing back, as she'd been swarmed by those things.

"*Lucas! Lucas? Lucas, help me! Lucas, where are you?*"

"Emily? *Emily!*"

"*Somebody? Anybody! Help me! Lucas! Lucas, help me!*"

It was her. It was her! She must have escaped – God had given him another chance. This time, he wasn't going to lose her.

He darted for the door, flinging it open.

****

BAM!

"*What the bloody hell*?!"

Silas nearly jumped out of his skin and fell off the couch; having been awakened by a very loud slam in the midst of a terrifying dream.

Picking himself up off the floor, he glanced around, his eyes happening upon the front door, which now lay on the kitchen floor, having left a very large dent in the wall.

He was confused for a moment, until he remembered that Lucas had taken it off its hinges so it would close.

A faint echo reached his ears.

"Emily! Emily! I'm coming sweetheart, keep running!"

It was Lucas. He was screaming his deceased lover's name. Was he completely deranged? They both knew she was dead.

And where the hell was he?

Two and two suddenly came together in Silas' exhausted brain.

"Door, Lucas gone, screaming from far away – Duh."

He walked over to the door, peering out cautiously, first one way and then the other. All clear on the one, just the fires from earlier still burning bright, but what he found in the other direction was absolutely strange.

Lucas was running down the street, faster than Silas had ever seen anyone move before and moving in from the opposite direction; a young woman half running, half limping down the street. It looked like Emily. Behind her were three Drillers, scuttling along at a moderate pace.

Silas blinked, speaking aloud.

"Whaaaat...? I guess she got away? "

Suddenly, the girl tripped and fell on her face and Silas caught a glimpse of her back; Raw and bloody, it had been torn to pieces, the shirt tattered and ripped, drenched in blood.

Something clicked in Silas' mind.

<It's a trap.>

Eyes widening, he called out to his friend.

"Lucas, no!"

Pushing off the door frame, Silas ran forward and leaped over the railing, dropping like a stone to the ground, three stories below.

CHAPTER 6 – RENEGADE

<Y ou humans are so strange – *Why do you bury your dead?>*

<*It's a symbol of respect.>* Silas grunted, digging his fingers into the dirt, ripping up clods. <*If we bury the body deep enough, the body isn't ravaged by scavengers.>* He grunted again, plunging his claws deep into the ground.

<*I see – And is that the only reason?>*

<*That and we don't have to deal with the smell.>*

<*Ha. How amusing. Tell me – Why are you – <Digging a grave' for this girl? Out of all the ones we've killed together, of all the ones we've watched die, why does this one affect you in such a way?>*

<*Because she's a child. She doesn't deserve this. And though we've killed children before – It just doesn't feel right.>*

<*So? What does her physical maturity have to do with anything? Our dead young are left to rot with the rest. They are dumped and left to float to sea, to rejoin the planet's cycle of life.>* The Parasite sounded confused.

Silas grunted again, tearing up more dirt as he replied. <*Yeah, well same concept really.>*

<*I do not see the parallels. From what I see in your mind, you typically bury your dead in boxes, some of which are metal – this is in no way returning them to the planet.>*

<*It wasn't always that way – Personally I just want to be burned and thrown in the ocean.>*

<*So – you respect us in some ways, then?>*

<*It's something we've been doing for centuries.>*

He felt a small flicker in his brain, memories being pulled up. His upper lip curled in irritation. He wasn't fond of the feeling, it kind of tickled.

<*So I see. Cremation? How tidy. Further proof that you humans*

aren't as backwards as we first thought. Not all of you at least –Having you as a host has shown me that quite clearly. Strange thing really, I don't know why we assumed Earth would be so simple to take. In many ways, Earth is an extremely well evolved planet, humans being one of its few masterpieces.>

<Yeah?>

<Yes.>

<Hm.>

<Oh and Silas... I have seen respect for us in your mind, whether you acknowledge it or not. You admire us, don't you? I think you do.>

<Good to hear. I think I'm done digging for now though, so just give me a moment.>

<As you wish. Oh –By the way, Silas. I have something to tell you...>

<Oh yeah...? What's that?>

<I've found a way to link to the Hive Mind... Without you noticing.>

Silas froze.

<Thought that reaction might be elicited –However –You do not need to worry. I'm not going to report you, or what you are, or your whereabouts.>

Silas couldn't believe his ears. How could the parasite possibly expect him to believe such a thing?

<And why would you EVER do that? You could crush me. You've said yourself; I am probably the only real threat to your race that you have ever even heard of. Besides the Ancients, of course.>

Another tingle in his brain, though this one was physical, as the parasite twitched in annoyance at the mention of their ancient enemy.

<Well, yes – That is true. However, I and many of my brethren – Have grown very tired of this war. That is why you see so many Renegades recently. We have grown sick of this endless existence, this span of hatred across the galaxy, grown tired of the wave of destruction our species has become – Some of us, while observing earth, indeed thought that you are a brilliant species – One worth saving, regardless of what the scout was telling us. Worth passing over, passing by. But the Hive won't have it. The Raknila are too set in their cause. They believe that humanity will be our keys to victory over

the Ancients. *Some of us no longer even believe that the Ancients exist. Others, like myself, believe that they may have once, but are now just a story to further the Raknila's evil. None but the Raknila can even claim to have seen them any longer But regardless of that – The time has come to make a stand...>*

Silas smiled, his monstrous face twisting into a horrible grimace, as he hopped up out of the now huge hole.

<Are you saying what I think you're saying?>

<Yes. I am going to become a "Renegade," as you humans so call them.>

<Fuck yeah! That's what I'm talkin' about. You know what? You aren't so bad, once you stop being so emo.>

His fingers tickled as endorphins released from within the parasite, spreading a message of happiness through him.

<It's going to cause you a great deal of pain you know. And you may have some memory loss. I may have to destroy part of your central nervous system.>

<I don't care. Do it after I finish the burial.>

He glanced at his feet as remembered his solemn task.

<Time for that later...> Silas remarked.

<Indeed...>

****

She crouched down low behind the rock, staring. The Hunter, as she'd decided to name him, seemed to be digging a hole – A grave?

<I don't get it,> she sent to Ragger.

<Don't ask me.> He replied.

She peeked over the rock top, listening to the Hunter grunt, peering at his tiny package that he had carried all the way to this spot.

It appeared to be a little girl. Her left leg looked as though it had been snapped in half. She was still and quiet – Roach could smell no warmth coming from her tiny body. She was dead.

There was something else, however, a slight scent that seemed acidic – Even poisonous.

Had she been killed by way of venom? She knew that it was common practice nowadays among humans to kill their own by way of snake venom. This was usually done to people they were planning to eat, the ones who were injured beyond repair, the sick and the elderly.

It was useful, as venom cooked out of meat. Still, it didn't smell like anything she'd come across before.

Suddenly, dirt flew up from the hole, showering them both. She squeaked slightly in involuntary protest. As she did, a hand flew up to her mouth and her eyes widened in anticipation of a quick and furious death. Ragger crouched low, ready to attack.

Nothing happened. The Hunter continued to grunt, tossing dirt up out of the hole. He had to be about twelve feet down at this point. He'd just hurled a hand full of dirt almost 20 feet up and out of said hole.

<Completely uncalled for,> she thought to herself.

The noises stopped and time seemed to stand still. Neither of them moved and no sounds emanated from the hole.

<What do you think he's doing?> She asked.

<I don't know – But his heart rate just went through the roof. Something just scared the lahndeel out of him.>

She blinked. What could possibly scare a creature of that size? Something the Hive had told him, possibly.

<A Renegade Tanker?> Ragger suggested.

<Haha – Maybe. I don't know. He looks like he could handle himself quite easily.>

<How about this then?> He replied. *<You, when you wake up in the morning!>*

<Hey! Not funny!> She glared at him. He stared back, a doggy grin plastered on his face.

Several long moments passed, before Ragger's eyes widened as he suddenly said *<Get down.>*

She crouched quickly, just in time to hear a slight rush of air and loud thud as the Hunter leaped out of the hole and landed heavily upon the mound of dirt which he had created.

She peered over the rock, staring. A hideous grimace was plastered upon his face – A demented smile of sorts.

It sent a cold shiver through her very core.

****

Bending his knees, he leaned down and scooped up Natalie's body into his massive hands.

He stared at her wistfully for a moment. Things like this just should not be.

    <If it means anything – I feel I understand. I am sorry for this loss, as much as I can be, anyway. You humans are truly magnificent creatures. Not many species achieve intelligence like they have on Earth, as individual beings. Hive creatures are far more common throughout the universe, like ourselves.>

    <But you do have individual intelligence.> He turned, looking back towards the hole.

    <Yes, yes we do. But not all of us did, not always. We used to have a much more strict caste... Similar to ants, or bees. Hence the remnants of the Hive Mind. However, as we took more and more intelligent species, our own DNA structure mutated into a less stable form, and we evolved into the creature that I now am perhaps three hundred thousand years ago.>

    <So – What? You evolve with each species you take?>

    <Essentially, yes. We absorb DNA as we go. Our most recent acquisition was a primarily aquatic world. This is why you view us being close to the cephalopods of your world. It's really a convenient form. There was talk of giving our evolution an inhibitor to keep us at this stage.>

    Silas stared at the hole a moment longer and then took a stride forward, placing his foot on the edge, his claws overhanging. Bending his knees slightly, he hopped gently down into the hole.

    <That's creepy.>

    <Perhaps to you, but for us, it's rather natural. That is how we exist. Though recently, it appears we've become able to 'Give birth' through our hosts, creating interesting new branches.>

    <That's even creepier.>

    <Yes, we are rather disturbed by it as well. None of the creatures born are controllable by the hive. They have all been slaughtered.>

    Silas paused a moment.

    <I'm not sure how I feel about that. It is not their fault that they were born.>

    <It is what it is.>

    <Wait, you guys use the hosts to have sex?>

    The parasite sat in uncomfortable silence for a few moments, choosing his words carefully.

    <I think it's an experiment on the part of the Raknila. There

have been tales of coupling, but nothing ever comes of it. We too, are capable of love. As you said, we do have individual intelligence, feelings and reactions.>

Silas grunted, focusing on the small body in his hands, tilting his head to the side. What a meeting of moments. Here he stood, a monster in the flesh, a being born of a child's most depraved imaginings; now holding that child's broken body as he prepared to bury and mourn her.

<The Raknila, eh? I'm beginning to think those guys are real assholes.>

<Yes, they are – They are monsters of the worst kind.>

Bending his knees, Silas slowly lowered Natalie's body to the ground, cradling her head in the palm of his hand. His knuckles brushed the earth and he pulled his hands away from her body, letting her gently slide the remaining distance to the cold, hard packed clay.

He crouched over her body a moment, reaching out towards her miniscule face. With a single talon, he brushed a strand of hair away from her face. Death had begun to set into her skin, causing it to turn cold and pasty. The cheeks which had been so flushed just an hour or so before, had turned pale white, tinged with blue.

His hackles rose in anger.

Heaving a sigh, he stood, turning towards the wall, tossing a hand up in the air, latching onto the ledge, heaving downwards and propelling himself up from the hole. Making his way over to the large pile of earth he'd made, he stood by its side, shoving both hands in deep and then heaved sideways, pushing several hundred pounds of dirt towards the hole.

Pausing before the edge, he peered down once more, viewing Natalie's tiny body lying upon the ground. With a final sigh, he closed his eyes and heaved the dirt into the grave. Her bones crunched as the immense weight landed on her frame.

Without warning, a low growl sounded from behind him.

****

She huddled, staring, trying to make sense of what she was seeing. He was *burying* the child. It defied anything she could think of. Each idea that popped into her mind was just as unlikely as the one before it, if not more. She looked to the side.

Bullard

<Ragger.>

He glanced back at her. He seemed unusually focused. <What?>

<Could he be a Renegade of some sort?> she asked.

<Possibly. Still doesn't explain why he'd be burying a human. Renegades tend to be feral.>

<Well – You're not.>

<True – but I've been around for a very, very long time.>

Something clicked in the back of her mind.

<He smells like you.>

<What?!>

<He smells like you! Like a Ripper.>

Ragger's tone came through a bit strangled and indignant. <He does not! He can't smell like me, it's impossible.>

<Yes he does! Take a whiff real quick. You catch that pungent scent, almost like cedar?>

He pulled in a sharp lungful of air and then glared at her.

<Whatever. I think he smells like you. Reeking of petrol. Filthy half breed.> He smiled, baring his teeth.

She furled her eyebrow.

<I do not! And take that back, mutt!>

A noise caught her attention and she looked back. He was scarily close at this point, less than 10 feet away. It was a miracle they hadn't been seen. He must be really focused on the task at hand – the only reason he hadn't smelled them yet is that they'd rubbed themselves in Aloe and sage. For some reason, it acted as a scent blocker for *Mayans*. It was viscous enough to catch all other bodily scents and they just couldn't smell it.

He had thrust his arms into the dirt pile, almost up to the middle of his biceps and had gone to shove it towards the hole.

He paused at the edge, peering down. A spasm of what appeared to be pain flitted across his face, as he closed his eyes and grunted in exertion.

A dull thump and several sharp cracks issued from the bottom of the hole as the dirt hit.

Out of nowhere, Ragger sent her a thought.

<I'm not going to sit here any longer. Something isn't right with this, that thing is unnatural and it's going to hurt us. It's obviously deranged.>

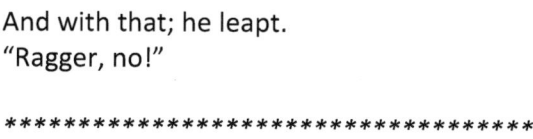

And with that; he leapt.
"Ragger, no!"

****

"Ragger, no!"
A shout issued immediately after the growling ceased and something suddenly slammed into his back, pitching him forward, down into the hole. The fall was short, but with it came a feeling of nostalgia.

****

Dec. 21, 2012 10:28 p.m.

Silas awoke slowly, dirt in his mouth and pain in his soul. Everything hurt and he was having trouble seeing, shapes and shadows weaved in and out of his vision. The iron clad taste of blood filled his mouth, mixed in with the bitter taste of dirt and gravel. Propping himself up on one arm, he attempted to spit, drooling, half coagulated blood spilling from his mouth onto the ground.

His stomach turned at the sight and his head swooned. His gorge rose and he struggled to keep it down.

Looking about slightly, flashes of thought came to his mind. Broken buildings, an arm impaled on a sign, flooded streets, a woman screaming in pain, Lucas running.

"Aghhh shthit." He couldn't speak and as his lips moved, he could feel they were swollen and tender.

He tried to prop himself up a little more and gasped in pain as he did so, almost fell back down in pain once more. Several of his ribs had been broken.

<What in the blue hell did I do?>

He backtracked in his mind, speaking aloud as he went. "Okgh weclht thhhfere gwask..."

He winced in pain as his lips mangled the words.

<Ok, well there was the hospital...> He shuddered.

<The walk back, sleeping on the couch... What happened after that?>

His eyebrows furled in the center as he concentrated, trying to remember the last few minutes of his life.

<The door on the floor, Lucas running, the girl – Oh.>

He turned slightly onto his side, looking up into the air at the overhanging balcony.

He had foolishly leaped from nearly thirty feet in the air. He was lucky to be alive.

<You know, Silas, you do some of the stupidest shit,> He chided himself.

He looked around and found that he was alone on a deserted street. He might have been out for some time. Last he'd seen, Lucas was about halfway down the street.

He put both hands beneath his body and quickly shoved his weight upwards, gasping in pain as three of his ribs and his left wrist sent bolts of pain through him. He must have busted his wrist too.

Pulling his legs underneath him, he pushed up onto his knees, grunting.

He looked down the street again, to see if he could see anything more from this vantage point. Still nothing.

"Damnit."

Throwing up a single leg, he planted his foot on the ground and laid both hands atop it. Using his knee as leverage, he staggered to his feet, gritting his teeth as bolts of pain flew along his nerve endings, causing his head to pound.

Taking a few weary steps, he fell to his knees again, wincing in pain as rocks dug deep into the flesh. Falling forward onto his hands he pushed his legs forward and struggled to his feet once more.

Looking down the street in which Lucas had run, he began to walk, shouting his name.

"LUCAS!"

Fires crackled in the several buildings around him; beyond that, all was silent.

"LUCAS!"

Still nothing.

"LUCAS!"

He pulled up short standing before a gaping hole in the street, probably where the sewer had fallen in. The sound of rushing water came from its depths. It sounded like a thousand whispers on the wind.

He had probably gone about fifty yards down the street by this point. It was eerie, the streets empty, flames cackling in windows of empty buildings, not a soul in sight.

"LUCAS!"

"I'm here!"

Lucas voice suddenly rang out from a side alley.

Blinking rapidly, Silas threw a glance off in the direction of the voice.

Lucas was standing about fifteen feet in, hidden in the shadows, bent over slightly, one hand on his thigh.

"Shit. Thank god." Silas started towards him, half jogging. "What happened?"

Lucas didn't move; said nothing.

Slowing to a walk, Silas moved his head about, trying to see. "Bro?"

Silence still.

"Come on man, talk to me."

"I wouldn't come any c-c-closer if I were you."

Silas walked to the edge of the hole, judging the distance.

"Are you ok?"

"I s-s-said stay the f-f-fuck away!" Lucas' voice had an odd tinge to it. And a stutter. Lucas never stuttered. He might repeat himself, but he never stuttered.

Silas jumped, landing precariously on the other side of the hole. Catching his balance, he stepped forward, peering at Lucas, a few feet away now.

"Nah man, I saw you chasing Emily. Are you ok?"

Lucas turned, facing Silas. His eyes had rolled into the back of his head, leaving only the whites showing. Blood dripped from his nose, rolling down his lips and chin. His tongue flicked out several times, swiping at the blood. His face twitched randomly, moving through various expressions; from fear to anger to ecstasy.

Silas stopped cold, staring. A knot of fear and panic grew in his stomach.

Lucas pushed himself away from the wall, standing unsteadily.

Silas noticed that his lower back and legs were drenched in blood. The knot in his stomach tightened.

"You n-n-n-need to leave. No, wait stay! Don't go I didn't mean it. LEAVE N-NOW!"

Bullard

Silas took a step back minding the pit behind him; as Lucas took an awkward step forward. It reminded Silas of watching his younger sister learn how to walk. It disturbed him.

Lucas eyes suddenly focused, narrowing. His face froze, locked into a grimace of hatred, his teeth bared. His head twitched slightly side to side, jerking. He opened his mouth slightly and spoke and then snapped his mouth shut once more, resuming the snarl.

"S-s-silas?"

His body clenched up and he brought one hand up to his face. His whole frame shook and a low groan escaped him.
A single word escaped his teeth.

"Run."

CHAPTER 7 – RUN LIKE HELL

Silas' eyes widened in fear and panic, as he turned to heed the warning given by his friend.

Unfortunately, he'd forgotten about the gaping hole in the ground that was located directly behind him. As it was he had no time to run anywhere at all. As he teetered on the edge of the hole, an iron grip clamped down upon his shoulder blade and yanked him backwards, throwing him several feet farther down into the alleyway. He landed face down in the dirt.

Stunned, he laid there a moment.

"Silas, it's in me, get away from me, I can't control it."

Grunting, he glanced back over his shoulder, just in time to see Lucas take an unsteady step towards him and attempt to bend over to grab him. He lost his balance and crashed down atop Silas.

Seizing his chance, he pushed himself up, scrabbling in the dirt, wincing in pain as his ribs screamed in protest. Lunging to his feet, he took a single step before that inhuman grip found his person once more, latching onto his ankle.

He toppled, one hand reaching out towards the wall, his fingers sliding down and along it, skin tearing. He slammed into the ground, chest first. He screamed and curled into a ball, balls of pain white hot and burning, popping before his eyes as his broken ribs took the force of the impact.

With huge amounts of adrenaline flooding his system, he quickly regained his composure and rolled over, kicking, lashing out with his feet. Lucas had pushed himself up onto his hands by this point and was grinding Silas' leg into the dirt, putting pressure on his ankle. He looked up staring at Lucas.

Lucas' face was more composed now, flashes of discomfort and displeasure and occasionally; fear, flitted across it.

But his eyes... His eyes would forever be burned into Silas' memory.

Bullard

Bloodshot and crazed, the pupils had dilated to fill almost the whole iris, leaving the center of his eye pitch black. Light from fires burning around them glinted within the pupil and Silas could see hell in them, the hell his friend was trapped in.

He lashed out with his feet, kicking hard. Once, twice, three times and his free foot connected with Luke's face; giving off a soft crunching noise, followed by the sound of blood pouring on the ground, like water spilling from a pipe. Lucas grunted and let go. Silas scooted backwards quickly, his butt dragging on the ground, jeans sagging down as he did so. Bracing his feet he quickly pushed himself up, turned and began to run.

Within a few steps, his pant legs caught under his feet, causing him to stumble and fall to his knees. His ribs were killing him and his ankle was raw and bleeding. He couldn't run on it very well. He scanned the area ahead of him, searching for a place to hide. He spotted a doorway a little ways ahead of him, maybe thirty feet. It looked like the back entrance to the cafeteria. If memory served him right, it was never locked.

Gritting his teeth, he climbed to his feet once more and staggered forward, forcing himself to move. He could hear Lucas moving in the dirt, grunting, pulling himself up. He screamed out in a hoarse voice.

"Come back here you schlackna! Lahndeel!"

Silas' blood ran cold upon hearing the alien words spill from his friend's mouth.

He pressed forward, veering slightly for the opening, hands outstretched. Closing in on it, he grabbed at the corner of the wall and threw himself around it. He almost ran straight into the door. Flinging out a hand, he grabbed the handle, praying that it wasn't locked. It turned underneath his grip.

"Thank God. " He threw the door open.

He had been right. It was the back entrance to the college cafeteria. He glanced around the empty kitchen, filled with gleaming pots and pans. Nooks and corners provided plenty of places to hide. There were knives and cooking pots everywhere. Perfect for weapons. His stomach turned at what that thought implied.

His darted around, searching for a place to hide. Cabinet doors, ovens and counters all jumped out at him. Deciding that behind a counter was probably his safest bet; he dived over a standalone, knocking some utensils to the floor with a loud crash. He cowered in a small ball behind the counter.

Crouching there, he heard Luke run into the door, grunting, heard him curse, fumbling with the handle. It took him a moment to get the hang of it. Then with another grunt, the jam clicked and the door flew open. A long shadow fell across the floor, wavering with the light of the burning campus. Silas listened with bated breath. A few cautious steps were taken. A snorting and snuffling noise sounded, almost like Lucas, or whoever he was now; was sniffing for him, searching for his scent.

The footsteps stopped. Another grunt was heard, followed by a clattering of cooking utensils crashing to the floor and skittering along the tile.

"Where the hell are you? I know you're in here. I will find you. SILAS RUN!"

Another grunt, more clattering; this time not too far behind him – He was moving closer. A pot skidded into Silas' shoe. He jumped slightly. The snuffling and footsteps stopped. His eyes widened in fear and anticipation.

A low growling began, echoing around the kitchen. Silas muscles tensed.

"I heard you move little human. Soon I will taste your flesh – How do you humans taste? I see much curiosity in this human's mind on the subject – I will teach him. I WON<*T* LET YOU!"

Another clatter, another crash, this time the utensils landing on top of Silas. A knife bit into his flesh and he yelped. An immediate crashing noise issued forth as Lucas dived over the counter. Silas looked up as he scampered forward, catching a glimpse of his friend's face, twisted into a grimace of hate. His eyes were glowing a slight yellow around the edges; the iris shot through with purple and gold.

Darting forward, Silas pushed himself to his feet, designer shoes slipping slightly on the cold tile. He could no longer feel his ribs; his ankle. He could only feel the fear rushing through his veins. Adrenaline clouded his mind, tunneled his vision.

He ran for the kitchen door.

Grabbing the handle, he blasted through, running through the cafeteria and past several people who shouted in alarm. He weaved in and out of tables, pressing forward. He heard the door slam open behind him once more, followed by a crashing and yelling and growling as Lucas ran into several chairs and tables.

A thought occurred to Silas and he began to turn tables and chairs over as he passed them by, creating a blockade behind him. Curses continue to issue forth as Lucas stumbled and crashed over objects in his way.

He was almost to the door. Several people stood in the way, screaming at him to stop, that he couldn't go out there.

"Those things are out there!"

He raised his arms, preparing to push his way through. Two large guys caught him.

"You can't go!"

He struggled against them, kicking and flailing, catching one of the guys in the jaw.

"Let me go! He's gonna fuckin' kill me! He's one of them! Let me go!"

Their eyes widened and they let him loose, backing away quickly. They glanced at one another and then looked at the oncoming Lucas. They ran, heading in different directions.

Silas slammed into the doors. Locked. Panicked, he turned around, glancing at Lucas, who was getting better at picking his way through the chairs. He was almost to the edge of the chair line.

There was an open path through the cafeteria, which led back towards the kitchen, coming out near the still open door. He ran for it, pushing himself, feeling his muscles burn. Fear bated his breath, pulled it short, coming in short ragged gasps.

A clatter came from right behind him as Lucas threw a chair out of his way and burst into the aisle, hard on Silas' heels. He snarled. Spittle hit Silas in the back of the leg.

Reaching a hand out, he snagged a chair and hurled it sideways as he passed it; hard as he could. Direct hit. Lucas went down, smashing face first into the floor, screaming unintelligible words of hatred – But among them still, was Lucas, screaming for his friend.

"Silas! Run, don't stop – You can't see what they want! Run, run and never stop!"

Silas' eyes teared up and he choked.

He reached the door and blew through it. He looked around, searching for a weapon. Sick as it made him, he knew what he had to do. He spotted a large vegetable knife lying on one of the counters. He jumped towards it, hand outstretched. His knees banged into the cabinet as his fingers curled around the hilt. It was heavy in his hand, as if it were made of lead. Getting a good grip on it, he ran back towards the alley door.

****

Jan. 8, 2014

Silas fell face first into the pit, something snarling and snapping at his back. It wasn't a very far fall and he didn't have time to flip over in the air. His face slammed into the dirt, mouth open. More cracks issued from under the earth as Natalie's body was pulverized by his weight. The foul taste of deep earth filled his mouth as pain seared through his back, claws and teeth laying him open. He rolled to the side, reaching behind him. Swatting at whatever it was, he knocked it off. He continued to roll onto his back; bracing his feet against the wall he pushed himself up onto his butt, looking around for what had attacked him.

Standing before him, on the lip of the pit above him was a full grown *Hellhound*; snarling, teeth bared and drooling. It was a beast of immense proportions for its species.

The hound snarled at him as he leaped to his feet. He snarled back, hunkering down, minimizing the amount of his body exposed, hands hanging near the ground.

Taking a deep breath, Silas noticed something that confused him. There was no scent in the air.

<Why can't I smell him?>

He pulled a deep breath through his nostrils. A slight scent was there, barely detectable, an earthy scent, like a deep wooded forest. A Renegade, then?

<My question is – As big as it is, how did you not SEE it?>

Its hackles raised as it paced back and forth, staring at him. It had the higher ground and it knew it. He stared at it, waiting for the moment it would strike. If he didn't catch it in time, it would rip his throat out. Its back legs tensed and his eyes widened. It leaped at him, front paws outstretched. He swatted at it, catching it in the ribcage, knocking it to the side. It flew up out of the pit and landed on its side, where it lay disoriented.

Taking his chance Silas leapt up and backwards off the dirt

mound, landing on the opposite side from the *Hellhound*. It climbed to all fours, shaking itself, clearing itself of the pain, the broken ribs it had just suffered cracking as they healed. Its eyes glowed softly as it stared at him. It moved to the side – He mirrored its behavior, moving to the other side, beginning a circling motion between them. He studied its movements.

It didn't move like other *Hellhounds* he'd seen and it didn't really look like others either.

It was bigger; standing at about 5 feet tall at the shoulder and it lacked the usual six to eight eyes possessed by most *Mayan* species; it only had four, like himself. It had long, sweeping, pointed ears that stood tall and rigid, curving over its back. It was shaped differently too. Sleeker, more muscled. Walked with more grace. Overall, in look and stature, it rather reminded him of a big cat. Terrifying as it was, it possessed a particular beauty. Was this indeed a *Hellhound*?

The parasite spoke in hushed awe. He sounded almost reverent.

<No. That's no ordinary Hellhound. That's a Ripper.>

Silas sighed inside, keeping an eye on the Hound. It paced back and forth, waiting for him to make a move.

<That doesn't tell me shit. What the hell is a Ripper?>

<A Ripper is a legendary creature among our species. We don't know what causes them to be born and we don't know where they come from. It is said that one arises every fifty thousand years or so, again, for reasons unknown. They are thought to just be a genetic anomaly, but they are magnificent creatures. You could possibly be classified as Ripper, as I have not an idea as to what our Viral form actually is. As it stands... I never thought I'd have the honor of meeting a Ripper.> Wary, Silas stared at the beast.

<Well, maybe you'd classify this as a meeting, but usually when I ask to MEET someone for dinner, I'm not trying to fucking eat them!>

It leaped again with no warning. Silas was ready this time, even if caught a bit off guard by the sudden movement. He leaped a split second after it did, colliding with it in midair, hands outstretched, slashing. Slamming into one another, his momentum carried them over the pit and several yards past. They crashed to the ground, scratching, biting and spitting at one another.

They rolled about on the dirt, tearing into each other. It had sunk its teeth into Silas' shoulder and was tearing its head side to side attempting to tear off the flesh. Its eyes were staring directly into his – He could see the iris, deep ochre in the center and flaring with gold and purple around the edges. He pounded on its back with one massive fist, brought his spiked knees up into its back legs. It yelped around his shoulder and then scrabbled at him with its massive forepaws, tearing into the flesh of his chest and upper abdomen. He screamed and growled in rage and pain.

Bringing one hand down, he curled his fingers around part of its chest, pushing upward. He brought his feet up as well, kicking into the stomach of the creature. It flew off of him landing on the ground several yards away. Silas' claws scrabbled in the dirt, pushing himself up.

It was already back on its feet, charging towards him, back feet pushing off the ground. It flew through the air, aimed at his head. Reacting quickly, he reached out his hands and grabbed it by the head moments from it reaching his face. Enraged jaws snapped inches from his eyes, spittle and foam flying everywhere.

<I convinced myself you weren't real eons ago! Leave! My hope is gone, do not reignite it!>

A strange voice resounded in his head. Alarmed, he dropped the creature and threw one of his lower knees into it, stabbing it in the shoulder. It screamed in pain, flying back away from him once more.

Landing on its feet, it circled him again, this time limping. He watched it, waiting for the moment to strike, the moment to land a death blow. It was doomed and it knew it. It stood straight and stared at him one last time, its eyes meeting his.

It rushed at him, leaping with all the enraged strength of a cornered animal. His massive hand swung out at it, claws outstretched. He caught it with one hand, fingers curled around its neck. He began to squeeze as it kicked and struggled as he cut off its air supply.

He hesitated a moment, his grip relenting.

<Seems such a waste to kill, doesn't it?>

<Yes, quite – Did it speak to us? How is that possible, with you blocking the Hive Mind?>

<I... I don't know.>

A shout rang out and a young woman ran out from behind a rock about fifty yards away.

"NO! RAGGER!"

He stared at her, eyes focusing on her. She froze, her eyes wide, her body rigid.

Silas snorted. <*I think my sniffer is broken. Because – I see her – But I sure as hell can't smell her.*>

<*Curious.*>

"Don't kill him! Please! I don't know who or what you are, but I know you don't mean any harm! We saw you bury that little girl."

He stared at her a moment longer, relinquishing his grip a little, allowing the beast to breathe. It coughed.

"Please let him go – He's the only friend I have. *Please.*"

<*She's lying.*>

<*Why would she lie? If you let it go, it would kill her too.*>

<*– Good point. Should we trust her?*>

<*I don't know, the last thing we couldn't smell tried to kill us – In fact, you've still got it in your fist!*>

The *Hellhound* struggled once more and the strange voice echoed through his head a second time.

<*You have my word; I will not harm you again!*>

His gaze returned to the beast which he held at arm's length.

Wondering a moment, he tried something. He opened his mind, searching for a tendril in the environment around him. He found it almost immediately.

<*Your word?*>

<*Yes! Please, let me go!*>

Another voice rang through his mind. It was the girl's this time.

<*You have both our words!*>

<*Very well.*>

He released his grip and the *Hellhound* fell to the ground, choking, gasping and wheezing. The young woman ran to it, throwing her arms around its neck, sobbing. He stared. It was possibly the strangest spectacle he had ever seen.

The Parasite prodded him questioningly.

Silas looked up, staring into the horizon.

<*What did you just do?*> The parasite prodded once more.

<*I'm not sure.*> Silas shrugged.

<*It was almost like you created a sub hive connection. We normally use that for troop communications, but it's rare and all*

information is still sent through the Raknila. Renegades are said to be capable of doing something similar, but you are not a Renegade. I demand to know how you did that.>

<I don't know. I've done something similar before, while trying to sense Renegades. Normally I just do it through you. You know how it goes.>

Linnerat was silent a moment, thinking about the new development.

<Humph. You humans are so strange – Your willpower alone changes things set in stone for millions of years.>

A sudden high pitched noise issued from where the two were lying. Dropping the internal conversation, he turned to the girl and the...

<Where did the Hellhound go?>

In its place lay a slightly smaller than average sized German Shepherd looking sort of dog, the girl clinging tightly to its fur. He stared yet again, the hundredth time in just a few moments.

Realization dawned upon him and he relaxed.

* *

Roach stared at the scene before her in horror, watched Ragger take one earth shattering blow after another and heard the wet, hollow thud that the *Hunter's* fists made as they pummeled into Ragger's pale grey flesh. Watched as the *Hunter's* spiked knees slammed into Ragger's shoulder, saw them tear a hole in it, heard Ragger's anguished cries of pain... and then, finally; she watched him leap into the jaws of death, saw him dangling by one powerful hand of the beast which he had enraged.

He was going to die. This monster was too much, too strong, too powerful. She couldn't watch him die.

She ran out, screaming.

The *Hunter* turned to look at her, his golden and violet eyes blazing, staring at her. She felt paralyzed by the stare. It wasn't the typical hateful, angry stare of a *Mayan,* it was deeper than that. It had anguish, it had pain – It had humanity.

Struggling to remember how to speak, she cried out, finding her tongue.

"Don't kill him! Please! I don't know who or what you are, but

77

I know you don't mean any harm! We saw you bury that little girl."

Out of the corner of her eye, she watched as Ragger squirmed, choking and gasping. The *Hunter* didn't move, just stared at her. Suddenly, Ragger heaved a sigh of relief in her mind.

<His grip is loosening. Oh god, Roach, I'm so sorry. I don't know why I did that. For the love of Raknir, keep talking to him. I don't want to die.>

She'd never heard Ragger speak like that and as the words reverberated in her mind, tears welled up in her eyes.
Suddenly, his gaze snapped to Ragger, eyes curious.

She opened her mind, listening. A powerful voice echoed in the recesses of her skull.

<... word?>
<Yes! Please, let me go!>

She spoke up in her mind, sending the beast an urgent thought.

<You have both our words!>
<Very well.>

His hands released and Ragger fell to the ground, body convulsing, coughing and hacking. She ran to him, throwing her arms around him and held his neck close to her chest, cradling his massive head.

All the while, the *Hunter* simply stared at them. She didn't care. She buried her face into Ragger's smooth grey skin, felt her face tickle as his hair began to sprout once more and felt her arms grow tighter around him as he slowly shrank.

She snuck a look at the *Hunter*. He was staring off into the horizon now, arms slack. Blood dripped from his right hand as it ran down his arm, leaking from his shoulder.

She snuggled her face into the now dog like Ragger, feeling his pulse, moving her fingers through his fur, finding wounds here and there, rubbing them softly. She moved her fingers towards the gaping hole in his front left shoulder. She found it, stuck her fingers in, felt the flesh pushing her fingers away as it quickly rebuilt itself. He whined in protest.

She removed her fingers, pressed her face harder into his fur, let out a soft sob. She'd almost lost him. Almost.

She heard a soft footstep and snapped her head back up to the look at the *Hunter*, who was slowly approaching them.

Bullard

Unable to believe her eyes, she stared in amazement.

CHAPTER 8 – STAR-CROSSED

Dec. 21, 2012, 10:57 p.m.

<G*ET OUT GET OUT GET OUT GET OUT!>* Lucas screamed.

Ateneran laughed in reply. *<This body is mine now.>*
<GET OUT OF MY HEAD! I WON<T LET YOU HURT HIM!>

Ignoring the human's anguished screams, Ateneran hobbled quickly and unsteadily towards the door, chasing after the human his host called *"Silas."*

He bared his teeth in what might have passed for a grin. Perhaps twenty humans lined the walls around them, watching in silence. Several of them shuddered at the grin. His teeth were covered in blood, the Human just having caused him to smash his new-found face into the floor. His nose stung and bled profusely.

<I will kill him and I will feed on him, do you like that idea? I see morbid thoughts in your head, human. Thoughts of killing, thoughts of feasting on your own. How delightfully disgusting a creature you are. I believe we will get along just fine.>

Of course, he had no such plans; he was going to lure the human to the breeders. However, he enjoyed playing with this fear steeped mind. He was regarded as a monster by most of his kin, but they were simple minded fools. There was a reason he was taken from planet to planet with the *Raknila*. It was even rumored that the next Ancient to be taken would be given to him. He would take his place among the Gods, the *Raknila*: the High Priests and Judges of the Galaxy.

<GET OUT OF MY HEAD!> Lucas roared.

<No, I think I'll stay – This mind is so rich, so vibrant! You humans are simply delectable, much better than any of my last hundred hosts or so.>

<I DON<T CARE! GET OUT GET OUT! GETOUTOUTOUTOUT!>

Ateneran chuckled softly, focusing on balancing the body he

had come to possess. So strange, this race, these – Humans. They were magnificent, but so far different from anything else in the galaxy. They walked on two legs, completely upright, much like the Ancients. They were this world's dominant species, technologically light years ahead of many other species congruent to this sector of the galaxy. They were amazing, really. With this planet, they would destroy the Ancients. The original plan had been to invade the home world – But Ateneran had other ideas.

The complete annihilation of the Ancients was all he desired. He would be the last God. And in time, he would be the Only God. All life would be his.

****

Stepping towards her was the Hunter. Up close his size was awe-inspiring. Muscles rippled across every inch of his body. Just looking at him, she knew he could rip her in half with ease. She crouched back, fearful, her fingers tensing as her claws extended. She watched him warily and he stared steadily back. Her soul quailed under that gaze. If ever there were a king among creatures and then here he stood.

She flinched as he suddenly brought up a hand, staring at it. Realizing that he had stopped, she warily took her eyes from his face and looked curiously at the hand he was holding forward.

As she watched, what she saw would be a sight she'd never forget.

His hand was slowly changing color, going from the dead grey to a familiar fleshy pink, the muscles stretching and bulging slightly, the claws retracting. He flicked his head to one side and a loud crack issued forth across the plains.

A surge of irritated energy flew through Roach's mind and at the same time, a low huffing noise reached her ears. It appeared that he was laughing. Her eyebrows knit together. Ragger growled low in his throat. Her fingers kneaded into his fur reassuringly.

The Hunter took another step forward. He appeared to be shrinking in size. The tattered rags of clothing he wore, hung loosely about his form now.

With another step, another loud crack sounded and he stumbled forward a little; as his knees reversed position. Catching himself, he stood up straight and arched his back, body twitching slightly as his ribs popped back into place. The spikes on his shoulders quickly retracted inward and he rotated each shoulder and then shrugged twice, shaking himself. His arms shrank quickly, dwindling like spaghetti noodles into a child's mouth. He continued walking forward, each step coming closer and closer to her and to the ground.

He opened his mouth wide and with a pop, the jaw snapped back farther on his head and skin began to form in the gaping maws on the sides, forming cheeks. Pink lips began forming and his mouth closed a little. He grinned with pointed teeth, running his tongue along them as they flattened out into their regular shape, gleaming and white. Hair started sprouting from the top of his skull, shooting up like strange little fountains, reaching their pinnacle and falling down, laying along his head.

He was only about ten feet away now, and she began to grow weary. Seeming to sense this, he drew to a stop, watching her.

He rolled his neck and shoulders once more and then thrust out his chest, stretching his back and twisting. Letting out a huge sigh, he returned to a regular standing position, his weight shifted slightly to his left hip.

Standing before her was a young man in his early twenties; medium length, light brown hair, one foot forward and staring at her. She examined him momentarily, taking him in. He was maybe six foot three, with a generously athletic build. Well defined muscle showed through the ripped and torn clothing he wore and his tattered jeans ran low on his hips. She blushed slightly, looking back to his face.

Looking slightly to one side, he raised an eyebrow as his irises flickered from the gold and purple of the *Infected* to a tawny brown.

He smiled and then he spoke. It was the same deep timbre which she had heard echo through her mind while speaking to the Hunter.

"Hi."

****

"Hi." Silas' voice reverberated across the plains.

He stared at the girl. She was crouching, hiding behind the dog, eyes wide, peering over the German Shepherd's form.

<She must be very small.> The Parasite remarked.

Bullard

<Witty observation there, Sherlock. Did you notice that the dog is a bit bigger than most too?>

<I did in fact, but what is this Sher...? Ah. Sarcasm.>

<Hey! You're getting better at this.> Silas laughed.

<Must you be so rude? I didn't get a clear look at her when she ran out the first time. I was busy focusing on the Hellhound, same as you. I really hate how what you're focused on is inevitably what I'm focused on. There's some form of mental symbiosis going on here and I don't like it. I think, in truth, if ever I were to try and extract myself from you, it would kill me.>

<You mean I'm stuck with your whiny ass forever? Shit.>

Stony silence ensued.

<Oh, I was just kidding.>

Movement caught his eye and he returned his attention to the girl. She stood. She was rather small, standing at approximately five foot, five foot two. Silky brown hair cascaded down and across her shoulders. Stark green eyes stood out from a pale, freckled face with high cheekbones and a tiny rosebud mouth sat pursed above a small pointed chin. She tilted her head curiously to the side, staring in silence.

Silas gave a silent gasp. *<Damn, she's beautiful.>*

<She is, isn't she?> The parasite agreed.

He took a step forward, speaking. "My name is Silas."

He was greeted with only another stare.

<I'd suggest that she can't speak, but we already have seen different.>

<Yeah, that's a little strange – I'll try the thought thing again.>

Reaching out with his mind, he found the now familiar tendril of thought. It was like a crystal bell in his skull, like the essence of her voice, soft and clear.

<I'm not going to hurt you.>

She gave no response, and Silas withdrew.

<Maybe she's in shock.>

He took another step forward and without warning, she rushed at him. He threw up his arms, alarmed. She stopped just short of him, eyes wide and wild. Lowering his guard a little, he stared at her carefully. Dashing forward the last foot or so, she threw her arms around him.

<Well, that was a little unexpected.> Silas remarked in his

head.

<Quite.>

She sobbed into his chest and clung to him. He patted her softly on the back, completely bewildered.

"I'm not alone," she cried.

He pushed her back a moment, looking at her.

"What?" He asked.

"I'm not alone!" She shouted, a smile crossing her face.

"What do you mean?"

The smile grew wider. "Watch."

She took a step back and held out her hand. He stared expectantly. "– What am I supposed to be watching?"

She held a finger to her lips and then pointed at her hand.

Still staring, Silas suddenly noted that her fingers were growing longer, the fingernails blackening and growing thick as they pushed outward. The skin grayed and took on a dead hue.

His eyes widened as he looked at her face and he saw her irises swirl with purple and gold.

****

Dec. 21, 2012

He stumbled through the doorway, tripping and falling to his hands and knees. Fresh pain exploded through his ankle as it jarred against the ground and as his hand which clenched the knife pounded into the ground. The knuckles had split wide open. He grunted, gritting his teeth, yanking himself to his feet. He glanced both left and right, looking down the alley. He bolted left, heading farther in, looking for a place to hide. It was dark, stars shining over head. The glow behind him, coming from the campus fires, seemed to have died down since he'd last been in the alley. He couldn't see more than ten or twelve feet ahead.

A slight shelf jutting out from one of the walls looked absolutely perfect. It was about a foot and a half wide and went all the way up to the roof. It was probably a gutter outlet. He pushed himself harder, his breath coming in rattled gasps, his throat burning. His muscles ached, his ribs and ankle screamed in pain; but the fear in his mind drove him onward.

Bullard

He brought one hand up, reaching for the corner. His arm fell down again of its own accord. He was so exhausted. He pushed his body around the tiny corner, pressing his back up against it. He sat a moment, listening, trying to catch his breath. He'd been right about hiding there. If he held his arm across his hip, he was completely hidden. He leaned forward a moment, breathing heavily.

The door slammed open behind him and a low laugh echoed through the alleyway, followed by a piece of a familiar nursery rhyme.

"Run, run, run, as fast as you can."

His eyes widened and he quickly stood up straight, drawing his arm across his pelvis. The laugh echoed once more, followed by slow, steady footsteps.

"Trying to keep from being found, are we? Don't bother. I can hear you breathing; hear your terrified heart pounding. Where are you little human?"

Silas held his breath. The footsteps paused.

"Clever."

A lump formed in Silas throat and he squeezed his eyes shut tight as a tear leaked down his face. It sounded just like Lucas. He said the word "Curious," all the time in that same tone. He'd cock his head to the side and scrunch up his eyebrows. Silas was very tempted to stick his head around and look. But he knew it would be a death sentence if he did.

The footsteps resumed.

"You're not making this easy, are you? Come out, come out, wherever you are..."

Lucas chuckled.

"You humans have the most DELIGHTFUL euphemisms. So – sadistic."

While he spoke, Silas exhaled through his nose and inhaled slowly, holding his breath once more. His life depended entirely on his timing now.

The footsteps were crunching closer.

"Thump thump. Thump thump. Thump thump. What a strong heart you have. With every step I take, the louder it grows – I know you are near."

Silas took another breath and another.

Crunch crunch crunch. Lucas couldn't be more than five feet away now.

Suddenly, the footsteps stopped and another chuckle emanated from behind Silas – This one close enough to send his spine crawling for cover.

"Now, now, Silas – Lucas is disappointed in you. Behind the corner? Really?"

Silas eyes widened as another step was taken. Tensing, he let out a hoarse yell and threw himself around the corner, knife raised.

CHAPTER 9 – DUEL TO THE DEATH

Silas stared in silence as her skin rippled and shifted from pink to grey, the tendons making soft squishing noises under her skin. The tendons disconnected and snapped back in different positions, roiling just under the surface of her flesh. It was eerie to watch – Even as many times as he'd seen it under his own skin. The hairs on the back of his neck stood up. Here was a sight he'd never expected to see anywhere else.

The fingers cracked as they finished elongating, snapping into place as the claws reached their final length.

From the middle of her forearm to her fingertips, her arm looked exactly like his while evolved, only smaller. The grey flesh slowly faded into pink from her elbow upward. He glanced at her other arm. It too, had changed.

He looked her up and down. She was now much taller, closer to his standing height while in human form. Her shoulders were broader and her stance farther apart. She smiled and showed pointed teeth. Her eyes flared gold; and purple swirled in the iris, the retrovirus reacting with her human cells, giving off the characteristic bioluminescence of the liquid that was carried within the viral cells; releasing among the human cells and alien cells alike, constantly repairing them, regenerating them. They flared gold with energy as human cells were turned and purple as the alien cells were repaired. After some time, *Mayan* eyes eventually faded from gold with purple to entirely purple, as the DNA was completely turned.

He stared at her. She stared back, eyes intense. He leaned back a little and then reached out and grasped her forearm.

"You're like me. Why don't you finish changing?"

She sighed, speaking in a guttural voice.

"I can't. I'm not like you. This is as far as it goes for me."

He raised an eyebrow and nodded his head at her arm. She sighed again and then slowly began to change back, fingers turning soft and supple once more, shoulders shrinking, teeth realigning.

She looked up at him.

"What did you say your name was again?" A hint of distrust colored her tone.

"My name is Silas."

The Parasite suddenly spoke up.

<And my name is Linnerat.>

She threw herself back in alarm, gasping. "You're infected?"

Silas paused a moment before replying, speaking inwardly at Linnerat.

< – Asshole. You've been in my head for nearly two years and have never had the courtesy to give me your name. Along comes a pretty face and you're all awww. Screw you man.>

Turning his attention back to her, he countered with a question of his own.

"Umm – Aren't you?"

"NO!" She shouted.

Ragger limped to his feet and came between the two of them, growling. He looked much more intimidating in this form, oddly enough. Maybe because Silas was smaller and less able to defend himself at this point. Silas' shoulder's tensed.

"Then what are you?" He asked.

"I'll ask the questions here." She replied in a venomous tone.

"No, let me get this straight. You travel with a *Renegade*, but you're scared of me?"

She eyed him suspiciously. "What are you?" She asked.

He shrugged. "I really don't know, girl."

She glared at him as the last word escaped his mouth. "I asked you a question. WHAT are you?"

It was his turn to sigh.

"Like I said. I don't know. I can give you my story, if you like? It might take a while. Would you care to listen? I can't tell you everything – But I can tell you most of it."

She continued staring a moment and then tilted her chin up in a steely nod.

Sighing, he plopped himself on the ground, crossing his legs, staring up at her.

"I was infected a little over a year and a half ago now. I guess,

Bullard

I'll just start from the beginning... It was December twenty first, two thousand and twelve – You know the day. We all know that day – I woke up at 11:32 a.m. I couldn't forget if I wanted too – That memory is burned into the very makeup of my brain. It was a bright and sunny morning in Miami –"

****

Dec. 21, 2012, 11:22 p.m.

A flash of purple and gold greeted him, glowing in the dark; the only distinct features on the otherwise dark silhouette that was his former friend. White teeth flashed in the darkness.

He swung the knife, slashing towards the eyes. He felt the blade scrape along flesh, catching bone.

Lucas howled in pain and agony, stumbling back, throwing his hands up to his face. Silas jumped back, dancing away and raising the knife high once more. Lucas moved back a few paces, one hand clenched to his face. He walked backwards slowly, staring at Silas. The creature seemed to realize that the upper hand had been taken.

"You'll regret that," it spat.

Silas didn't reply, he simply advanced.

"You have no idea what you're dealing with. Why kill me? Let me live and I'll give you a place at my side. This human seems to think highly of you. It will keep him co-operative, at the least."

Still no word from Silas. His mind was incapable of forming any coherent thought at that moment.

"Fool! You will not live out this night!"

Suddenly, Lucas lunged at Silas, reaching for his neck. Caught off guard, Silas flailed the knife wildly, connecting a few times, but causing no lasting damage. Fingers found his throat, squeezing.

Spots immediately burst before his eyes as his blood supply was cut off. He struggled wildly, purple and gold dots floating before him. The last thing he was ever going to see would be those eyes. He feebly tried to make a few more slashes at his attacker, but then an idea occurred to him.

Swinging his arm sideways and downward, he brought the full length of the blade directly into Luke's hip, hacking into the flesh, biting deeply into the bone. Warm liquid gushed across Silas' hand as he yanked the blade back.

Lucas screamed, letting go and falling to the ground, writing in agony. Silas fell backwards, one hand to his throat, coughing and hacking. Lucas began to crawl away, screaming unintelligibly. Silas too pushed himself away from the demented creature that once had been his friend.

Judging Luke to be a safe distance away, Silas stopped retreating, massaging his throat, staring at him. The creature rolled over onto its back and used its arms and right leg to push itself backward, left leg dead and dragging on the ground. It hissed in anger, staring at Silas.

Silas stared back stonily. He felt numb, his fingers and toes tingling. He pushed himself up, using the wall as support. Lucas crawled backwards even faster, screaming alien words at him.

He took a steady step forward, lips set in a mask of sorrow and hate.

The creature screamed at him, spittle flying from its lips.

He took another step and another, watching Luke's every movement. No. Not Luke. It. It.

Lucas looked over his shoulder, seeing how far away he was from freedom. Silas glanced upward a bit, looking. Lucas was about fifteen feet from where the pit.

Silas stepped past the cafeteria door, pushing it closed as he passed. It bounced, opening once more.

Lucas was pushing himself to his feet now, using the wall, following Silas' example. It grunted in pain as it discovered that its left leg was completely useless.

Crunch. Crunch. Crunch.

Silas was closing in. Lucas was only about five feet away now. Seeing an opportunity, Silas lunged forward, knife raised, a yell rising in his throat.

Blinding pain was waiting for him. He slammed into the wall, nose bleeding, teeth broken. He spit chunks of bone, holding his mouth in pain. The knife clattered to the ground.

He looked up, seeing that Lucas had picked up a rock and had slammed him in the side of the mouth with it. It grinned, its canines and front teeth strangely pointed.

Silas stumbled backwards and then let out a cry, hurling himself into Lucas' body, meeting him in the hip. It cried out with fresh pain. They crashed to the ground, the Lucas creature pounding the rock into Silas' upper and middle back. Each blow was like being hit with a sledgehammer. Reaching around, he grabbed a piece of rubble from the edge of the pit. He slammed it into the creature's already damaged left hip.

A fresh scream of pain reverberated through Silas' skull, piercing his ears, threatening to drive him mad. Part of his heart wanted nothing more than to rush to Luke's aid: to hurt whoever was hurting him. The other part of his heart drove on in grim determination, knowing what had to be done.

He struck again mercilessly. The creature convulsed beneath him, screaming, pushing at him, tearing at his body, slamming the rock into his back, his neck, trying to reach his head. Focusing, he brought down another blow.

Taking a chance, while the creature was preoccupied with pain, Silas pushed himself back and up, onto his knees. With a final look into his friend's eyes, he swung the rock directly into the side of its head with all the force he could muster. Blood spattered against the wall and the screams abruptly ended, though Lucas still struggled weakly under his weight.

Reaching to his side, Silas felt for the knife. Finding it, his fingers closed slowly around its hilt and he brought it above his head in fluid movement. Closing his eyes, he whispered softly. "Forgive me."

He plunged the knife downward, driving it deep into Lucas' skull with a crunch.

Luke's head slowly fell backwards, followed by the rest of his body, thudding against the ground, arms spread out. Blood pooled around his skull, leaking from the gash which marred his face and from his smashed temple. The area where the knife sat did not bleed. Silas stared at him for a long moment and as he did, the golden liquid color of Luke's eyes faded away, leaving only the crystal clear blue Silas had known for so long. Light from the remaining fires flickered in those eyes, lending them a hint of life, but still, Silas knew – He had murdered his friend.

A soft sob escaped him as he bowed his head over Luke's body.

CHAPTER 10 – ORIGIN OF THE SPECIES

Silas finished his tale and then sat in silence, staring at Roach. They had built a fire partway through his tale, stopping to collect some brush and tinder. The scrubby bushes and raggedy weeds worked surprisingly well. The fire burned strong and bright, crackling between the two parties, Silas on side, Roach and Ragger on the other. Silas tilted his head back, staring up at the stars. At night it was too cold in the atmosphere for clouds to form. The Earth had been cursed to exist without blue skies anymore, but they had been blessed with the clearest night skies the world had ever witnessed. He sighed, gazing at their beauty.

Roach spoke and he flicked his gaze back to her quickly.

"So – You've never been under infection control?"

"No. Well, that's not true, actually. I have been. But it's only when I, for whatever reason, lose consciousness. I usually awoke to dead bodies at that point. That hasn't occurred in over a year now though, and Linnerat and I have come to an agreement since then."

She looked at him suspiciously. "I want to talk to the parasite."

"What?"

"I want to speak with Linnerat." she stated.

He stared at her. "I'm not even sure that's possible."

"Can't you surrender control?" she asked.

"I mean, I suppose I could, but – Alright, give me a moment."

<Are you okay with this?> Silas asked Linnerat.

<Me? I'm positively enthused! I haven't had a run in a while. You ought to let me out of my cage from time to time you know.>

<I don't like how it feels.>

<And you think I like being a disembodied voice? If we're going to work together, let's actually work together.> Linnerat countered. Silas realized he had a good point.

Bullard

Hesitating, Silas made an offer. *<...After we destroy the hive link. We'll work out some sort of schedule. Ok? But if at any time we get into trouble, you give control back to me, you understand?>* Silas shifted uncomfortably with this thought.

<That sounds reasonable. What if I want to kill something?>

Silas chuckled. *<We'll see.>* He sighed. *<Alright – let's try this.>*

Silas leaned back, taking a deep breath and closing his eyes. Rocking back and forth slightly, he reached inward and found a spot to hold onto.

His eyes opened of their own accord and he gasped, yanking back control. Linnerat's voice echoed through his mind.

<Relax.>

<I'm trying!> Silas shouted.

<I know, just – take it easy.>

<OK.> He relaxed again, closing his eyes and finding his center once more.

His eyes opened again and this time, both he and Linnerat were ready for the involuntary response. Silas controlled his urge to jump back and Linnerat shoved Silas' consciousness to the side. Suddenly, Silas was not only aware of what he was seeing, but that it was very dark. He was confused for a moment.

Instinctively, he tried looking around him, 'twisting' his body. Suddenly the view of the world he had got a little larger, as Linnerat widened Silas' eyes.

"What was that?" a voice boomed, sending vibrations through Silas.

Another voice echoed, this one just coming to Silas through – his ears? Something? He didn't know. "What?"

The second voice was female and had to be the girl. He assumed that the first must of have been Linnerat using his body to speak.

He replied silently in his mind.

<What?>

<Something just moved in your head. That would be my body, but– >

Silas was very suddenly aware of the fact that he had limbs. Too many limbs. They all seemed to be encased in some sort of squishy, semi tight material. He tried moving them and the view of the world got larger again.

Bullard

<You're in my body? I see what you mean by it tickles. Odd that I've never been able to sense the tickling sensation. I always thought you were just whining.>

Silas waited a long moment before replying. *<This is weird. Why am I in your body? Did you know this would happen? And are your tentacles IN MY BRAIN?>*

A low chuckle rolled through his body as Linnerat laughed quietly.

<Yes – yes they are. And no, I had no idea. Don't worry, I'll keep my promise– >

<– Ok.> said Silas.

The window that was the world refocused and he peered across at Roach and Ragger. The view looked strange.

It was more vibrant and flickering than he was used too. It was like watching the world through an old computer screen; one that was trying to play a DVD quality film.

Silas voice rolled through the world again as Linnerat spoke to Roach. It sounded oddly clipped to Silas.

"Hello. You requested to speak to me?"

She stared curiously a moment before replying.

"You are Linnerat?"

"Yes – What did you say your name was?"

She looked him up and down, setting her hands on her hips. She looked like a cocky little shit to Silas. He didn't know if he liked that or not.

"Roach." She replied.

"Roach? Like the insect? Why would a girl as attractive as yourself carry such a name?" Linnerat sounded surprised. Silas could think of twenty reasons why she'd have that name.

She blushed at his words, turning away slightly.

Silas groaned in his mind. *<Oh my God. Are you hitting on her?>*

<No!> Linnerat declared.

<Yes you are.>

<Whatever.>

<Don't you whatever me! Since when do you use whatever?> Silas demanded angrily.

Linnerat ignored him. Silas steamed silently. Roach appeared to have gotten over her embarrassment, as she was replying.

94

Bullard

"Because I'm very small, quiet and I seem to be very hard to kill."

"Oh – I see. Is there any reason you called me out here? I sense that Silas is getting antsy. Thank you, by the way. It's been a very long time since I was allowed out."

Linnerat stretched one of Silas' arms.

"You have no idea how good it feels to do this." He remarked.

She laughed. Both Silas and Linnerat stared, attentions focused. It was a sound they hadn't heard in a long time.

"No, I do, actually," she said. "I was under infection control for some time, as you might imagine. Regaining control was like a breath of fresh air."

Linnerat started at the statement.

"Yes, about that. I mean – we, were wondering how you cannot be a symbiotic being like Silas and myself and yet still retain the abilities of the retrovirus."

She sighed and her expression grew somber. She glanced at Ragger and then looked back at them.

"It might surprise you, considering my choice of traveling companion, but I am actually terrified of *Hellhounds*." She paused at the look on their face.

"Long story short: I managed to hide out for nearly a year and a half in my area; long after both Human and *Mayan* troops had all but destroyed the place and moved on. It wasn't too hard. I was a bit of a tomboy beforehand and found it easy to rough it. I hid out in old buildings, barricaded doors, made runs for food once every other day, rationed things out. I lived rather comfortably, actually, picking up things here and there that had been left behind. I had the best of everything, except for food. But even then, after the stores ran dry, I would just hunt."

Silas suddenly became aware of a sudden warmth running down his back and through his core. A small tube had extended from what he assumed was his 'lower back' and into the flesh of the spinal cord.

<What the hell?> he said.

Linnerat held up a hand, stopping Roach. She paused, eyes curious.

<What?> he prodded Silas.

<What is this?> Silas wondered.

Linnerat paused a moment, analyzing what Silas was talking about, before suddenly bursting out in laughter.

"What's so funny?"

<What's so funny?>

Both Roach and Silas asked the same question at the same time.

Linnerat, still smiling, explained aloud to them both.

"Silas' consciousness appears to have been shoved into my parasitic body. Much of what our bodies do is completely involuntary. Working our way up an animal's brain stem, for example; mostly involuntary. We come with preprogrammed instincts. Our bodily functions are much the same – entirely involuntary and occurring on a regular schedule. Silas has just discovered feeding time. We extend a tube which lodges into the nearest, largest and juiciest vein and extract our fill of nutrient filled blood. Then through the same tube, excrete our waste products. It is also how we deposit the retrovirus into the bloodstream, as well as various muscle enhancing amino acids."

Roach's expression was one of mortification and disgust. Silas' mind recoiled in horror. Linnerat just laughed.

<You shit in my bloodstream after feeding off of me?> Silas asked in horror.

Linnerat only laughed harder.

As he laughed, Ragger sat up and started huffing along with him.

A voice entered their mind. <Poor human, dealing with our systems. I always did find our species rather distasteful. It's part of why I became a Renegade.>

Linnerat replied slowly and carefully, no longer laughing.

<Yes – About that. If you are a Renegade, how can you speak to us?>

The answer was surprisingly simple.

<Through Roach. Her hive connection is still intact, though – broken, I suppose would be the word. I don't know how to explain. She is cut off from the main Hive mind due to the impairment, but she is able to connect Renegade minds together over a range that they have never achieved before. I really have no idea how it works. It's amazing really; she has the ability to create an entire, self sustaining sub hive, all on her own. And at any rate, Renegades can still speak mind to mind, but only from very close range, within fifteen feet or so of one

another. You should know this.>

Linnerat thought about this for a moment before replying. *<I have a theory, but first – where is her parasite?>*

Ragger replied with another, even more simplistic answer – *<Listen.>*

They looked back at Roach. "Please; continue."

She threw a strange glance at Ragger, who looked over his shoulder at her and cocked his head to the side, giving a shrug. It was very odd for Silas to see a dog do that.

"As I was saying – I had things pretty good." Roach resumed. "Except for one thing: About – two months before the invasion, I was diagnosed with stage one cervical cancer."

Silas perked up. *<Cancer? Really? That's odd. Hmmm.>*

<What?> Linnerat asked.

<Nothing, I'll tell you later.> said Silas.

"They gave me pills and such to treat it, I went in for radiation the whole two months we were able – All but killed it. I ran out of meds about eight or nine months after everything went down. I would just head to the local super center and take what I needed from the pharmacy. Was easy enough. Nobody else was in that whole town anymore. But after I ran out, I realized that we hadn't beaten it. The cancer was still there, just suppressed by the medicine. The radiation was what I needed. I started getting tired, lethargic. Couldn't move as fast, couldn't run as long. Got cramps really easily." Her voice choked up.

Silas could see where this was heading.

"It was about six months ago, maybe seven. I'd been out hunting. I'd seen a couple deer running, followed them down to a ravine – It was stupid, I knew I should have found somewhere else, but I hadn't eaten in like two days, I was so hungry – I snuck down near an old bridge, taken aim and was about to take my shot. And then I heard them – the Drillers. You know the sound they make. That dreadful clicking?" She shuddered.

"Several of them had been hiding out, waiting for stupid passerby like myself. I tried to run – but..."

Her voice trailed off.

Linnerat walked up to her and gave her a hug. It was strange for Silas, very strange. He could feel her skin against his, but it was like it was through a thin screen. He could only assume that it was because his brain – *<How strange,>* he thought – acted as a filter for all the electrical signals, which were weakened by the time they reached Linnerat's brain. He poked around in Linnerat's brain, seeing exactly what he could do.

Linnerat pulled away, looking at her.

"So you were infected." he said.

She stared up at him.

"Yes. I was under its control for about three days. I'd started to change, patches of my hair fell out, my skin began turning that nasty pale grey. I didn't know where it was heading, never did either; we'd been walking for almost the three full days and we'd passed through a few cities, all of them abandoned. It was searching for others of its kind, I think. It didn't talk to me at all."

Linnerat interrupted.

"Yes, you are correct. Our orders are to search our others of our kind so we may join the troops, should we find ourselves alone."

"Yeah, I thought so." said Roach. "Anyway." She shook her head. "We'd come into another city and we had spotted a *Hellhound* pack, started making our way towards them. When we'd reached about fifty feet from them, it realized the others were all dead and slain, propped up. It was a trap, obviously and it didn't take very long for the parasite to figure that out. We'd run almost immediately, but not before some *Renegade Hellhounds* from behind the corner discovered us."

Linnerat looked at Ragger. Roach shook her head.

"No, Ragger wasn't one of them. It was just a random pack. It wasn't a very long chase, they were all full grown and I wasn't even halfway finished changing. It was no contest. They caught us, slammed us into the ground and –" Her voice trailed off.

She stopped, turning around. Leaning slightly forward, she tilted her head downward, staring at the ground. Raising one hand up to the back of her head, she pushed all her hair upwards and forwards, revealing the base of her skull. Linnerat gasped and both Silas and he stared in silence.

At the base of her head was a bare patch of dead grey skin, glistening and oily. Several small tentacles protruded from the skin, twitching randomly.

"T-t-they – they ripped the Yahntil out from the back of your skull? And it didn't kill you?" Linnerat stuttered.

She let her hair back down, turning back to stare at them. "Yes. And no, obviously."

Linnerat looked at Ragger, questioning him silently in his mind.

<My theory was correct then? She still has the hive connection open through what remains of her parasite. The portion of her brain which hosts the hive mind connection must not have fully evolved, leaving her able to; in essence, create and access any <Channel' she chooses. She is able to tune into what's specifically in Renegade brains. This is unheard of. How far does her ability extend?>

<About two miles, is as far as I've gone from her and still maintained contact.>

<Amazing...> Linnerat sighed.

Silas was thoroughly confused by all this conversation and decided he wanted control back. He shoved at Linnerat, who stepped down quickly. The eyes closed and Silas surged his consciousness forward. The first sensation that reached him was the smell of dirt. He smiled.

Linnerat huffed.

<After being in control of your body, this is really pathetic.>

At this, Silas felt slightly bad for him. He felt he better understood the Yahntil now, having essentially been one. Frowning, he apologized inwardly. *<Sorry mate. Call it a trade off for the fact that you shit in my bloodstream.>*

<Whatever.>

<You know, I like it better when you're all formal.> Silas thought.

<Whatever.> Linnerat didn't drop the snippy attitude.

<Oooooh sometimes you make me mad!>

<Whatever.>

<Fine, be a little emo bitch.>

<WHATEVER.>

Silas sighed, laughing silently.

He turned his attention to Roach and Ragger, looking at each of them before speaking.

"This is Silas again."

Roach raised an eyebrow at him. He ignored the look.

"I have a question for you. You said you had cancer? What happened to it?"

"Well – I woke up about two days or so after being attacked, so far as I could tell. I noticed while I was under control that little things, like my back aches, had disappeared and all that. When I woke up, my head was healed and I guess it just healed my cancer, too. It's never been an issue since."

Silas was beginning to get excited. His face lit up as she spoke. When she was done, he opened up with enthusiasm.

"I had cancer too. Leukemia, stage two. I dealt with it pretty much my whole life. When I was infected, it vanished too. I wonder if that has something to do with our ability to change?"

He glanced at Ragger sitting there.

"Do you know if your host had any form of cancer?"

<I don't know what you mean. What is cancer?> Ragger asked, tilting his head to one side.

Silas suddenly noticed one of the dog's ears was shredded.

In infected creatures, the regenerative properties they gained healed all old wounds and in some cases, even completely healed the scar that was potentially left by infection. As Ragger had all his fur, Silas assumed this was the case with him.

<So why didn't his ear heal?> He wondered. Thinking on it, he realized that the ear had been the same way even while Ragger was in Viral form; one of the long, sweeping ears had been ripped and ragged. Perhaps this was his name had originated from.

Looking at Ragger closely, Silas now realized that Ragger wasn't even a German-Shepherd at all, though he had similar markings. He was too small and his legs and snout were too long. He looked more like a Dingo, if anything. *<Dingo ate mah baby!>*

Giving an internal snort, Silas returned his attention to the conversation at hand, thinking quickly about the question he'd been asked.

"It's – It's a disease in which particular cell's DNA is corrupted and cells grow at an uncontrollable rate. It's normally fatal. Nobody really knows what causes it."

A momentary pause sat between the four of them, as Ragger thought about his answer.

<I have no way of really telling you – However, the animal does have memories of having severe abdominal pain and regurgitating blood.>

Silas snapped his fingers, staring at Roach.

"That makes a lot of sense. I never had any idea why I would be able to switch between forms and neither did the para – neither did Linnerat."

<Sorry to intrude,> at the mention of his name, Linnerat spoke up, broadcasting through Roach to all three of them. He sounded surprised that the link worked. <By Raknir, it really works. At any rate, this does make sense. If this is true, as Silas has said and the DNA of your cells were corrupted, part of what our retrovirus does is align all cells to a particular DNA structure, injecting them with our creator's DNA.>

Roach interjected. "Creators?"

It was Ragger that answered her question, projecting his words slowly and carefully.

<Yes. Our creators. The Ancients.>

He looked at Silas with a stony stare. Silas knit his eyebrows together, unsure of why he was being stared at.

<We were created by The Ancients, the Rakniran; long ago, far into the forgotten past.> Ragger began. <They were a dying species, destroyed by their own advancements. War and famine had ripped their society to shreds; all that were left of them were their bio-soldiers and scientists. They were a race of intellectuals; war, weapons and death were not their strong points. A risk run in such a society is that one insane individual will manage to get a hold of a weapon of indescribable power and spark a war which ends only in genocide. In a last ditch effort to save their species, they created us, the Yahntil. It means 'little one' in their tongue. We were little more than slugs, so they modified an insect on their planet, created the Drillers, took away their brain and placed us inside instead. The Drillers are little more than biomechanical suits. Silas – > He gestured with his head, pointing at Silas <—at first glance, looks like a perfect recreation of an Ancient super soldier. Upon closer examination, that isn't true... He's something far more. But I did not realize that until after my watching him for some time. To tell the truth, not until after fighting him. I simply didn't want to believe.>

Silas blinked, half opening his mouth. Ragger continued on, not stopping for questions. <Let me show you.>

Silas and Roach gasped in unison as the world before them changed suddenly, or so it seemed. Red shrubs surrounded him and a soft gold light bathed his flesh. Confused, Silas looked around, seeing that he was standing beneath a yellow sky, in a world clothed in green and red plant life. Small creatures wandered about. Silas' chest seized up as his adrenaline kicked in, not knowing where he was. Noticing this, Linnerat spoke softly with a soothing tone.

<It is alright. He is projecting to us his memories. Be honored children,> Silas assumed he must be speaking to Roach as well, <as this is something rarely done – and something which takes a great deal of energy. Many Yahntil are not even capable of doing such a thing. Ragger, as he calls himself, must be very old indeed, to be able to do this. What you are seeing now are the only recorded images we have of the Ancient's world before the Fall. We have no pictures from after.>

Ragger paused, nodding towards Silas, presumably to acknowledge what Linnerat had said.

The scene changed without warning, disorienting Silas. They appeared to be looking at a new world this time. Bleaker than current Earth, lightning crackled overhead and in the distance, lasers could be heard as they seared the air. Static made his hair stand on end as massive explosions sounded in the distance, sending pulses of electricity past him.

Before Silas' eyes, two armies stood at the ready, one very small, composed of huge creatures he could only assume were the Super Soldiers that Ragger had mentioned.

<Is that really what I become?> He asked silently. Roach's voice was the one that answered him, echoing quietly in his mind.

<Yes. That is almost exactly what you become. You, however... Are much larger. Much stronger. I could defeat a Rakniran on my own. You, I could not.>

Silas stared intently as his flesh crawled.

The other army looked all too familiar, even though they were entirely alien. Golden and purple eyes flashed all around and massive four and six legged creatures roared and yelled into the air. At the sound of a horn, the two armies rushed one another.

Another flash, this time to standing in a vast metal hallway, bathed in soft blue light. Massive statues gilded the walls, staring down at them. These creatures were unlike anything he had ever seen before. They were reminiscent of the creatures he had just seen on the battle field, but these ones were different, in many ways. They looked soft. Kind and benevolent, soft golden light fell from their eyes and Silas felt as though they were watching him. He felt unafraid in their gaze. It was a good feeling, one he had not felt in a very long time.

    <I had the privilege of walking one of the ancient temples, several hundred thousand years ago. They had massive statues of the Ancients there – I think they've all been destroyed now. That was while we still worshipped the Ancients. I also took it upon myself to look through the libraries left to us. I was always searching for more answers than were given me. This is the only reason that I have knowledge of what the enemy looks like. Not many of us are old enough now to remember even that we are a created species and many would be appalled to learn that we ever worshipped the enemy. I myself have only lasted so long, opting not to reproduce in some vague hope to become a Judge. That too is part of why I attacked Silas. Only an infected Ancient can create a creature of such power as to be one of the mighty Raknila. The new generations are arrogant and cruel. Some of them, though, have developed a sense of compassion – Humans and other species like them, I think have contributed very much to that.>

    Ragger paused, pulling himself back on track. Another scene met Silas' mind's eye, one that brought warmth to his heart. A fully grown *Snapper,* standing over a cowering child, staying its hand from killing him and his family; walking away from the carnage that he no longer wished to take part in; lying on the ground in the woods, writhing in pain as he made the transition to becoming a *Renegade.*

    <After our creation, we were placed on massive spaceships, lined with temples, rules written on walls, countless factories to create new Drillers, holding cells to travel with created life forms and libraries of all the technology ever created by the Rakniran. These ships are the asteroids you've all witnessed. Over the millennia, they have collected so much debris they are now indistinguishable from a space body. Sixty Eight ships were sent out, towards a nearby planet in another solar system; that was believed to have rudimentary life forms, nothing intelligent. The Rakniran went the opposite direction from you humans. If you were as old as the Rakniran, you would have conquered the galaxy and moved past it onto others, by that point in your evolution. The Rakniran, however, took an interest in the nature of things. They didn't know much about space, or other planets or civilizations. They had the ability to reach them, but outside terra-forming their solar system, they had no interest in expanding beyond it.> He paused momentarily once more, gathering his thoughts.

    <They were content in their space and this is what destroyed

them. They were confined to one space... You humans are not. It is part of why you frighten the Judges so.> He stopped at the look on Silas' face. *<Oh yes. They are afraid of you. Your species and you in particular, though they do not yet know that you exist.>*

<As for us and our purpose; Our ships reached the planet we were originally sent too and apparently, we slaughtered an entire intelligent population, comparable to that of your planet around the year 4000 B.C. From there, we built new ships and sent them out to a new planet. Upon hearing reports, our creators realized exactly what they had unleashed on the universe. With the last of their technology, they bred two-hundred super warriors. They were bigger. Faster. Stronger. Tougher than anything they had ever created before – or so they thought. They called them Syar, meaning destroyers – and then sent them into deep space after us. We greeted our Gods with open arms and they slaughtered us all on that first planet, as we had slaughtered the indigenous species. When we discovered that our creators had turned on us, we built up our defenses from another planet we had acquired, made a haphazard stand against the invaders when they came. We crushed a great many of them with ease and the first two Raknila were born. The super soldiers that were sent after us were incredible creatures. Not only were they biologically enhanced, but bio-mechanically enhanced as well. With the birth of the Raknila, came the birth of the true Hive mind. The mechanical and computerized portions of the enhanced Rakniran allowed and amplification of the natural telepathic ability found in all Yahntil to an unimaginable degree. One Yahntil could see everything occurring on a planet at once. Through the Raknila, we grew extremely powerful, having a command center that had thousands, even millions of eyes and ears. We would send probes into space with single drillers; find planets with life, taking individuals, studying their culture from afar, with just a single creature. Even we don't entirely understand how the Hive Mind works. It is a stroke of Genius from our creators.>

More strange memories in his head. As Ragger spoke, Silas 'saw' various images fly before his eyes. An Ancient super soldier falling, being crushed under the feet of some massive beasts. Another being ripped apart from all four limbs as a humongous squid creature wrapped its tentacles about him. And yet another, falling to the ground, reaching for his back as a Driller found his spine. Then, the very same, standing to his feet, blue blood running down his legs as he looked up at the sky and let out a roar, being the first true *Raknila*.

Ragger paused another moment, gathering his thoughts, thinking of how to continue.

<For example, there has been a Hellhound on Earth for almost 5300 Earth years, gathering information, sending it back through the hive link. Forever spreading through the galaxy, we are forever fulfilling our mission, it is our drive. But now, we had our own agenda. We would hunt and kill our betraying Gods. The Syar use guerrilla warfare, following us from planet to planet, attempting to kill the Judges, as that would cripple us in a way that we would never recover from. Last that I heard, there are twenty remaining Raknila and from estimates, around fourteen remaining Syar. When all of them are crushed, the Raknila plan to return to the Ancients home world and crush them all, take them, make many Judges and begin universal conquest. This is something I cannot abide by. We are an evil flood and one that must be stopped or put in check.>

This time, as Ragger spoke, Silas was met with a very strange scene, one that flickered and was gone in an instant. He had a feeling it wasn't meant to be seen at all. A sand filled desert, a pyramid rising over a crowd of dark skinned peoples; all bowing to a *Hellhound* with sweeping ears, one torn and waving in the wind, as the blood red sun sank beneath the dunes. As Silas' eyes widened, he felt the memory be ripped from his mind. He looked at Ragger, who pointedly did not return his stare.

<Linnerat. Did you see that?>

Linnerat's tone sounded grave as he replied. *<Yes. I did. I have a feeling our four legged friend here may be hiding something. I do not know if he is trustworthy or not.>*

Ragger sat a moment, thinking, trying to avoid any pressing questions.

<What does this "Cancer" do, exactly?> He asked.

Silas couldn't respond and it looked like Roach couldn't either. What had just occurred fit directly under the categorization of "Information Overload."

Linnerat answered for them.

<In Earth species, it appears to be a corruption in cells, in which they begin to act much like our own. They generate and regenerate at speeds unnatural for the body which they are in. It spreads and infects other healthy cells, corrupting their DNA. It seems

to me, that if such cells were to be infected with Yahntil DNA, the corruption would be increased tenfold, bringing out unknown facets of both ours and the human's DNA. We obviously change our hosts form anyway, but what if this cancer allows such rapid changing of cells that either specimen can be accessible? This is what appears to be the case of us three standing here.>

Ragger sat a moment longer, thinking about what he'd just heard.

<This seems likely, yes. The corrupted DNA and whatever causes it could ignite like a wildfire the moment the virus came into contact with it, spreading to the whole of the host body, changing cellular structure. This in and of itself would be an effect that would go beyond our ability to really understand. For example, why does your host appear as a Rakniran while in Viral form? How many others like us are there? The war has so consumed our race, that to my knowledge, we have yet to tap any of the Ancients' knowledge given us besides what is needed for weaponry. Yes – cancer, cancer indeed. The added regenerative ability would have interesting effects as well. Perhaps this too, is the cause for why you are unable to control your host, as is the norm,> Ragger told Linnerat. *<Somehow or another, the structure of his central nervous system will not change.>*

<Perhaps; I do not know. I have a feeling that will be a mystery that remains as such. This one has a very strong mind...> He left the thought hanging.

Ragger stared at them, nodding his head slightly, thinking slowly.

<He is different, yes. Be glad to be his, Linnerat. This boy is important. He is The Hunter, of that I am now sure.>

Silas snapped out of his stupor at this, staring at Ragger and his strange statement.

"What do you mean?" Silas demanded.

Ragger just stared at him blankly and then looked to the side disinterestedly.

Turning inward, Silas prodded at Linnerat.

<What did he mean?>

<I really have no idea, Silas.>

Silas grunted in annoyance, speaking aloud. "You Yahntil are fuckin' irritating."

Roach turned, giving him a funny look.

Bullard

Linnerat chuckled. *<As are you humans.>*

CHAPTER 11 – SORROW

Dec. 22, 2012
1:15 A.M.

A sob escaped Silas' throat, forcing itself into existence. His frame shook and all was black in his mind, spots circling about in his consciousness, sounds fading in and out, the outline of Luke's bleeding face sputtering and blurring before his eyes. Heaving backwards, he pulled in a quavering breath and then huddled back over once more, physical and emotional agony racking his body and mind alike.

Soft and wet, tears spilled from his eyes, rolling gently across his face and plopping softly onto the motionless form lying underneath him. The stars watched coldly from above as he writhed in pain above his friend's corpse, unfeeling and uncaring. He was nothing to them; they acknowledged neither his pain, nor his existence.

Another heavy sob uttered itself without warning, followed by a rattling gasp. He lay low, pressing his hands against Luke's ribcage, pressing his face tightly against the chest, feeling the skin beginning to grow cold beneath his cheek; felt a mixture of his and Luke's blood seeping into his hair. It coated his face, some drying, some still running in rivulets down his cheekbones. Silas' fingers twisted in the dead flesh and he whispered softly against Luke's chest.

"I'm so sorry – I'm so sorry. Forgive me, I'm so sorry, Oh God, what have I done, I'm so sorry. God *forgive* me."

The tears flowed, hot and fresh, pouring down his face and leaking onto Luke's breast, mingling with the blood. From there, they rolled towards his lips, getting in his mouth. Grimacing, he sat up, staring downward at Luke's body. His tongue flickered to his lips and the iron clad taste of blood filled his mouth and with it, came a feeling of rage. His teeth ground together as his jaw clenched, the bridge of his nose crinkled as he scrunched his brow and bared his teeth. Leaning his head back he let out a yell of anguish and anger, challenging the sky with his pain, daring it to look at him.

Reaching his hands high above him, he clawed at the air, screaming unintelligibly, tears streaming down his face until he ran out of air. Several moments passed, his agonized screams echoing about him, making their way towards the ears of anyone nearby.

Sucking in breath after breath his screams continued, until he could scream no more, could barely even breathe.

Bowing his head once more, he focused on Luke, whose eyes were still wide open, glimmers of purple and gold flashing about in the irises like lightning in the dark. Reaching out a hand, Silas ran his hand across Luke's face, closing the eyes and then slowly sat back, leaning on his heels.

Putting his hands on the ground, by his knees, he slowly pushed himself to his feet, wincing in pain. Reaching his full height, he turned his back on the still bleeding corpse and walked stolidly into the night.

May 2, 2013
Nashville, Tennessee
6:22 PM

Flinging his foot outward, Silas kicked the door off its hinges, guns pointed, semi automatic shotgun in his right hand, nine millimeter in his left. Roars immediately sounded forth from the darkness, purple and gold flaring all around him. Muzzle flashes lit up the room as he pumped the triggers over and over, swinging his weapons forward and back, loosing round after round into the dark room. Blood spattered his face. He was glad that the virus could only transmit through biting or blood transfer – skin contact posed no danger.

His fingers stayed and his arms fell to his sides as a rattling gasp rolled around the room, several creatures trying to crawl away to heal. Looking around the room, he pulled a clip from his belt and slapped it into the now empty pistol. Raising the weapon, he fired seven more shots, each of which were followed by a crunch and splatter as his target's skulls burst and painted the walls.

He stared around a moment and then reaching up to his face; Silas pushed the night vision goggles up and away from his eyes. Holstering the shotgun on his back, he turned and waved to the group standing outside the store, yelling.

"It's alright, they're dead. Come on, come get what you need. Keep your eyes peeled and guns at the ready –but nobody shoot each other this time, god damnit!"

Slowly and cautiously, the people filtered in, stepping around Silas, who stood silently in the doorway, monitoring what was going on both in and outside the store. A young girl of about ten years old came and stood by him, clinging onto his waist.

Looking down, he smiled. "Hey Alisissy. Why don't you go on in with mom, grab some food?"

She stared up at him with big brown eyes, speaking softly. "I don't wanna see the monsters. I've seen enough monsters. They freak me out."

Silas' face twitched in discomfort. Crouching down he embraced his sister in a hug. "Yeah, I know, I've seen enough monsters too."

Whispering softly in his ear, his sister asked, "Silas?"

Pulling away slightly, holding her at arm's length. "Yes?"

Her voice quavered as she spoke. "We're all going to die, aren't we? We're going to lose. Me and you and mom, we're all going to die, I know it."

She began to cry. Silas pulled her back into his embrace, speaking in a soothing tone to her. "Oh no no no, honey, we're not. I won't let that happen. Nothing's going to happen to us, I promise. I won't let it."

"But, how are you going to do that? You can't save the whole world."

He chuckled softly, pulling away from her again. "You never know, Alicia. I might. Can't give up hope, right?"

She stared at him, sniffling, tears running down her dirt covered face. Reaching up, Silas licked his thumb and then applied it to her face, rubbing some of the dirt away.

Pushing his hand away, Alicia protested. "Ewww!"

Silas laughed, standing. "Go find Mom hon; we need all the food we can get. Don't worry about the monsters; I blasted all their brains out. Go on, shoo, I need to keep watch, ok?"

Turning away, running inside the store, she called back over her shoulder. "Alright. I better not have any new nightmares, or mom will have your ass!"

Bullard

He yelled back at her. "I told you not to use words like that, you little shit!"

Her giggle echoed back from within the store.

He smiled and then turned around, looking out through the doorway, scanning the broken buildings and their hollow windows for movement, be it human or otherwise. He and his group were always on the lookout for survivors.

He sighed, turning slightly, looking back through the doorway in which he stood.

His group. He never really liked that idea; he didn't like feeling responsible for so many lives. But he supposed he couldn't help it. He had after all, brought them all together, in one way or another. The group was comprised of about seventy members, men, women and children all. Their oldest member was a feisty old man of seventy, who went by the name of Matthias, their youngest was an 8 month old child named Joshua.

Every single one of them looked to Silas to lead them, to protect. And so it was. Silas did his job to the best of his ability, keeping them safe, keeping them fed and clothed. The latter wasn't too hard, there were canned goods and abandoned clothing stores everywhere. If none of those were nearby, they raided houses. The former, on the other hand, was a nightmare. They'd lost six members just a week prior, due to Silas' inattentiveness. He'd walked away for less than one minute, to investigate something and had come back to a slaughter. He would probably never forgive himself.

Turning back to look outside, his thoughts turned back through time.

After leaving Luke, Silas had traveled up to Troy, Illinois, his home town, finding his mother and sister safe and sound, hiding in their home. Nothing had quite reached them yet, but they were scared, hearing rumors and without power. His father had been on business in Chicago, which had been hit. Silas had wanted to go try and find him, but his mother, sister and logic all told him it was pointless, he was probably already gone.

From their hometown, they'd stolen a moving truck packed up what food and survivors that they could, scavenging along the way, traveling southward, hoping that with less major cities nearby, the infection would take longer to reach them. They'd been right, but the infection spread faster than anyone could have ever predicted.

Bullard

A shrill scream echoed from in the store behind him, interrupting his thoughts. Turning, eyes wide, he ran into the store, a single worded shout reaching his ears.

"DRILLERS!"

A scream tore from his throat as he ran forward, guns raised. "ALICIA!"

****

"I need to go back to the fortress."

Roach stared at him incredulously.

"You just barely escaped with your life. Now you want to go back there?"

Silas tossed his head back and laughed. "Barely escaped with my life? Oh ho ho, no... That, my dear, is a story for another day."

She raised an eyebrow. "Why do you need to go back?"

He smiled at her. "For my stuff, of course."

"And what would that be? Why are we going to go and risk our lives for your 'stuff'?"

Silas rolled his eyes. "You're going to wait outside, while I scale the wall and go get my shit. No risking of lives or anything James Bond. Get in, get out, get gone."

Her eyes widened.

"Wait, what makes you think we're traveling together at all? Why don't we just go our separate ways? And what makes you the leader?"

Silas was thrown by the question. Why wouldn't they? "I-I-I – Um."

She laughed at the look on his face. "You sure you wanna be the leader? Sure are easy to confuse, ain't ya?"

Catching on to her ruse, Silas glared at her. "You think you're funny?"

She shrugged, grinning at him. "Oh... It happens on occasion."

Smiling at her, he replied sardonically, "Ha. Ha. Ha. Come on, let's go. I don't wanna stick around here much longer; don't like staying in one place."

She frowned. "Really? Why not?"

"Sitting target."

Her facial expression changed, twisting to the side.

"Yeah, guess you're right. How far are we from your fort?"

"Well, I was running for about twenty minutes at full viral form—"

He paused at the questions look that crossed her face.

"Viral form," he explained. "I don't know, it's just what Linnerat and I call it –when I'm –morphed, or whatever you want to call it. Transformed. Everything else just sounded stupid."

Roach's lips formed a silent O. "I gotcha."

"Anyway," he continued. "We were running for about twenty minutes in full viral and then another twenty walking? I'm not entirely sure. Linnerat, what do you think?"

<What? Hm, oh, I'd say about forty minutes total, yes, you are correct.>

Still speaking aloud, Silas addressed Ragger and Linnerat.

"You two have been rather quiet. What's up?"

Ragger turned his head slightly, staring at Silas, not replying. Linnerat answered briefly. *<We are discussing some important issues. Our friend here has a very long and interesting history.>*

Silas was a little mad at hearing this.

"What the hell? You two can talk without either of us hearing you?"

Roach looked at Ragger with a slight look of hurt.

"You are using me to talk to each other? Why would you –"

Silas held up a hand, cutting her off. "No, I don't think they are. Linnerat is still a fully functioning Yahntil. We'd agreed that after burying Natalie, he'd go ahead and convert himself over to *Renegade* status."

At his words, Roach backed away slowly. "He's not *Renegade*? How do you know he hasn't already betrayed us?"

"He wouldn't. I know him too well."

She blinked at him, fear in her eyes.

A sigh resounded through all their minds. It was Linnerat. *<Silas, I haven't been entirely honest with you.>*

At the words, Roach tensed in preparation to run.

<I disabled myself not too long after infecting you. Maybe two of your months. I decided that it was entirely pointless for me to continue in keeping in contact with the Hive. Watching this world fall from your perspective, watch you struggle and fight and rage against the war machine that is my species... I decided that I hate my species. I

hate what we do, I hate what we are. I decided that our mission is folly and what you do is far more a noble cause to devote myself too. Mere survival, more noble a cause than what my species has become. Of course, you had the same hatred for me that you did your species, how could I blame you? I was one of the creatures that destroyed your life, took from you your best friend, your mother, your sister and probably your father. Took from you all who was important. I was one of the creatures which has taken your world and turned it upside down. I lay no blame to you for the hatred harbored against me. I knew that in time, either we would die, or you would move past the resentment which you held. And so, I disabled my own link to the Hive.> He paused momentarily before continuing, letting what he had said sink in.

<I left yours alone, because in all honesty, I was never able to access it until recently; you had so well cut yourself off. Those first few days, in which we fought one another, I was able to use it, but once you took control, I was never again able to even come near it. Even during times when you were unconscious, that part of your mind remained untouchable to me. When I finally did, I heard words of slaughter, blood, murder and laughter. It seemed so foreign to me, that I was repulsed by it. After so long living inside your mind, Silas, full of kindness and selflessness, I knew that I would never again be able to return to that world. And so I set about trying to earn your trust, choosing to tie myself forever to you and your endeavors, rather than be a part of the evil that my species has become.>

Silas sat in stunned silence. "You chose to be a part of me, instead of your people? Even though I hated you? Why?"

<As I said; I figured either we would work things out or we would die. Either way, I had nothing to lose.>

"What of telling me we would have to destroy part of my brain?"

<Well, for the charade to work, of earning your trust, I would have to do something to prove to you that I was doing something, wouldn't I?>

Silas laughed aloud.

<Yes, I suppose you would.>

Taking control of Silas' eyes for a moment, Linnerat aimed them at Roach and Silas felt his lips pull into a smile, before being given back control.

<Perhaps there is some credibility to this thing you humans call

Bullard

Fate.>

CHAPTER 12 – FAMILY MATTERS

He pounded through the doorway, glancing left and right, throwing the night vision goggles down around his face. The group was in complete disarray, running left and right, making their way towards any and all exits. Panicked as he was, he knew he couldn't let the group fall into any traps.

"Make for the side entrance!" He cried aloud in a hoarse voice, pulling short in a quick stop. "Do you hear me? Avoid all side exits; make for door we came in ONLY! Gather together in a circle, protect the old and the young, get the flame throwers from the back of the truck and fend off the drillers! Kendall!" He pointed at a young man who looked to be about seventeen. "Bring me one of those throwers. Now." The boy nodded, dashing towards the front door, flashlight beam bobbing.

Pushing forward, leaping over debris and slain enemies, old skeletons Silas made his way through the store, shouting for his sister and his mother. "Alicia! Alicia! Mom! Where the hell are you guys?"

Peering through the green light that was his vision, he searched the corners for his family. He could see no one, everyone in his group had already gone streaming past him, save for eight. The store wasn't that large, he couldn't see where they could be. Perhaps some had slipped by without his notice, though it wasn't likely. Glancing up, he noticed a black set of double swing doors, which most likely led back through into the storage area. The store wasn't nearly as spacious inside as it appeared to be on the outer. Silas assumed that a great deal of the space must be contained in the backroom. He veered towards the doors.

Stopping short just before them, he holstered his pistol, reaching back for his shotgun, bringing it to bear and holding it up to his shoulder. Using the muzzle alone, he pushed the doors inward, stepping forward cautiously. Taking another step forward, he let the doors swing shut behind him.

Bullard

An ominous clicking sounded about him and a scuttling noise came from his left.

A whisper dropped from his lips. "Shit."

Glancing around, he saw that he was surrounded by large metal frames, pallets and boxes. There were many hiding places there in the shadows, for friends and foes alike.

Taking a chance, he called out for his sister and mother.

"Alicia? Mom? Are you in here?"

The clicking noise sounded again, this time from directly ahead of him, followed by a loud squeal. His eyes widened.

A Driller flew through the darkness, its four legs spread wide, ready to tear into Silas' flesh. Gritting his teeth, he swung the gun upward, pulling the trigger. The blast deafened him in the tiny area. The driller screamed, flying backwards through the darkness. Silas heard it hit the floor, skittering across the floor, heard it kicking its legs as it tried to bring itself back upright.

Pumping the chamber, Silas backed away, moving through the swinging doors, searching back and forth with his gun.

Stopping a good five feet from the doorway, he let out a yell. "KENDALL!!! WHERE THE HELL IS MY THROWER?"

A huffing came from behind him as the young man ran up. Turning, Silas saw that hugged to his chest was a large tank with a hose and nozzle attached. Matthias, who had been on active duty during both World War II and the Vietnam War, had had the brilliant idea of using modified electric power washers filled with gasoline and lighter fluid as portable flame throwers. The idea had been their group's saving grace. It was the only effective weapon they had against Drillers.

Drillers were immune to all conventional weapons; melee weapons broke on their hide, projectiles simply bounced off of them. It had been said that a shotgun blast at point blank range would kill them, but it was well known that if you got close enough to shoot one at point blank range, you were already dead. The little fuckers traveled in packs.

However, they'd discovered that while the armor was projectile resistant, they did not like fire, in the slightest, keeping away from burning buildings by a full twenty feet or so, straying away from even small sources of heat like embers. With a flame thrower, a person could literally cook a parasite in its shell.

Bullard

Handing the shotgun to Kendall, Silas gave him a curt order. "Help me put it on."

The boy nodded, reaching out a single hand, he snatched the gun and placed it between his knees. Loosing a grunt, he heaved the heavy tank up with one hand, the liquid sloshing around inside.

Grunting, Kendall managed to sling the pack up high enough for Silas to quickly turn and slide both arms into the straps which had been secured to the makeshift outer chassis.

"What's in it? Fluid or Gas?" Silas queried.

"Uh, I'm not sure. The last station we passed was full up on diesel, low on regular. It might be a mixture of diesel and fluid."

Silas raised an eyebrow. "Diesel? We've never tried using diesel, have we?"

"No sir."

"God Damn – Alright, well we'll just have to make this its test run, eh?" Silas winked.

A smile crossed Kendall's face. "Damn straight sir."

Silas cracked a grin and then reached out a hand and slapped the boy lightly on the cheek, his look turning sober. "Eight minutes."

The boy nodded curtly, reciting the burning motto. "I know the drill sir. Eight minutes and then we torch the building with or without you. No ifs, ands or buts. Survival of the species. We are the last."

"Damn straight. Now go."

The boy turned on his heel and ran for the exit. Silas watched him silently for a moment, a bad feeling growing in the pit of his stomach and then called out. "Kendall? I love you, I hope you know that."

Turning while running, jogging backward, Kendall threw up a salute, calling back to him. "I love you too, bro. Now go get our family." With those final words, he flipped back around and bolted out the door.

Tears in his eyes, Silas threw a salute, watching his brother's figure recede. He had a deep feeling that it was going to be a very long time until he saw him again.

Shouldering the pack, he turned back to the swinging doors and took a step forward.

****

Bullard

"So, where do we go from here?" Roach asked.

"It's about another three miles to the fort. You see the forests off to our right? Those start about five miles out from the fort and continue right up to about a hundred feet from the outer fortifications. If we were to head into it from here, we would travel about seven miles, coming out by the city ruins. We will be heading through those after we collect my belongings." He glanced at Roach, her arms hanging limply by her sides. "Speaking of which, do you even have any belongings?"

She shook her head.

"I scavenge. I've found it to be easier. Cities are almost always empty, only *Renegades* and drillers inhabit them. We get along with the one group and the other pay no attention to us."

Ragger turned his head, looking at Silas, his shrewd black eyes unreadable.

<*When you have lived for so long as I, you realize that material possessions are of little consequence. And beyond that, how inconspicuous would I manage to be carrying a satchel?*>

Silas raised an eyebrow. The mutt had a point.

<*He always has a point.*> Linnerat laughed.

Silas laughed inwardly. <*True dat.*>

After about twenty minutes of the, the group walking in silence, Silas in the front, Roach in the middle and Ragger bringing up the rear, Roach asked a question.

"Alright." Roach said. "So the plan is to... what? Grab your shit and run? Where do you plan on going?"

"We're headed to Chicago."

This time, when Roach spoke, her voice sounded a bit higher than usual.

"You say you have a hard time getting into forts, but you want to try and get into a shielded city? And not just any shielded city, you want to try and get into the new capital of the world resistance? You're insane. Why the hell am I traveling with you?"

Silas smiled, turning to her.

"My dashing good looks." He winked and she laughed aloud, tossing her head back, small, white teeth showing. Silas stared.

"You're cute, but you're not that cute. Brad Pitt isn't even that cute. Johnny Depp, maybe, but I don't think so. I think the answer is that I'm plum nuts too."

Relaxing, she looked at Silas, catching him staring. "What?"

Turning quickly, looking at Ragger, Silas' eyes went wide and he shook his head. "Nothing."

This time, it was Roach who raised an eyebrow, opening her half grinning mouth to ask a question that Silas had no intention of answering.

Suddenly, she stopped, pointing ahead, her expression changing.

"Look! The trees stop just a little ways ahead! That means we're close, right?"

Nodding, Silas answered softly. "Yeah, it does. And keep your voice down. There are sentries out this way. I don't know about you, but I've already been shot once in the past few days. I'd rather not have it done again."

Roach's eyes widened and she pursed her lips.

"You got shot? When?"

"About three hours before I met you."

<What? Three hours? That's impossible. Not even I can heal that fast.> Ragger this time.

Silas opened his mouth to answer, but Linnerat cut him off.

<He's not lying. His body heals from major trauma within time frames that seem almost miraculous. I remember approximately six months ago, we had a run in with a Leaper; Silas had his arm completely ripped off at the second elbow. The healing process was almost instantaneous in beginning, less than a single pint of blood was spilt. Within one planetary rotation, his arm had fully regenerated. He's also been shot in the head and made a full recovery. That one I remember quite vividly. Had the bullet penetrated any deeper, my body would have been hit.>

Ragger just stared.

Irritated, Silas let out a growl. "What, did I grow a third head? We all get it; I'm a freak, even by the standards of brain invading aliens. Stop being surprised by every little god damn thing. Now, let's move. I want my stuff so we can get a move on towards the city. We might be strong, but I do not like being out in the open longer than I have to be."

Turning, he stomped off into the woods, heading towards the fort.

CHAPTER 13 – DEATH AND DENIABILITY

The darkness lit up by the luminescent lenses which sat upon the bridge of his nose, Silas moved forward silently through the doors, his breath bated and tight, each one coming in a shallow, ragged gasp. His finger was pressed tightly against the pressure washer's trigger, small spurts of fluid spilling from the nozzle as he trembled, each drop falling short of the flame, splashing on the floor, casting a distinctive echo about the room.

Grimacing, he eased up on the trigger, but almost instantly, a skittering noise sounded off from his left. Jerking to the side, he pulled the trigger, a jet of flame flying through the air, coating boxes of canned food and bags of flour in a burning film of gasoline.

A curse flew from his lips. "God damnit."

A screech issued up ahead and another skittering, coming towards him. Looking ahead, he could see nothing, the light from the flames blinding the goggles, white noise before his eyes. Quickly reaching up, he pushed the goggles up across his face. With the goggles off, he could see far better by the light of the fire, but he still couldn't find the source of the noise.

Placing his hand underneath the barrel of the flame thrower, he leaned forward slightly, creeping further into the darkness, trigger finger at the ready.

****

They traveled in physical silence, though Silas was mentally fuming.

<Why you gotta go and spill shit all over, eh? Can't I speak for myself? What reason did you have to tell him anything like that?>

<I do apologize, Silas, though I do not understand your anger. Are you irate for me speaking over you, speaking in your place? It was

not my intention to be rude or un-empower you. I am sincerely sorry.>

<Whatever. Lemme be. Go talk to your hero.>

<What is the point of this hostility? My hero? Who, Ragger? He is a great and admirable character, this is truth, but he is far from being any sort of hero to me. Not in the slightest. My hero is nothing like him.>

<Ahaha, right, whatever. You big alien types just love a killer. I can see it in him. He's a killer to the core. Even if he's decided to change his ways, he is still a killing machine. I have no doubt you...>

<Admire him? Absolutely. I admire him to a great extent. He is a Ripper, after all. They take millennia to evolve. In the beginning, he would have appeared to be nothing more than just a regular Hell hound... However, if a Yahntil remains in a singular body for a long time, living, fighting, surviving, they slowly evolve into what is known as a Ripper. They are beautiful, perfect creatures. Perfect fighters. For him to be a Ripper, means that he must be upwards of three thousand years in that body. He may well have been THE original scout for this planet. Yes. Yes, I admire him. But as I said, he is not my hero.>

<Oh really? Who is then?>

<I'd rather not say. We all have our dirty secrets, Silas. I will keep mine and you may keep yours.>

<What? You're in my head! I don't have any secrets, you can see practically everything!>

Linnerat laughed. *<Yes, quite. Practically everything. The key word in that sentence is 'Practically.> You have many secrets, Silas. Things which your subconscious has sealed off; protected, not only from me, but from yourself. Your family. Your friends. Many gray areas in your head, many small pockets of emptiness, which I cannot penetrate. I see them in your dreams, sometimes, but never otherwise.>*

<Really? Like what? What can you not see?>

<Your sister. Your mother. You didn't even bring them up when speaking to Roach. The last half of your story was a lie.>

Silas gasped, stopping short in his tracks, the memory flooding back to him.

****

She leapt, flying out from behind her hiding place, a makeshift stack of boxes, probably food that she and their mother had been gathering.

A screech in her throat, she collided with Silas, knocking him sideways, sending both he and her crashing to the ground. Silas snatched at his lower back in panic, fearing the worst.

She leaped to her feet immediately, circling around him.

Struggling with the heavy pack, he managed to push himself to the side, cursing, dragging the barrel of the flamethrower along the floor, unattended. The lighter had closed and gasoline flowed freely from the now damaged tip.

"Damn! Alicia?"

At the sound of her name, she froze, her face flickering in the harsh light of the fire.

He pushed himself to his feet, grunting. With dismay, he noticed that the right shoulder strap had broken on his flamethrower. Snarling, he threw it to the ground and looked up at his sister.

"Thank God you're alright. Where's Mom?"

No response.

"Alicia? Are you ok? We need to get out of here. Where is Mom?"

A sudden, minute movement caught his eye, as blood ran down his sister's bare calf into her sneakers. His eyes followed the trail upward to her blood soaked shorts, widening as they went.

Sudden realization hit him as tears filled his eyes and his gaze flickered back to her face, which he could now see was twitching violently; eyelids fluttering, her mouth uttering voiceless words. It was an all too familiar sight and in his mind's eye, her face slowly morphed into that of Lucas'.

Silas felt like someone had punched him in the throat. "No. God damnit. No."

Alicia's eyelids flickered one final time, before she straightened and another screech emitted from her mouth.

She leaped again, arms outstretched, fingernails aimed for his eyes and he brought up the pistol which he'd had hidden in the back of his jeans and squeezed off a single shot,

The impact of the bullet threw his sister's frail body through the air, slamming her into the pile of cans and boxes which she'd been hiding behind.

Stepping forward cautiously, pistol gripped tightly, Silas stared at where his sister had landed. A single pale white hand trembled against a can of corn and one blood drenched shoe was held aloft in the air. The fingers twitched and he paused. The movement stopped and he stepped forward again, peering at her small, near lifeless body. A hole about the size of a soda can was in her chest and blood flowed freely from the wound in all directions. As he watched, he could see swirls of blue appearing in her blood, floating to the surface and then swirling down once more.   Her fingers twitched again and she struggled to turn her head to look at him.

No longer worried, he crouched beside her and reached out a hand to lay it atop hers. With a sudden burst of strength, she snatched at it and pulled it down to her side. Startled, Silas brought his gun up, but at the look on his sister's face, he stopped. There was nothing she could do to him now.

"Alicia..." Her name left his lips unbidden.

She smiled and coughed, her beautiful green eyes peering up at him.

"I'm d-dead, aren't I?"

Tears ran freely from his eyes and he fought to keep his voice steady as he answered.

"No, no baby, you're not."

"Silas, you sh-sh-shot me. My heart isn't beati-ing. I can feel it. Or can't. Can't feel it." She laughed, blood leaking from the corner of her mouth.

A twitch of a smile crossed Silas' face, but then, thinking, he froze.

"Wait, how are you in control?"

A look of annoyance crossed her face and she narrowed her eyes.

"I don't k-know. Maybe it's unconscious. I hit my head pretty hard – why do you care?"

A look of pain and humor crossed Silas' face. Still the same old smart ass, even as she lay dying. The emotion quickly passed and he whispered to her softly.

"I'm so sorry sissy. This is entirely my fault."

Her breath rattled, as she struggled to breathe. The bullet had ripped a hole in one of her lungs and each breath was a death rattle. Silas fought the urge to run away, to turn his head in shame, to break down and cry.

"No, it's n-not. They got mom. Go find her. P-p-please."

Another look of pain crossed Silas' face, this time without any trace of laughter. "I was afraid of that."

"Silasss? It hurts."

"I know baby."

Her hand slid from his and her eyes pleaded with him, warm and caring, they invited her death by his hand. Biting his lip, Silas stood, staring at her.

"Please, Silas. Please. D-don't let me live like this. It hurts. Don't let me become one of them."

She coughed again, blood leaking from her lips and nose and agony filled her eyes.

He raised the weapon, his face a mask of agony and fear. "Alicia…"

Closing his eyes, he turned his head to the side and pulled the trigger, aiming for her throat.

The shot echoed around the room, followed by a choking gurgle, which faded within a few moments, it too echoing about the room.

"I'm sorry."

Gasping for air, Silas hit his knees, the gun clattering to the floor. A deep stillness fell and all that could be heard was the crackle of flames and the racking sobs of a heartbroken man.

CHAPTER 14 – INITIATIVE

<Y*ou killed them yourself? That must have taken strength untold.*>

Silas scowled. <*You're really not helping my mood. If it were possible, I'd tell you to stay out of my fucking head.*>

<*My apologies. Should I "shut up," now?*>

<*Yes. Please do.*>

A third voice intruded. Roach. <*Silas, are you alright,* why'd *you stop? Is there something nearby?*>

He sighed, resuming his former pace.

<*I am fine. Linnerat brought up a painful subject, bad memories.*>

<*Oh. Ok. Just making sure you're alright. Don't go nuts on us or anything.*>

He chuckled. She reminded him of Alicia. <*I'll do my best. No promises.*>

<*You'd better, mister!*>

"Mister?" He turned his head to the side, looking at her, speaking aloud. "Mister? What the hell."

She laughed, shrugging her shoulders. "I don't know, I used to say it to my Dad all the time, whenever he got mad he'd point and say "Listen up little lady!" so I'd say "Something something Mister!" And it would always crack him up and he couldn't yell anymore."

Silas' eyebrows raised a little and a small grin crossed his face. "Interesting. If my dad was ever pissed off, I'd just avoid him. He's a bit of an angry man, my father. I love him, but damn... It's always his way or the highway. Military man, through and through."

"Is he still alive? You talk about him as though he is."

"He's the only one I'm not sure about. He and my brother, Kendall. I haven't seen either one in a long time. If they are alive, they will be in Chicago. I've been slowly making my way there, to see if I can find them. My mother and sister are dead, that I know for sure."

"For sure?"

He nodded. "For sure."

"How can you be so sure? You should never give up hope, you know!"

He turned his head to look forward once more, his eyes blurring a bit. "No, I know for sure. There is nothing to hope for."

"Really? How could you possibly know? Did you see them die? I thought you told me you were separated from your family. And if they're anything like you, they could have escaped. They could be out there, living, happy! In one of the sheltered cities! Ok. Well, probably not happy, but you know what I mean."

Pulling up short, Silas turned and grabbed Roach by the shoulders, startling her. She yelped and Ragger let loose a low growl in his throat. Silas ignored both, staring Roach in the eyes.

"No. I know, because I killed them both with my own hands."

Her eyes grew wide and her mouth worded silently as he let her go and turned on his heel, stalking in the opposite direction.

"Again, come on, let's move!" he said, breaking into a run.

Roach stood a moment longer, thinking and then she too broke into a run, chasing after Silas, Ragger close on her heels. "Hey, wait! Wait up, I'm sorry!"

****

What seemed like hours had passed in Silas' mind, though he knew it had probably been less than a minute or two.

He opened his eyes and tears spilled out onto his face.

Through the watery film, he caught a glimpse of his sister's hand, torn and bleeding, droplets of purple tinged blood falling slowly from the fingertips and his eyes snapped shut once more.

His hands rose to his skull and his fingers dug into his flesh as he began to scream, rocking back and forth. Convulsions took him and his hands flew from his head and into the air, slamming into anything they could reach, the floor, his abdomen, the metal frame which he sat beside, his sister's legs. He pounded and pounded until his knuckles were a bloody mess. How long this lasted, he had no idea, the episode only ending when he flung his body forward and smashed his head into one of the metal leggings of the shelves.

Stars filled his mind and he rolled onto his back, gasping for air, his throat raw, heart choking. He opened his mouth to try and scream once more, but only half hearted yells and moans escaped him.

A voice echoed about the room. "Silas dear, what's wrong?" His mother.

Taking a huge breath, Silas forced himself to sit up. He stared at his sister's body, thinking long and hard about how to tell his mother what he had done. "I killed her mom. I killed her."

"Who?"

"Alicia. My sister. Your daughter. I killed her!" Another low moan escaped him and he brought his hands up to his face, tears leaking freely through the dirt.

"Aww, sweetheart. It's okay. You did what you thought you had to do. It was for the best, right? You always do what's for the best, Silas. You're a good man and I'm proud of you."

Relief filled his heart at her words.

"I know Mom. She was infected, she was – infected. Oh God." His eyes grew wide and he looked about frantically for his gun, but saw that it was nowhere to be found. Fear gripped him, as reality set in once more.

"It's a shame. She would have made a good soldier. Attacked too early, wasn't used to the body. Foolish. But you – You'll make a FINE soldier, won't you Silas?"

Scooting backwards until his hands found the metal rack, Silas began to slowly push himself up off of the concrete floor, glancing about, searching for his gun. The flamethrower lay about five feet to his right, his sister's body just to the left. Right where his gun should have been. How close had he come to being taken? His infected mother must have literally walked right up next to him and taken his weapon.

Foolish.

Movement caught his eye and he glanced upward. His mother came out from behind one of the racks, pointing a gun at him, her head tilted curiously to the side.

<Just like Lucas.> He thought.

"Looking for this, dear? You know, I never did like my children playing with guns. Someone could get shot!"

Loathing filled him. It was using the voice his mother used when they were sick or being playfully bad as children. Light and carefree, it was now heinous and evil. He snarled.

"Get out of my mother."

The creature laughed.

"Now, why would I want to do that? Her screams in the back of her own pitiful mind are wearying, to say the least. But beyond that, I don't particularly care to leave this body. It's not exactly the best for combat, but for now I've got firearms to get by with. At any rate, my body will change soon enough. This is my body now, after all." It smiled, bloody teeth glistening in the firelight.

Silas' lips curled with hate.

"Your body now, is it? In that case, I'm going to rip your fucking throat out."

Her eyes narrowed as the smile dropped off her face. Playtime was over. "I think not."

She pulled the trigger.

Silas jumped to the side, ears ringing as the bullet bounced off the metal frame. Hitting the ground and rolling, he jumped to his feet and burst into a sprint, arms and legs pumping as fast as he could make them.

"You can run, but you can't hide!"

<Run run run, as fast as you can!> Lucas' voice echoed through his memory. These monsters were all cut from the same cloth. Despicable.

Searching, his eyes sought the darkness for a place to hide, a weapon which he could use to fend off or kill his... the creature. He knew he wouldn't be able to kill her if he thought of her as his mother.

A small opening to his side caught his attention. Darting left, he headed for it.

A bullet whizzed by his leg, ricocheting off into the darkness.

"You can't hide from me, fool. I can see just fine in this light. You think hiding in some hole is going to save you? This place isn't that big, you know. And that fire is growing. I can either search you out, or wait you out. Depends on my mood, I guess. What do you think?"

It paused. "Not up for games, I see. Well, at any rate, I saw you go into that little hole. I guess I can wait you out..."

"Shit." Silas silently cursed. He put his hands on the ground and leapt to his feet ready to run.

Mistake. His head slammed into the top of the space he was in and for the second time in ten minutes, he saw stars. He fell back, landing on his butt and skidding a few inches. Reaching his hands behind him in an attempt to steady himself, he felt something cold and metallic. Gripping the object, he pulled it out and in front of him, unable to believe his luck.

****

"Hey! Wait!"

<God damnit Silas, wait. I'm sorry.>

He slowed, turning. "It's just something I don't care to talk about, okay? It's why I didn't tell you before."

"I get that. I understand. I'm sorry; I didn't mean to hit a sore spot."

He sighed, shoulders lowering. "It's fine. Come on though, we're almost to the fort. See? Look there."

They'd run for probably close to half a mile and the fort now loomed before them, a little less than a quarter of a mile from the spot they stood.

Roach shook her head. "I saw it. It's huge for being in the middle of nowhere. I guess it had to have been built around a town that was already there?"

"Actually, no. It was built from the ground up, from what I understand. I wasn't here during the main construction. I've only lived here about six months or so. Before that, I was a nomad; I went wherever I could find food and shelter."

"Yeah, I remember..."

They stood for a moment in silence, staring at the fort, both thinking about how life was before all of this. Hatred rolled off the both of them and Ragger whined.

<I wish I could apologize, on the behalf of my species, but I can't. Your hatred is warranted, but it pains me to see into your minds and see that you hate us all. Even myself.>

Silas threw a silent glance at the dog and licked his teeth, sucking at them momentarily, while Roach turned and knelt to throw her arms around him.

"We don't hate you, Ragger! I just... It's hard not to remember how things used to be. Things were so grand, so perfect... Blue skies, light breezes, warm summer days, clear winter nights."

<Yes, I remember. Your world was magnificent. Absolutely

magnificent. I hope to perhaps see it restored one day.>

He looked at Silas. *<In fact, I plan too. With the biological technology my species possesses, combined with the amazing innovative human mind... It could take less than fifty years to restore Earth to the way it looked before the Industrial Revolution.>*

Silas stared at Ragger a moment and then turned away, snorting. "Wouldn't need that if you and your ilk hadn't shown up and taken less than ONE year to destroy it all, now would we?"

Ragger hung his head and Roach gave the back of Silas' head a dirty look.

"You're kind of an asshole, aren't you?"

Silas ignored the comment.

Sighing, Ragger answered Silas' question. *<No. I suppose not. Shall we move on now?>*

Silas nodded, still sucking at his teeth. "Yup. Sounds good to me."

<Silas, why are you being, as Roach said, an asshole?> Linnerat chuckled at his use of the word. *<Asshole. What a quaint insult. Fitting, really. I love humans, I think.>*

<Oh God, Lin, I don't need you ganging up on me here too.>

<No one is... Lin? Did you just call me Lin?>

<Yes.>

<Why? It sounds ridiculous. And Female! I am Male, I'll have you know.>

<It's called a nickname, numb nuts, and it's a hell of a lot easier than saying your real name. And good to know. I feel kind of gay now, knowing I have a dude inside of me. At least you're in my head, not in my ass.>

<Oh, I don't know... Your head tends to be pretty far up your ass.>

<Was that a joke?>

<Perhaps. Why are you being so cruel to our new companions?

<Bad memories floating around in my head, man.>

<I see that. They are affecting your mood?>

<Yup.>

<Why?>

<Because they do, okay? Jesus Christ, shut up and leave me alone for a while.>

<As you wish.... Anyway I could help?>

Silas growled. "NO, NOW SHUTUP."

<Sorry.>

Turning to Roach and Ragger, who had stopped at his sudden outburst, Silas remarked, "You know what, you two are lucky." He pointed at Ragger. "A dog's brain can't be too much worry, or too hard to placate. And after how god knows how many years you've been in that thing, it probably loves you wholeheartedly."

Ragger nodded and Silas turned his finger towards Roach.

"And you're lucky because your parasite is dead. You know why?" His finger pointed towards his own head. "Because these things are fucking annoying!"

Pain and hurt washed through his emotions, but he didn't care. He turned on his heel and then sat down. "We're stopping."

Roach looked at him like he was retarded. "Here?"

"Yes, here."

"The fort is RIGHT THERE!" She shouted. "What is your issue?"

He sighed, starting to feel bad. He'd just met these two and they were already dealing with his crap,

<This is why I travel alone,> he thought to himself. "I'm just having a bad week, that's all."

"Well, don't take it out on us."

"Sorry. Just the thing with Natalie kind of brought back some painful memories, that's all."

"Natalie...? Oh. The little girl. Was that her name? You never said." She sat down beside him. "I'd already forgotten about her. Wow... I feel really low saying that out loud. Guess it says more about our times than me, though... Right?"

Silas nodded in silent agreement.

She sighed. "Alright. I guess we can chill here for the night. Don't you want to move towards the forest though?"

He shook his head. "Place is full of *Renegade*s. Not very friendly towards groups of humans. Not exactly hostile, but certainly not friendly."

"Gotcha."

This time, Silas was the one to sigh. "Actually, I think I'll probably go in alone tonight and snatch up my old supplies myself and that way we can be off in the morning, towards Chicago. If you still want to come with me, that is. Asshole that I am."

She smiled, chuckling and punched him in the arm.

"OW." He rubbed his shoulder. "That hurt."

She ignored him.

"Of course we want too." She looked at Ragger. "Don't we?"

<Absolutely. Fate brought us together, it will be fate that draws us apart.>

****

Smooth and dark, Silas could not believe what he held in his hands. It had to be the store owner's; no other reason would explain its placement here in the back room.

In his hands lay a double barreled shotgun. Cracking it open, he looked to see if it was loaded and as he did, a silent prayer of thanks went out to whatever God was watching over him. He snapped it shut once more and pushed himself onto his knees, shuffling out into the open.

The light of the fire had grown tremendously, he could see fairly well and a sweltering heat had begun to fill the room. He could feel a tickle in the back of his throat, telling him that he needed to get out of there soon, or he was going to never be able leave.

A sudden thought struck him and he paused. He'd given Kendall orders for eight minutes. Could everything that had happened really have taken place in less than eight minutes? Impossible. Chances were that the group had run into further resistance outside, or that, more likely, Kendall was foregoing orders, hoping to see his brother come out. If Silas did get out of this, he was going to strangle the kid.

Turning his attention back to his immediate time and place, he peered about. He couldn't see his mother, which worried him.

He pushed himself to his feet, cradling the gun to his chest, wrapping his arms around it, doing his best to hide it from view.

"Where are you, Mom?" The second the words left his lips, her laugh echoed about the room.

"Oooh. Come out to play, have we? Oh, I'm over here, by your sister. I'd hoped maybe I could help the poor sap in her out of her skull before it's too late, but if you're coming out to play and then I think he's just... how do you teens say it? Shit out of luck? Yes, that's it. Shit out of luck."

Silas stared towards the source of the voice, which now was

sitting behind a thick sheet of flame.

As he stared, he saw a figure begin to materialize in the flames and his eyes grew wide.

From within the flames stepped his mother. Her hair was aflame, almost complete burnt away and but for a few scraps of still burning cloth, she was completely naked. Silas fought the urge to look away, struggling to keep his eyes on her still mostly human face, and away from her oozing, burnt flesh.

"Ouch, that hurt," she said, laughing. She shook her head and as he watched, the angry red skin began to return to normal, the blisters popping and fading. Well, almost normal. From where Silas stood, he could see that where her skin had burned, it now appeared to be gray and leathery. Like almost like that of an elephant, but less wrinkled, more supple.

The skin of a *Mayan*.

She caught the look on his face.

"Oh, you just hate this, don't you? Seeing me like this? I guess it's probably not my best look, but you'll come to love this too, dear! I promise. *Mommy* wouldn't lie to you." She took another few steps forward, laughing at him. "You'll be one of us soon, Silas. There are Drillers all around this building. We already got the rest of your crew. It's been fifteen minutes since you came in here, Silas. Fifteen! A full seven minutes past orders. You know that not even Kendall would wait this long. "

She'd almost reached him and her tone of voice suddenly changed, to something soft and kind. She reached a single hand towards his face.

"Nobody would ever believe you're still alive in here. We got them. He's one of us. They're all one of us. Just join and make it so much easier, Silas! We don't even have to use a Driller, but only if you come with us quietly. No pain. I swear. It doesn't have to be this way."

His teeth grit with each step she took, waiting for her to come into range. Close enough. He snarled. "Hey *mom*? Fuck you."

He swung the shotgun up and pulled the trigger.

CHAPTER 15 – THE BEGINNING

Silas sat, staring out into the night, listening. *<I can hear them,>* he remarked.

<Yes, I can too,> Ragger replied, sitting softly at Silas' side. *<They have no care for their lives anymore. They no longer feel a need to hide their presence. They realize that they cast themselves off from the only thing they know. Some of them are happy, content, like me. But they tire of being hunted. In their minds, they simply want to live their lives as they wish. If they die, they die. If they are caught and slaughtered then that is their fate.>*

Silas sighed. *<It must be a hard life. I know that being all alone, surrounded by people who I pretended and maybe even not so much pretended at times, were my friends, was lonely enough. I absolutely despised the time periods when I was by myself. Can they at least speak to one another?>*

<Oh yes. We have a spoken language, it's guttural and harsh, but it gets us by well enough. They still also possess the ability to speak to one another mind to mind. But they have to be fairly close to one another. Their connection is not like the one that Roach and I share. Hers is a unique gift. Also, many Renegades I came across began to adopt a form of English as their mainstay of speech.>

<Really now? That's interesting. What purpose does that serve?>

This time, Ragger sighed. *<You must understand our species, Silas. We are NOT monsters. We are merely what we were designed to be. And some of us hate that, very much. When a Yahntil chooses to become a Renegade, they are literally casting aside everything that makes them a part of our species, besides their looks. They are no longer able to reattach to a driller, to inhabit another body. If the body they currently inhabit dies then they die with it. The process of becoming a Renegade literally fuses our body with the brain of the host. It's a painful process and most Yahntil that choose it are friends*

with their host... Much like you and Linnerat.>

<I would say it's stretching it to say that he and I are friends. This is a rather new state of mind for us.>

<You two are friends. Enough said. At any rate, it serves the purpose of maybe communicating with humans to get them to stop hunting them. Not that it will work.> Warmth swelled through Silas a moment as Linnerat took the statement to heart.

<Ooook.>

Silence fell yet again between the two beings.

Uncomfortable, Silas stirred, attempting to make small talk.

<Is she asleep yet?>

<Yes.>

<And you are going to stay and keep watch?>

<No. I am coming with you. I have a sense of unease in my stomach.>

<That's just the cancer, remember?> Silas teased. Ragger did not respond, and Silas sighed. This guy was about as dry as they came.

<... Wouldn't it be better for you to stay here with Roach, then?>

<No.>

Silas blinked. *<Why not?>*

<Because, it simply wouldn't.>

Silas shook his head, sighing. *<You're terribly cryptic, aren't you?>*

<Yes.>

<I hate you.>

<That's unfortunate.>

Silas chuckled. *<Alright then. We still have a few hours left before daybreak. Would you care to go now, or wait?>*

<We are going into that fortress to retrieve your things, not mine. It's up to you when we leave."

Silas nodded, leaning back a little, looking up at the stars. *<Where is your home world?>*

Looking up at the stars as well, Ragger replied wryly, *<If I had fingers, I would point it out to you... And at any rate, we don't really have a home world.>*

<Haha... I forgot.>

<It's alright. Linnerat, would you care to show our friend from where we come?>

Linnerat stirred, causing Silas to wince slightly.

<That feels so strange.>

Ragger turned his head slightly, looking up at Silas' face.

<What feels strange?>

Silas squinted and drew his eyebrows together, resisting the urge to try to reach into his brain and massage it. *<When he moves in my brain. I can feel it.>*

Linnerat spoke. *<Would you care to let me direct your eyes for a moment, Silas?>*

<Sure… And hey. Sorry about earlier. That was in bad taste. I was just in a foul mood.>

<Really? I didn't notice.>

<Another bit of sarcasm? We'll have you humanized before the week is through, buddy.>

Warmth passed through him again as Linnerat glowed at Silas' use of the friendly term.

<I just need your eyes for this one.>

Silas nodded. *<Alrighty.>* He relaxed, letting Linnerat take partial control.

<Hmmm. Let's see.>

Silas' eyes flicked suddenly to the left and then rolled across the top of his vision, searching, focusing. They moved about for several moments and then stopped on a particularly faint star, directly above them.

<That one, there. That is the home world of the Rakniran. Our birthplace.>

Silas smiled. *<That's a long way away.>*

<Yes… a long path of destruction from here to there.> Sadness rolled through him as Linnerat dwelt on the crimes of his people. *<Destruction I was all too ready to take part in. I'm glad I ended up inside of you, Silas. I'm not sure what kind of being I would be if I hadn't. I would probably be evil and cruel. You took that from me and for that I'm grateful.>*

Momentary silence ensued once more, as Silas felt heat crawl up his cheeks. *<Between you and Ragger, you make me feel like some sort of hero or amazing person. I'm really not, you know.>*

Ragger spoke once more. *<Perhaps not. But you are exemplary of your species and their capacity for greatness.>*

Looking towards the ground, Silas kicked at the dirt. *<Thanks,*

I'll take your word for it. Should we go now?>

> *<If you wish.>*

Silas thought about it for a moment. *<One more question. I think I might have figured something out.>*

> *<Yes? What's that.>*

> *<I have a question, first... What was the last species you took like? Linnerat said they were akin to our world's cephalopods?>*

Ragger blinked. *<You would have to ask Linnerat about that. I have no idea. I've been here on Earth for at least the conquering of three worlds now.>*

> *<Oh? Well then, Linnerat? Tell me about the last species taken?>*

> *<I do not know much... But I will share what I know...>*

> *<Awesome, thanks. I'm going to start walking towards the fort while you share. Shouldn't take too long, so make it short.>*

Taking a step into the darkness, they began to head towards the fort, both Silas and Ragger listening intently to what Linnerat had to say.

> *<As I said, I don't know much. From what I understand, the world was primarily aquatic. The dominant species of the planet was a creature much like what you humans call an octopus. It had twelve limbs, tentacles, all of which had three small digits on the end, which they could use to make tools. They had communities, made primarily from plants and shaped stones. They had knowledge of stonemasonry and had crude musical instruments. They were probably akin to your species five to six thousand years ago in terms of civilization and learning. In terms of intelligence, they were similar to your own. There was a land based life form, similar to your hippopotamus. A large, lumbering animal that lounged in water and occasionally went on to land to forage. We don't know when, but at some point, the octopi forged a sort of symbiotic relationship with the land based life forms –*
>
> *>*

Silas cut him off. *<That's what I was looking for. How does your species reproduce?>*

Ragger stopped walking for a moment, seeing where Silas was going with his thought and then resumed walking, letting Silas explain. Linnerat appeared to not have caught up yet, though.

> *<What? Shouldn't I finish my analysis of the last world?>*

> *<No, I've heard what I need. How does your species*

reproduce?>

<*Ok... When members of our species reach a certain age, they are allowed to choose to enter the breeding pool. We have male and female varieties and sometimes, the Raknila choose specific members who have shown great honor to the species and who are very powerful and place them there, but often, two members who have become attracted to one another, or who have fought side by side for many years choose to enter the pool. Once placed in the pool, the two members allow their cells to co-mingle and the female absorbs the male and his DNA structure and every cell in her body becomes a viable embryo from which each new member of our species is born. After impregnation, the female is– >*

Silas interrupted once more. <*You told me once, that you absorb the DNA of each species. That every member of your species absorbs DNA from their host.>*

<*Yes. Are you going to let me finish anything?>* Lin was getting aggravated.

<*No. Is it possible that your parents had inhabited different creatures? Like, could one have inhabited the octopus and the other inhabited the hippo?>*

<*I suppose, but what does that have– >*

<*So, is it possible that instead of breeding a parasite, they could have bred a symbiote?>*

<*... Yes.>*

<*So, does that mean that perhaps, you are not a parasite at all? That you are something new and different.>*

<*...Possibly.>*

Ragger interjected. <*He's right, Lin.>*

<*You're calling me that, too? Rakna! You know, I would make a wager... that is the correct term, right, Silas? Ah... No, make a bet. I see... I'd make a bet that your name is long and complicated too!>*

Silas and Ragger laughed and then spoke at the same time. <*Hey, it's catchy.>*

They looked at each strangely for a moment and then laughed again.

Ragger chuckled a moment and then answered Lin's unspoken question. <*No, even my real name is fairly short. I merely like to keep my secrets... My name is well known among our race and humans, as well.>* Silas shot him a strange glance, curious. <*I prefer it not to be.>*

<Whatever,> Linnerat sulked. <But yes, that could be quite true. It would explain a lot, in fact. Why I can't control you unless you allow it or are rendered unconscious. It would also explain why your DNA profile is a bit different. I could be an evolved form of Yahntil. More than just my physical appearance might have been affected. Very good, Silas. This explains many things I'd been wondering about. Between this new idea and the idea of your cancer, this covers pretty much everything...>

<Sweet.>

They walked on in silence, Silas' question answered.

After a few moments, Linnerat posed his own question.

<Would you care to hear about the rest of our breeding process?>

<Hell, to the no. Hahaha.>

****

The blast caught his mother in the stomach, throwing her back, blood spraying through the air, hitting Silas in the face.

She screamed, hitting the ground and skidding towards the flames, bent in half, cradling her midsection, words of unintelligible rage spewing from her open mouth.

Grimacing, tears filling his eyes, Silas stepped forward, staring cautiously at his mother, but paying attention to his peripherals too, watching for any Drillers that might be looking to take advantage of the situation.

****

"Kendall! Kendall! We have to go!" Matthias shouted at him, grabbing his shoulder.

"No! I'm not leaving without them!"

"Kendall, they're dead, or worse!"

Turning, Kendall screamed at the old man, rage and pain in his eyes. "That's my family in there, you doddering old fool! My whole shitting family! My Mother! My Brother! My Sister! I'm not leaving them, god damnit! Look, see the flames? Silas had to have done that! He's in there, alive, rescuing them, damnit! Eight minutes is such a stupid rule!" He turned back around, his eyes frantically tracing a continuous line between every exit he could see and the back of the building.

"Silas can do it. I know he can." He whispered. "That son of a bitch can't die, he's too stubborn. He can't die. He won't. He would never just lie down and die, even if there were a driller on his back, he would save Mom and Alicia." He turned, screaming at Matthias again. "You hear that? Even if there were a fucking Driller on his back, he wouldn't leave the rest of my family in there! You don't know him like I do!" His voice cracked.

Waving his hand, Matthias turned his back, throwing his hand in the air and twirling it in a circle, signaling the rest of the crew to grab the gas cans and rush the building. Seeing this, Kendall went into a rage, screaming and running at the various gas carrying members. A few other members rushed out and grabbed him, holding his arms behind his back and kicking his legs out, tossing him to the ground.

Shaking his head, Matthias walked over to Kendall and knelt down, grabbing the young man's face. "I know what it's like, son. I burned my own daughter and wife alive, in our home, after they had been taken. I hid in a closet while they were taken, like a coward and then torched them before the driller managed to fully take them. Poured gasoline on them and threw my favorite Zippo lighters on them. Stood and listened to them scream, watched the Driller's pop. Worst thing I've ever endured and I was in <Nam, boy. I know your shame, your pain. You defied his orders, gave him extra time, but we can't do anything else now. It's done. We all heard the gunshots, the screams. We know what's happened."

"But we haven't heard him. I haven't heard him screaming. I haven't heard my brother!"

"Son, who do you think the shots were? Silas isn't the kind who would scream, but he would turn the gun on himself. You know what he's seen. He would never let himself be taken. If he was taken down, Silas would end his own life. We all know that."

Tears streamed down Kendall's face. "I can't. I can't, he's my brother. If there's a chance he's alive..."

"Son, we all love your brother just as much as you do. That young man is the bravest son of a bitch I've ever met. You don't think I remember how he saved my ass, coming in, guns blazing? Most beautiful thing I've seen in my long years, your brother coming in that door with a hundred guns strapped to him, shotgun in both hands, bloody and bruised, ripping the throat out of one of those god damned things with his hands. He's the bat shit craziest man I've ever seen, I owe him my life. We all owe him our lives, five times over. He's a saint. He's insane, but he is the reason we're all still alive. And I love him like a brother, a son. And we all love you. We're your family and we're his. But we know what has to be done, Kendall! You know what has to be done!"

Kendall just lay on the ground, sobbing, his captors having let him go. His fist pounded the ground weakly and his breath came in short gasps. "They're all I have."

"No, son, you've got us now. And we might not be much, but we'll do what we can." Turning, he gave the order. "Light the sucker up. And bring me that grenade. We'll give Silas a hell of a going out party. It's the least we can do."

****

Reaching his mother there on the ground, he gave a vicious kick to the side of the head, stunning her, stopping her screams. He crouched down, staring at her.

"Mom, if you're in there, I'm sorry."

The purple and gold eyes stared back at him, cold and lifeless and a weak laugh escaped through her teeth.

"Oh yes, she's in here. Screaming bloody murder in hatred and pain. You see what you've done to her? To your mother...? You see what you've done? Everyone close to you dies and by your hand no less! You're more of a monster than I am." It chuckled once more and then closed its eyes and the breathing stopped.

Silas' focus wavered as his eyes filled with moisture and hatred for himself consumed him. He closed them for a second and was greeted by a sudden tug at his leg. Gasping, his eyes flew open and he looked down to see that the creature inhabiting the body of his mother had grabbed his ankle and pulled herself towards him and was poised to bite him.

Time seemed to slow down for Silas and everything happening at the moment took on a perfect clarity he'd never known before. The fire crackling took on a stereo sound; the light glistening from his mother's teeth blinded him, the purple in swirling in her green eyes popped out at him, vivid in the extreme.

Bullard

He knew exactly what would happen to him if her teeth penetrated his flesh. First, the area would go numb. Then, within a few hours, he would lose his sense of direction, start seeing things that weren't there, hear voices in his head. A few hours after that, he would become delirious, feverish. After twenty four hours, he would be bedridden; his eyes would begin to change color. And after forty eight, his mind would have surrendered to the call of some unseen force and he would begin walking towards the closest city. To them.

Her teeth closed on his flesh and searing pain shot through him. He kicked forwards, snapping her head back and cracking several of her teeth. She howled in pain, amidst fits of laughter. "I told you, son… You'll be one of us soon enough. Too bad you killed your sister. Otherwise, we could be a happy little family! Hahaha…" She choked, blood leaking from her lips. "Schlack, this is going to take a while to heal. But I don't think I'm going to be getting out of here. I'll burn before healing. Which sucks, but hey… It's for the greater good. We'll have you… and oh, what a fighter you'll be. What a prize. The hive has been trying to get you for a good long time, Silas dear. They want to make a general out of you. Lucky little shit."

Standing, Silas walked over to where the creature was lying and placed his hand on her throat, pulling her up into a sitting position. Her oily gray skin felt disgusting under his fingertips. He squeezed slowly, crushing her windpipe, causing her to choke more.

"What, Silas, are you going to kill your mother? Hahaha."

Silas lips curled up over his lips and he slammed her head against a box. "You're not my mother." He looked deep into the creature's eyes and spoke to his mother one last time, knowing she was watching, listening. "I love you, mom." His clenched his fist, fingers penetrating deep into the flesh and he yanked, ripping the esophagus away in his tightened fist.

Surprise filled the creature's eyes and it gurgled, blood pouring out of it's now gaping throat.

Standing, Silas spit on her. "I told you I was going to rip your fucking throat out." Releasing his fist, the clump of flesh fell wetly to the ground. He raised the gun over his head, swinging it downward as hard as he could and slammed the butt directly into the side of her temple, cracking her skull and rendering her unconscious. She slumped, falling sideways onto the concrete. Her head hit the floor with an audible "crack" and blood pooled onto the floor. Within

143

seconds, the choking and gurgling stopped. She was dead. The flames inched closer to her. Within minutes, they would consume her body.

Silas stared down at his mother's body for a moment and hatred filled him. How could these creatures just so casually destroy lives? For what agenda could this possibly be? What could possibly be to gain from all this? Pointless questions, he would never know the answer. He wasn't even going to be alive in another few days. He was going to die and become one of the creatures themselves.

Sudden noises interrupted his thoughts. Shouts. Eyes widening, he brought the gun to bear and crouched down. If he was going to die, he was going to take out at least one more little shit with him. He had one shot left, and the pistol still lay on the other side of the flames.

Turning to look at the flames, he debated how bad it was going to hurt and whether or not it was going to hurt. It was worth it. He wasn't going to let his friends live like that.

Tucking and rolling, holding the shotgun close to his chest, he threw himself forward and into the flames, doing his best not to scream as flames licked at his face, ignited his hair. It only lasted one second, but the heat felt like it lasted an eternity. Coming out the other side, he leapt to his feet and batted at his skull, putting out the hungry flames.

More shouts reached his ears, closer this time and he tensed once more, listening.

"Get those gas cans down here. Kendall held this shit off long enough. Light this place up, now! Chances are those two girls are going to be coming out of here any time now. We don't want to be around when that happens and God forbid Kendall sees."

A huge feeling of relief came over Silas and a sigh escaped him. The creature in his mother had been lying. Not a single other person from his group had been taken. Kendall had just disobeyed. He was going to kill the kid... Or not. He glanced down at his ankle, watched the blood spilling out, leaking into his sneaker. He wasn't going to get out of here. Might as well find that gun and end it for himself, if nobody else needed it. A shotgun suicide just didn't appeal to him. A small caliber bullet would be so much cleaner.

Not paying attention to the immediate surroundings, he stepped forward and tripped over a can. Landing flat and rolling, he realized that he had come out right by his sister's body, laying only a few feet from the fire.

Sighing, he stepped over to her and knelt down, staring at her face. He frowned, realizing that there were claw marks all across the side of her face and back of her skull.

"I'd hoped maybe I could help the poor sap in her out of her skull before it's too late," his mother's voice echoed through his head and he sucked at his teeth in disbelief. She'd tried to rip the other parasite out of his sister's head.

Suddenly, Alicia's head moved and he hopped up, pointing the gun at her, trigger finger poised. It moved again, a little tiny pop and along with the movement came a crack. Focusing, he suddenly realized that the back of her skull was moving. Under the scratches and blood, he could see a bit of bone, with a deep crack in it. It popped again and the crack grew wider. A small black tentacle pushed out from inside it. Silas eyes grew wide and he crouched down, a fit of rage taking him.

Grabbing Alicia's head by the hair, he yanked her up and flipped her onto her side, grabbing at the crack in her skull, digging his fingers in, relishing the sting of pain as the jagged bone tore into his fingers. Wedging his fingers into the crack, feeling her brain on his finger tips, he grabbed her hair with his other hand and yank, ripping the section of bone away, flinging it into the darkness.

By the flickering light of the fire, for the first time, he beheld his enemy's true form with his own eyes.

His first impression of it was that it was small. Too small. Maybe three inches long at the most. Twenty or more tentacles surrounded a small black body, which pulsated and quivered. Many of the tentacles were sunk deep into the cracks and wrinkles of the brain it sat upon and the body itself appeared to have been flattened out and smashed into the crevasse between the two halves of the brain. Upon the hot air touching it, it tried to pull away. Four red dots sat on the top of its body, which it moved back and forth, appearing to look around. Upon seeing Silas, the thing's movements suddenly became very frantic, it's tentacles flailing about, pushing against his sister's now exposed gray matter, trying to escape its prison.

Teeth bared, Silas snatched the creature, which let out a high pitched keen of fear. Standing, Silas flung the creature against the floor, where it slammed with a splat and green liquid leaked from it. It lay stunned for a moment and then weakly tried to squirm away, but to little avail.

Stepping forward, Silas stomped on it, listening to its tiny screams of pain in satisfaction. He stomped again and again. Finally, unable to stand any longer, he hit his knees and scooped the remains of the creature up into his hands and slammed it with his fist again and again, until there was nothing left but green and black ooze. And still, he pounded.

****

Matthias stood, staring at the building as they lit their matches, one by one. Turning to look at the still sobbing boy on the ground, sadness filled his heart.

This was the fifth war he'd taken part in. World War Two, Vietnam, Desert Shield, Project Freedom. What was the point of fighting one another? he'd believed in the cause before, thought he'd seen crimes against nature, seen cruelty. How wrong he'd been. He'd fought in the war to end all wars, come home, turned around and went right back into another one. He'd killed many, many people, women and children and even one of his traitorous friends, all in the name of his country. He saw how pointless it all was now.

Now, in the name of his species, he'd killed his friends, his family, his spouse… His own daughter. People from his own country. People from his life.

And now he had consigned to death the man who had risked his own skin to save Matthias' ass from the fire more times than he could count, in a world that just didn't give a shit about anyone anymore. Silas was a saint among men and what Matthias had to do now broke his heart. He said a silent prayer to whatever God might be listening, that Silas was already dead and to forgive him if he wasn't.

"Here's that grenade sir." A young man tapped him on the shoulder. "Ready to give Silas that send off?" The boy's voice choked at the end in pain. Silas had touched all their lives in a way they'd never be able to forget. Every breath they took was a reminder.

Matthias reached out with both hands, one taking the grenade from the boy, the other patting him on the shoulder. "Damn right, son. He's gonna go out with a bang, if it's the last thing I do." He smiled briefly and then began the short walk to the building.

It seemed like a million miles away.

146

Bullard

He didn't know how long he sat there pounding. It could have been mere seconds, it could have been years. All that filled his soul was rage and hate. Nothing else mattered. There was nothing left for him here in this life. After stopping, he sat a few more minutes, listened to the flames crackle and noted the sweat pouring off of him. Funny he hadn't noticed it before. Looking about, he realized that the building was beginning to fall apart. Rafters fell and boxes filled with canned peas exploded here and there as their contents boiled. The whole place was on fire. The crew must have finally lit the place. This small grocery store was going to be his tomb.

He thought about his life for a few minutes, chuckling now and then. It was true, what they said. Your life really did flash before your eyes when you were about to die. It wasn't his last moment, but it was his last thoughts, that he was going through. In a few minutes, he was going to end his own life. He refused to live as a monster. He sighed.

Looking down at his hand, at the slimy mess that resided there, he blanched. He shook his hand, flinging the guts and gore off of him, grimacing and then placed both hands on the floor and pulled himself to his feet, wincing at the pain that shot through his ankle. Bitch had gotten him good. Turning, he looked at the floor, finding his sister's body again and pain shot through his soul once more. He stepped over to her, kneeling down again and flipping her body gently back onto its back, looked at her tenderly. She didn't deserve to go that way, murdered by her own brother, in a place that no person should ever die. He scooped her into his arms and stood, cradling her to his chest, rubbing his chin softly against her blood matted hair.

Walking over to the fire, pulling away from the heat, he spoke gently to his sister one last time.

"I love you, Alicia. I always did. And I'm so sorry for the way things ended here. You always deserved the best in my life. You'll live in my heart, always." Looking into the fire, he spoke to the flames, where his mother now undoubtedly rested. "You too, mom. I love you guys." And with that, he kissed his sister's forehead gently and then tossed her body into the flames.

Turning back into the darkness, he searched for the gun. There, he spotted a glint in the corner. He smiled. How fortunate.

<Fate has a sense of humor,> he thought to himself.

****

Matthias stood before the now flame engulfed building, paying his last respects to the man to whom he owed his life. The heat of the flames burned his face, forced him to look away and he knew that nothing could still be alive within the fiery pit. Still, he couldn't help but feel a nagging in the back of his mind that Silas might still be alive. Something telling him to withhold his hand.

He sighed heavily and then jumped back as a portion of the roof fell in, leaving a large hole. He smiled sadly. Perfect. Lifting his hand to his face, he grabbed the pull pin with his teeth and yanked back.

Reaching up and back, he chucked the grenade at the rooftop, watching it sail up and towards the hole. Just short. He twisted his mouth to the side, watching for a second. No harm done, it rolled right into the hole, falling right into the center of the establishment.

"So long, Silas my friend. I'll take care of Kendall. I promise." With those simple words of farewell, he ran, heading back towards the caravan and away from the assured explosion.

****

He started for the gun, a small grin on his face. Death suddenly seemed so welcome. He'd been running from it so long, been so afraid of it, that now, turning to face it, embrace it, seemed as natural as hugging an old friend after a long absence. He was tired, empty. He just wanted to lie down here and end his life. And he planned too. All it was going to take was one little tiny piece of metal and all his troubles would finally be cured. All the pointless questions he'd asked himself and such a simple answer. One bullet, would answer all his questions.

His faith had taught him that suicide was a one way ticket to hell. He figured that he was already in hell and he'd dealt with it pretty okay thus far and just didn't give a shit. Anywhere but here.

A creak sounded above him, shaking him from his momentary reverie and he looked up, dread knotting in his stomach. A section of roof, which had caught fire early on, set from his flamethrower, had finally decided to relinquish its grip on the rest of the structure. His eyes followed it downward, even as he leapt away and anguish filled him as it hit the ground. Right on top of the god damned gun.

He hit the ground hard, face first and tasted blood. Agony shot through his jaw and he knew he'd broken teeth.

"Ok, fate has a SICK sense of humor!" he shouted, spitting blood and bone.

A clunk sounded on the roof and Silas rolled onto his back to see what fate had in store for him this time. Something had landed on the roof and was now rolling into the now aerated ceiling; he could hear it against the metal rivets, clacking as it rolled.

He knit his eyebrows together as a small, round object fell from the ceiling, hit the ground and bounced towards him. It bounced twice and then rolled gently, stopped a few feet from him. A grenade.

He released the muscles in his neck with a sigh, letting his head hit the concrete with a crack. "It fuckin' figures."

He sighed, staring up through the hole at the sky one last time. The stars were beginning to show, wavering through the heat of the flames. He smiled and closed his eyes. At least he got to see his favorite sight one last time before slipping into the void. He never imagined it would end this way. He reached his right hand up to his throat and gently rubbed at the silver cross bound to it.

A muffled thump sounded from somewhere nearby, sudden pain ripped into his side and then –

****

Matthias and Kendall stood at the top of the hill, staring at the building, now completely ruined. The grenade had destroyed the entire store, knocking out its structural support and collapsing it. Only the back wall remained standing. Piles of rubble burned and pops could be heard as cans of food exploded.

"I want to go look." Kendall said.

"Oh no, son. You don't. Trust me." Matthias replied, placing a firm hand on Kendall's shoulder.

"I thought I saw a body go out the back. I seen it, I swear." Kendall tried to move forward, but Matthias' grip was not going to be broken.

"Son... You probably did. It's not something you want to see.

Let's move on." Kendall relented, turning his face into the old man's shoulder, letting out a weak sound of pain.

Turning to the rest of the group, Matthias shouted. "Nothing more to see here, folks. A good man died for us all today, let's not waste his sacrifice. North! To Chicago! It's what he would have wanted. Let us honor the sacrifice of our Saint Silas! The best way to show him our thanks is to live on. To fight on. It would not do to die now, not after all he has done for us. Another two hundred miles, people. It's not that far. Another two weeks if we push ourselves, that's it. Let us honor Saint Silas with our lives!"

One by one, the group members nodded, looking towards the burning building, many with a prayer of thanks on their lips and then turned away, moving into the distance.

"Saint Silas… I like that." Kendall looked up at Matthias. "I don't think he would have, though."

Matthias chuckled, wrapping his arm around the boy, leading him towards the rest of the group. "Are you kidding? he'd skin me alive if he ever heard me say that. Skin me alive, I tell you."

****

The blast threw Silas' body into the air, through two metal racks and then through a wall, landing a good ten feet from the building and skidding another ten. Unconscious, he didn't feel a thing. The pain would have rendered him catatonic almost instantly anyway.

Blood pooled into the dirt about his broken body, his face smashed into the dirt. His teeth all broken or missing, blood leaked from his ears and his eyes, as well from a long gash that stretched from his left ear to his hip. His heart fluttered weakly, shrapnel filling all his organs. One by one, his vital systems began shutting down. Silas was dying.

Nearby, another life form moved weakly, one of its legs broken and blue hydraulic fluids gushing out onto the ground. Its scanners flickered and went in and out. Pulling itself onto its three remaining legs, it searched its surroundings the best it could. Three out of four of its mechanical eyes had been destroyed in the blast and its casing had been broken. Fluids were leaking fast, it was going to dry out and die unless it found a host quickly. Its vision was blurred and static filled. It shouldn't even be conscious in this body. It should still be in stasis. In emergency, the suit awoke its cargo to let it assess the situation.

Its scanners picked up no other Yahntil nearby, nor any drillers, infected or cocooned. No rescue. It was alone. Despair washed through it. It was going to die before even obtaining a single host.

The scanners beeped, indicating a nearby possible host, off to the left. Shuffling sideways, it turned to get a better scan and look. It appeared to be an unconscious human, one of the dominant species of this world. Sudden hope filled the bug and it scuttled towards the human. As soon as the hope had arisen, the hope disappeared. The human was dead. Blood leaked from every orifice on its head and great gouts of blood had hemorrhaged from its side. It was the one that had killed the two infected in the building. Greignan had said something about this human being an important one. One that the *Raknila* themselves sought after as a prize.

The gods frowned upon him this day. If he had taken this human, greatness could have been his.

The scanner beeped once more, as the human's fingers twitched. A heartbeat had been detected by the scanners and a faint brainwave. Small symbols ran across his field of vision, naming variables. Disbelief filled the creature as it weighed its options. Chances were that if he took the body, it would die before completely healing, but it was a sure thing that if he were to stay in this suit, he was going to run out of fluid and die soon. Dehydration was a terrible thing. At any rate, he had to act quickly, he wasn't even sure that his suit had enough hydraulic fluid to complete the transition. Drilling took a lot of power and he'd lost a lot of fluid. About ten gallons was compressed into the carapace, but it only went so far after a crack or leak was breached.

He had a two percent chance of survival in the human and less than one fifteenth of a percent of a chance at survival staying in the driller suit.

Making his decision, Linnerat crawled up on top of the human and settled on his back, activating the hydraulic drilling process.

CHAPTER 16 – THE FOLLOWING

"Alright," Silas whispered, crouching down, looking at Ragger. "I'm gonna go in. My pack of stuff should just be right over the wall here. I put it here for a reason... No moat here, easy entrance, easy escape. No real guards either... I always did warn them about this hole in security, but they don't care. I just jump over and grab it. Easy enough, right?"

<If you say so. As I said, I have a bad feeling about something. My hunches are never wrong.> Ragger whined.

Silas smiled and reached out and roughed up the dog's ears, noting the strangeness of his single torn ear. "I'll be fine. Take me less than two minutes, I promise."

<Go, then.>

"Right." Turning and standing, Silas rolled his neck first to one side and then the other, sighing in relief as the bones cracked once more.

<I'm seriously going to have to do that one day when you let me in control just so you can see how uncomfortable it is.> Linnerat complained.

<Sorry buddy. It's just habit.>

<Buddy. You use that word towards me a lot, lately. Are we friends, Silas? It's been less than two days since we started talking, you know that, correct? I think it's probably some stretch of the imagination to say we're really friends. I know how I reacted when Ragger said what he did, but I really don't know what you think.>

Silas smiled. *<Yes. I would call you friend, Lin. And why do I feel your emotions? I've been meaning to ask that.>*

<We're a very hormonal species. We were originally in the form of an aquatic slug... Our emotions trigger a hormone release. It could be picked up by other members of our species in whatever medium we were in and let them know how we were really feeling. In our natural bodies, it's almost entirely impossible to lie to one

another.>

> *<Ah. That would make sense.>*

In the midst of the conversation, Silas had released his claws and approached the walls and as he spoke his last bit, he grunted and jumped into the air, latching his claws deeply into the rock of the fort wall, finding purchase.

> *<Mmm... I really love this. Have I ever told you that? I used to love rock climbing, as a regular human. Never a better workout.>*

> *<No, I don't believe you've ever mentioned it. Though, I have picked up on your thorough enjoyment of climbing. It's usually accompanied by guilt, but not on this occasion. Why is that?>*

> *<Because I've accepted what I am. There is no need to feel guilty for using the abilities I've obtained.>*

> *<I see.>*

He reached the top of the wall. Looking left and right, he searched for guards. None. He shook his head. These people were all going to get killed without him here. Bunch of idiots. Grunting, he pulled himself up and over the side, vaulting himself slightly up into the air, landing lightly atop the wall. Stepping forward, he peered down into the darkness, looking for the tell tale jutting stone that he'd hidden his stash under.

Spotting it, he smiled, jumping down from the top of the wall. Still in the air, he noticed his error. Camouflaged guards. With guns. Hidden from the vantage point of the wall. They'd taken his advice after all. The smile left his face.

> *<Um, shit. Ragger?!>*

> *<What?>* The dog's tone was overlaid with nervousness.

> *<Your hunch was right!>*

> *<...You fool.>* The tones were now infected with irritation.

> *<Help?>*

No answer. "Fuck."

He slammed into the ground, bending his knees to take the shock, one hand slamming into the ground, the stones beneath him cracking with the force of his impact. It was a little harder a landing than he had expected and it jarred his bones.

Standing with a small groan of pain, he realized with shock, that the soldiers hadn't done anything. They simply stood, guns at the ready, staring silently at him. A knot formed in Silas' stomach. He should have been more careful with letting people see where he kept his stash.

"Shit. I guess this is my welcoming party?"

Two men stepped out with M-16's at the ready, one aimed at his face, the other aimed at his torso. If he moved so much as an inch, they would have removed his head and cut him in half. They weren't taking any chances with him. Apparently, the council had told everyone what he was and what he was capable of.

He wondered who had been publicly hung. Someone had to be the scapegoat. Probably the oldest council member. He would have then been roasted and eaten. Because of him. He sighed. How many people were going to die because of him? He was sick of living with that sort of guilt. Deep down, he knew it wasn't truly his fault, but he couldn't help but feel that part of the burden was his.

He studied the men before him. He'd never seen them in town before and he'd memorized every face, followed every person and been in every dwelling. He didn't recognize a single one. They had to have come from the bunker below. He counted, slowly. Sixteen individual soldiers, all in full camouflage and armed to the teeth with the best weaponry goods could buy.

A man stepped forward, dressed in a suit and began to address Silas in a thick English accent.

"You sir, are being detained for crimes against humanity, for which the punishment is death. By firing squad, ironically enough. We figured you would return for your belongings, so we simply waited for you."

"Oh, how nice of you. Saves you and me time both." Silas smiled. "How thoughtful."

The man stared at Silas and then returned the smile. "Yes, it really is, isn't it? This way, we minimally damage your body. We will put one clip after another into your heart until you are dead. Several may go into your brain, but not if we can help it. We've been itching for an excuse to kill you and cut you open for months now, boy. You could be the key to winning this entire war!"

Silas snorted. "Not dead, I'm not. I could certainly be while I'm alive though."

The man looked at his fingers, picking at his nails. "That's possible. But as far as I – we, are concerned, you're the enemy. And killing you is just killing one more *Mayan*." He raised a hand, tapping two fingers forward, motioning to one of the men to step forward.

Bullard

The man stepped aside, allowing the soldier to take his place, who raised a .357 magnum, aimed straight at Silas' heart.

"Shit." Silas whispered. He closed his eyes, bracing himself, focusing more urgently on his slow transformations.

Unseen to the rest of the group, Silas had slowly been thickening the muscle and bone layer in his abdomen, torso and brow. His shoulders slowly bulged and his pectoral muscles became harder than common iron, while the bone in his forehead slowly piled on underneath his eyebrows. The bullet was going to hurt, but it wasn't going to penetrate through into his heart. <Unless it's an armor piercing round... Oh damn.>

The man fired.

The force of the shot spun Silas around, blue blood glistening in the air, spattering against the wall. The man had loaded his gun with armor piercing rounds, but it still hadn't quite managed to hit Silas in the heart. It had stopped about halfway through one of his rib bones. Another shot to the same area would surely hit the organ, potentially ending his life. Even if it didn't kill him, it could still render him defenseless and free to capture.

His blood ran cold as he thought of how long his body could linger on an operating table. How long it might take before he finally died from the sheer pain. Or just lost his mind. They could keep him alive for years.

He gasped, holding his hand to his chest. The man fired again, this time hitting Silas in the side of his rib cage, where there was less dense muscle to protect him.

This bullet ripped into his body cavity and penetrated one of his lungs. He spun again, back arching in pain and a howl of pain escaped him. Ignoring everything else now, he focused on his transformation, feeling his legs reverse direction and his hands crack and grow, his bones lengthening, tendons snapping and reattaching to accommodate his growing stature. The group of soldiers backed away, startled by his sudden transformation.

"Not going to go easily, are we?" questioned the suited man. Waving to another soldier, this one wielding a slightly smaller caliber gun, he said "Shoot him in the head. We can't use the magnum; we don't want to damage his brain too badly."

The soldier nodded and stepped forward, taking careful aim and then fired. The bullet hit Silas squarely in the forehead and ricocheted, hitting another soldier in the face, killing him instantly. Silas twitched his head, growling. Fully transformed, he stood, staring around the now pitiful looking group which surrounded him.

The man yelled something, waving to another soldier. The soldier stepped forwards and took aim. This one was wielding a small caliber weapon as well. Silas shook his head. Didn't these people learn?

The soldier fired and Silas fell forward screaming as one of his eyes was obliterated by the small bullet. The bone behind his ocular cavity was too thick for the bullet to penetrate, but the pain was enough to completely throw off his focus. Out of his remaining three eyes, he saw the Englishman wave to another soldier, who stepped forward and fired three times in rapid succession. Apparently they did learn, and quickly.

Silas screamed again as two more of his eyes were taken out, leaving only one functional, his left peripheral. Seeing the soldier that had shot him first raise his weapon, Silas stepped forward and grabbed the man by the face and swung him backwards over his head, catapulting him over the wall. The man screamed for a long moment, but stopped rather abruptly when he hit the ground on the other side.

From either side of Silas, three more shots rang out and agony caught him once more as his last eye was obliterated. Shielding his face, Silas swiped back and forth, trying to catch the soldiers. Blood ran down his face and pounded in his skull.

"Not so tough from a distance, are you? Or blind, for that matter." The man mocked.

Silas bared his teeth and growled, stepping towards the direction of the voice, flinging his claws outward. He was rewarded with a small yelp and the sound of a man landing flat on his ass. He smiled, taking a few steps backwards feeling around in the air behind him, searching for the wall.

"Open fire!" The accented man yelled. Silas' empty eye sockets widened in sudden fear. He had no idea what a barrage of heavy artillery bullets would do to him.

At the same moment that his claws found the cold stones of the wall, he heard a huge crash and the wall vibrated under his hands. He could hear the soldiers step back and the man in the suit say "What the bloody hell?"

The wall vibrated once more and Silas blinked, trying to regain his vision. His first destroyed eye had already mostly healed, the bullet clinking to the dirt below, but all he could make out were blurry lights and darks, nothing substantial.

He heard a rush of air and one of the soldiers screamed in pain as they were crushed by whatever fell from the sky. He blinked again, trying to see what was going on. As best as his muddy vision could tell, it appeared that a large object had been flung over the wall and had landed on one of the soldiers, possibly a tree. The soldier closest to Silas had been flattened, and the thrown object was now forming a minimal barrier between him and the rest of the bullets. They could of course, just fire through the branches, but it kept him less visible at the very least. The wall boomed again, vibrating, chunks of stone dislodging and falling to the ground.

Blinking once more, Silas finally regained some clarity in his sight. Taking in the immediate scene before him, he found that he'd been correct. A large, dying oak tree had been ripped up from the ground and now sat between him and his malefactors. Turning to look at the top of the wall, he couldn't see anything, but behind it, he could hear a great many growls and groans.

<Again!> Roach and Ragger's voices echoed through Silas' mind in tandem. BOOM. The wall vibrated again and a hole began to appear behind Silas as the stones were ground to dust by whatever forces were behind the wall.

The British guy lost it. "He's going to escape! Get over that tree and kill him! I want him in my labs, god damnit! Kill him!"

The wall shattered and Silas dove forward to avoid being crushed by the rubble. Spotting his haversack among the rocks, he reached down and scooped it up. Turning, he looked out through the new entrance to the fort and found a sight he certainly hadn't thought to find. Before him stood Roach, Ragger, five *Titans*, three *Snappers* and a single *Hellhound.*

The *Hellhound* leaped, bounding through the hole and past Silas, over the tree and into the fray of soldiers. Screams and gunshots followed almost immediately. Moments later, the three *Snappers* pushed their way past him and they too leapt over the tree and laid into the group of soldiers. As Silas stared out the hole and into the night, the *Titans* looked at Ragger a moment, before nodding and turning back to the forest, stomping away.

<Remember, only the ones with weapons.> Ragger voiced to

his remaining allies. *<No innocents! If we want to prove that we can be allies then you cannot murder those who cannot defend themselves! And try not to kill the soldiers, either... Just wound them.>*

A soft mental rumble of agreement passed through Silas' mind and he felt confused. Leaping over the tree, he stood in disbelief to find each soldier disarmed and bloodied. Two lay dead, but the rest seemed without critical damage. The *Snappers* had taken their weapons and tossed them into a pile and then stomped them flat.

Roach and Ragger came up behind him softly. *<Go now. And guard this hole until the humans can fix it.>* Ragger ordered.

<Yes, ancient one.> The *Renegades* spoke with one voice, all leaning forward and doing a strange little bow in Ragger's direction. Then, turning to Silas, they all too leaned forward and bowed even lower than they had to Ragger. *<Hunter.>* They then turned and bounded out through the hole which they had just created, heading swiftly back to the safety of the forest.

<What the hell?> Silas gaped, staring at Ragger.

<You said help. So I went and found some.> Ragger looked at him like he was stupid. Why did everyone look at him like he was stupid, Silas wondered.

<In Renegades? But, but... how?>

<I went into the forest; I called out to them, told them that a fellow Renegade and warrior was in trouble and that I needed their assistance. Those friendly to peace heeded my call.>

<They seemed like they knew you.>

<They did.>

<Care to share how?>

<No.>

<Dickhead.>

Something slammed into the back of Silas' skull and stars wandered before his eyes. Stepping forward, his knees buckled and he fell onto his hands. Ragger leaped to his feet and growled in a manner that made his skin crawl. Rolling onto his side and holding his head, Silas turned to look at whatever had attacked him.

Dangling in the air by his tie was the Englishman, held aloft by Roach, whose teeth were bared and claws extended, looking the man in the face. His suit arm was torn and deep scratches in his flesh could be seen where the fabric parted. Blood dripped from Roach's hand and small strips of flesh could be seen buried under her claws. The magnum lay on the ground beside her feet, spattered in blood. The bastard had shot him in the head from behind.

Woozy, Silas pushed up, staggering to his feet.

A low growl built in the back of her throat as she brought him down towards her face. "Never, again. Never, never again, you coward." Her voice was harsh and deep, it sounded more like a growl than words. Still, the malice and disgust was apparent in her tone.

Raising a single hand to the man's forehead, she dug her claws into his temples as he whimpered and tears ran down his face. Almost delicately, she pulled one of her fingers down the side of his face, tracing a line of blood across his features.

"Roach," Silas said sternly, testing his ability to speak while in form. He was surprised to find that the words came easily enough, though his voice sounded like something out of a nightmare. "Don't."

She turned to look at him, her eyes glowing soft yellow in the darkness and in them, Silas saw a touch of madness. She couldn't control the transformation nearly as well as himself, it overwhelmed her, drove her to the edge of her sanity. He also noted that she had lied to him before. She was more in form than she'd shown him, whereas before, she said all she'd shown was all she could do. She was taller and broader, perhaps ten feet tall, and her arms were far more bulky than they had been and all her hair had fallen out.

"Roach," he said again, this time more softly. "Put the man down. He can't hurt us; we have no business with him."

Her coarse, pointed tongue flickered out and ran across her lips once and she looked up at the man once more. Growling, she set him on the ground and stepped away from him, turning towards Silas. Then, with a sudden roar, she spun and hit the man in the side, sending him flying through the air towards the stone wall. He hit it with a sickening thud and then fell to the ground moaning, cradling his shredded arm, blood leaking down his face.

Silas looked at the man for a moment, assessing the damage. He would live with medical attention, which Silas was sure would swarm the area within moments of their departure. He would be fine. Turning to look again at Roach, he noticed that she had already begun to release the transformation, her features softening, her hair growing swiftly out once more, her fingers cracking as they returned to their normal size and shape.

Finishing the form, she stood looking weary, surrounded by

broken men. Stepping towards Silas, she stumbled and fell. "I can't. It's too much. I hate doing that. I hate what I become. I just get so angry and I can't help it." She said, her words aching with disgust for herself.

Hopping over the debris, Silas scooped her up in his arms. <*It's alright. I remember how it was in the beginning. It takes a few months to get used to.*>

Surveying the now broken portion of the town surrounding him, he shook his head. He brought a hand closer to his face and opened his palm, looking down at the small haversack which he had come for. All this for that? She was going to be pissed. He shook his head again and then tossed the package at Ragger. <*Catch.*>

Leaping into the air, Ragger caught the sack easily in his open jaws. Standing before the hole, he looked at Silas silently and then walked out into the night, followed close behind by his new companion.

****

2013: Silas

Amidst the burning remains of the building, Silas awoke to more pain than anyone ever had a right. His first thought was that he was in hell. He couldn't remember a single thing, he didn't know his name and he didn't know where he was from or what year it was. All he knew was unending, agonizing pain. His side and his back were the worst. They felt like they were on fire and a million hot pokers had been jabbed into his side, again and again. He didn't know why he thought he was in hell, but he knew that for some reason, he deserved to be. Something told him that was where he'd planned to go all along. That he'd been trying to escape something worse.

Waves of heat rolled across him and he could tell that parts of his skin were cooked, just by how raw and disgusting they felt in some places, and in others, by the way that he couldn't feel anything at all. Occasional cool wisps of air across his skin told him that he was nearly naked, covered by only a few burnt scraps of cloth, here and there.

He had to be in hell. Oddly, relief bubbled up from within him at the thought.

Spitting into the dirt that filled his mouth and nose, he tried to get a good breath, but every gasp of air set his insides to screaming. The iron clad scent of blood filled the air around him and trying to move, he found that he absolutely could not. Agony filled every muscle and his left side in particular screamed for release. But there was nothing he could do but lie in the dirt and do his best to breathe.

Choking on the dirt, he tried to force his head to the side, but doing so caused a grating in his neck, the bones grinding together. His neck had been broken. Was that the case? Was he in hell for committing suicide? Yes, that seemed right. But not by hanging himself. He'd planned to shoot himself.

Flashes of memory came back to him, wielding a gun, pressing a pistol to his throat. But that seemed eons before and besides, in the memory, a little girl came in the room and screamed at him, running to him and hugging. That could not be his last memory. He didn't believe he was the kind of person to off himself in front of a little girl. But then again, perhaps he was. That would certainly explain why he thought he deserved to go to hell.

He tried moving his head once more, this time getting a little force behind the tiny movement and his head flopped to the left, giving him a view of his body. He immediately wished he hadn't.

His body had been completely destroyed. Lying helpless in a rapidly spreading pool of his own blood, he lay in the dirt on top of a shattered arm, blood oozing from every pore in his skin that hadn't been ripped to pieces. Deep gashes and burns rested atop his skin bare skin, from which blood and clear fluid leaked. He could see two ribs, bent and broken, piercing out through his flesh and every time he took a breath, he could swear that he could see his exposed lungs. His rear was in the air and one of his legs had been twisted up beneath his stomach. A gaping hole just above the small of his back was evident even from the angle at which he lay.

The more he saw, the more he felt, the more he felt, the more he wanted to scream, but his lungs simply wouldn't let him. Blackness swam in his vision and his heart fluttered, threatening to give out. His cells screamed for blood, they needed their nourishment, their oxygen. He could feel his body shutting down.

He didn't understand how he was alive. By all rights, he absolutely should be dead. No living body could take this much trauma and survive more than a few minutes. Maybe that was the case. Maybe he just wasn't dead yet. Maybe these were his last few minutes. Bitterness filled him. He was going to die here alone and he didn't even know his own name. What cruel world had he lived in?

Trying to take his thoughts off his pain, his body and his impending death, he tried to look at his surroundings, even though he couldn't see much with one eye in the dirt. He could still feel heat and hear flames, though he couldn't see their source. The heat that he could feel rolled across his raised thighs and back, so he assumed it must be behind him. Smoke filled the air and he began to notice that it was burning his lungs and that he was getting lightheaded, from lack of oxygen, and lack of blood.

Looking desperately for anything that would tell him where he was, or what his name was, he tried to flop his head up, to get a better look. Agony filled him, but he ignored it. His head popped a little bit, allowing his other eye to look about.

The first sight he caught was of an oblong, black object lying on the ground near his body, almost on top of his leg. He hadn't been able to see it before because the way his head had been laying, with his neck popped sideways.

His blood ran cold as he studied it, something tugging at the back of his mind, memories of running, huge walls of water and packs of black... <Driller.>

Everything came back to him in an instant and his eyes grew wide as he began to scream, wishing he had instead found himself in Hell.

Then again, perhaps this was Hell, for Silas could think of no crueler way for him to exist.

****

2013: Caravan

They walked in silence, Matthias' arm wrapped around Kendall's shoulder, the whole group moving through the night without a word spoken between them. Some had tears streaming down their face, other's lips moved in internal prayer, but all of them wore an expression of despair and anguish. Every heart felt the same emotion; every set of eyes hid the same thoughts. Not even the animals uttered a single noise, the dogs and oxen walking side by side with their masters, they too seemingly mourning the loss of the man.

Bullard

How would they go on each day without the man who brought them all together? Who would lead them? If a man such as he could be defeated, the hero risen from the dirt and grit of circumstance, could fall and be beaten by this enemy, what hope did any of them chance at seeking?

Matthias and Kendall sensed this overall sense of despair and looking at one another, turned around to face the group and held up a hand, walking backwards, waiting until everyone had stopped. Matthias spoke first, allowing Kendall to gather his thoughts.

"I know how you all feel. We all were touched by Silas. In one way or another, each and every one of us owe him our lives. He saved every single one of us individually. In the past five months... God, has it really only been that long? He waged a war by himself to gather and lead this group, against an enemy that, I'm not proud to admit, I have wet myself facing. We knew him and loved him. He found us, brought us into his fold, fed us, clothed us and called us his family. In a time like this." He waved an arm about, gesturing to the dying landscape.

"That's something more miraculous than anyone else in the world has ever seen. We are the luckiest group of people in the world, for ever having met that man. Where was the Government? Where were our families? Where were our friends? I'll tell you where. They were exactly where we were, running for cover, hiding in their individual holes, praying to God to save our ass, to forgive us for all the wrong we did. The difference is that our prayers were answered, in the form of a young, crude, vulgarly spoken young man, who kicked ass and took names on a daily basis. You don't think we're a pain in the ass? Don't get me wrong, I love each and every one of you like a brother, or a sister, but I'll be damned if you're not the whiniest bunch of sons of bitches I've ever met."

The crowd chuckled, as Matthias smiled, looking down at the ground. The moment passed and Matthias looked up once more, his tone sober again.

"But you don't think he could have left us? You don't think he could have struck out on his own for Chicago, for the safety of the city? You think *he* needed *us?* Yeah, like a pig needs stucking, he needed us."

Several people hung their heads in what appeared to be shame. Others in the crowd were silently shaking their heads and others pointedly looked away.

Bullard

"He could have –" Kendall held up a hand, cutting Matthias off, speaking softly but clearly, his low voice carrying across the crowd.

"If a single one of you in this crowd think that my brother could have walked away from this group, taken just those that mattered most, myself, my sister and mother and left you all to die then you never saw him for the man that he is... was." A single tear sprung from his eye at the use of the past tense.

"If a single one of you can think about him and all that he did and say that he didn't care and love about each of you as an individual then I want you to pack your shit and get out of this group. You're not worth the rest of us." He stared around, meeting as many eyes as he could "You're an insult to his memory. No... That's not what he would have wanted. Better yet, if a single one of you can turn and look back at those flames and have a bad thought towards him then don't speak to me. Don't speak to anyone. Come with us to Chicago and then never interact with any of us ever again. Silas had a heart of gold. He stopped and saved your asses because he *wanted* to. Because it was the right thing to do. Because he couldn't bear to let another person live on their own in this dirty hell like he did for some time. He saved you because that's the man he was."

He stepped back again and this time, glancing around, saw even more ashamed faces, but saw determination too, among other emotions. Fear, hope, loss, despair. All of them were present.

Matthias let silence reign for a long moment, let the people think about what they'd heard before speaking again.

"We were truly blessed to have such a man enter into our lives at such a time. And even more blessed to have him as long as we did! He was indeed a saint. Saint Silas. I will live and wake by him, as long as my years last. And if by some tiny miracle, he survived... When he finds me, as I know he will if he lives, I will follow him until the ends of the earth. If he lives, he will find us. You know this as well as I... Let me ask you this. Would you die for him? I know that I would."

Silence once more.

"I asked you a question. Would you die for that man? If the answer is yes, then I tell you, you can live for him too. Live for that which he died."

Stepping forward, Kendall answered quietly. "I would. I would die for him in an instant, no matter the situation."

Another man from the group, Keaton, stepped forward,

gripping his rifle so tightly his knuckles had turned white and spoke just even more quietly than Kendall had, but with no less conviction. "Aye... As would I. He took a bullet for me and my own and then dragged my unconscious ass to safety. There's no way I could turn my back on his memory. Not one." He turned and melted back into the crowd, making his way towards the back.

A woman stepped forward this time, bouncing a young child on her hip. Theresa. "I was pregnant and in labor when Silas found me... I thought I was going to die and my baby with me. Then Silas kind of came out of nowhere, diving down into our basement, dragged me out of the ruins of my home while shooting over my shoulder and then hid with me in a hole for seventeen hours while I delivered Jonathan amidst gunshots and explosions."

"He was my support, my nursemaid and my guardian. He had ten clips of bullets, two belts of shotgun shells and two grenades. How he got us out of there, I'll never know. He made every shot count – I think when we got back to the group, he had about five bullets left and that was it. He'd also taken several wounds –I never thanked him. But I'm glad he did. And yes... I would die for him. Gladly." Her free hand clapped to her face as the tears spilt forth. She turned and buried her face into the shoulder of her boyfriend, sobbing quietly. He ran a single hand through her hair before beginning to speak quietly as well, telling his tale.

One by one, the group stepped forward and shared their story of how Silas saved them and one by one, pledged their allegiance to their hero, their patron saint, their martyr of humanity.

CHAPTER 17 – JOURNEY

"I still can't believe you went back for a shotgun, a Selenidi, a couple changes of clothes and a bottle of Southern Comfort." Roach had been pissed when she'd found out what he'd risked all their lives for.

"I still can't believe you *smacked* me when you found out! And you know what? We could use this damn shotgun!" He snatched it from his back, waving it under her nose. "Oh, and! My recipe book was in there too. I've been building that up for almost two years. You liked that deer stew well enough last night. And you drank half my booze anyway! You're not even old enough to drink!"

<*It's been two days. Are you two going to shut up any time soon?*> Ragger moaned.

"No," Roach snapped. "He risked our lives for a couple of stupid little things. And technically, since we don't age, you're not old enough to drink either!"

Silas leered at her, moving his head back and forth in a mocking manner. "Well, aren't you clever? I'll have you know that this here Selenidi keeps me sane. It's got all my music on it... Just wish I had a way to charge it. You broke the god damned laptop when you came through the wall."

"ARE YOU COMPLAINING ABOUT US SAVING YOUR ASS?!"

Ragger shook his head. <*Chicago can't be too far away, can it?*>

Half grimacing, Silas shook his head. "It's another good four hundred fifty miles from here. We still have to pass through Saint Louis and it's about fifty from here. We can make about fifteen miles a day at this pace. If we run, probably fifty. So another nine days, at least. Eleven, more likely."

A feeling of mental despair washed across the group as Ragger whined.

Feeling bad, Silas decided to try and change the topic. "Hey

Ragger, what's up with your ear? Why does it scar like that? I thought the only scar ever left on an infected was the one from being drilled."

Perking up at the prospect of being able to have a change of subject, Ragger spoke enthusiastically.

<Well, it was a subject I was planning to broach later, but since you asked...>

"Seriously? A Selenidi. I can't believe you. Irresponsible jerk. I should slap the shit out of you again." Roach wasn't having any distractions.

<Roach, if I may kindly interject?> Linnerat appeared to be fed up with the argument as well.

Roach glared at the side of Silas' head, presumably glaring at Linnerat. Silas fought the urge to laugh. <She's giving you the stink-eye, dude.>

<I noticed.> Lin replied.

<What?> She snapped.

Pausing before answering – almost like taking a breath, Silas thought – Lin spoke quietly in Roach's mind. <That little piece of equipment really does keep him sane. He has an attachment to music that is quite admirable. You should hear him sing! I think it's quite good. Of course, I am somewhat biased.> Warmth emanated from him.

Roach continued glaring at the side of Silas' head for a few moments and then cracked a small smile. "If you say so... I still think it was completely irresponsible of him. Three men died and I almost ripped the head off of another."

<Yes. Yes they did. And how unfortunate a happening. However, regardless of what was in the sack, they were there to greet and murder Silas. And we would have killed them, regardless. That is how war works. And darling, this is war, no matter how you cut it.>

Roach hung her head sadly. <I wish none of this had ever happened. I wish I hadn't...> She trailed off.

<We can all wish many things, Roach. And sometimes, we get what we want. Sometimes we don't. Did you know that once, Silas was the one thing I desired above all else?>

"What? Really? Why?" Roach asked the questions in Silas' mind for him.

<I was dying. And so was he. Silas very well near killed me. I woke in my suit to a shotgun blast and hitting a hard concrete floor.> A

memory of bringing the shotgun to bear and blasting a Driller into the darkness in a warehouse bubbled to the surface of Silas' mind. He chuckled under his breath. "Son of a bitch. That was you?"

<Yes. And you broke my suit, very nearly killed me right then.> He turned his attention back to Roach. <Soon after, a grenade went off a few feet from the two of us. Blew us both through a brick wall. He was dying and I was dying. Ironically enough, we saved each other. If I had not entered Silas, I would have died. If I had not entered him, he would have died. And you know what? I got my wish. And in some ways, so did he. He wished at that time to die. I wished at that time to live. Sometimes, wishes don't go as we plan. For example: I did not really get what I wished. I am completely and utterly powerless in this body. I did not gain the prestige and power I so longed for...> He paused, thinking on how to word his next sentence.

< But, I am alive, and living an adventure I could never have otherwise imagined. Silas however: now has super strength and cannot die by normal means. Yet, he'd wished he'd died. In some ways, he did. His life ended. But his existence in this particular plane of life endured. So, both wishes granted, but neither of us really got what we want. But we make the best of it. Such is life.>

Roach nodded slowly. "I think that was a little deep for the situation, LinLin, but that's ok. I understand where you're coming from. Thank you. Silas? I'm sorry for slapping you."

He laughed. "It's cool. It's not like it hurt, anyway."

She huffed and turned away. He reached out, placing a hand on her shoulder. "Thanks. Really."

Withdrawing, Silas spoke silently to his internal counterpart. <You already knew about my mother and sister, didn't you? You have to have, having been there.>

<—Yes. Not all of it, mind you, just bits and pieces. Your mind was wrapped around it when I merged with you. And I heard some of the proceeding – but overall, yes... I knew.>

Silas nodded. <Thanks for not using it against me.>

<You are most welcome.>

****

Roach's stomach growled audibly and she looked at Silas. "I'm hungry..."

He cocked an eyebrow, laughing. "Really? You don't say. I don't think you are; I think you're faking."

She glared at him. "You're a dick sometimes."

He frowned. "I'm sorry. I'm just playing."

"Yeah, well..." She huffed. "I know. But we haven't eaten in like, two days. I get cranky when I'm hungry. That cow didn't last very long."

"... It's been like twelve hours and we'll find something soon enough, don't worry – St. Louis is fairly close by. Thirty minutes, no more. Just keep this pace and we'll be there soon. You should be able to see the city skyline soon enough. Just keep looking for it."

Ragger just shook his head. Silas shot him a glance.

"What?"

<Oh, nothing...> Then, privately, Ragger spoke in his head. <You two need to knock it off with the pheromones. You're making my nose hurt. If you can't just turn them off, stop talking to each other!>

Silas yelped. <Pheromones?!>

Roach jumped at the sudden noise and exclamation, slowing her pace and forcing Silas and Ragger to the same. She turned slightly, looking at Silas. "What?" She looked back and forth between he and Ragger, a strange look on her face.

"Nothing," Silas said aloud. "Just a sudden thought."

"What?" She pressed. "Tell me! I want to know. Can't hide things from me."

He scowled. "The hell I can't."

She huffed once more, turning away from him, resuming her previous pace, muttering. "Asshole."

He smiled quietly and Ragger sent him a mental nudge. <Like that. Stop it. Hormones roll off of you like – like – like – like I don't know, but they stink. Just quit.>

<I don't know what you're talking about.> Silas replied indignantly. <I'm not giving off any pheromones. Neither is she. I'd smell them!>

<No, you wouldn't... Actually, yes you would. You do, it's helping drive your behavior!>

Silas paused, thinking, ignoring the topic at hand. <Why can't I smell either of you? I mean, now I can, up close. And maybe a little further away, now that I recognize you.>

Ragger's eyes widened. <I forgot.>

169

<Forgot what?>

<That we need to slather you in tree sap or aloe, sagebrush and clay.>

<What? Tree sap and clay?>

<It eliminates our scent.>

Silas rolled his eyes. *<No shit, but I wouldn't have thought tree sap and clay would do much. Sagebrush sure, that stuff reeks. And maybe Aloe. But that sage explains it, for sure. Don't know where we'd find any out here in the burbs, though. Maybe a kitchen?>*

<Burbs?>

<Suburban areas.>

<Oh. Strange little humans... Yes, that is normally where we find it, in various kitchens.>

They all three strode on in silence for a few moments, Silas throwing glances at Roach occasionally.

Ragger piped up with his own question this time.

<What is Linnerat doing? He's so quiet so often. He's a very intelligent individual of our species. I'm surprised he doesn't partake in our conversations more often.>

Peering inward momentarily, Silas checked on his inner self. *<He's sleeping. He sleeps a lot. I think he must get very bored sometimes. And... I used to be very mean to him. I mean... I really, really hated him. I think he went to sleep to escape me a lot of the time. I think it's become something of a habit; an escape.>* He frowned.

<It's understandable. On both accounts.> Ragger reassured him.

They had traveled probably less than twenty paces when another thought struck Silas, this one seeming of fairly grave importance, considering the context of their previous conversation.

<We're speaking through Roach, right? As you're a Renegade, you can't connect to me unless you go through her?>

<Yes and no.>

<Like I said before, I really hate you sometimes.> Silas glared.

<Ha. I was merely thinking of how to explain this process to you. You see —> He seemed to struggle for words for a moment, something Silas had never seen him do before. He raised an eyebrow.

<Ok, yes, that makes sense. Yes, you see, Renegades can speak to one another mind to mind and to non-Renegades as well. They

merely have to be within a few feet of one another, in fact, I'm at range for speaking with you mind to mind right now. Think of all the times we've spoken. The first time, you were physically touching me. Has my voice ever come through so clear that first time?>

<No, but I figured that was because you were terrified I was going to pop your head off...>

Ragger laughed aloud, a short barking noise. Roach turned again, looking at them quickly before looking away again, flipping her hair.

Silas glanced at her. <Does she know?>

<I don't think so, given her earlier question about using her to speak. No real need for her to, after all. Now, about speaking through her —>

Silas interrupted. <One more question.>

Ragger waited a moment and then replied stiffly. <Yes?>

Silas laughed. <Sorry if I'm bugging you, just curious. If we can speak through her... how is it that she can't process what we're saying?>

<That's what I was figuring out how to explain. The closest way I can figure it is this: You obviously know how when a Yahntil infects a brain, the host can no longer control the brain?>

<Yes.>

<Well, the closest I can figure the process out is this: When the Yahntil was ripped from her head prematurely, whatever tentacles were left within her brain, still function and effectively cut off whatever sections they sit in off from the rest of her cerebellum. We block signals from neurons with our own neurons. Our entire body is a neural unit. It has to be. Our intelligence could not be kept in such a small central unit that our body would require. We do have a central brain, but it is not the seat of our intelligence or personality. Even our organs and skin are capable of processing thought and memory —>

<— that's freaky.> Silas interjected.

<Maybe to you, yes.> Ragger agreed. <For us, not only is it natural, but at times very convenient. The older and larger we grow, the more intelligent we become. At any rate, I assume that for all intents and purposes, that part of her brain is dead. I was mistaken in telling you that she is able to create any channels she chooses... I think that she is capable of such a thing. But at the moment, she is merely open to all thought speak near her, no matter how weak. In fact, she

may be acting much as the Raknila, routing enemy thoughts through her brain, without ever knowing. Of course, she cannot pick up the offworld Raknila... Only they have that power, and that is due to the quantum machines in their hosts brain.>

<At any rate, I've been attempting to teach her to access this part of her brain to override the foreign neurons, force them to do what she wants, but she lacks the discipline. It's irritating. This canine managed to overpower me as a whole, several times, and that girl can't overpower a few tentacles.> He snorted.

<Huh. Maybe we can do something about that.> Silas thought.

<What do you mean?> Ragger queried.

<When first dealing with the taunts of Lin in my head, I discovered that sometimes mental discipline comes from physical discipline.>

He accelerated his stride, reaching out and grabbing Roach by the shoulder, stopping her. Ragger slid to a close stop behind her.

Skidding to a stop, Silas turned to Roach, looking her in the face.

"We need to teach you how to fight."

She shook her head, blinking rapidly. "I can fight just fine."

He shook his head in return, staring at her. "No, you can't. You know how to hit and flail and maim. You don't know how to fight worth a damn."

She looked at him like he'd just suggested she moon him.

"Ok," he said, "What is with that look? Why does everyone look at me like I'm retarded all the time?"

"Because you really say some strange shit and have some strange ideas sometimes." She replied. "Alright, maybe I don't know how to fight. But I've survived this long."

He glared at her, grabbing her arm, hoisting it up, squeezing it. "Have you ever actually had to fight a *Mayan* soldier hand to hand? You see your reflexes on me grabbing you? Non-existent. I guarantee you would lose, the way you handle yourself now. Not only do you have to learn how to fight, you have got to learn how to handle your transformations."

He flung her arm down. She rubbed at it, looking at him. "Fine. When do you want to 'train' me, then?" A strange look flitted across her face as she spoke and she laughed.

Blinking, he looked at her strangely. "What?"

She laughed again. "Never mind. When do you want to train me?"

"In there." He pointed. A small grocery store sat off to the side of the highway they were on by about half a mile. Looked like a Stop'N'Shop. "Might even find some canned food in there. This place was hit pretty hard, people evacuated pretty quickly. We'll eat and then we'll train."

She nodded. "Alright. Let's go."

He looked her up and down. "Alright."

As they began walking, Linnerat stirred, stretching mildly inside Silas' skull. Silas winced.

<That feels so strange, you know.>

<Ah yes, I'm sorry...> Linnerat apologized. <It's just... Haha, kind of tight in here.>

Silas laughed. <I can imagine.>

<What's going on?> Lin asked. <I heard something about fighting? Training?>

<I'm going to train Roach how to fight.>

<—That should be interesting. However, may I mention something? You need to feed, your blood is rather weak at the moment.>

<Oh, great, you just took a shit. Lovely.> Silas shook his head. <God, that's so disgusting! I really wish you hadn't told me that...>

<It would have come up sooner or later, I'm sure. Would you rather, perhaps, that we feed on your brain?>

<No. I suppose not. But yeah, you're right, I'm hungry.>

<Mm. Where are you planning to train Roach?>

Looking up so Lin could see, Silas looked at the building coming up before them. <There. I figure that hand to hand combat in an enclosed space is more difficult, more strenuous. I can't waste time training her. We have to make it to Chicago and convince them that we are more of an asset than a threat, to give us safe haven. Yet another council meeting, I'm sure.>

Lin cringed. <And more scanners to boot —Those things hurt.>

<Yeah —They don't feel too pleasant for me either, bucko.>

<Not nearly as bad as they hurt me. It tickles your brain, for me, it nearly electrocutes me.>

<Yowch, really? Damn, I didn't know that. I'm sorry.>

<Not much you can really do about it.> Lin said.

<True. But I can still feel bad about it.>

<You absolutely can. But what's the point of it?>

<—I don't know, it's just something humans do, we feel bad for things that aren't necessarily in our—'

"We're here." Roach announced, interrupting the internal conversation.

And indeed they were. Looking up, Silas realized he hadn't even been paying attention to where they had been going. They stood before a pair of decrepit sliding doors, plants and vines winding up along the edges of the glass. Stop'N'Shop. His mother had loved coming to this store chain. He never understood why. Sure, it was cheap, but the food was terrible.

"So we are. Let's see if we have any unwelcome guests hiding out in here..." He trailed off, reaching out through his mind, searching for any Yahntil presence with the store. After a few seconds, both Ragger and he spoke at the same time. *<The structure is clear of all Yahntil presence.>* "Nope, nuttin, all clear."

They looked at each other quickly, frowning and then looked away. Silas stepped forward, digging his fingers into the pliable material between the sliding doors and began to pull, heaving them to the side. After an initial creak and groan of protest at being moved after so long, they popped open easily enough under Silas' immense strength. Grunting, he pulled one of the doors clean off its groove, tossing it to the side, glancing at Roach as he did so. She didn't appear interested. He sniffed. *<Damn.>*

<What? What was the point of taking the door off of the building? It was coming open easily enough.> Lin asked.

<No reason.> Silas replied innocently.

<Right.> Lin sounded amused. *<That's why you looked at her, right? And then seemed disappointed when she didn't care? You forget, I can see almost every thought in your head. You were trying to impress her.>*

<Was not.>

<Were too.>

<Was not!>

<Were too!>

<WAS NOT!>

<Mhm. Okay.>

<I wasn't, I tell you!>

Bullard

"Are you just going to stand there, or are we going in? I'm really freaking hungry." Roach asked.

"Oh... Sorry, talking to Lin. Go right ahead, the place is clean." He stepped to one side, gesturing for her to go in. She stepped forward, shaking her head slightly. "I hope there's some food here." She wrinkled her nose. "It stinks in here. Like rotten meat. Probably the meat section... Well, that means that this place probably hasn't been looted. It's strange... We can see St. Louis from here. Why aren't there any people?"

Silas looked at the ground, answering slowly. "St. Louis was one of the first cities to be hit... And was completely slaughtered. There were three major battles here, the first one was won by sheer numbers, the second one was won by a strange occurrence where half the enemy army simply fell over dead and the third battle... Well, let's just say that St. Louis is almost entirely a *Mayan* city now, if anything. I think it's pretty much empty. Most likely filled with *Renegade*s. It's sad... I lived here, once. It's my childhood home. In fact, I'm pretty sure I shopped here once, stopped in with a friend to grab some beer." He waved a hand about them, indicating the store. At the thought, a sudden memory hit him, one that he hadn't considered in a long time. "Ah... Paul. I miss him. He didn't make it." He frowned. "He was with a naval unit in San Francisco, a corpsman... Went AWOL, from what I hear. Came back to try and fight for his home. Died the first week." He hung his head, examining the dirt once more.

Roach stood with a soft look on her face. "I'm sorry, Silas. You've lost a lot, haven't you?" She took a step towards him, reaching a hand out and placing it on his arm. "It's ok, though. Cause you know what? You're a good guy. And no matter what happens to you, I'm starting to realize, that you come through the other side just as good as when you went in. No matter what you have to do, or see, or endure, you come out the other side, just as wholesome and good looking as you were before going in." She winked and then dropped her arm and walked away. "Come on, we need to find something to eat. My stomach isn't the only one I can hear now."

Ragger padded softly past Silas, rubbing his head once against his hand, whining, before following Roach into the darkness of the store.

Heaving a soft sigh, Silas looked up, watching her until she turned around a corner, a slight twinge in his heart, one he hadn't felt in a long time. One that he couldn't let himself feel. He sighed again, following the two of them into the dark.

****

They sat on the ground, digging into their cans with some plastic spoons they'd found. Mounds of empty cans surrounded them, Silas' mainly of beef stew and corn, Roach's of green beans and peas. Several unopened cans of kidney beans sat between them. Off to the side, Ragger tore into case after case of Raman noodle cups, shredding the foam and showering Roach and Silas with crumbs.

Occasionally one of them would reach over and snag one from a case before he get to it, at which he would turn and glare at whoever had stolen it before going back to ripping open another case.

A small coal fire crackled in a grill to one side, something they found in the back room of the store, probably for employee appreciation day. A small pot of water boiled on top and several other small pots sat beside it, filled with various soups.

"God, I hate eating like this. There's never enough in the store to fill me up. It's like a blessing and a curse. I can eat all I want and never get fat – But I can never eat enough! I'd rather just hunt down a deer or two and eat them myself. Much more filling and frankly –Taste better than all this processed crap. I never realized how disgusting a lot of this tasted before I was infected." Silas complained. "And I wish I had some bread. I haven't had bread in so long. Or Pizza. I still love pizza…"

Roach nodded, stuffing her ladle in her mouth, sucking her clam chowder off, before dipping it back into her bowl for another go.

****

Several hours later, when they'd eaten most of the canned goods aisle and a mountain of cans lay in the middle of the floor; Silas stood and walked over to Roach, who'd gone to spread out and go to sleep there on the floor. "Alright, let's get some training in, while we still have all this energy from the food. Best time to fight, right after a meal."

Roach looked up at him and frowned. "Right now? But I –"
Her words were cut short as Silas kicked her in the face,

sending her flying. She yelped, landing hard on her hip about ten feet from where she had sat, trying to scramble to her feet. Ragger growled for a moment and then realizing the situation, went back to gnawing on a can of stew.

"What the hell?" Roach screamed at Silas.

"You think the enemy cares what you want? You're soft. Come on, show me what you got." He extended a hand, waving her towards him. With a snarl, she ran at him, leaping. It wasn't something he was expecting.

She hit him square in the stomach, knocking the wind out of him, sending them both flying back another ten feet in the opposite direction. Silas foot hit the grill as he tried to shove her off of him, knocking it over and scattering still smoldering coals across the floor. Several touched his skin and he gasped, leaping to his feet and regaining his balance. To his surprise, he found that Roach had already gotten to her feet and was about five feet from him, watching him warily. He took a step towards her and she took a step back.

Suddenly, the smell of burnt flesh reached him and he looked down, wondering what it could be, thinking perhaps he had burned himself worse than he thought.

Sudden, blinding pain shot through his mind as Roach thrust the hot coals she held in her hand directing into his face. Batting at the heat, he ran backwards, holding his face and eyes, tripping over a small pile of cans.

In an instant, Roach was on top of him, her hands pounding at the side of his head, ribcage, upper arms, leaving deep scratches in his flesh.

Getting angry, Silas slammed his arms upward and into Roach's chest, sending her flying upward into the air. Leaping to his feet once more, Silas punched straight outward, catching the still airborne Roach in the side of the stomach, propelling her forward and into the grill, spilling the rest of the coals, igniting her hair. She screamed, batting at her head. Walking up to her, he gave her one, two, three vicious kicks in the stomach, ribcage and face, sending her spinning across the floor and curled into a ball. A trail of blood followed behind her, pouring from her nose. She came to a full stop and lay there.

"Never, let your surroundings distract you from your enemy! We both made the mistake; you used it against me first and then foolishly fell for it yourself! The fire was inconsequential. It would have burned your hair away and then the fire would have gone out. The flesh would have grown back. Were I really the enemy, I could have just ripped your guts out... Learn from your enemy and yourself! Some of the biggest lessons you can learn are from your instincts!"

He walked towards her, realizing she wasn't moving. Suddenly worried, he darted forward, kneeling down next to her, reaching for her neck to check for a pulse.

Her hand darted up, grabbing his wrist. His eyes widened as she sat up and yanked on his arm, throwing him through the air. He hit a merchandise rack and then fell hard to the floor onto his head, cracking the tile. She jumped up and ran at him, kicking him several times in the side, jamming him into the rack, denting the metal shelves with the force of each blow.

Rolling, he swiped an arm out and slammed it into her feet, knocking her to the floor and winding her momentarily. Pulling himself up and forward by the metal shelves, he staggered to a standing position, holding his severely bruised ribs momentarily, gasping for air and then leaped at her, thinking to stomp on her. She rolled out of the way and got to her hands and knees, crawling away at an inhuman speed. She disappeared around a corner. Silas' foot met only hard floor, the tiles shattering under the force of his blow.

"Yes, very smart." Silas said. "Hiding is half the battle against a *Viral*." He listened intently as he walked forward, trying to get a bearing on her position. He could hear her pained breathing when he stopped, but couldn't get a lock on it much more than it was coming from his left. "Try listening for my footsteps and only breathe when I'm walking. Breathe as softly as you can and hold it when I hold still. When I stop, you can guarantee I'm listening for you. My own footsteps can help mask your position." The breathing stopped. He began walking and the breathing started up again, but this time he couldn't even tell what direction it was coming from. "Very goo—" He was cut off as hands came through a rack, grabbing him by the throat and yanking him backwards into a shelf, cold metal biting into the back of his head. Stars wandered before his eyes and he slid to the floor.

Roach vaulted over the rack, landing lightly before him. "Don't know how to fight, eh?"

"Nope." He kicked outward, his foot connecting squarely with her kneecap, shattering the joint. She screamed long and loud, crumpling to the floor and holding her injury, giving Silas time to pull himself to the side and run, hiding several aisles over.

Her agonized scream went on several moments and then he could hear snapping and cracking as her bone realigned, plus several groans as the inevitable heat and prickle of the healing occurred. She pulled herself to her feet, calling out to him.

"You're going to pay for that, asshole."

"Good. Use your anger." He called out, staying put. He was going to allow him to find her and then the real fun would begin. He'd specifically chosen a wide aisle with nothing in it. Perfect for one on one, hand to hand, body blow combat. Should make things interesting.

<Don't hurt her, Silas.> Came Lin.

<He's two aisles over.> Ragger.

Outraged, Silas yelled aloud. "What the hell, Ragger! How is she supposed to learn if you're helping her?"

<Maybe you need to learn that sometimes the best advantage in a fight is a friend.>

The words struck him in a way he wouldn't have expected. The mutt was right. Silas had never had someone to fight with, he'd never really considered what an asset another mind or set of ears or hands might be worth. Lin didn't particularly count; Lin's thoughts in head were like his own. Usually, if Lin noticed something, Silas had the same information in an instant, reacted to it just as if he had been the one to notice. A physical companion there to help could change things entirely.

Roach had managed to sneak up on him and he noticed too late. She hit him square in the small of the back with a well placed kick, sending him sprawling, hitting his face against the floor. Rolling over, choking on blood, he held up a hand. "Wait. Wait. Alright, I want to explain something."

She pulled up short from a determined walk towards him, staring at him for a moment and thinking. Coming to a decision, she snorted and took another step forward, slamming her heel down on his knee, effectively snapping his leg in half. He groaned, leaning forward, holding the spot where her foot had landed.

The bone cracked and snapped back into place immediately and he glared up at her. "That hurt."

"I told you were going to pay for it. I could have broken your femur. That would take a few hours to heal."

"So you did, yes, I suppose so. Alright, now, I brought us to this aisle for a reason. Can you see what that is?"

She looked around briefly and then answered questioningly. "There's nothing in it? It's big?"

He extended a hand and she grabbed it, pulling him to his feet. He patted at her hair, some of which was still smoldering. "Sorry about that. But yes. You see, *Mayans* don't like closed spaces. They're so big, you know? They often like to lure you into a large, open space, in which they can just tear you to shreds. Well, most humans they can anyway. We can fight in either form. I usually only ever resorted to morphing if I was outnumbered, but that was before I became comfortable with the changing. For now, I'm just going to teach you to fight as a human. You don't like the change either, you said it yourself, so that's fine with you, I'm guessing?"

She nodded.

"Very good. Alright, now, you come here." He walked forward; pointing to a spot in the middle of the floor and then took a few more paces, standing in a spot of his own, waiting for her to move.

Taking a few steps, she stood in the spot she indicated.

Lightning fast he stepped forward and threw a punch at her face, only to find himself blocked as she stepped back and threw an arm up, glancing his blow. "Good!" He said. "Now counter my next att-"

Her fist slammed into his ribcage, faster than his eye could see and he flew back several feet, gasping for air. She smiled and winked. "I know how to fight just fine."

"Very well," He said. "Let's go." He leapt forward, swinging an open hand at the side of her head. She ducked and pulled away, kicking out at him in the same instant. He pulled back and grabbed her foot, flinging it upwards, throwing her into the air.

She tucked and rolled, landing hard on the ground, rolling away from him before jumping up. He ran at her, leaping into the air. His foot connected with her ribcage as she popped onto her feet, sending her flying away once more. He landed lightly on his feet, crouching slightly to soften the landing.

She was already on her feet. "You're fast." Silas remarked. "Linnerat says you're almost abnormally fast."

"I know," she said and then leapt, doing a sort of mid air pirouette, aiming a kick at his face. He stepped easily to the side and punched her in the kidney as her leg went rocketing past. She crumpled to floor in pain, rolling about, trying to scoot away. He walked over to her, staring down.

"Not bad," he said. "Though you could definitely use some improvement."

She rolled to look at him, her eyes flaring gold in the darkness. He extended a hand down to her, proffering help in standing.

Pain shot through him and his eyes bulged as her foot extended with a whoosh, moving through the air and catching him in the crotch. The force of the blow was enough to lift him several inches off the ground, from where he then fell back down onto her still extended foot, doubling the pain.

He gasped and held himself, falling backwards to the floor.

Roach stood over him, leering at him once before walking away. "Good thing those will grow back."

He struggled to his feet, still holding himself, staring after her. Rage bubbled up from the pit of his stomach. *<Now Silas, all's fair in love and war,>* Lin remarked.

<I don't care!> he replied. *<That was a cheap shot!>* Regaining his composure, he ran at her, leaping headfirst at her back. Hearing his footsteps she turned with a grin on her face, but by that time, he was already in the air. Her eyes widened as he plowed into her stomach, wrapping his arms around her and sending them flying through a merchandise rack.

They hit the floor amid a clatter and boom of pots and pans falling from the shelf, their bodies cracking the very concrete.

A flurry of fists, teeth, punches and bites followed, both trying to do the most damage to one another. Rolling about on the floor, several punches landed on the ground, missing their target and sending resounding booms throughout the entire building, shaking dust from the rafters. Occasionally a bite or scratch would land, tearing through flesh and muscle and an ear piercing scream of rage would follow. Anyone listening would think that a congregation of demons armed to the teeth within the store had turned on each other.

Gaining the upper hand by shoving a hand in Silas' face and digging her fingers into his eyes, Roach yanked him to one side, rolling atop of him.

She straddled his midsection, landing blow after blow into his chest, wincing at the pain that jolted through her hand as it landed on his iron hard frame. He began to laugh, a deep, low sound that caught her attention. Relinquishing her grip on his face she sat back for a moment, looking at him and then leaned forward until she was looking him in the eyes. She gasped softly, staring into them, so low not even she could hear. They were a soft, tawny brown, with gold specks floating about them, a soft glow and sheen that captured her entire attention. He laughed again. She blinked.

"What's so funny?" She asked. "I kicked your ass."

He laughed even harder. She punched him in the head and he laughed even harder.

"What's so funny?!"

He trailed off laughing, still chuckling every few words. "Ha-ha, oh... You're one of the feistiest fighters I've ever come across. *Leapers*, *Hellhounds*, *Titans*, *Stalker*s... They all would have been dead a long time ago, if they were in my shoes. Ha-ha." He laughed again. His eyes were gorgeous. He was the only human she'd come across in months. Probably the only person who would ever accept her for what she was. And he was perfect. But she couldn't do it, not knowing what she did. She'd never be able to live with herself. "I was wrong. You do know how to fight... You just don't know how to control your viral form. That's something we're going to have to work on, if we—"

She kissed him.

CHAPTER 18 – THE FALLEN CITY

Silas sat perfectly still for a moment, shocked and not knowing what to do, Roach's lips pressed to his. On spur of impulse, going by instinct, he reached up and wrapped his hands in her hair, digging his fingers in and pulling her face to his, kissing her back. He lifted his face slightly, tasting her lips hungrily.

Her lips moved from his, down to his neck, sucking at his skin, nipping lightly with her teeth, working her way down across his chest. He groaned lightly, working his hands down across her neck and to her back, kneading his fingers into the taught, lean muscles of her body. She moaned against his chest, pressing her body tightly against his, making his flesh tingle in a way he'd almost forgotten. And then – a voice.

<Should I – go to sleep or something?> Lin sounded unsure, excited and confused. Silas sighed, realizing what was happening couldn't happen.

Roach sat up, running a hand through her hair and clearing her throat, an embarrassed look on her face. She pushed herself sideways and sidled off of Silas. He pushed himself up and back, sitting and looking at her, an apologetic look crossing his features. He pulled his knees up and lightly wrapped his arms around them, hanging his hands out in front of him.

<No, Lin...> he thought <You're fine.>

<I've upset you. I simply know that it is customary for humans to copula—'

<Nope, you're good. Nothing happening here. No "copulation" happening. It's all good!> he sighed again.

He looked at Roach, speaking a single word. "No."

She looked at him, hurt in her expression. He grimaced. "I don't mean it like, no –I don't –want you," He swallowed. "I mean it like no, we can't."

She scooted closer to him, almost touching him. "Why not?"

She flipped her hair back slightly, staring at him.

"Because —" She reached one hand out and ran it along his arm, up to his face, where her fingers traced his lips. She leaned in and kissed him again. He pulled away for a moment, biting his lip, but found himself unable to resist and gave in.

****

They sat across from each other in the aisle, purposefully not looking at one another, but stealing furtive glances at one another when they thought the other wasn't looking. Ragger, sitting between them, caught every glance and shook his head every time, gnawing on a large haunch of meat. He'd gone out hunting while they'd found themselves busy.

The entire store lay in shambles. Not a wall remained un-cracked and not a single shelf was left standing. Rubble lay on the floor in several places where large chunks of wall had fallen and now lay on the floor. Silas was glad he had grabbed several bottles of liquor earlier. Alcohol was as rare as gold and was useful as a bribe. He doubted that he'd find any intact bottles now.

Silas looked at Roach, who was staring off to her left.

She was topless and flushed; a slight purplish-red tinge on her cheeks and breasts. Lin had just finished explaining to him that while their blood was blue, when it rose to the surface, such as in a blush, the virus would retreat from the extra oxygen at the surface of the skin, allowing the blood to return to an almost normal red color. He didn't really care; he was just trying to distract himself from what happened.

She moved slightly and his eyes widened and he turned away, looking off to his left. Ragger shook his head again before standing and padding towards the door.

He looked back, glancing around the store and spoke wryly. *<Well now we know how you two can defeat an enemy who has overpowered your battle skills... Mate with it.>* He laughed, turning away again and walking out the doorway.

Silas' faced burned and while he couldn't see Roach's, he knew that hers did as well. He stood up, dusting his hands off on his now even more ripped pants, glancing at Roach.

"We need to find some new clothes. If memory serves me

correctly, Delmar Loop isn't too far from here. We can find some clothes there; the Galleria Mall is over there. And maybe some sage... Lots of kitchens and fancy eateries down there."

She nodded, standing, crossing her arms and covering herself. She looked down at herself, asking in a pathetic tone, "How far?"

Silas glanced at her with a small smile on his lips and then looked away before she would notice. "About ten miles."

She sighed, pouting and then dropped her arms down to her sides, baring her chest. "Well, I'm not walking that far like that... You walk in front."

Silas shook his head, stepping forward towards the door, muttering. "Nothing I haven't seen before."

His comment was greeted with a sharp blow to the back of the head. He smiled and walked out the door.

****

Walking through St. Louis had injured Silas in his heart. The entire city was decrepit and silent, chunks of buildings missing; scorch marks on the majority of them, parts of the street were missing, torn away from the ground by bomb blasts. Steel girders and guts of buildings showed through deep gauges in the sides of the buildings. Here and there, massive steel structures lay twisted and destroyed, rubble in the streets lay in giant piles.

St. Louis wasn't the biggest city, but it had been home to over two million individuals. Not a breath stirred the air near the ground, not a breeze or noise except their footsteps. Skeletons lie on the ground, charred and broken. Half rotted bodies lie everywhere, some mummified by the eternal layer of soot and ash, some rotting away, falling apart. Dust sifted about in the street, caught by intangible eddies of air. It covered everything in a thin blanket. He could trace their footsteps back about fifty paces, but then the dirty settled again... Like they'd never even come into the city. St. Louis was dead. Silas grieved silently with every step they took. And he wasn't the only one.

Everyone had grown silent, weaving their way in and out of burnt shells of cars. A single tear had slipped down Silas cheek as they'd had to leap over the top of a destroyed tank, a single blackened skeleton lying atop of it. Not even a soldier, by the looks of the clothing that remained. A civilian, trying to flee, caught atop the tank as it had burst into flames from enemy plasma fire. A horrible way to go. His skin had prickled as they'd passed some fire stormed buildings, the virus repairing the radioactivity damage he was suffering. Busch Stadium had been all but completely destroyed. Entire sections had collapsed; craters filled the stands and pocketed the outside of the structure. The field was covered in tiny crosses. It was unmistakable as a cemetery.

Silas grit his teeth with each desiccated corpse they passed by. Upon walking past the telltale skeleton of an infected, with the pointed teeth and depressions of newly formed eye sockets, he gave into his anger and kicked it as hard he could, shattering it, sending the fragments spinning through the air. They hit the side of a building and burst apart. The sound echoed through the empty streets for several moments before fading into distant memory. It did nothing for Silas' pain.

Coming across the body of a child, Roach had stopped a moment, crouching down, touching the leathery skin that lay atop of the skull, running her hand lightly through the hair. She looked up at Silas, pain in her eyes.

"I've never been to a fallen city before." A tear formed in the corner of her eye and her voice went up a notch. "This –This is disgusting. So much death. How—" Her words failed her as she spoke, tears leaking angrily down her face. Silas turned away, sitting on a curb, looking down at his new clothes.

They'd stopped at an American Eagle store down by Delmar, picking out some outfits and grabbing a bag to carry it in. Much to his disgruntlement, Ragger had been chosen to carry the bag. Silas had slung it over his back like a rescue dog's pack. However, the ancient dog had agreed to the idea, feeling the perhaps he should pull his weight.

At Ragger's behest, they had also grabbed all black or extremely dark clothing to wear. Silas was wearing a pair of dark blue, loose jeans and black hoodie with a black compression shirt underneath. Roach was wearing the same, her hood up and hair tied into a ponytail. It was getting colder the farther north they went.

Ragger's ears perked up suddenly and Linnerat stirred. <We're being watched,> Ragger said.

<Indeed we are,> Lin replied. <I think if they meant us harm,

they would have attacked by now, though.>

<You sensed them before?>

<You forget that Silas' entire brain and everything he hears and sees is at my disposal to pick apart at my leisure. I don't have anything else to occupy my time, like remembering to breathe...>

<Ah, yes. I forgot. You think they mean us no harm?>

Silas shook his head and his eyes widened. He hadn't meant to do that. Lin must have done it on accident.

Silas had gotten the impression several times before, that when Lin was speaking, he pantomimed in his mind a physical reaction. It was interesting. And now he was actually taking control of Silas at small intervals. It wasn't anything duly worrying.

Silas had thought it over several days before. The closest thing he could figure was that either, one; Lin had been lying about not being able to control Silas, which Silas had brushed off immediately, knowing that it was false, or two; Silas had relaxed about Lin being in his head and the thought that he would try to take control. He'd begun to trust the creature. He wasn't so on guard and when Lin imagined doing something, it happened. So long as it didn't happen in the middle of a fight, he figured it was something he could live with.

He turned his attention back to what Lin was telling Ragger.

<No, they've been following us since right after we left the clothing store, so at least two miles, about thirty minutes.>

Ragger nodded, looking around, curious as to where the creatures were. Silas assumed he must have heard them. But he hadn't heard anything...?

Lin spoke quietly in his mind. *<You saw them, Silas. Their eyes, in the darkness of a building adjacent to the entrance. You were just hurting because of our situation and didn't notice. If I would have thought them a threat at any time, I would have mentioned them.>*

Silas' eyes widened at the idea that he could have missed something that endangered them all. Ragger was right; sometimes the greatest advantage in battle was an ally.

A thought struck him and he stood, sighing and slapping his thighs. Roach and Ragger turned to look at him questioningly.

He laughed and then spoke quickly. "I think that we need to find a gun store." Ragger's eyes grew wide as he nodded.

<I think that would be wise. Our little friends may not be so friendly. And there are more of them than us. Of that I am certain. Do

you know if there's a gun store around here Silas?>

Silas sucked at his teeth a moment and then shook his head. *<No I don't, unfortunately. However, we may be able to salvage some weapons from police and army vehicles, though I doubt it's likely. Most everything has probably already been stripped. Let's go look.>* He pointed. *<There's a patrol car over there. Hell, if we get really lucky, we might even find a working car, though it's unlikely. These plasma marks... All the ignitions are likely fried. We'd be better off looking for a car across the river.>*

<Yes,> Ragger remarked, *<I noticed those too... Though, if you noticed, that tank back there is a testament to your species' ingenuity and intelligence. That tank was coated with a Lithium-Titanium alloy. Absorbs most of the shock from the plasma and fires it into the ground through the treads. This city must have been the first city to develop that technology. They saved thousands of lives, if not millions. That discovery all but rendered our plasma weapons useless. Why do you think we stopped using them as handheld weapons?>*

Silas looked at the ground, his mouth twisted to the side. *<Yeah, probably. Nice thought, but a bit bittersweet, you know? Most of my friends lived here. Most of them died here.>* A strange look crossed his face and his knees threatened to give out. A small hand touched his back.

"It'll be alright, Silas," Roach said. "It'll be alright." She rubbed his back softly before patting him and walking past him. "We need to move. I don't like the fact that we're being watched."

Silas nodded, following her. "Wait up. You don't know where you're going." He laughed.

She turned with her hands on her hips and glared at him. "Sure I do!" She said, turning and pointing with one hand, the other remaining firmly on her hip. She was pointing nowhere.

He laughed again. "Really? And where is that?"

She frowned at him. "I don't know. This is your town. Where do you suggest we go?"

He stood, thinking for a moment. "Well, I know we need to get across the river. That's about all I've got right now—" A sudden clicking rang out and a scuttling noise sounded from a small alley off to their left. Silas grimaced, sucking at his teeth. Drillers. He reached up and grabbed his shotgun from off of his back, stepping onto the sidewalk and towards the alley, pumping the chamber.

Bullard

A sudden, guttural voice rang out. "Do not harm our little ones. We have not harmed you. They would not harm you, nor can they anyway, changelings. Why do you wish to harm ussss?"

Silas turned, searching for the source of the voice. From across the street, a *Snapper* jumped out an open window, landing hard on the sidewalk below. Training the weapon on the creatures, Silas stepped forward, guarding Roach and Ragger. It held its hands up and walked towards him slowly. Silas examined it.

It was a rather large specimen, standing at about ten feet tall, as opposed to the usual eight. It looked pretty much like any other *Snapper*, hairless, ugly grey skin, rippling muscle, boxy head on top of huge shoulders, four eyes in a row across the top of the face, doubly elbowed arms, clawed hands with two extra digits and wide grimacing lips hiding a mouth full of teeth. One odd thing about it was that it wore pants, seemingly woven from scraps of ripped apart denim. They looked like they fit well enough.

It spoke again. "I know you are jussst as capable of battle as I am, changeling. That weapon is an unfair advantage. We will let you Hive-Sssservants passsss in peace, as we always have done."

"So?" Silas said. "I don't trust your kind. And what do you mean, changeling?"

<Our kind? Don't you mean your kind? Just because you can change between forms does not make you better than the rest of our race.> The voice echoed in his head.

"No. Not my kind. I am human. She is human. Only the dog is truly infected. He is *Renegade*."

The *Snapper* hissed, lowering its hands. "You are not human. If you were human, you would not have heard that." It bowed slightly to Ragger. "Brother."

"I am human." Silas said. "I am infected, but I have complete control over the bug in my head."

The *Snapper* took a step backward. "How is that posssssible?"

At the question, Lin spoke up. *<I am defective. I am a symbiotic life-form, rather than parasitic. A fortunate genetic defect occurring from my parent's hosts.>*

The *Snapper* stared at Silas. "Fortunate? You enjoy your imprisonment? My hossst is my friend, but he sssstill complains."

<Oh no, do not mistake me in that. I hate this, though Silas does allow me control from time to time.>

"Ssssilassss. What a pain in the assss to ssssay. What is redeemable, then?"

Ragger spoke this time. *<He is The Hunter. The Syarantil.>*

Again, the *Snapper* took a disbelieving step backward. He aimed a final question at Ragger. *<And who are you, to be able to say that you know The Hunter when you see him? Name yourself. Your true name. Not this, "Ragger." What a shameful name, to be named as a pet. Renegade you may be, but have pride!>*

Ragger looked at his companions and then hung his head, letting out a small sigh before whispering his reply in all their heads.

<My name is Anubisarius.>

The *Mayan* gasped and stared hard at Ragger. *<That's not possible. Anubis is dead! I heard the report from Isis myself! Prove it!>*

"Wait wait, what?" Silas said. "Anubis, like the Egyptian God? You're a *GOD?*"

<No, fool... I was the basis for the legend of the god. Several of us were. Myself, Isis, Osiris, Ra. We were the first scouts. I killed Osiris and Ra... They were men. Osiris was portrayed as a falcon because he kept one as a pet. Isis was a Hellhound like myself. She escaped. You see why I like to keep this information privy? Too many questions.> He sighed again. *<Now, get this pack off me. I have to show him my form, or he and the rest of the Renegades surrounding us will rip us to shreds for blasphemy.>*

"What, that you're a Ripper?" Roach asked. "What will that prove?"

<I am not A Ripper; I am one of THE Rippers. One of the Thousand Torn. The originals. Rippers come from a particular strain of Yahntil. The DNA marker is all but lost, but it crops up from time to time. There were a thousand of us. We tried altering our own DNA from what the Rakniran gave us. But the results were too unstable, too unpredictable.> He shrugged.

<Not only did it cause our DNA to mutate much too quickly, the Thousand Torn, as we were called, often went insane. Many of us found ourselves unable to attack the Rakniran super soldiers. We were torn between the survival of our species and the survival of the Rakniran. Messing with the DNA tripped a kill switch inside some of us, which ironically, should have been tripped long before. It left us unable to attack our creators. Hence the Thousand "Torn." Torn between our orders and our internal directions. We were still formidable foes

against anything else that opposed us, though. Still, disappointed, The Judges ordered most of us destroyed. However, a few of us were left alive, those of us most loyal, most lethal. We were sent out as scouts, all of us. I came to Earth, sent to accompany Osiris and Ra, as their guard in this new world.>

<Ah.> said Lin. *<That makes things make much more sense.>*

The *Snapper* stared at them expectantly, his fists clenching and opening.

<Yes. Now, remove this pack from me.>

Crouching down by his side, both Silas and Roach grabbed a strap and unhooked it. The pack slid softly to one side, landing in the dirt, sending a puff of dust swirling down and along the gutter.

Silas stood, looking at Roach, speaking to her in his mind. *<Incidentally... What's your name?>*

She set her face towards the ground, looking up at him from the corner of her eye. *<Ava.>* She replied.

Silas smiled and extended a hand across Ragger's rapidly growing form. She took it and shook it, smiling back at him, though for some reason, she looked slightly saddened. From the corner of his eye, Silas saw the *Mayan* look at the two of them strangely, shaking its head.

<Pleased to meet you, Ava.> He winked. *<Probably should have gotten that out of the way before we uh. Yeah.>*

She blushed, crushing his hand. His eyes grew wide and mouth formed a silent *<O'* in pain. Releasing his hand, she huffed and turned away.

Silas suddenly realized that Ragger was getting much bigger than usual. He stepped aside, Ava doing the same. Ragger had already reached what Silas had thought was his full size, standing somewhere near Silas' shoulder on all fours and approximately ten feet long at his rear hip, not including the long, whip like tail.

Silas stared, watching Ragger take on transformations he'd never seen before. His ears grew out and out and out, sweeping along the length of his back, reaching halfway along the length of his body. His skull grew and grew, as did his body, until he stood at approximately seven feet tall on all fours and had a body length that was somewhere around thirteen feet long.

His tail extended another five or six feet behind him, thick and powerful at the top, shaped like a whip at the end. He flicked it through the air above him, cracking the air, snapping it mere inches from the *Mayan*'s face, who flinched in fear.

His skull piled on in thickness, growing wider and longer, until his snout was probably two and a half feet long, with rows of shark like teeth filling his mouth, four or five inches long a piece. Silas took a few fearful steps backwards. Ava reached out and laid a hand on Ragger's bare grey skin, which shivered and twisted, like a horse trying to rid itself of a horsefly.

Even if he were in full viral form, this being was one that could, without a doubt, kill him. Yet, Ragger said earlier that he didn't think that he would be able to kill Silas in battle. Silas frowned. Surely he didn't seem that powerful, or large. Then again, he had also said that he didn't believe that anyone had ever seen Silas in full Viral form. He hadn't paid much attention to it at the time, but now, thinking on it, it seemed absurd. But — he'd seen Roach become more than she said she could, perhaps she'd thought it was all she could do? Perhaps she didn't even realize she had become more than usual. And now Ragger was becoming more than he ever had, too.

The *Mayan* was slowly creeping backward, fear in its expression. Ragger twisted his head to one side and a loud crack issued forth. As they did so, two small impressions formed on either side of his head, sinking into bone, four eyes rapidly growing, until six fiery purple orbs resided on the sides of his skull.

Stepping forward, he swatted the *Mayan* to the ground, who made no attempt to get up. Ragger roared and a puddle spread out behind the *Snapper* as it urinated.

"Holy shit!" Silas exclaimed, staring at Ragger.

<*Is your challenge met?*> Ragger's voice resounded in their heads, deeper, louder and far more feral than they'd ever heard it before. Silas resisted an urge to grab his skull, an instant headache occurring at the sound of the dog's voice.

The *Mayan* nodded slowly, climbing to its feet. <*Yes. My challenge is met. I have no doubt that you are the great and mighty; Anubis. What do you want? Why do you come here? And why have you waited so long to step forward?*>

Ragger snorted at the question, blowing hot air across the alley, stirring up gusts of dirt, small tornados of dust swirling across the street, smacking into cars and dying.

He opened his mouth and spoke aloud. Silas stepped back. He

had never thought that Ragger would be able to speak with an actual voice. Then again, he supposed, he would have to be able too, to communicate with regular humans.

"What would have been the point? I would have been killed. The Empire would have slaughtered me and Isis too, for falsely reporting my death." He looked to the side and a wave of pain crossed through Silas' mind.

Linnerat spoke quietly in Silas' head. <I've heard *this tale. I know who he is; I know who they all are. I was nothing more than a pool-slug at the time, clinging to the inside of a maternity tank, but even I heard the stories. All the youth did. They were several of our greatest warriors, revered almost to worship. All five were set to take over as a Raknila. Then one day, they all vanished. We heard some years later about another planet having been discovered, but it never crossed my mind that perhaps they had been sent as advance scouts. It makes sense, a Rakniran hadn't been seen in over a thousand years, and it was almost another thousand years after that time when another was finally captured. At any rate, yes, things are beginning to fall together, at least for things I've been wondering for several thousand years.>*

Silas choked. <*Several thousand years? How old are you?*>

<*I am just under seven thousand years old. You are my first host. All Yahntil are required to hunt and obtain their own hosts, as a rite of passage.*>

<*Oh. What is wrong with Ragger?*> Silas asked weakly, head spinning.

<*Anubis and Isis were lovers. It appears that one betrayed the other.*>

CHAPTER 19 – ALLIANCE

The *Mayan* stood staring at them for a long moment, taking in all that it had learned. It shook its head, setting its hands on its hips. – <Very *human*.> Silas thought to himself – It began to laugh.

<I have in my presence, not only the Lost Warrior and Seer, but The Hunter of whom he spoke! Today, the stars truly smile on us. War is on the Horizon. Peace rides swiftly in on the Daystar.>

"Wait, what? The prophet? The Hunter of whom he spoke? What is he talking about?"

The *Mayan* looked at him strangely. <You don't know your own prophecy?>

<Don't tell him. Let his fate be his own.> Ragger said. <It's not something I wish to speak of anyway.>

The *Mayan* bowed its head in Ragger's direction. <As you wish, Anubis.>

"Wait, no." Silas said. "I want to know. Tell me what you're talking about, now. If it's about me, I deserve to know."

Turning, Ragger looked at Silas, lowering his head to look him in the eyes.

"I foresaw your birth, existence and death almost seventy six thousand years ago. Now, speak of it no more."

Silas stood in shock, not knowing what to say. His mouth fell open slightly and Ava laughed at him.

Ragger turned and looked back at the *Mayan*, addressing it once more. <What is your name, friend?>

It bowed its head to Ragger once more, who became irritated. <Stop bowing to me. I am nothing to our race anymore.>

At this, the *Mayan*'s eyes grew wide. <No, that you are not. My birth name is Gegnan. But I have forsaken that name and have taken my host's name. Call me Scott.>

Silas blinked. <Scott?> he thought to himself. <What the hell.>

Scott continued speaking after a moment's pause. <And *no,*

great one, you are nothing to our 'species.> But to our people, the Renegades.> He extended an arm and indicated the city. Looking around, Silas noticed that hundreds of eyes were watching from the Shadows, some large, some small. *<You are everything. You were the first of us. The first to suggest the very idea of becoming a Renegade, hundreds of thousands of years ago. You are our king, our inspiration!>*

Ragger shook his head. *<I am no king. I ruled long enough on this world. I am done. I no longer hold an interest in any such thing...>*

Scott nodded. *<And we revere you all the more for such a thing. Come. I will take you to our stronghold. You can eat and rest there. There aren't many of us, a few hundred, but we get by well enough. We have cows ready to roast. Come! We will prepare one for you.>* He looked at Silas, frowning. *<How much do you usually eat?>*

Silas shrugged. "I can eat half a deer by myself in this form."

He pointed to Ava. *<And her?>*

She raised an eyebrow. "I eat about the same."

Scott nodded again, turning, waving over his shoulder. "Two cows then." He held up two fingers to the buildings about them and a sudden shower of rocks could be heard as something or someone ran off, leaping from rooftop to rooftop. He motioned at the group. "Follow me."

****

They walked in silence, following Scott, wondering where he was going to take them, Silas and Ava stealing glances at Ragger occasionally, who was still in his hulking viral form. He was gorgeous and terrifying. Ragger kept his eyes on Scott, watching for a single sign of betrayal. Silas seriously doubted the creature was foolish enough to do anything of the sort with a creature like Ragger walking ten paces behind him.

They traveled for probably ten minutes in this manner, when Scott suddenly turned and began to speak. *<May I –a'* Ragger growled at the sudden movement, but the noise died in his throat as soon as he saw that no harm was meant.

Hesitating with fear, Scott spoke again. *<May I – may I see you in full form, Hunter? I do apologize, but we grow up hearing tales of you, how you will lead us to peace over the Evil leaders of our race, call*

our brothers and sisters away from the evil campaign which they serve. It would be a great honor.>

Silas was taken aback. He wasn't used to being treated like he was something special. Most people and creatures went out of their way to try and kill him, nothing more.

"Su-Sure, I guess that would be alright." He said. He looked at Ragger in one of his eyes, who sighed and nodded.

"Um, give me a moment." Silas said, poking around his head, bugging Linnerat. *<Hey, you.>*

<What?> Lin stirred. *<What is it?>*

<Scott wants to see me in full viral form.>

'*... And?>*

<I need your help! I'm not all pumped up I can't reach full form without being excited.>

<Oh. Hold on.> The parasite moved in his head a moment and Silas suddenly felt his heart rate speed up and his vision grow clearer, while at the same time, he suddenly began to feel the presence of all the eyes watching him.

<I pushed on your fear control center. Your adrenaline should be going now. Feel free... I'm going to feed and go back to sleep.>

Silas made a face at the feeding reference thanking Lin. Focusing inward on the changes; they began almost immediately, starting in the lengthening of his fingers and toes.

"Oh shit," he said, grabbing the shotgun from his back and tossing it to Ava, who caught it deftly in one hand. He kicked his shoes off and quickly ripped his hoodie and shirt off over his head. One of the sleeves got caught on one of his hands as he yanked and tore clean off. "God damnit."

His skin was already turning glistening gray and he felt the extra eye sockets drawing in, his skull thickening and his peripheral vision expanding as the eyeballs quickly grew. He bent over to keep his balance as his knees popped and reversed direction, grabbed his head as his radius and shin snapped in half as another joint grew between them, arms lengthening, legs getting thicker, larger.

His shoulders popped as they erupted out and away from his head, the muscle expanding immensely to support his now huge arms. Two extra fingers and toes grew on each hand and foot, giving him a total of fourteen clawed digits.

He stood and straightened his back as several large spikes

erupted from his shoulders and lower knees and tops of his ankles, signaling the end of his transformation.

To his surprise, he kept growing, past his standard twelve feet, growing another two to stand at fourteen. The top of his head itched momentarily and reaching up he found that a line of bony spurs had erupted from the top of his skull and down and along his back. One pricked his hand, drawing blood.

Squinting, he turned to look at Ragger, sucking at his massive teeth.

Ragger turned to look at him answering the unspoken question.

<*You still aren't at full form... However, willful execution of the transformation yields different results than when you're afraid. When you are afraid and willing the transformation, then you will reach your full form. Maybe. It may yet be many years before you discover your true form. You're almost there, though.*> He turned away again and Silas shook his head, speaking to Lin. <*I really hate that dog. He's so cryptic! It pisses me off.*>

<*Well,*> Lin replied, <*He did have good reason for hiding the other things from us. Perhaps this is much the same way. He says he "foresaw" you somehow. This was something I heard of vaguely, a prophecy of some mighty warrior coming to strike down our empire... It was something we all feared, but I had no idea that the prophecy said it would be one of our own, or that they would be called the "Hunter," or in our tongue, the Syarantil. Perhaps he does have an idea of what you will look at full form.*> He shrugged, making Silas' brain itch. <*Hm. I thought that maybe it would be roomier in here when you're like this, but sadly it isn't.*>

Silas laughed, a deep, choking like noise in the back of his throat.

Ava started towards him, "What's wrong?" she asked.

At the same time, Scott looked at him, asking, "Whatsss sssso funny?"

Ava turned and looked at him. "Is that what it sounds like when you guys laugh?"

Scott nodded.

"Oh." She looked back at Silas. "That sounds weird. Thought he was choking somehow." She looked him up and down. "You do look different." She turned around and went back to stand by Ragger, glancing at Silas from the corner of her eye, an occasional shiver running down her spine.

Silas suddenly felt bad and spoke mind to mind with Scott.

<Well, what do you think? I'd like to return to my normal form. Roach—I mean, Ava, seems very uncomfortable being the only human here.>

Scott looked up into his face, awe shining in his eyes, speaking to the whole group. *<Very impressive. If I were to die this day, then my life would have been worth it.>* He suddenly eyed the small cross wrapped around Silas' neck.

"You are Chrissstian? I am as well."

Silas blinked again, shaking his head.

<Wait, what? You're... Huh. No harm done, I suppose. No, I'm not. Not really, I was never much of a believer.> He reached up and tapped the tiny piece of silver against the massive hollow of his throat. *<This was a parting gift given to me by a very dear friend, who passed away.>*

<Ah. I see... That rope looks very flimsy. I'm amazed it does not break when you change.>

<It absorbs partially into my skin at the back of my neck.>

<Ah. Well, perhaps we can find something for it that will better suit such an object, something that will better to stand up to wear and tear? Come, we must travel faster. We are almost there. I do apologize, to both you and Anubis, but can you please both stay in form.> He looked over at Roach. *<Would you perhaps feel more comfortable in form as well?>*

She shook her head. "My parasite is dead. I don't know how to control my viral form."

Scott blinked a few times and then nodded. "Very well. Let usss continue." He turned and began walking again. Silas motioned to Ava, waving her over. She took a few steps towards him and then squeaked as he scooped her up in his arms like a baby. She hit him a few times and then gave up, leaning back against him. He started off, following Scott, who was now pointing at a building up ahead a little ways, off the main street. "We go there."

Silas began to laugh, recognizing where they were. He hadn't noticed, but Scott had taken them in a huge circle.

Scott turned his head slightly while still walking, look at Silas out of one of his eyes. "What is sssso funny, thissss time?"

Bullard

"You took us in a huge circle. I know that building. It's the old Anheuser Bush factory warehouse. They made beer there. Well, stored it there, anyway, to be shipped."

Scott's eyes widened and he stopped. "You know thissss ssssity? I took you on such a roundabout way to make you confused."

"Yes. I grew up here."

Scott stopped walking and turned to Silas, bowing low, his skull almost touching the ground before standing. "Forgive me, Hunter."

Silas brows knit together. "For what?"

Scott took a few steps back, still looking at the ground. "I am the one who led the final asssssault on this ssssity. I am the one who fell the ssssity and its armies. I killed them all." He looked off the side, regret in his expression.

Silas' jaw and fists clenched together, the muscles in his neck standing out as he struggled with the urge to rip the puny little creature's head off and fling it through the warehouse on his left.

<Silas.> It was Lin, the voice of reason, as always. Silas didn't want to listen to reason. The creature standing before him was the creature responsible for the death of almost every single friend he'd ever had, the one that had ordered their demise or worse.

<Silas.> More stern this time. <Silas!>

<What?> He replied stiffly, chewing on his tongue, rivulets of blood dripping down his throat. The base of his tongue began to itch as it slowly began to grow back. He swallowed the chunk of meat rolling between his teeth, glaring at Scott, who was still staring off to the side, refusing to meet his gaze.

<He is a changed creature. Look at him. Before he said anything, could you have imagined that this lowly Snapper led the assault on this city? The way you describe the fight they'd put up, I would have imagined that one of the Ravager would have been sent to raze the city. Look at him, Silas! He claims to have found religion; he's a Renegade, renounced the ways of our race. He is no different than me or Ragger.>

Silas bit through his tongue again, wincing, chewing on the resulting hunk of meat again.

<Stop that.> Lin said sharply.

<Stop what?>

<Biting your tongue off. You might be distracted enough to

have not it bother you too much, but it hurts me, damnit.>

Silas swallowed, not bothering to apologize, still staring at Scott. Lin had a point. As always. The creature had renounced as much as it could of its species, beyond what it needed to survive. What it had done in the past didn't matter. Was washed clean. That's what Christianity was about, right? He touched the cross once more, wondering. He sighed, reaching a hand out. Scott cringed as Silas' hand enveloped his skull and a small, high pitched whine escaped him. Silas twisted Scott's head, forcing him to look into his eyes.

"I forgive you. You were just following orders. I believe you're not the same person you were then, as you claim to be now. But, if you should ever –" Scott's eyes widened and he nodded, a muffled noise coming his mouth, covered by Silas' palm. "Ever, ever indicate otherwise, I will wear your skull on my belt as a trophy. Now, let us get to that warehouse. I'm starving."

He set Scott down and walked forward briskly, catching a smile on Roach's lips.

****

Scott ducked beneath the doorway, followed closely by Ragger and Silas. He called out into the darkness. "Ssssafe! I bring friends and good tidings."

Hundreds of eyes flared, most golden, some completely purple. Old ones. Lights flared and Silas was blinded momentarily. Hundreds upon hundreds of silent *Mayan* met his gaze, some laying on the ground, others leaning up against machinery, some clinging to walls and ceilings, *Snappers, Titans, Stalkers, Leapers*; everything he had ever come across, and several he hadn't. His hackles involuntarily rose, baring his teeth.

To his surprise, he saw humans mingled in with the crowd, sleeping on mattresses and sitting at desks with computers before them. He frowned.

<Are those...>

Scott answered his question before he even had time to finish thinking it.

<Yes they are. Some of them, anyway. Others are like you. Changelings. But many of them are regular humans. We find travelers and take them in. Some choose to allow our Drillers attach, others opt

to have us surgically implanted. Others are merely content to live among us, once they know what we are. Some run, most that do, die crossing the River.>

Silas nodded, peering around, wondering what he had meant by *"Die crossing the river."* Was the bridge not there anymore?

Not a single Renegade had moved up until that point, not until Scott waved some of them forward, to which they responded cautiously, walking slowly towards Ragger, examining him, wary of his side. Rolling his eyes, Ragger suddenly just flopped on the ground, laying his head on his massive front paws.

Several *Mayan* which had been walking towards them vanished, leaping away and running as fast as they could in the opposite direction.

A few moments passed and suddenly loud, chuffing laughter could be heard resonating through the room as the frightened creatures poked their heads out of their various hiding places.

Seeing that Ragger had done nothing more than lie down, making himself more vulnerable, several other *Mayan* found the courage to come forward and take a look at their visitors.

<My friends,> Scott said. *<This'* he gestured to Ragger, *<Is the great Warrior, Anubis.>*

A murmur ran the room at his words and several more *Mayan* came forward, forming a crowd standing about fifteen feet from them. Several of the shorter ones were craning their necks to get a good look at Ragger, though several of them seem fixated on Silas.

Noticing this, Scott smiled. *<Yes. Anubis. And this,>* he gestured to Silas this time, who had just set Ava down. *<This is The Hunter. Syarantil. He has come.>*

The entire room exploded.

****

After the commotion had died down, many *Mayan* came forward and bowed to Ragger and Silas both. Ragger found it annoying immediately; it took several hours of praise to get under Silas' skin. But at the end of the day, Silas was just as sick of it as Ragger, if not more. By nightfall, most of the crowds had had their look and left them. The occasional return came through and some stragglers, those who had been too fearful in the beginning.

Bullard

Silas was beginning to realize that Yahntil weren't as heartless and cruel and scary and fearless as he'd thought. They were just like humans, only really big and really ugly. One odd thing that he had noted was that not many humans seemed interested in them. While they had met several, most seemed just more interested in the fact that Silas was infected but in control, but once it stopped being a novelty, they stopped caring. There was one scientist named Wimble that kept coming back, but he never had anything substantial to say.

Silas figured that the humans just didn't attach as much importance to their presence as the Renegades did. Upon finding out that they were traveling to Chicago, several Renegades had offered to go with them, but oddly enough, not a single human asked to go. As far as Silas could tell, they were happy living here. A sudden thought struck him and he turned to Ragger.

<You ruled?> he remarked.

Ragger looked at him surprised. <Oh yes. I ordered the building of the pyramids.>

Silas sat dumbfounded, finally grasping exactly how long Ragger had been around. Grasping how old even the human God Anubis was. Ragger had to be far older than even that.

<How old are you, Ragger?> he asked.

<I don't remember.>

Silas blinked several times, sucking at his teeth.

<So you've seen a lot then eh?>

<I was the start of your civilization. I have been here from the beginning. You guys were nothing more than rudimentary animals when I came.>

<So why even bother with us?>

Ragger laughed. <I don't know if you've ever noticed, but we dogs don't have thumbs and it's not very comfortable being a dog out in the wild. My last host had been a Darkoun, Ravager is what your military calls them; complete with wings. I was a guard of the Raknila, as all Ravager's are. I was used to the best of things. So I set out to make that my way of life once more. We all did. You humans obviously had intelligence. It was merely a matter of getting Ra and Osiris to convince them that we were gods. After that, they did anything we said.>

<What are Ravager's?> Silas asked. <That's the second time I've heard them mentioned today.>

Bullard

<Dragons.>

Silas looked at Ragger, who nodded.

<Yes, you heard me. Dragons. Darkoun. The language became garbled after several hundred years. Who do you think started most of your culture's myths? Ravagers were something we took thousands and thousands of years ago. Less than a hundred remain. They only live about two hundred thousand years or so when infected. In their natural state, they live perhaps ten years. Their metabolism and bodily functions are so extreme that it destroys them from the inside out, so much so that it wears them out even with constant repair. We never really figured out how or why they evolved in such a self-destructive manner. Magnificent beasts, though.>

Silas began to get excited. Dragons were one of his favorite mythological creatures. When in the hospital for his Leukemia, he often lay with a mythology book during the procedure, distracting himself. *<So, do they breathe fire and all that?>*

Ragger laughed low in his throat. *<No. Not in actuality. They spray a substance similar to your napalm from glands in the back of their throat, which they ignite by creating sparks with their teeth. They unhinge their lower jaw, much like a snake, which then slams forward at speeds upward of a hundred miles an hour, slamming teeth into one another. They can only do it for short spurts, though. Still, it's an awesome sight to see. And it is far more awesome to do.>* He smirked. *<Though some – and this was what I was consistently jealous of, are able to empty their second stomach, which fills with an organic acid stronger than anything we've been able to create in a lab to date. They could destroy entire armies in seconds. I think all of those are passed away by now, though. The ones that still remained while I was a Ravager were near death as it was.>*

Silas sat in awe, envisioning in his mind's eye what the Ravager must be like.

<Do they look like Dragons in tales?>

<Somewhat, yes. They are thick, scaly, with massive wings. They are around eighty feet long and stand close to twenty feet tall at the shoulder. Long necks, fearsome teeth, jet black color. They don't look much different when infected than when wild. The legends haven't changed much. The Chinese kind of diverted, but other than that, your lore is still intact.>

Silas nodded, daydreaming.

Bullard

<We invented a great deal of your mythology and legends. I invented a great deal, that is. I was the one who was most attracted to your race. Told them stories, gave them information, taught them. The others stayed very true to our race. ... I wish to no longer speak of this.>

He sighed, looking away, inviting no argument.

Silas reached a single hand out and lay it on Ragger, careful to not disturb the sleeping Ava between them.

<All in good time, friend. All in good time.>

CHAPTER 20 – EMPTYING THE ARSENAL

Silas awoke with a start, forgetting where he was. Everything was dark, but gold and purple flared far and away in the darkness and his night vision showed him the hulking forms of *Snappers*, igniting his heart rate.

He tensed to jump and run, but then remembered the previous day's events and lay his head back down. Something tickled his face and he felt a weight on his arm. Looked down he found himself looking at the top of Ava's head. She was lying next to him, her head on his bare arm, halfway curled into the fetal position.

Pressed up against her back was Ragger in his regular dog form, sleeping. His ears pricked up and he turned to look at Silas.

<Easy.>

<I know. Just forgot where we were for a moment.>

<I guessed as much. By the way, I'm not happy with you right now.>

Silas' eyes grew wide and he became momentarily worried. *<What'd I do wrong?>*

Ragger huffed. *<YOU didn't do anything. She did.>* He gestured with his head at Ava. *<Roach did. But I still blame you. You've gone and stolen my sleeping buddy.>*

Silas laughed softly then lay his head back down, whispering. "Sorry."

Ragger whined and lay his head down on his paws, staring off into the darkness, his ears swiveling every few moments, picking up sounds not even Silas could hear.

His ears suddenly swiveled forwards and stayed where they were, pointing forward. Following their direction, Silas peered out into the darkness, looking for whatever had drawn Ragger's attention, wary of danger.

Ragger stood, head cocked to the side, staring into the

darkness, padding forward slowly, towards a group of small glowing eyes.

Laying Ava down softly, Silas got up and followed him. The closer he got; the more shapes he could make out. They looked like small humanoids, though oddly shaped. He reached along the wall, searching for a light. Finding a switch, he flipped it and gasped in awe as several small *Snappers* looked at him, confused.

They were almost perfect miniatures of fully grown *Snappers*, but Silas had no doubt in his mind that these were children. They ranged in size from under about two feet tall, to around four or five. One even wore a diaper.

While they had appeared to be miniatures at first glance, he began noticing differences between them as he looked them over. Some had various differences in facial structures. Small tufts of hair appeared on the top of some of their heads, blonde and brown, little patches that stuck straight up. Some had a slightly red tinge to their skin, while others sported a very light blue sheen.

The longer Silas looked, the further his jaw dropped and the wider his eyes got. They stared back at him, just as curious about them as they were. One approached Ragger, the one wearing the diaper. It had a healthy blue tinge to its cheeks and was very chubby. A baby, Silas had no doubt.

It swung an open hand towards Ragger, claws extended. Silas gasped in fear, though whether it was for Ragger or the baby thing, he wasn't sure.

Ragger caught the hand lightly in his teeth and the baby giggled; a high pitched alternating noise. It wasn't as cute as a human child's giggle, but as far as noises from *Mayans* went, it was adorable. It patted Ragger on the head with its other hand. "Soft!" it exclaimed. "Soft!"

At the word, the other children came up and lay a hand on Ragger, talking animatedly amongst themselves while they stroked his fur, an odd mix of gibberish, alien and English. Ragger was loving it, rubbing his head into the kids, licking at their hands, jumping up and looking into their faces and wagging his tail.

Scott came up behind Silas and stood, watching the spectacle. *<They've never seen a real dog before. Only Hellhounds.>*

Startled, Silas turned and looked at Scott, wondering how he had approached so quietly. Disregarding the question, he replied softly. "I don't think Ragger has ever seen Children like this before. Even infected human children reach their full height within a few months. How old are they?"

<The oldest is a year and a half, the youngest is six months.> He pointed at each of the children in turn, starting with the smallest and ending with the largest. *<Gesha, Saa, Jennie, Fernal, Tanch and Caro. They are our pride and joy. A rare thing, our children are.>*

Silas nodded. "I'll say. A year and a half...? So they grow quickly then?"

<The first year or so, they grow at about the same rate as a human child. After that, they go through a huge growth spurt. After that, we don't know.> He spread his hands in a shrug. *<However, we estimate that they will reach adulthood within eight years.>*

Silas nodded in stunned silence, staring at the children. One approached him, reaching out a single hand, the other stuck firmly in its mouth, drool running in rivulets down its chin. Scott bumped Silas with one hand. *<This is Saa. He wants to play with your hair.>*

Crouching down, Silas took a few squatting steps towards the child, not wanting to scare him. He turned and looked at Scott. *<Saa... Male, right?>* Scott nodded.

Silas turned back, looking into the child's face. Startled, he moved back a few paces, finding himself staring into two pairs of very bright blue eyes. *<They don't have the virus!>*

Scott nodded once more, his mouth cracking into a fearsome grin. *<They do, actually. Some are born with a dormant form of the virus, which only activates when they are scared. Saa, for example. His name means blue skies in our tongue. His birth caused much rejoicing. You see, these are true hybrids of our species, created from the Fetuses of infected human women, infected in vitro. We believe that this is what our creators meant to happen. There was never a real need for us to continue, just our offspring. They will rebuild our creator's race. This is our purpose. The end of this war begins here, with these babies.>*

Silas found himself unable to speak, the enormity of what these children meant threatening to overwhelm him.

His attention turned back to the child as its hand suddenly touched his face, the skin cool and slick. He sighed, pressing his face into the palm of the hand, which traveled up the side of his head and ran through his hair. It giggled, chewing on its other hand.

Silas stared at Saa, taking him in. In some ways, he was cute.

Bullard

He stood at about three feet tall, a small nose sitting on his face, replacing the usual two gaping holes that formed the nostrils of a *Mayan*. A small tuft of blonde hair sat atop of his boxy skull and he only had a few teeth, all of which were far more uniform than a regular *Mayan*'s, though just as sharp. He smiled at Silas, drooling around his fingers, small blue gums showing through.

<Whass yor name?> A small voice echoed in Silas' head.

Silas smiled. "My name is Silas."

<Oh. Selas. My daddy was talkin bou you. He says you're hur to stop the bad guys.> He beamed at him.

Scott chuckled behind him. <Saa is my adoptive son. We found him wandering the streets about three months ago. No one knows from whom he was born, or whence he came. It's not uncommon, many of these children are left on our doorstep.>

Lin stirred at the voice. <What's going – Holy shit!>

Silas laughed, startling the child, who moved back a few steps, his eyes flaring purple. It watched him with wide eyes.

"It's ok," he said, waving his fingers at the child, urging him to come back. "It's alright," he said, both aloud and internally to Lin.

Internally, he chided Lin. <This is why you need to be awake more often.>

Lin grumbled. <Well, you were sleeping, why shouldn't I?>

<Point taken, but why don't you start waking up when I do? That would work out well, I think.>

<Because I'm bored most of the time. What is this thing?>

Silas laughed silently in an attempt not to startle Saa, who had his hands back in Silas' hair, running back and forth.

<This "thing" is named Saa. He is a human and Yahntil Hybrid. He is a year and a half old.>

Silas' eyes grew wide once more as Lin's hormonal surprise spilled over into the tissues of his brain.

<A-a-a child? A CHILD?!>

Silas looked up at the rest of the group of kids, who now had Ragger on his back, all four legs motoring in the air, tongue hanging out. Silas laughed. <Children, actually.>

Silas felt Lin reach out to Scott immediately.

<How is this possible?>

Scott laughed. <Search your host's memories. I just explained it all to him.>

Bullard

Lin shifted, digging through the memories, settling himself in for a visual tour of the last few minutes. Silas' face twitched in discomfort.

After a few moments, Lin came back. *<Ah. In-vitro infection. That makes sense.>*

Scott pointed towards another of the children. *<Actually, not all of them are a product of such a thing. Gesha is actually a product of six months of pregnancy, carried by a female Infected.>*

Silas eyebrows knit together. He hadn't known that *Mayan*'s reproductive system worked. The thought of a *Titan* on the rag tore through his mind and he bust up laughing. Saa scampered away from him, towards the rest of the group, looking resentfully back at Silas, eyes glowing. Turning, he rediscovered Ragger and quickly forgot about Silas.

Silas stood, running a quick hand through his hair, laying it back down. He turned to Scott and looked at him.

"This... This means something. I don't know what. But this is important. This changes everything."

Scott nodded in agreement, hands clasped behind his back, watching the children play with Ragger. They were chasing him now, Ragger running out in front, turning and barking at them every ten feet or so. They thought it was hilarious.

Movement caught Silas eye and he glanced forward, seeing Ava coming forth out of the darkness, the same look of amazement on her face that had been on his. He smiled at her, beckoning her closer.

****

After the initial shock had worn off and once they were done playing with the children, Scott had led the group back to the dining hall, where they had eaten the night before, saying that they needed to speak privately.

Almost immediately upon entering, several large roasted pigs were set out and the *Infected* cooks scurried away. The human cooks; unable to hear thoughtspeak, remained, busying themselves with preparations for that night.

They sat at the tables and tore a few hunks of meat off the pork, munching for a few minutes, listening what Scott had to say.

<There has been talk among the dregs of our group of handing

you over to the "authorities." They feel that your presence here, us harboring you, will bring the full force of the Empire down on us. And while I'm wont to agree with them, I'm afraid I must. Especially if one of the cowards were to go and tell. I guarantee we would be flushed and out and murdered within the week. And this isn't the only stronghold. There are thirteen more around the city. All of them would be killed. I'm sorry. You can't stay here any longer.>

Silas nodded, while Lin spoke for him, his mouth being full.

<That's understandable and we discussed something of the nature last night. We picked up on several shady characters, Ragger and I. Dresnan, in particular, seemed to dislike us.>

Scott raised his brow. *<Observant bunch, aren't you? Yes, Dresnan is the ringleader. If anyone were to leave and bring forces here to take you, he would be the one. As it stands, I haven't seen him this morning. I fear for his whereabouts. You must depart from here with all haste. Your packs have been made ready. Also, we have opened our arsenal to you. Come, finish eating, quickly. I will take you to the armory.>* He turned and headed for a door at the back

Ava and Silas stood, smacking their lips, both reaching for another hunk of meat, ripping it out of the side of the pig and then hurried after Scott. Ragger padded slowly behind them, yawning.

Dashing through the door, swallowing whole chunks of meat, Silas choked at the sight that greeted him. Rows upon rows of weapons lay on tables, lined up against the walls, hanging from hooks by the ceilings. There had to be thousands of different weapons. Some he recognized others not so much, though they were clearly man made projectile weapons.

Against the far wall lay rows of plasma and heat weapons, all alien. He recognized the variety of gun carried by the Snapper and Stalker and several that could only be carried by a Titan and one that looked too big for even a Titan to carry it. It was the size of himself at full viral form. He pointed at it, eyes wide.

Catching the gesture, Scott told him that it was a Hulken Gun, carried by Hulkens only. Silas had never encountered either a Hulken or their Gun. From the size of the Gun, he doubted he ever wanted to come across one. Especially not one with its Gun in hand.

He stepped forward, examining the weapons on the table. He picked up several, ranging from an AK-47 to an M-18. Nothing felt right. Continuing down the line he came across a sawed off shotgun.

Bullard

He weighed it in his hands and then held it at arm's length, staring down the iron sights. Smiling, he strapped the gun to his back and then stepped further down the line, finding four Sig Sauer's, which he strapped to his waist and upper legs.

Ava picked more dainty weapons. Drawn to a table along the right wall, she picked several small metal objects off of a belt designed to hold them. Shuriken. Upon realizing what they were, Silas had begun to laugh, until one struck him in the left shoulder and buried itself in the muscle.

Gritting his teeth, he grabbed it and yanked it out. He held it aloft, dripping blood. "You still need real weapons," he said, dropping it to the table. "That thing is great for inflicting pain, but it won't kill anything."

Ava looked at him icily. "I meant to hit your shoulder. If I'd meant to hit your left eye, I would have. Likewise, if I had meant for it to cut your throat, it would have. And either way; it would have killed you. Instantly and then I could have retrieved it, using it and it alone to kill everyone in this room."

Silas shut up after that, searching for more weapons.

By the time they'd worked their way across the room, they'd picked up a total of sixteen pistols, two sawed off shotguns, four Uzi's, twelve grenades, twenty five shuriken and well over five hundred rounds of ammo.

Scott had tried to place a plasma emitter on top of Ragger's head, but he wasn't having it, telling Scott that while he wasn't a <God' anymore, he still had his <God' damned dignity.

Working his way over to Ava, something caught Silas' eye on the table that contained the shuriken. Stepping over to it, he frowned slightly, picking up the object that had caught his eye. It was surprisingly heavy, but not so much that it was clumsy. He swung it through the air, listening to the blade sing. He smiled.

He admired the weapon a moment, taking it in. It was a beautiful two handed sword, well over six feet long, with a polished blade. It was a weapon he could use while in viral form. It would still be at close range, but it certainly would increase his kill zone.

Turning to face Scott, he held it up. "Where did you find this?"

Looking at the weapon, Scott frowned for a moment, thinking. <The museum, I believe.>

Silas nodded, looking the blade up and down. Reaching across his back, he yanked the shotgun out of its holster and threw it across the room to Ava.

"I won't be needing this."

Lin just laughed.

****

Armed to the teeth, they grabbed their duffel bag of ammo and headed for the door, weaving their way through the now lit warehouse, whispers and grunts being made their way. They now attracted much more human attention than they had before. They were carrying more weaponry than most body builders could handle.

Upon reaching the door, they found Scott and several other Renegades waiting for them. Recognizing several, Silas spoke firmly.

"We told you last night, we refuse to take anyone with us."

Scott replied to this just as firmly.

"And I'm telling you now that we refuse to not come with you."

Ragger looked at Scott in surprise. <You're *coming?*>

"NO, he's not." Silas shouted. "None of them are!"

<Let them come if they like, Silas.> Lin said.

<They'll be killed, the moment we reach Chicago!>

<Who says they have to come in? They can simply accompany us if they like. Once we reach the city, we may even just send them back.>

Silas fumed silently, glaring at Ragger, who was looking at him expectantly.

"Fine." He said, pushing Scott aside and walking through the door. "I'm not responsible for any of your lives."

He knew it was a lie, but it made him better to say it anyway.

The group moved quickly and silently after him, Ragger in the lead, Ava following close behind.

****

They moved quickly through the city, trying to ignore the bodies they came across. Passing through several areas that they had been in the day before, Silas realized some of the bodies were missing.

He mentioned this to Scott, a sneaking suspicion in his the

back of his mind

<Yes. We collect bodies every day and take them to the baseball stadium to bury them there.>

Silas sucked at his teeth, throwing a glance over his shoulder in the direction of the stadium and then looked at Scott.

"Thank you. That means a lot to me." He stopped, staring at the rest of the group, pulling up to a stop behind him.

"So what are your names?" He asked. "I obviously know Scott, and I recognize Zendil, but the rest of you never gave me your names." He stared at the last creature in line. "In fact, some of you never even spoke to me."

The creature looked away as the others began to speak.

<I am Claudia.> Came a gentle voice from the smallest of the group.

<And I am Qend,> said another.

<Jason.>

<Farhan.>

<Michael.>

<Brecktan.>

Silas walked up to the last creature in line, who still hadn't spoken, peering into its turned face.

"And who are you, eh?"

The creature turned to look at him, a look of something like shame on its face.

"My name is Glenten. My hosssst's name is Paul. Paul Broshaw."

Silas felt like someone had punched him in the stomach.

"Paul?" Tears filled his eyes. "Paul? Are you serious? Can I speak to him?"

It nodded, standing straight, leaning its head back. It stood like that for a several moments before a sudden shiver ran through it.

When it opened its eyes and looked at him again, there was a difference in its eyes. Something softer was looking at him this time.

"Paul?" Silas asked.

<Aye, it's me buddy.> Paul's voice filled his mind

"I thought you were dead!"

<Technically, I am.> A sad smile crossed his face. <I kind of just disappeared. I think everyone preferred to think of me as dead, rather than worse off. I guess I kind of lucked out in some ways. I'm still a

213

good guy this way, and I look really badass.>

Stepping forward, smiling; Silas threw his arms around the huge body of his friend. Clawed hands wrapped around his shoulders.

"I missed you man. I looked for you, last year, with my caravan. Wanted to take you with us. I knew you wouldn't be able to resist coming back to your family. Your house was destroyed, man... Burned to the ground."

Paul hung his head, and huge tears formed in the corners. *<I know. That was me who torched it. I found my folks dead inside. Dad had turned the gun on him and mom before I got home, rather than end up like everyone else.>*

Silas looked up at his friend's face, and a giant tear plopped down on his shoulder. He pulled away, taking a few steps back.

Addressing Glenten in his mind, Silas asked a question. *<Will you let him be in control the remainder of your time with us?>*

<Yes.>

<Thank you.>

<Anything for you, Hunter.>

Silas shook his head, speaking to his friend once more. "Man. With all the shit that's gone down in the past two years or so, that's the best news I've had in a long time."

Paul laughed.

<Good news, is that what you call it? You must have had a hell of a ride to think that my condition is good news.>

Silas shook his head again, looking Paul in the eyes. "You have no idea."

Paul frowned. *<Where is your family? Are they good?>*

Silas looked away.

Paul nodded. *<I see. I'm sorry.>*

The moment past, Silas looked off to the side. "We should get moving."

Paul and Scott nodded in unison. *<Yes, we should. It's a long way to Chicago.>*

"Indeed it is... What is the quickest, safest route out of the city?"

The group all looked at one another, rather uneasily. Scott spoke softly.

<Would you prefer the safest? Or the quickest? They are two completely different routes.>

Bullard

Silas thought a moment, looking at his rag-tag group. "Quickest, first."

Paul answered for the group. <Martin Luther King Bridge.>

"Alright." Silas replied. "I know where that is. And the safest?"

Scott answered this time.

<North, one hundred fifty miles upstream to cross.>

Silas shook his head, confused. "Why so far north? Why not just use one of the other bridges?"

The group stole glances around at each other again, and Silas began to get uneasy. "Is there something wrong with the bridges?"

Paul spoke again.

<There's only the one bridge left in the city... And... No... But anyone who tries to cross the bridge is never seen again.>

CHAPTER 21 – LEGEND

Silas sat for a moment, weighing the options. North by a hundred and fifty miles was quite a ways to go out of the way. It would at least a full three days to their travel, even if they were to run.

Looking back at Paul, he asked "What do you mean nobody is ever seen again? Don't you go near the bridge?"

Paul shook his head, pointing towards the river. Silas followed his finger, and for the first time, realized that a thick, swirling wall of fog sat at the edge of the city. Scott spoke in a somber tone.

<We don't go into the fog. Anyone who ventures into the fog, the last thing we hear from them are their screams. No one returns. Not humans, not Snappers, not Titans, not Hellhounds, and not even our one and only Hulken. That was his gun back there that you saw. It was thrown back into the streets. Nothing else of him was ever heard or seen again, nothing but screams and the sounds of tearing flesh.

Silas shuddered. What could possibly be hiding in the fog?

He plopped down to the ground. He didn't know what to do. He couldn't add another three days to the schedule, but he couldn't sacrifice the lives of these Renegades, either. Especially not the life of his friend, not after finding out that he was indeed alive.

He looked up at the group, despair on his face.

"What do you suggest we do?"

They stared at one another for a few moments before looking back down at Silas.

<We go where you go, Hunter.>

Silas threw his hands up, looking at Ragger.

"What do you think, eh?"

Ragger shook his head. *<There are few things I can think of that could be as destructive, large or as lethal as they've described. And only one creature that I know of that can create a fog like that to hide itself. But they're extinct, unless they began breeding them.>* He shook his head again, looking at Silas. *<If it is what I think, then we*

should go north. We would not survive crossing the bridge'

Silas nodded in agreement. "That's good enough for me."

He jumped to his feet, wiping his hands on his pants. "We go north."

<Very well,> Scott said for the group, stepping to the side and allowing Silas to walk through. As he passed, he threw the ammo bag that he'd been carrying to the Renegade that had named itself as Farhan. He caught it in one hand, looking at him strangely.

"This is heavy. Carry that for me?"

Farhan's eyes grew wide and then he nodded vigorously.

<It would be my honor, Hunter.>

Silas shook his head in slight irritation and walked on, heading for the northern half of the city.

****

They'd been walking perhaps twenty minutes, heading north along I-70, when a sudden thought struck Silas. He pulled up short, turning to look back at Scott, who glanced at him questioningly, slowing and stopping his walk.

<What happened to the Arch? We weren't that far from it, and I just realized, I didn't see it. At all.>

Scott didn't answer, just looked to the side. A gust of wind blew through the group. Ava shivered, pulling her arms to her chest. "It's cold."

"Scott," Silas said demandingly, "What happened to the Arch?"

Scott began walking again, pushing his way ahead of Silas.

<First, we used it as a snipers nest. Then, after that became unnecessary, I tore it down. We used the metal to make more weapons. Your army torched the rest to render it unusable.>

Silas stared after Scott, a sick feeling in the pit of his stomach.

He used to tell people that St. Louis was <His city.> He loved <His city.> And now the entire thing was gone. The St. Louis Arch had been something that had dominated the skyline of his life for nearly ten years. He turned back, searching, finding nothing.

Feeling queasy, he stumbled to the side of the group and threw up.

Bullard

After Silas had recovered, they'd continued their journey, though this time Scott led the way, keeping himself away and the group.

Ignoring him, ignoring the feelings growing in the bottom of his stomach, Silas had attempted to distract him by getting to know the rest of the group, first going around in the order which they'd introduced themselves and then just talking to whoever he wanted. Ava joined in, talking animatedly to several of the members, making friends.

It turned out that only two of the group had hosts that were originally from St. Louis. Claudia and Jason. Claudia, who had been an eighty seven year old African American woman from south side, was very pleasant, and very opinionated. Her host was much the same as her, and they worked well together, so much so that Silas couldn't really tell the difference between the two.

Jason had been a Marine from the nearby town of Kirkwood, infected several weeks into the conflict. Both he and his host were very similar as well, both very quiet and spoke only when called upon, or when they felt that they had something of worth to say.

As he went around the group, Silas began to see a pattern. Many of the parasites and their hosts were very similar in their demeanor or outlook on things. He wondered if it was a factor in the choice to become a Renegade. When he voiced his question, it had been Jason who had answered him.

<Something to do? It has almost everything to do with the choice. It's hard not to have a second opinion in your head, commenting on everything you do, without it affecting how you see things.>

Silas had smiled at the alliteration. He nodded, understanding all too well.

Michael and Brecktan had been brothers, both the parasites and the hosts. They had been a couple of foster teens from the streets, hiding in the same warehouse that Silas and the group had stayed.

Farhan had been an Engineer from the Karachi, Pakistan, flown into St. Louis by the US government before the invasion to work on plasma weaponry for the Army. He had been the one that had discovered the break-through in lithium plating armor. Upon discovering this, Silas turned and shook his hand. Farhan beamed at the gesture.

Qend was rather quiet, and didn't speak much, even less than Jason. Silas hadn't pushed her too much, leaving her to her own devices.

At about ten miles out of town, Scott suddenly stopped.

Coming up behind him, Silas peered ahead along the broken freeway, not seeing anything.

"What's wrong?"

<Sh. Look. Ahead and slightly to the west. Change your eyes, if you must.>

Silas blinked, willing his eyeballs to enhance. His eyes tickled, and his jaw popped, his face changing a little.

Scott nodded his head forwards, and Silas looked in the direction indicated.

"Ah, shit. That's not good."

A platoon of probably seven hundred Viral soldiers were coming towards them. Leading the pack were two titans, Dresnan shackled between them, looking miserable.

The others followed Silas' and Scott's gaze and hissed.

<Traitor.>

Scott looked at Silas, speaking urgently.

<I do not think they have spotted us yet, they have no reason to be looking out for danger. If we turn back now, we can escape them. We can head south along the river, and cross at a safe point.>

Silas thought about it for a second and then shook his head. "No. I'm not putting another week onto this trip. We go back. We'll cross the river."

The group stared at him.

Ava stepped forward, taking his arm. "Silas. You heard what Ragger said. If we cross the bridge, we die."

Silas shook his head again, pointing behind him. "And if we go that way, I guarantee we're going to die. Now, Ragger doesn't necessarily know what is in the fog. Maybe the fog is natural!"

She hit him in the chest with her free hand. "You heard what the others said, too! That big ol' gun, whatever carries it, got eaten! Silas! Come on! Let's just go south."

He shook his head again. "No. I've been working my way towards Chicago for almost two years. If anyone is left alive, they'll be there. My father, my brother, the rest of my caravan. I can't start going backwards, not now. Not when I'm this close." He kept shaking his head. "NO."

Pushing Ava to the side, he set a brisk pace back towards St. Louis. She stared after him, disbelief on her face. "You did NOT just—" He ignored her.

Ragger called out to him in his mind, padding behind the quick moving group. *<Silas, this course is unwise.>*

Lin agreed with Silas, speaking up suddenly. *<Silas, he's right. This course is unwise. It is foolish, even. Stupid! You're going to get us all killed. Think of Paul.>*

Silas looked at his feet as he walked, replying to the both of them.

<I can't. I have to make it to Chicago. I'm sick of running, sick of hiding. I might actually be able to make a difference in the city.>

<You can't make a difference if you're dead.> Ragger retorted, placing heavy emphasis on the last word.

Silas snorted, ignoring the comment.

<I can't die, remember, not here. You'd have already seen it, right?>

<God damnit, Silas. Don't push that issue, and my visions have been wrong before. You don't look like The Hunter in my dreams, anyway, not in your human form. Similar, but not exact. These things are never exact! Do not throw your life away. Do not throw ours away! Since when is that the kind of person you are?>

Silas turned around, shouting, startling several of the members of the group, who backed out of his way.

"What do you expect me to do, huh? What do you want me to do, you stupid fuckin' mutt? You want me to just protect all your asses all the time? I didn't ask for this!"

<Easy, Silas,> Lin warned.

Silas ignored him, continuing. "I never wanted to be infected; I never wanted to slaughter my own family. You think I wanted to kill my sister, rip my mother's throat out? You think I wanted that, any of this? NO! NO! I never wanted to force my brother to burn me alive, I never wanted this to happen to the world, and god damnit, I hate to say it, but I don't want the burden of having to go out and save the whole damn thing! I don't want to be <The Hunter' I don't want you to be Anubis," he pointed at Ragger and then to Paul "I don't want him to

be an alien, I don't want to be overjoyed that one of my friends is living, even if it's as a prisoner in his own head; I just want to wake up and go to school tomorrow and tell Luke about this screwed up dream! Call Paul and tell him I had a dream that we were aliens, and listen to him laugh about how stupid I am."

He walked up on Ragger, his fists clenched, claws erupting into the flesh, blue blood dripping from between his knuckles. He'd begun to cry somewhere in the middle of his tirade, and tears slipped fast and furious down his cheeks.

"I don't want this! All I want to get to Chicago, and find the rest of my family. I just want to wake up." Silas fell to his knees and held his head in his hands.

Ragger stared at Silas with a strange expression on his face. Slowly, he began to nod his head and then looked at the rest of the group, addressing them brusquely.

<*We go back to the warehouse. Each of you gather up as many weapons as you can. Plasma, projectile, blade; it doesn't matter. We cross the bridge, and hope that I'm wrong. A group this large with a full arsenal should be able to fend off most anything that attempts to attack us.*>

They bowed slightly and then turned and back began walking once more.

Ragger stepped around Silas and followed them, looking back after a few steps, whining before continuing.

<*I'm sorry for this, Silas. I blame only myself. For everything.*>

Ava came up to Silas and crouched down in front of him, tears forming in the corner of her eyes. She reached out and hand and placed it on his chin, lifting his face to look at her.

His eyes flared gold, brimming with water. "I don't want this." He said.

"I know." She said. "None of us do. But Silas... We need you. I need you. To be strong for everyone."

She kissed him softly before standing and stepping around him, following after Ragger and the rest.

Silas sat alone for a few minutes, contemplating everything. Lin spoke to him briefly, telling him that even if he were to have a choice, he would stick with Silas. Silas didn't reply, and Lin said nothing more.

With a heavy sigh, he pushed himself up off the ground,

arching his back and cracking it.

Slowly, he turned and began to run, catching up to the group.

****

Silas, Ragger and Ava stood outside the door of the warehouse, waiting patiently for Scott and the others to come back from the Arsenal. Ava leaned against Silas' chest as he stood against the wall, Ragger sitting by his side, pressed against his leg.

Silas ran his hands through Ava's hair softly, talking to Ragger.

<What do you think this creature is?>

Ragger looked up at him, panting.

<I believe it is a Klendeken. It would roughly translate to something along the lines of 'Water lord' in your tongue. It's a massive water beast that spends most of its time underwater, feeding on fish, debris and dirt. But, when occasion arises, it is capable of standing on its end tentacles and removing itself from the water to snatch prey. It's a massive... Rakna.> He looked away from Silas, towards the River.

<I don't know how to explain it. Think of something like an octopus crossed with a monkey. Well over a hundred feet tall when it stands; a large, bulbous head, a humanoid face, giant teeth, one massive jelly-like eye. Almost no bones. Hundreds of tentacles. It exhales steam and fog from hundreds of pores from all of its body. They are extremely difficult to obtain, and it is impossible to take one by infection. As it stands, I thought they were extinct. Perhaps the Raknila finally saw wisdom in tapping into the biologic research available to us from the Rakniran, more than to just try and enhance ourselves.>

Silas eyes had gotten bigger and bigger with each word that Ragger spoke.

<Let's hope it's not that,> he replied. *<I have a feeling that we wouldn't make it.>*

Ragger moved his body back and forth slightly in agreement.

<We would all be eaten alive.>

Scott and Paul came through the door suddenly, ducking out and under.

<God, that's a tight fit.> Paul said, smiling at Silas. Silas looked him up and down approvingly. Three or four ammo belts were strapped across his chest, and multiple plasma weapons were

strapped to various joints and limbs.

"Looks like you're ready to go," Ava giggled. "God, you have so much ammo on, it might as well be armor."

Paul laughed. *<That was the point.>*

Silas laughed with him, hugging Ava before stepping away from the door.

The rest of the group slowly filtered out, all of them just as well armed as Paul. All of them seemed to be in high spirits, minus Scott.

Frowning, Silas sent him a thought. *<Why are they so upbeat?>*

<Defense mechanism against the fear. They know we're going to die. As it says in the bible, some men state, Eat, Drink and Be Merry, for tomorrow, We Die.>

Silas swallowed before replying. *<Are we going too? Do you really believe that?>*

<Oh no. You're not.> Scott turned to look at him. *<But we are. We are going to die for you. And don't you ever forget that sacrifice, Hunter.>* He turned away again and turned off his connection, ignoring Silas.

Silas sucked at his teeth and bit his lip, staring at the ground, weighing things. Looking at the group and the small weapons depot they had strapped on them, his confidence grew, and his fear abated.

He stepped forward and smiled at them. "Come on, let's go kick some ass."

Paul threw a fist up in the air. "Hells yah bro." He winked at Silas.

Turning away, Silas began to walk quickly towards the bridge, his mind on reaching Chicago. Any sacrifice was worth it at this point, he thought.

****

They moved quickly through the streets, the group in a great mood, kicking cars aside and flipping them into buildings, causing a great amount of noise. Silas saw small pairs of eyes poke out from buildings and look at them. Several drillers came out of the cars that were disturbed, running about in a confused frenzy. Silas resisted the urge to grab one of the guns and unload a clip at some of them.

Lin laughed. *<I think that would be a bad idea, Silas, given who we're with. These drillers are undoubtedly already devoted to the cause. No other drillers would stay in an area so thoroughly dosed with the hormones of Renegades. These drillers may well be conscious in their suits, choosing to live their lives as such a creature.>* He paused a moment. *<Yes, Scott says that is exactly the case. They do not attack humans, they are fully conscious, and only take humans who choose to become infected.>*

Silas laughed slightly. *<I guess that makes sense.>* He took a deep breath. *<I never imagined it could be like it was in that warehouse. Humans and Yahntil, sleeping, eating, dining together?>*

<Scott did say they have their skirmishes.> Lin pointed out.

<That's true, but still. That was almost... If the whole world could be like that. I'd do anything to achieve that.>

They both fell silent, daydreaming.

Paul laughed suddenly and slapped Silas in the arm, snapping him out of his reverie.

"Ow! What, asshole?"

Paul laughed again and pointed to a sign. Silas peered at it for a moment and then laughed with sudden recognition. They were right beside the Scott Trade Center. It had been hockey season when the invasion began, and the St. Louis Blue's slogan could still be seen on a giant poster. "Do YOU bleed blue?"

Silas ran his teeth along the back of his hand quickly, a blue line appearing, and held it up to the sky, laughing.

"Damn right I do. This is my city, bitch." He looked at Paul and held out his hand for a high five. Paul slapped it, knocking Silas backwards.

<Oops.>

He held out a hand and helped Silas up, yanking him to his feet. Silas yelped as his shoulder came out of socket. Landing lightly on his feet he flung it out and grimaced as it popped back into place.

<Damn, I'm sorry man... This is only like the tenth time I've been let out. And this is def the longest. I don't know the strength of this body very well.>

Silas laughed. "Don't worry bro... I remember all too well."

They began walking again, and Silas' mind turned to his first few days of infection, his hundred attempts at suicide, the first few days of cruel taunting from Linnerat.

Bullard

<Hey, Lin.>

No answer.

<Lin!>

Damn thing was sleeping.

<LENNY.>

<Ok, I can deal with Lin, LinLin, whatever, but LENNY is not going to fly. I am not your one handed homeroom teacher.>

Silas chuckled silently. *<I forgot all about that guy till just now.>*

<Yeah, well you can forget about him again, because I am LINNERAT not LENNY.> A snorting noise resounded through his brain. Silas frowned.

<Are you making sound effects at me?>

<Yes.>

Silas stopped, beginning to wheeze with laughter. Ava turned around and looked at him.

He just pointed to his head, laughing. "This... conversation... Oh god."

Ava shook her head and walked away.

Silas spent the next five minutes trying to ask Lin his question without bursting into laughter, but failing.

In the midst of his laughter, however, he suddenly noticed that they were quick closing in on the bridge. Clearing his throat, he regained his composure.

<Lin.>

<You finally done?>

<Yeah – I have a question for you. Two, actually.>

<Go ahead.> Lin replied.

<Why didn't you use my mother and sister against me? You used Luke. You used leaving my caravan alone. You used everything you could against me to make me miserable. Why not use the one thing that might have destroyed me?>

Lin was silent for a long moment.

<Because it would have been beyond cruel. I couldn't bring myself to do it.>

Silas nodded. *<Yeah.>*

<What's your other question?>

He bit his lip.

<Since... Well, since we might not make it out of this alive, will

you tell me who your hero is? You know all my secrets now.>

A warmth rushed through his body as Lin listened to the question.

<Ha-ha. Oh yes. That. Are you sure that you want to know?>
He nodded.

<Very well. It's you.>

Silas lost his footing, tripping and landing on his knees. The group looked at him as he pushed himself to his feet, dusting himself off.

"I'm alright," he said to them. "Meant to do that."

Then to Lin, *<What? Me? Why?>*

<How could you not be a hero to me? I live in your head, Silas. Inside of your skull. I see all your thoughts, your hopes, your dreams, and your amazingly few fears. They pass through me, and invigorate me. Give me a purpose. You live in a world that is barely your own, you watched your world be ripped apart by an enemy that you still barely understand, even after learning so much. You fight for that which is right; in a world that no longer has a solid grip on the meaning of the word <Good.> You fight for others in a world that seeks to kill everyone living in it. In a world that is survival of the fittest, you stand with atop a hill with your middle finger up, saying I am the fittest, I will survive and then you turn and help those less fortunate than you, saying I'll be damned if they don't too.> He paused, thinking.

<Out of all the creatures now on this planet, you are the most likely to survive. You're smart, you're strong, and you know how to fight, hunt, and survive. It's like you were designed for this life. But even when your own life is in danger, you turn and help the weak, the sick, the dying. You show kindness in a world which has none. I've seen it. You do it every day. Every day, you make at least one decision that requires you to forego what you want, and help someone else. You, Silas, are an exemplary figure of what it means to be strong, not just physically, but in heart and mind. You must understand, Silas. I watch this world through your eyes. I get to sit and watch your life play out as if it were on a screen. Each day, each thought that crosses your mind, is an adventure to me. You think I sleep all the time? You're wrong. I get so caught up in you, get caught up in this legend in the making that is you; that sometimes I forget to think. To speak. I watch everything through your eyes; I feel your fear, your pain, and your immense strength. You think that I gave that to you? You're wrong.

You already had it, deep inside you.> He paused again, a tremor running through him. A single tear sat on Silas' cheek as he listened.

<Fear. You are full of fear, Silas. You fear to wake in the morning, dreading hearing my voice in your head. Dread to wake up and find those dreary gray skies, long to wake and see the sun in your window, and you feel like crying every day it isn't there. But you don't. You grit your teeth and pull yourself to feet, once again, against all odds. I feel that fear, constantly. But through thick and thin, it never fails, through every horror and desperate situation, I feel your resolve. Your damnitall attitude that makes you so resilient. In the same moments in which I watched other, lesser men crawl away on their hands and knees like little children, blubbering and crying for their lives as they faced their last moments; I tasted the joy of battle as you and I leaped over their backs, bellowing at those who would take the lives of those lesser men.>

<I have heard your screams of rage as I watched you rip an unrighteous, murderer of a man in half with your bare hands and then, with the same hands, lay a small child down to rest for the night, singing a lullaby to them. Watched the same fearsome talons which have slaughtered countless thousands, lay a young child in a grave, to sleep for eternity. After all the horror you've witnessed, you are still a kind, loving soul. To steal an apt human phrase, Silas, you blow my mind.>

<I seek through your memories, searching through those days before I clawed my way up your spine, and find exactly who you are today, lying dormant. Nothing more than a mere teenage human, still with the same strength, same resolve. You attribute your power to me, but all I have done is given you another form with which to defend this world. And that is what you do, Silas. You defend. You defend all those that come into contact with you. Take them under your wing, give them shelter, and show them that getting up tomorrow to fight isn't a self-defeating concept.>

Silas was crying silently by this point, and he had stopped moving, standing still. He didn't notice that each and every other person in the group was stalk still, listening to the now open thought broadcast.

<When this world met its likely demise, you were nothing more than a child. A child. And you took charge of adults and children alike; found them in the holes and the ruins of their homes which they still

hid, and drew them together. Brought them all into one place, and taught them how to survive in a world that wants to dance on their graves. You give everyone who comes near you strength, Silas. You give them hope. Give them reasons to get up and fight on, even when all seems lost, to move forward at all costs. Give them reasons to believe. Give them reasons to hope.>

Silas bowed his head, tears streaming down his face.

<You are my hero, Silas, because you give me hope.>

CHAPTER 22 – DEMISE

Thereby traveled the rest of the way to the bridge in silence, coming to a standstill a few feet away from the fog, staring into the swirling white. Ephemeral shadows moved within, like ghosts of those who had entered before them, appearing and disappearing in the same instant.

<Oh, Hunter.> Scott said. <I forgot.> He tossed something sparkling through the air. Silas raised one hand and caught it, examining it quickly. It was a long, thin silver chain. He looked at Scott and gave a quick nod of thanks. Shoving the chain in his pocket, he turned his attention back to the bridge.

A shiver crawled down his spine as he took his first step the fog, letting the cold mist envelop him, his clothing instantly clinging to him. Ava and Ragger followed close behind. She reached forward and grabbed Silas' hand, pulling herself to his side.

After a long moment, the Renegade group heaved a collective sigh and stepped forward as one onto the bridge.

Reaching into his pocket, Silas pulled up a single headphone and twisted it into his ear and pressed the tiny button on the side of it, speaking aloud. "Play all tracks."

A small beep issued from the speaker, and music began blaring in his ear. He smiled. Earlier, at the warehouse, he had managed to convince a human with a computer to let him charge his Selenidi.

Roach looked up at him as he spoke and then shook her head as she realized what had happened. She squeezed his hand once and then pulled away, looking around her as they worked their way across the bridge.

It was eerie. Even with his enhanced vision, Silas couldn't see much further than ten feet in front of him. No foreign heat signatures danced across his vision, everything was the same pale, grey shade of cold.

Bullard

The bridge creaked under his feet, and the now ancient looking steel supports screamed their distress at the newcomers.

Hollow cars stood a watchful guard as the group picked their way through the street, some with doors still hanging open. There were no bodies, something which Silas found worrisome. Various weapons littered the ground. A sick feeling began to grow in his stomach.

He coughed as a sulfurous scent tickled the back of his nasal cavity. Covering his nose, he looked over his shoulder at Ragger, whose fur had begun to stand up on the nape his neck.

<It's a Klendeken.> Ragger said. <Look sharp.>

Silas nodded.

The cars grew closer together, some tipped on their side and blocking the road, forcing the group to spread out. Scott, Qend and Jason climbed over the separating barrier between lanes, giving everyone else some room to walk. Jason led the way slowly, Qend close behind and Scott bringing up the rear. Silas followed them with his eyes for a few seconds and then looked back ahead, watching his footing.

They had walked less than twenty feet when Jason suddenly cried out, sounding panicked. <Where are Scott and Qend?>

The rest of the group turned and peered towards Jason, looking for any sign of the two other party members. He was greeted by nothing but swirling mist. As it was, he could barely see the outline of Jason.

"Scott? Qend?" He called out, drawing a pistol from his thigh, checking the chamber. "Come on guys."

No response. Jason stared at him, his wide, glowing eyes shining through the mist.

Fear creeping into the edges of his voice, Silas motioned to Jason. "Why don't you come back over here?"

Jason immediately hopped over the wall, stepping close to Michael and Braxton. He shivered, his skin vibrating.

Ragger growled and slowly began to change; growing with each step they took. Silas followed suit, allowing himself to slip into his viral form.

He glanced at Ava, who had grabbed onto his arm.

<You should think about changing too.>

<Yes,> Lin agreed. <It would be better for all of us if you were

able to fight, rather than us feeling we have to defend you.>

She shot the side of Silas' head a dirty look, snorting in derision. *<If we change, we can't use hardly any of the weapons we brought.>*

Silas realized she was right, even as the various ammo belts and weapon straps began to restrict against his growing body, biting into his flesh.

Weighing the options, he thought for a moment, halting the progression of his body. If he were to change, the only weapons he would have available to him were the sword and the single plasma weapon he had on his leg.

If it was truly a *Klendeken,* his size wasn't going to be of much assistance. In fact, it could be a hindrance.

Sighing, he reversed the changes, shrinking down to his former size.

Out of the corner of his eye, he caught a smirk on Ava's face.

This time, he snorted, focusing on changing once more.

He closed his eyes momentarily, and when he opened them again, his peripheral vision had expanded to twice its previous area, two extra eyes opening on the side of his head.

Ava turned to look at him in disgust.

Baring a toothy grin, he winked at her with one of his right eyes.

She rolled her eyes and shook her head.

Ahead of them, Ragger in his full *Torn* form stopped and flicked his tail, telling the rest of the group to stop.

They slowed and looked around. Turning, Silas counted the members of the group. All still remained, minus the two previously missing members. He sighed in relief.

Turning back to Ragger, he drew another pistol, checking its chamber as well. He knew they were loaded; it was just something that came from force of habit. He'd tried firing an empty gun a few times before. It never worked out very well, for some strange reason.

When Silas had begun estimating that they were probably a quarter the way across the bridge, sudden noise rang out from behind them; a sort of slithering and clattering. A car door slammed shut.

The whole group whirled around, looking for the source of the sound. It was no use; they couldn't see anything through the fog.

Another noise, this time from the direction they'd been facing before. They whirled around again, pulses racing. Still nothing.

Ragger began growling low in his throat, rising and falling in pitch, a menacing noise that stood the hair on Silas' neck up. Not for the first time, Silas was very aware of how lucky he was to have Ragger on his side.

Suddenly, Ragger whipped around and ran into the fog, barking. Silas' and Ava's eyes widened and she ran forward, calling after him.

Silas darted forward after her, grabbing her by the wrist. "Don't!"

From the white, there was a sound of tearing flesh, a rumble and a sudden yelp.

A crash sounded as something heavy crushed a car. A low whining came from the fog, and Ava tore free of Silas' grip and ran forward. "Ragger!"

Silas ran after her, the rest of the group following in quick succession.

The fog began to clear, and Silas able to see a little further in front of him. A sight greeted him that froze his feet to the ground, causing Brecktan to crash into him. He didn't budge, staring.

Ragger lay in the ruins of a car, moaning slightly, Ava clinging to his neck. The last half of his tail was missing, and a bright blue line of blood stood out against his grey skin, trailing the length of his body. A dark, leafy green tentacle lay by the car at Ava's feet. It twitched and flopped, green slime oozing from the torn end.

Ragger lifted his head and looked at Silas. The eyes on the right side were missing, and it looked like someone had taken a strip of duct tape and ripped it off his face, tearing away the flesh. Raw and oozing, Silas could see the pale blue layers of muscle underneath.

<It's *here. Don't worry about me, I'll be fine.>*

From the back of the group, Claudia screamed. Turning, Silas saw a thick, ropey tentacle wrapped around her neck, dragging her into the fog.

Raising the pistol, Silas walked forward, shooting after her. A crunch sounded and Claudia's screams stopped as her skull burst, Silas having hit his target. Aiming up and to the left and right, Silas squeezed off several more shots.

An ear shattering shriek split the air, and several tentacles shot towards them from their left side.

Bullard

Michael and Brecktan jumped into action immediately, acting as one, running and jumping over cars, ducking and rolling, firing shots into the empty air, shouting their satisfaction every time they heard the sizzle of wet flesh.

The fog continued to clear, and Silas began to be able to make out a monstrous shape on the left side of bridge.

It stood at least a hundred and fifty feet high out of the water, towering over them, and almost over the bridge. A dull red glow showed from its center, shining through the fog, lighting the landscape in an eerie manner. As Silas watched, it began to expand and contract; and a fetid wind began to blow, smelling of rotting fish and death.

Grimacing, he swung up both pistols and aimed for the red glow, pumping the triggers, emptying the chambers. Tossing them to the side, he grabbed for his sides, grabbing the two Uzi's strapped there.

He ran and leaped atop a car, shooting at various tentacles aimed his way, squeezing first one trigger and then the other, cutting the offending appendages off.

The creature screamed once more, and moved closer to the bridge, close enough to be seen through the rapidly dissipating fog.

Several plasma shots fired off as Jason leaped atop the car next to him. Silas heard ripping and tearing from the direction of Ragger and Ava, followed by Ragger's harrowing growls.

Ava screamed and several shots were fired. Ragger roared and a gun clattered to the ground. Silas' eyes widened and he resisted the urge to look and see what had happened.

He ducked as a tentacle swept past him and took out Jason, knocking him to the ground. A roar tore from the back of Jason's throat and he grabbed the tentacle and bit it in half, jumping back to his feet.

Three tentacles shot out of nowhere and pierced the Mayan through the abdomen, eliciting a long howl of pain. Silas turned his gun and shot through the tentacles with the last of his clip and then tossed one of the Uzi's to the side and reached into his pocket, grabbing another ammo bay, slapping it into the chamber.

<Thank you, Hunter.> Jason said.

Silas ignored him, focusing on the matter at hand. "Farhan!" He yelled. "I need that ammo bag!"

<Yes, Hunter.>

Bullard

A grunt issued from his left and the ammo bag flew out of the fog and towards his head. He snatched it with one hand and redirected it towards the ground in front of the car.

He jumped down and tore the bag open with his fingers, reaching inside and grabbing a flare gun. Reaching up, he fired it off, illuminating the entire scene.

The creature was massive. He'd seen that much before, but now, laid bare by the dissipating fog and the light of the flare, Silas' skin began to crawl.

Ragger's description hadn't done its hideous nature justice. It stood almost as tall as the bridge, one massive, jelly fish looking eye dominating the center of its head. Its head itself was surrounded by hundreds of variously sized mouths, all opening and closing, venting steam and showing thousands of teeth. Mud and slime covered tentacles waved from every part of the creature.

Two humanoid arms extended from its sides, ending in hand like appendages, which were covered in hundreds of long, whipping tentacles. Two massive tentacles extended from its middle and down into the water, like pillars of pure muscle.

From the corners of his vision, he could see that Michael had fallen and Brecktan stood over his body, firing madly with two plasma guns at the creature's eye. Jason was on one knee, firing with one hand and ripping at the tentacles which had pierced his body furiously with the other hand, desperately trying to heal and rejoin the battle.

Farhan stood by himself, two blades in his hands, whirling like fans of death, nothing coming within several feet of him. At his feet lay hundreds of small tentacles.

Paul stood with four modified Uzi's, two in each hand, laughing maniacally as he fired off round after round.

Ava and Ragger stood off to the other side, Ragger snapping at every tentacle that came near them in half, either with a gnash of his teeth or a thunderous whip of his tail, nothing came near Ava, who stood with her teeth bared, flinging star after star into the darkness, twinkling red in the glow of the monster's eye. Every once in a while, she aimed and fired a few precision shots from her laser sighted pistol.

Silas' attention was rerouted after another tentacle shot for his head and he leaned to one side, the tentacle grazing his skin, tracing a deep groove in the flesh of his face. He bared his teeth and snapped at the tentacle, biting it in half. A disgusting taste filled his mouth and he struggled not to vomit. He spit, the severed tentacle falling to the ground.

The *Klendeken* screamed once more, swinging both hands towards the bridge. Hundred of tentacles descended upon them, and Ava screamed. Glancing from the corner of his eye, he saw that her arm had been pierced. Ragger had been pierced several times, but still stood his ground; blood running in rivulets down the tentacles sticking through is body and pooling on the ground.

Silas jumped down and ran towards the two of them, throwing his guns to the side and drawing the sword from his back, swinging it back and forth, chopping and hacking, tentacles shredding before him like foliage. They pulled away momentarily, seeming distracted.

<Follow me!> he cried aloud in his mind. <While its unfocused!>

Paul replied. <It's only me and Farhan, now. Michael and Brecktan are dead.>

Silas glanced to his left as he ducked and rolled. He saw two bodies being dragged towards several of the gaping mouths. <That's why it slowed the attack.> Lin remarked.

Silas grimaced and a said a small apology in his heart.

Reaching Ava and Ragger, he hit one knee and asked Ava if she was ok, but didn't wait for an answer.

He grabbed the tentacle sticking through her arm and yanked as hard as he could. She screamed once more as the tentacle came free, flesh tearing away with it. A gaping hole remained, the edges undulating with instant reparations.

He stood and rushed to Ragger, where he attempted to do the same.

<Do not!> Ragger shouted. <Those tentacles have pierced vital organs. Leave them, and I may be able to survive, absorb them. Rip them free, and I will surely bleed to death.>

Silas stared at Ragger a long moment and then nodded, standing and jumping back as a tentacle made its way for him. Too late.

It pierced him through the stomach and he groaned, doubling over. He swung the sword once and chopped the limb in half.

He stood again, regaining his composure, his sword twirling above his head. He danced towards Ava as several came her way, severing them in half.

<How many tentacles does this thing have?>

<It's a plant.> Ragger replied. <As many as we chop off, it can grow them back just as quickly, using the material found inside it's body, anything it's just eaten, even material in the river. To kill it, we have to attack the body directly.>

Hearing this, Farhan turned and bowed to Silas.

For the first time, Silas noticed that the Mayan was covered in deep cuts, and several tentacles pierced him. He must have sustained them while running.

<I will not live out this day, even if no more injuries are inflicted upon me.>

Silas, understanding, nodded.

<Thank you, Hunter. I shall die knowing my life has meant something.>

Bellowing, Farhan stepped forward, letting several tentacles pierce him.

The *Klendeken* screamed in delight, having found its next meal. Several attacking tentacles diverted, wrapping around Farhan's body, squeezing him. Pain rolled out of the Mayan's mind in waves, causing Silas to cringe.

He waved to Ragger, Ava and Paul. "Run! Run, while it's still focused on Farhan."

They turned and bolted, shooting and hacking at any tentacles still coming their way.

They'd gotten around five hundred feet when the *Klendeken* suddenly screamed in a way they'd never heard before.

Turning, they looked back to see what had happened.

Farhan had cut himself loose and now stood atop the creature, his blades flying in a whirling message of death, cutting deep into the creature. Hunks of spongy green flesh flew through the air, and Farhan slowly descended into a hole he was cutting through its hide.

The *Klendeken* raised its arms and batted at its head, screaming again as one of its hands were nearly severed by Farhan's blades.

The other hand came crashing down moments after, and the link with Farhan's mind was severed as he was crushed.

They turned and began to run again. The end of the bridge was nearing, less than five hundred feet away.

Bullard

They pushed themselves, putting on an extra burst of speed. Tentacles came from the fog, each one snapping at their backs, most of them not reaching, though Paul screamed in his head a few times as strips of flesh were torn from his back.

Ragger pulled ahead, bounding away towards the shore line, leaving a thick trail of blood behind him. Following behind, Silas suddenly slipped in the trail of blood and fell to the ground.

Paul grabbed him by the seat of his pants before he could hit the ground and flung him into the air.

Pin wheeling, Silas landed on his feet and rolled, jumping back up and running, covered in Ragger's blood, his feet pounding the pavement, flying forward with each stride.

A loud thud issued from behind him, and the ground shook. Several shots were fired. Instinctively knowing what had happened, Silas stopped on his heel, turning and skidding several feet, digging his fingers into the ground, leaving four long furrows. Coming to a stop, he sprinted back towards the fallen Paul.

Jumping in front of his friend, Silas spun and chopped, slicing the twenty or so small tentacles which had wrapped around Paul. He reached down and grabbed Paul by the arm and yanked the giant to his feet.

Turning, they ran side by side, Silas slipping the sword back into its makeshift strap across his back, snatching another pistol from his hip; Paul slapped at the still writhing tentacles attached to his midsection, groaning as he ripped them away, chunks of skin tearing away with them.

Ava and Ragger stood a hundred feet in land, three hundred feet from where Silas and Paul now found themselves, calling out to them, panic in their tones. Silas understood immediately, pushing himself even harder. Ava and Ragger must have seen something behind them.

The bridge suddenly vibrated, and the ground shook. Ragger and Ava fell to the ground as Silas and Paul flew forwards, crashing to the concrete.

Their mouths full of blood, they turned and looked behind them, finding an entire wall of tentacles coming their way, the *Klendeken* having crashed through the bridge. Huge chunks of concrete broke apart and fell to the river and road far below, sending huge plumes of water and sound through the air.

Bullard

They scrambled back to their feet, turning occasionally to fire off a burst of ammo into the writhing mass that chased them.

Gaining ground by leaps and bounds, Silas looked up and saw that Ragger and Ava had turned and run further inland before turning to assault the *Klendeken* from afar once more.

The more ground they gained, the further away the tentacles seemed, until finally, with a scream of rage at having lost its meal, the *Klendeken* gave up and retreated. A roiling fog immediately began to set back in, steam venting from the creature furiously.

Silas skid to a stop, sliding into Ava. Ragger turned sideways and stopped Paul cold as he slammed into him.

Crying, Ava threw his arms around Silas, and Paul patted Ragger affectionately between his ears.

They stood like that for a few moments, Ava squeezing Silas tightly, her face pressed to his chest, and Paul gently scratching Ragger behind the ears. As he scratched, Ragger arched his head into Paul's hand, just like a domestic dog. Silas laughed at the sight.

Turning her head against Silas to look, Ava caught sight of the spectacle and began to laugh along with him. Ragger grinned sheepishly, showing his teeth.

Paul shrugged, beginning to laugh.

Silas turned away, burying his face into Ava's hair, smelling her, reveling in the fact that he was still alive. That they were all still alive.

The moment was short lived as a crunch sounded. Silas frowned, turning back to Paul.

His curious gaze quickly became a horrified one as he found Paul staring down at his chest, which had just sprouted a green tentacle as big around as a coke can.

Choking, blood gurgling in his throat and leaking from the corners of his mouth, Paul grabbed onto the tentacle with one hand, trying to rip it apart, but it was no use. Ragger backed away from him slowly, eyes wide.

Silas started for Paul, snatching at the tentacle, drawing his sword, but it was too late.

Paul looked up at him one last time and smiled, the light in his eyes dying.

<Good to see you one last time, broski. Love ya man. No homo.>

Bullard

And then he was gone, yanked back into the swirling fog.

Eyes wide, Silas staggered forward, one hand outstretched towards the wall of white.

Ava wrapped around his waist, clinging tight to him and dragging him to one knee.

"Paul!" He shouted. "Paul!"

He turned and placed both hands on Ava's shoulders and shoved her down, grimacing as her nails tore long lines into his clothing and flesh.

He struggled to his feet and took a few steps forward, preparing to break into a run, when a dark shadow appeared in the corner of his vision, racing towards him.

Pain exploded across the bridge of his nose as everything went black.

CHAPTER 23 – RISE OF THE GODS

Silas came to slowly, staring at a clear night sky. The stars shone brightly, glaring at him.

He sat up and rubbed his head, which was pounding harder than it had in a long time. Thinking on it, it hadn't pounded this hard since the time he'd been shot in the face.

He looked around, finding a crackling fire ten or twelve feet from him, Ava and Ragger crouched by it, sleeping.

He frowned, his eyebrows knitting into one another. Something had happened. Something important, something tragic. He just couldn't remember what.

He pushed himself to his feet and walked over to his slumbering friends.

Ragger pushed up onto his front paws, staring at him as he plopped down by the fire, staring into it.

Silas was silent for a moment, watching the flames jumping skyward. Glimpses of memory flashed through his mind. The bridge, the fog, being pierced.

He shook his head, reaching inward for Lin.

<Hey Lin.>

He waited a few seconds before trying again.

<Lin.>

He reached up and smacked himself in the back of the head.

<Lin.>

<He's sleeping.>

Silas looked at Ragger.

<He's had a long day. We had to have him take control of you while you were unconscious. He's not used to such long excursions.>

Silas frowned again.

"How –"

Ava stirred. Silas glanced at her and switched to thought speak.

Bullard

<How long have I been out?>

<A little under twenty seven hours.> Ragger replied.

Silas ran his tongue along his teeth, nodding his head. That would explain why he felt the way he did.

<What happened?>

<You don't remember?>

He shook his head.

<Bits and pieces. I remember u top me and Paul running. Then... Things kind of just...> He shook his head again, trailing off.

Ragger looked at the fire, propping himself up more, sitting upright. After staring at the fire for a moment, he looked away, off towards the horizon.

<Perhaps it's best you don't dwell on it.>

<I know Paul's dead. He's not here. There's no other explanation. I just don't remember...>

Ragger sighed.

<Paul was eaten.>

Silas looked at Ava, watching her chest rise and fall.

<But, we almost escaped. The tentacles, they pulled away, I was holding Ava. I remember that. He was scratching your ears and then... Oh.>

Pain washed across him as the memories came flooding back.

<Oh. Oh.>

He stuck his head between his knees and stared at the ground.

Ragger whined and stood, walking over to Silas and licking his ear before plopping down next to him.

<Oh. Oh. Oh man. Paul.>

Silas pulled his head up and looked to the side, staring at the dog.

<I remember. I also remember trying to go after him. And then – nothing. What happened?>

<I broke most of your face and your neck. I hit you in the face with my tail. I couldn't let you go into the fog after a dead body. Not only did that tentacle pierce half of Paul's heart, it severed his spine. He was dead in thirty seconds.>

Silas drew a sharp breath and stood quickly. Ragger backed away from him.

"You what?"

Ragger backed further away from him.

Bullard

"YOU WHAT?"

Ava stirred and sat up, staring around.

Silas clenched his fists, taking several steps towards Ragger, who took several steps back in return.

"You couldn't possibly have known that he was dead! There's no way!"

<Silas, I heard his heart stop. Moments after you fell to the ground, I heard him get ripped to pieces, his bones snap and crack. There was nothing you could have done.>

"That wasn't your choice to make!" Silas shouted, his hands opening and closing. "Not your choice! He was my friend, *my* friend, *mine!* You had no right! I don't care what, or who you think you are! You're no God, you're a coward!"

Ragger looked away from Silas once more, not speaking.

"You think that you're some all powerful, God of death still? Huh, is that it? You're the almighty Anubis, weigher of souls, right? Nobody questions you, you do what you want! Decide who deserves to live, who dies?"

<No! It isn't like that. It never was. That was a myth perpetrated by Ra. I wanted nothing to do with it!>

"I'm sick of being lied to by you Ragger. Sick of your cryptic little manner, sick of –"

<What's going on?> Linnerat stirred suddenly, awakened by the shouting.

"Shutup, Lin. This is between the mutt and me. Stay out of it."

Confusion rolled across him, but Lin stayed quiet.

Silas kept walking forward, though Ragger had stopped moving, still refusing to look at him.

Reaching the dog, Silas kicked him viciously in the chest, causing a resounding thud. Ragger bared his teeth momentarily, but lowered his lips quickly, refusing to move.

"Look at me!" Silas shouted, clenching his fists once more. He kicked him again.

"Damnit, I said look at me!"

Another kick, this time a cracking noise sounding deep in Ragger's chest.

Ava ran up behind the two of them, laying a hand on Silas' shoulder. He shrugged, throwing a hand up.

Ragger sat down heavily, whining, his breath coming up short.

Bullard

"Silas," Ava said, "Don't. He did what was best for you. All of us. After you passed out, the... the sounds... They were horrible. Paul didn't even scream. Nothing even came across the connection. He was dead, gone."

Silas turned, eyes flaring in the darkness, gnashing his teeth, turning his rage on her.

"Best for us? Best for me? He was my last! Living! Friend!" He punctuated each word with a shout and short pause, "The last one! I thought he was dead and then found him and then you think you have the right to rip him away from me again?!"

He shoved her to the ground and turned back to Ragger, whose breathing had returned to normal. The dog still refused to look at him, staring into the far horizon.

Silas gathered the strength to kick the dog once more, when a sudden heaviness came over him, and all he wanted to do was sleep.

He sat heavily, narrowly missing Ava's foot, staring at Ragger, waiting for a response. Ava scooted back, hugging her legs and setting her chin on her knees.

Slowly, Ragger turned to look at Silas, something like sorrow reflecting with the fire in his eyes.

<Silas, I know you think that I have no idea what it's like to be you. But you're wrong. I know you; I know your life, your feelings. I may not have lived your life... But I have lived a very long time, and this is just one more thing in a very, very long line of things that I am not proud of.>

<I am over five hundred thousand years old, Silas. And I have forgotten half of the grievous terrors I have inflicted. The ones I remember are still enough so that they keep me awake at night. I haven't had a good night's rest in years.>

Silas just shook his head, keeping his silence a few moments longer, wondering what had happened.

Lin prodded him softly. *<Sorry bud, had to up your serotonin. Couldn't let you go on a rampage.>*

He nodded slowly. Lin was right. No use in letting things go to shit now.

Ragger took the silence as a sign to continue.

<As you now know, due to Lin, I was set to be a Judge. A Raknila.>

Silas nodded tiredly once more.

Bullard

<And, as you can obviously see, that never came to pass. I'm sure that Lin also explained that a Rakniran hadn't been seen in almost a thousand years, when the orders of a lush new world came. Around the same time, I saw you in my dreams, Silas. Or someone similar to you.>

Ragger examined Silas for a moment.

<The hair was different. And the eyes. And some of the facial features. But it doesn't matter. You are the Hunter; I feel it in my bones. As I said, the visions are never exact.>

<The visions. Something I hadn't had in a very long time. The only other visions I had ever had was of me becoming a Ravager. They – the visions, – They sparked something inside of me. A desire for more than the primal brutality of our race. Even in vision, I aspired to fight by your side, Silas. Seventy six thousand years before you were born, I desired to live, fight, and die by your side. And I will, in time.>

<At that same moment, the idea for becoming a Renegade came to me. At that time, I told no one but a select few. And when they asked for Volunteers to go to the new world, I volunteered to go. I wasn't chosen. So I killed the two guards who were. They were never seen, or heard from again. And I killed every single other guard who was chosen. Not even the Raknila would dare to challenge a Ravager one on one. Not even ten to one. And nobody was going to find those poor souls in my stomach without killing me and cutting me open.>

At the mention of the dragon creatures, Silas' heart rate jumped up a little bit. He simultaneously could not wait to come across one, but hated the very thought of a confrontation.

<The Raknila knew what I was doing. They tried to pry into my mind. I shut them out, let them see nothing. Sensing this, they decided to go ahead and grant my wish, to send me to the new world, along with, Zeig, Osiris and Ra-ahgan, as a primary escort. At that time, Isis, my Geishnan, another of the Thousand Torn, begged to go with me.>

Silas and Ava frowned. <Mate in waiting,> Lin said to them, not allowing them to interrupt Ragger, whose eyes had glossed over. <The word itself means, "Meant to Be.">

Ragger continued his tale.

<As she was my Geishnan, and it is looked down upon to separate Geish's, she too was granted passage.>

<We were removed from our bodies and placed back into Drillers, put into stasis and fired towards the planet.>

Silas frowned again, unable to resist asking a question. He opened his mouth, but was interrupted by Lin once more.

<When scouts are sent out, no more than eight Drillers are placed into what we call a "Pod." It's a self sufficient space, which keeps Drillers healthy and maintained and keeps their cargo alive in the cold of space. It's like a large, hollow rock, with several spaces which static Drillers are placed in.>

Silas closed his mouth, nodding. Ragger had not slowed his speech, but Silas hadn't missed more than a few words, his communication with Lin being almost instantaneous.

<– traveled almost seventy one thousand years in stasis. We crashed down in Northern Africa, atop a large boulder. Zeig was killed on impact, his suit crushed. Isis nearly died, but to her luck, a pack of Hyenas came by within an hour or so, curious about our scent. We worked together to wound one, and let her take it, that she might survive. Ra-ahgan suggested that we take them as well, but I disagreed. Primary scans of the planet before touchdown had indicated a large, somewhat advanced civilization less than five hundred miles from us.>

<Along the way, my suit sprung a leak. One of my legs had cracked, and as you know, Drillers are our only form incapable of self repair. The crack soon became a geyser of blue fluid spraying across the African landscape. I began to become dehydrated. It soon became apparent that I would not survive the trip. At my behest, Isis ran off to search for a suitable life-form to inhabit. She first attempted to take on a lioness, but was severely wounded, having underestimated the creature. After sitting aside for several hours to heal, she went out again, this time dragging back with her a creature similar to her own by its legs. A jackal. At first, I was displeased, as it was so small.>

<But I had no choice. I infected the creature. It was exhilarating. Earth has such a rich sense of life to it. Not many other worlds have creatures that see in so many frequencies of light, and at first, the sense of smell almost overwhelmed me. The minds are very strong as well. This Jackal I inhabit has overpowered me twenty seven times to date.>

<Several more hours later, as dusk began to fall; my host's legs had healed enough that we could begin walking again. Isis was pleased, as we were now much in the same form. Once we reached our full forms, we would be nearly identical. We had always strived to

inhabit the same species. She too, had been a Ravager. It makes the sexual encounters not only more enjoyable, but easier, as the instincts of the host are still intact. They know what to do.>

Silas raised an eyebrow, trying to imagine the scene that the thought presented him. He laughed silently, and Ava laid a hand on his shoulder, hushing him.

<However, as the hours progressed, she began to become irritated, as her host's changes were apparent, and rapid. Mine were not forthcoming. My host was fully healed, but beyond my eyes changing shades, nothing else had shifted. Not one of us could fathom why this was. But, I quickly found that if I focused on what should be happening, it slowly began to. I'd never had to do such a thing.>

<Isis quickly overcame her irritation, figuring that it must have something to do with the immune system of my particular host. Some hosts have very powerful immune systems, which fight off our viral compounds for quite some time, but with us pumping pure viral cells into the bloodstream, every immune system fails eventually.>

<By the time twenty four hours had passed, I had reached my full form, as had she. We killed and ate everything that crossed our paths, studying innards, learning each species as well as we could. Being what we are, and who we come from, we have an innate understanding of biology. Isis tried to encourage Osiris and Ra-ahgan to inhabit a lion, as they were the most powerful life form we came across, but still I disagreed, and asked that they inhabit the dominant life form, which, by that point, was less than one hundred miles from where we were. Being that I was the oldest and most respected of the four of us, Osiris and Ra-ahgan agreed.>

<We reached the city by nightfall. The river first posed a problem, as it was a wet season, and the Nile was swollen. However, we soon discovered that our hosts were good swimmers, and water sources pose no problem to Drillers, as you well know. The suits have re-breathers built in which pull all needed gases from the environment around them.>

<We slunk among the dunes, and studied the humans from afar. At first, we couldn't understand why they had become the dominant species. But slowly, we came to see that you had a much higher intelligence than any other creature we had come across. Nothing else on the planet had the understanding of the mechanics of the world around them. Rather than moving, adapting to your

environment, you adapted your environment to you. It was impressive, a level of society we had seldom come across. Actually, to be honest, your species is one of the most advanced that we have ever enslaved. You are by far not the oldest. One of the youngest, in fact. Your solar system is very young. But you... Your species is very advanced. You weren't then, but by the time our main force arrived... Yes, you are one of the most advanced species we've ever enslaved.>

    <Isis and I hunted and trapped two humans. Both male, as were Osiris and Ra-ahgan. It took less than a week to convince the Humans that we were Gods. I rather enjoyed the proximity, as it allowed me to examine your race. Not only was the Hunter I had seen in my visions one of your species, you intrigued me anyway. You were intelligent, innovative, and creative. Something our species often lacks.>

    <After learning all that we could about your society at that time frame; we set about making ourselves immortal, invincible. We invented the legends of the underworld, our various powers and responsibilities as Gods. We ordered the construction of the pyramids, for our amusement. The sphinx was Osiris' tribute to Zeig, his Geishnan. We gave the Egyptians advanced mathematics, taught them how to irrigate and jumped your civilization forwards by almost a thousand years overnight.>

    <All of us stayed in Egypt for nearly a thousand years. Osiris and Ra left before Isis and I. We stayed and taught among the humans. I don't know why we are portrayed as such terrible, cruel creatures in later texts. We were the most benevolent of the four. We taught, showed, helped and walked among the people, told them tales, wove images of the great beasts we had fallen, spoke of the great civilizations that we had destroyed. Ra-ahgan and Osiris were the cruel ones, eating those who chose to worship them, demanding sacrifices, heavy taxes. Those who worshiped Isis and I were protected, and those who laid hands against them were punished in a manner not worth speaking of in civilized company. It saddens me to think that all I tried to do for your civilization was lost in the terrors that were perpetrated by my brothers.>

    <In the time that we walked and taught, I came to love your species. I saw the vast potential that they could provide the universe. Short lived, hot tempered and violent, yes, that you are. But compared to our long lived, wise, hateful species, you are like angels against

demons. You have a capacity for intelligence, wisdom and kindness not many of our species can even imagine. I began to hate my species more and more with each passing moment, becoming ashamed of what I was.>

<After another hundred years or so, Isis and I departed, traveling the world. We discovered within a few hundred years that Osiris and Ra had taken up new residences, new names. Zeus and Apollo, over the Greeks. Isis and I wanted nothing to do with them, and steered clear of them and the wars they caused for their amusement.>

<By this time, of course, we had discovered my ability to walk as a normal earth form, and this prompted me during our travels, to mention to Isis my ideas about becoming a Renegade. Of course, it was not called as such then, I had come up with the idea thousands of years before and discussed it with others, but no one had ever acted on it, and it was very much a taboo subject. I was punished terribly for that first dissent... However, unbeknownst to the rest, I had already done this to myself during our time on Earth. They never knew otherwise, as when we spoke we were always close enough to one another for me to speak with ease. The Raknila did not notify the others, as we had not had contact since a hundred years after our landing. They were unaware of my condition.>

<Upon learning that I had turned m y back on our species, Isis chose to leave me, to seek out Osiris and Ra-ahgan, believing me to be a traitor. I could never convince her otherwise. I believe that she became the basis of the Legend of Cerberus, as well as Athena. Kind, but terrible. They may have portrayed me as Hades. As my Geishnan, Isis could not have helped but to have spoken of me from time to time. Also, as my Geishnan, she could not help but to hold my secrets. Ra-ahgan and Osiris never knew the reason for our separation, nor my treachery; not for many years. An interesting observation; The Legend of Atlantis surfaced soon after Isis departed from me. I believe she encountered Plato on her journey, and told him of the world of Ahkind; the home world of the Klendeken, perhaps on a quiet night spent together. It was where we met, Ahkind.>

A tear formed in the corner of one of Ragger's eyes, a strange sight to see, a dog beginning to weep.

<I eventually settled down as a regular canine, in the midlands of Egypt, which I considered to be my Earthly home. I occasionally came to the aid of honest men, good kings, appearing as a great

shadow in the night, destroying the enemies of those whom I watched from afar. I never again came to rule, though I often appeared to Pharaohs and Queens in the middle of the night, to give them guidance.>

<After another five hundred years or so, I grew weary of walking the Earth alone, and so appeared to a Pharaoh and ordered him to build me a tomb, cut into a valley far to the north. After it was finished, I entered within and had the entrance sealed. For how long I slept, I'm not sure. I didn't exactly keep track of time for the years I was here. I believe it was almost two thousand years into my Earthly journey when I lay down to sleep, and I woke perhaps a thousand years later? Maybe less. I know that after another hundred years, I was awake during the birth of your Christ. I walked beside him during his life, he was an inspiring man. I walked beside the Mohammed, also. He too, was a great man. I found myself attracted to the great religious figures. Jesus, Mohammed, Buddha. I walked beside them all; learning from them, and teaching them also. But that is not important.>

Silas' eyes grew wide, grasping; not for the first time, how ancient the animal sitting beside him was.

<The world had not changed much, when I awakened, though my beloved Egypt was beginning to lose its splendor. My companions had vanished from the Earthly timeline, no longer reigning as physical Gods. They never really resurfaced in that capacity. I never learned why, but I speculated that they were contacted by the Raknila, who would have been displeased by this turn of events, ordering them to quit meddling.>

<I'm also sure that at that moment was when they received their orders to kill me. I encountered them again perhaps a hundred years after the birth of Christ, in the Amazonian rainforests. A fight ensued that lasted nearly ten days without rest. At the end, Ra lay dead at my feet, and Osiris and Isis fled, badly wounded. But not before Isis threw in my face that she had chosen Osiris as her new Geishnan. If two Geish's lose their own, they are allowed to choose one another as their new Geishnan. By Isis telling me that she had chosen Osiris as her new Geishnan, she was essentially telling me that I was dead to her, worth nothing. I no longer existed in her eyes.>

An immense sadness blasted across the connection Silas held in his mind, and a small lump lodged itself in his throat.

Bullard

<I lay down atop the carcass of Ra-ahgan and slept for many days, waking occasionally to tears and pain in my hearts.>

<For how long I lay there, I do not know. I only know that when my stomach cried out in great pain, did my host struggle against me, overpowering me and devouring the rotting corpse of Ra-ahgan. I did not care. My Geishnan had condemned me. I was alone, in a world that I loved, but which was not my own. I let the host wonder in my body for years, perhaps ten, withdrawn into myself.>

<After regaining control of my host, I fled west, across the ocean, to the comparatively uncivilized Americas. I found myself in the Gulf of Mexico, and traveled north, until I came across a rudimentary civilization. Picking up my old ways, I convinced their leaders that I was a God. Tired of being a destroyer, I brought Science to this society: Agriculture, Mathematics, Stonemasonry, Metallurgy, Astronomy and many others. I taught them of the cultures of the rest of the world, told them of my past, my companions and my species.>

<They took to astronomy with a passion, curious about other worlds. So I taught them of my species and told them of the impending doom I had brought upon them, gave them the approximate date upon which they would arrive. They drew up the years and alignments of the stars on a giant stone calendar, which they called the 'long count,> based in pairs of ten.>

Silas eyes grew large and he whispered under his breath, recognizing the description of the society being given to him. "The Mayans," he whispered. "That's how they knew. The end of the Mayan calendar, it was you."

Ragger turned his head slightly, looking at Silas and nodding.

<Yes. The Mayans. We lived in peace for quite some time. I demanded they pay me no sacrifices, but did not forbid them sacrifices to other Gods. They had their brutal sports, and priests who claimed to hear other Gods besides myself. It did no harm, I did not care. A thousand years passed in this manner, and the Maya flourished, creating a great and massive empire.>

<During this time, Osiris and Isis hunted me down once more, confronting me atop a temple. I snapped Osiris neck, throwing him down the many stairs, but could not bring myself to destroy Isis. She tore my ear to shreds and then fled.>

He shook his head, flopping his ears, drawing attention to the ugly holes in his torn ear.

Bullard

<I can heal this scar. I choose not to. I have let it become a part of me, because it reminds me of her. Before she disappeared into the forest, she told me that she had reported me dead to the Empire, that I was free to do as I wished. And that she envied me for that, but she could not bear to abandon our race. She also left me with a promise. That she would kill me.>

An image popped into Silas' mind, of a giant beast turning to look at him. A female voice rang in his head. <If we meet again, I will kill you, Anubisarius. But let it be known that it will be with love, for that is all I hold for you. I've tried to hate you... But I cannot bring myself to do so. Until we meet again, my love, and then may we never part, in death's embrace.> And then it was gone, leaving Silas with the feeling that he had seen yet another thing meant to be hidden, and Ragger was continuing with his story.

<Another hundred years or so passed in relative peace. But then the Spanish came, and began to slaughter my people. I fought as long as I could, but found myself disgusted by the joy I found myself having in the slaughter of men. I departed, ashamed by my actions.>

<I traveled South, across the length of the continents, crossing another ocean, until I found myself in another world, composed entirely of cold and white. No humans to rule, no lives to meddle with. I buried myself in a cave hundreds of feet beneath the surface of the ice, laying myself to sleep, to await the arrival of my species.>

<And when they finally arrived, when I heard the multitudes of screams echoing across the oceans, saw the bloodshed in my mind; I awoke, to protect my Earth. And I will not lie down and surrender until I have done so. I will die trying. By my life, I swear: This world will not fall to my race.>

CHAPTER 24 – THE SOUND OF MUSIC

Tired and dragging, the group had been walking for two days, travelling from town to town, searching for anything useful.

They hadn't come up with much, though Silas had found a netbook laptop in the ruins of an old home, and a working charger. He'd been pretty happy about the matter, meaning he could now charge his Selenidi anytime they came across a generator.

Ava and Ragger hadn't been so lucky, not finding anything they cared to keep.

Silas had led them from town to town, going from Granite City, to his hometown of Troy, and onward to Collinsville, scavenging. It was the area he'd grown up in, he knew it well. After passing through Collinsville, they moved on towards Glen Carbon and Edwardsville.

As they'd passed the local Stop'N'Shop, Ragger let a low laugh out in his throat and nipped at Silas' hand.

Frowning, he looked down at the dog, who raised an eyebrow at him and jerked his head towards Ava. Silas looked at her and then caught on to what Ragger was laughing about. He looked away quickly, blushing.

Grimacing, he aimed a punch at Ragger's head, just missing as Ragger ducked swiftly and stepped to the side, still laughing.

Silas nodded.

<You think you're funny.>

Ragger's laugh entered his mind as he replied. <I tend to think so, yes. Why don't you pop on over there and knock that one down too, eh?>

Silas slapped at the dog again, this time eliciting a strange look from Ava.

"What are you doing?" she asked.

Silas shook his head, pulling his lips into a tight smile.

Bullard

Ragger laughed again and Silas slapped at him once more.

Ava drew her eyebrows together and looked at the two of them out of the side of her eyes, shaking her head.

"You two are so strange. Good to see you've bonded. I was worried you two were going to hate each other forever."

"Nah," Silas said. "We reached an understanding."

"Good." She replied.

She stopped, frowning.

Silas' eyes widened, thinking Ragger had told her what they were talking about. His cheeks flushed and he opened his mouth to deny any involvement in whatever Ragger had hinted at.

She looked up at the sky. "Is it just me," she asked, "or are the clouds clearing?"

Silas frowned alongside her, the color receding from his cheeks, looking up at the sky as well. Ragger too, lifted his head, and cocked it to one side.

The clouds were indeed clearing, bright light pouring through.

The sun suddenly broke through and basked the three of them in warm light. It was only almost February, but to the three of them, having lived in a sunless world for nearly a year, the sun was like walking under a July evening.

Silas and Ava closed their eyes and let their hands fall loosely to their sides, reveling in the patch of sun, soaking up as much as they could.

The moment passed quickly as another roiling bunch of vapor passed in front of the sun's rays.

Silas sighed, his heart feeling suddenly heavy. "Hey Ava?"

"Hm?" She replied, eyes still closed.

"Do you ever wish none of this was real? That it was some big joke, that none of this ever happened? Do you ever get the feeling that maybe it isn't? That this is just some crazy dream? And after that thought, you pray to whatever God is listening, that it is?"

She opened her eyes slowly and stared at him solemnly. "Every day, Silas. Every day."

****

"Hey, look." Silas pointed. "Is that a school?"

Bullard

Ragger and Ava peered in the direction Silas was referencing, squinting. Ragger nodded slowly. *<It appears to be, yes. It may be a good place to stop. We aren't going to find anything around here, and that school is probably safe as anything we'll find. Nothing has been through here in months, all the scents are cold and dead.>*

Silas nodded in agreement, reaching across the dog and grabbing Ava's hand momentarily and giving it a tug before striding ahead. "C'mon."

She sighed and followed him, Ragger bringing up the rear.

The trip to the building took about ten minutes, which they traveled in silence, wary of the empty eyes of the houses that surrounded them. Silas had walked through ghost towns before, but they never failed to give him the creeps.

Reaching the school, they did a quick survey of the area, checking scents and looking for any tell tale signs of hostiles.

Finding none, they strode into the building, Silas and Ragger prying the double doors off their rusted and previously welded hinges.

Stepping forward into the darkness, they took in the scenery before them. Empty lockers hung open down the hallway ahead of them, dried, brown blood colored several otherwise spotlessly white pillars. A torn banner hung from the ceiling, plasma marks pocketed the walls. Bullet shells lay everywhere on the floor.

Silas bit his lip, tasting the still lingering pain and fear that hung in the air.

Ava came up behind him and laid a soft hand on his hip, looking about.

"No bodies," she remarked. "I think the Renegades must have been here. I didn't see any cemeteries though."

Silas shrugged, staring. "How many of them do you think were just kids?" He asked.

Ava shook her head. "I don't know. Probably a lot of them. The doors were welded shut; this was probably where the last survivors in town came. The young people are always the last to die, the longest to survive. You know that. And look at the walls." She pointed. "Look at where the bullet holes are. And then look where the plasma marks are." She gestured to their sides and behind them. "They were attacked from behind. The enemy found another way in. This is where they made their last stand, backed into this entrance. They knew this place better than anyone else; they knew that right here was their best chance."

Silas nodded, still looking around and taking a few steps further, Ava's hand sliding from his hip and to her side.

<Looks like they put up a valiant fight.> Lin remarked. <From the number of shells and bullet holes, there were many of them, and they fought for their lives with ferocity. They died with honor, I'm sure.>

Ragger padded softly forward into the darkness. <There must be some sort of cafeteria here, with canned goods. And if as many people holed up here as it appears, they probably had a stockpile somewhere.>

Silas nodded in agreement once more, following the dog, replying. <Maybe. But if there are indeed Renegades about, who's to say they didn't take it?>

Ragger paused a moment and then resumed walking. <Then we're screwed out of dinner. Can't hurt to look.>

Ava chuckled. "Well, you two go ahead. I'm going to find a restroom."

Silas turned to her and tried to hand her a pistol, which she pushed away. "I'm a big girl. Besides," she lifted her shirt, revealing an automatic pistol in the waist of her pants. "I'm packing already. We didn't use all our weapons earlier. Just most."

Silas smiled, tucking the pistol back into his own pants as Ava turned and walked down a side hall.

He watched her walk for a moment, worry tugging at his mind.

<She'll be fine, Silas. Like she said, she's a big girl.> Linnerat reminded him. <Figuratively.>

Silas shook his head and laughed before hurrying after Ragger.

After five minutes or so, Ragger stopped and looked over his shoulder at Silas.

<Why are you following me? We can look over more areas if we split.>

Silas stopped and stared at the dog for a second, a goofy grin crossing his face.

"Haha... Yeah, guess I didn't think of that. Alright, I'll go this way." He jerked his head to the side, gesturing down another hallway.

Ragger nodded once and then resumed sniffing his way down the corridor.

Silas walked slowly down the hallway, running his hands

across the crooked and bent lockers. Here and there, a plasma burn decorated a few of them. Others hung off their hinges. Looking closely, Silas saw that some of the lockers had four small cylinder prints at the edges.

Stepping close to one of the lockers with the markings and examined them. Turning his hand to the side, he arranged his fingers and laid them along the markings, matching them up. They were fingerprints, but he couldn't figure out how they would get on the lockers in the position. <Not unless –> he grimaced.

They were from people trying to cram themselves into lockers, to escape whatever horror had been coming down the hallway. He wondered how many had succeeded, only to be torn from their hiding places, like an oyster being scooped from its shell.

Shaking his head, he continued on, peering into doorways.

Passing one, he stopped dead in his tracks, the object within the room catching his eye, and his temptation was too great to resist.

****

Ava sauntered slowly through the school's halls, peering into rooms, looking at old chalkboards. Passing a near pristine room, she stepped in and looked around, drawing a finger along the dust on the teacher's desk. Walking over to one of the student's desks, she blew hard on the desktop and chair, sending dust cascading through the air.

Wiping the remaining dust from the seat, she turned and sat in the desk, staring at the board, running her fingertips across the cool surface of the writing top.

She sighed and closed her eyes, leaning back. She could almost imagine the sounds of being back in school. She'd been in her senior year when the invasion occurred. Ready to graduate, she'd wanted to go to law school. She'd even thought she would have a shot at getting into Harvard. She would never know, now.

She lost herself in a daydream for several minutes, recalling her friends and classes, tears forming beneath her lids.

As the first tear escaped the grasp of her eyelashes and slid down her cheek, a noise caught her attention.

Reaching for her gun, she sat straight up, straining to hear.

At first, she couldn't hear anything, but then the noise came again.

Bullard

Sitting stunned, she couldn't believe her ears. She stood, pushing herself to her feet, securing her gun in her waistband once more before rushing out the door.

She walked quickly down the hallway, searching for the source of the noise, looking back and forth, confused by the echo.

The sound grew louder and louder, increasing in speed before falling back to a slow, steady pattern, one she recognized.

She broke into a run, smiling with tears still on her cheeks.

****

Ragger followed close behind Ava, unbeknownst to her, as she was too wrapped up in emotion and disbelief.

He too, was curious as to where the sound was coming from. Would they find friend or foe at its source? Was it a call for friendship, a trap, or perhaps a warning? He didn't know

He picked up his pace as Roach broke into a run, keeping good time behind her.

As they ran, twisting up and down stairs and down hallways, the sound haunted them, teasing them, daring them to find its source.

Finally, they came to a hallway which unmistakably housed the source of the sounds.

Ava burst into a sprint, looking in doorways as she passed. Near reaching the end, she suddenly skidded to a stop, staring into a room.

A look of wonder on her face, she slowly walked forward and into the room.

Ragger heard her come to a stop and cautiously approached the door, peering inside.

Inside he beheld a large, expansive room with the general shape of an amphitheatre, with various musical instruments scattered about the floor and lying against the walls.

At the center sat a large grand piano, Silas seated before it, his eyes closed and a look of determination on his face as his fingers danced deftly across the keys, a mournful melody filling the air.

Ava stood behind him, watching him, a strange look on her face.

Satisfied that there was no danger, Ragger lay down and set his head upon his paws, watching in silence.

Bullard

As he watched, Silas began to sway slowly in time to the music sweeping forth from the keys he played. He didn't appear to be aware of anything other than the music, oblivious to Ava behind him.

She took several steps backwards and looked along the walls, searching. She arched her eyebrows and then stepped out of Ragger's sight momentarily. When she stepped back into view, she held an old, dusty case in her hands.

Kneeling down, she set the case on the floor and popped it open, withdrawing a beautiful violin and bow.

Ragger drew in a breath of slight surprise. He'd had no idea that either of his companions were musically inclined.

Ava stood and silently twisted the knobs atop the violin, running her fingers along the strings and testing the vibrations, careful to not make any noise she walked around to stand in front of the piano where Silas could see her if he opened his eyes.

Slowly and carefully, she raised the violin to her shoulder and set it atop her collar bone and rested her chin upon it, poising her bow above the violin.

She waited several moments, listening to the music as Silas played and then, finding the right moment, lay the bow to the strings in a single sweeping motion, causing the strings to weave their sweet voice in with the deep melancholic tones of the piano.

Silas' eyes snapped open, not missing a single note and seeing Ava before him, he smiled and closed his eyes once more, picking up a slow, sad melody, Ava keeping in perfect time. She walked slowly around to the bench where Silas' sat and perched herself on the end, watching him, her fingers swooning and crooning up and down the strings, creating a tune to match his, the piano seducing sweet notes from the violin.

How long they played, Ragger did not know, nor did he care. It could have been mere seconds or it could have been years. He could have listened forever. He sighed, closing his eyes and smiling softly to himself, immersing himself in the moment. Humans were one of the only species they had ever come across that wrote and played such complex music.

In the notes they sang to one another, he could hear their sadness, their anger, their fear, their pain and their loss. But through it all, he could hear their budding love.

And that was what would matter the most, in the end.

Bullard

Winning this war wouldn't boil down to firepower or guts or wits or numbers or technology.

The most inexplicable force in the universe had just found the two most powerful creatures in existence. And that would be enough.

Ragger fell asleep in the doorway with music in his soul and a smile in his heart.

CHAPTER 25 – A HEARTFELT BETRAYAL

Anubis awoke slowly, his dreams still ringing with the music his two friends had poured forth from their souls.

The light filtering in through the high windows in the room was dim and faded with the tinges of dusk. Night was approaching quickly.

He looked around the room, blinking slowly, searching for his companions. He located them quickly, propped up against a makeshift bed composed of instrument cases and torn curtains. Roach had her head laid across Silas' chest, whose arms were wrapped tightly around her. A hard look sat on Silas' face, vigilant even in his sleep.

Anubis shook his head in sadness. *<These young people shouldn't have to live this way.>* He thought to himself. *<We are a filthy race.>*

He shook his head once more and then sent a thought out to Lin.

<Lin. Are you awake?>

The reply came a few moments later.

<Yes, I am. I trust you slept well?>

<I did. The music was most relaxing; they lulled me to sleep within just a few minutes.>

Lin chuckled. *<Yes, it was much the same for me, though; I was too enthralled by the actions Silas was performing to really allow myself to sleep. The finger movements were just... Fascinating! Once they finished, however, I allowed myself rest. Have you been awake long? I heard you stir several moments ago.>*

<No, I just awoke.>

<Hm.>

They didn't speak for several minutes, Anubis closing his eyes once more.

<Did you want something?> Lin asked.

Bullard

Anubis leaned his head to one side, eyes still closed, thinking.

<Yes and no.>

Lin waited, allowing Anubis time to think.

<I am troubled. I wish to hear your thoughts on a matter, and perhaps glean some advice.>

Confusion flitted across the connection, as Anubis had expected.

<My advice? What could I possibly advise you on? You're almost seven hundred and fifty thousand years my elder.>

<Yes, I know. However, will you hear me out?>

<Of course. What's troubling you?>

Anubis rolled his head the other way, laying it across the other paw.

<These humans. They have troubled me so long, so many times.>

Confusion touched him once more, though Lin made no reply.

<They are so angry, so weak, so dim and so very near-sighted. They live their lives in the fraction of an instant, not caring where they go, or whence they came. They are lazy and predisposed to taking the easy way out. Genetically, they are nearly backwards. No natural defenses. No real predatory instinct. They are not fleet of foot. They are not strong of limb. They are neither the strongest, nor the weakest that this planet has to offer. Yet, they have come to the dominant position on this planet.>

He paused, waiting to see if Lin had any input. After several nanoseconds of silence, he continued.

<Half of their life is spent speaking, trying to communicate with one another, to convey their ideas. By the time they convince others, show other persons that their idea is valuable and venerable; they have wasted almost the full amount of time it would take to complete the project by themselves. After that, the project takes years to complete, due to other humans having to communicate the ideas to others. Nothing should get done on this planet.>

<Yet it does. Compared to us, humans are slow, backwards and genetically near despicable creatures. The only thing that they have going for them is that enormous neural center. And most of them waste it. Even those that choose not to, never achieve anything due to the mundane nature of the rest of their race. How has this race achieved anything?>

Bullard

<How is it that these creatures, with all their chaos, laziness and hatred have come to be the most technologically advanced species we have ever come across? Why is that we look at them and shake our heads in dismay, yet look at some of their achievements, leaps and bounds in awe? How does a backwards race like this, get anywhere at all?>

<And how is that we: a race designed, created, programmed and released by a race as intelligent, long-lived, and far-sighted as the Rakniran, are so weak in comparison to these beings? For all the technology, wisdom and long years we have in our possession, why do we fall short of being able to understand life like sad, pitiful, short-lived humans?>

He paused, waiting for an answer. Several long moments passed before Lin realized he was being waited on.

<Well, I cannot tell you for sure, for any of your questions. And I suspect this is not all that is on your mind... However – Your last question, of how do we fall short of understanding life like these humans, as a younger being I may be able to provide some insight. It is because we take life for granted. Being so long lived, we lose a taste for life. We lose a taste for living. Nothing is exciting, nothing is new. We have done and seen everything we can do in a lifetime a hundred times over before our lives are even a quarter way through. Humans, however, wake up each day wondering how things are going to occur. Each day, they wake up in fear that they may die, but in hopes that they may accomplish something as well. They wake up with the hope of a blue sky, rather than a cloudy day, even if they know better.>

Anubis nodded slowly, thinking about what Lin had said.

<You are wise beyond your years, young one. I think you are correct. However, I believe that we will never quite understand the wonderful disease that is the human condition. We can only hope that perhaps as we infect them, they will infect us in turn.>

Silence fell between them once more as they both nodded back into sleep.

****

A sudden noise stirred Anubis from his sleep once more, one that originated from within the room. Years of experience over rode his internal instinct to sit up and search for the source. Instead, he just barely cracked his eyelids apart, searching the room for any signs of danger.

The source of the noise was easy to identify. Roach had sat up and was looking about the room. Carefully, she lifted Silas' arms from her lap, where they had slid when she sat up. Silas grumbled and turned his head to one side, muttering in his sleep. Roach froze, staring at him a long while, holding completely still. Clearly, she didn't want anyone to see her.

After several minutes, Roach slowly pushed herself away from Silas and to her feet. She walked silently over to Anubis and stared down at him, even going so far as to crouch down and look him in the face. He had already snapped his eyes shut before she could come close enough to see.

Another several minutes passed, Anubis trying to alternate between regulating his breathing and letting out small noises of protest, as if he were dreaming.

Finally, Roach seemed satisfied and pulled up from her crouch slowly and turned on her heel, walking towards the door of the auditorium, careful to not make a single noise as she walked. Anubis marveled. He had never encountered a situation in which she had kept so quiet.

After passing through the doorway, her pace quickened as she walked down the hall and after a minute or so, Anubis heard the front door latch snap quietly as she left the building. Satisfied that she was gone, Anubis stood slowly, stretching and eyeing the window above the room. It wasn't that high, but he didn't think he would fit through the tiny space. It had glass anyway, and he didn't feel that he should wake Silas just yet.

He padded towards the door, stepping in Roach's footprints. He too quickened his pace after stepping through the doorway, flying down the hallway, searching through rooms for any open windows. Finding one, he made a quick u-turn at the end of the hall and doubled back into the room and bounded out the window. He landed lightly on the ground below, sniffing the air, searching for Roach's familiar scent.

He found it quickly, heading east along the side of the building and out into the deserted town.

He sat and stared at the stars for several minutes, allowing the girl to get a good head start, far enough ahead that he could track her without her having any way of knowing.

Bullard

He gazed at their home star with regret. How he wished that he had never been born, his species never created. So much pain could have been saved, so many more worthwhile species spared.

He sighed. Nothing he could do about it now.

He stretched once more, putting his paws on the ground in front of him and arching his back down. He yawned and then sniffed the air, finding her scent once more.

He followed along at a leisurely pace, taking in the surroundings. He passed by two gas stations and a supermarket, neither of which she had made any indication of going towards. He couldn't figure out where she might be heading.

Suddenly, the scent grew much stronger, pooling as she slowed down and stopped. Anubis pulled up short, looking around and following her scent more slowly.

She had wandered into an old abandoned house. He examined it. There was nothing special about it. Old faded paint, broken windows and a busted concrete patio, nothing made it stand out from any other house in this area.

His ears perked up as several voices wafted from one of the broken windows. Slinking over to the window, he crouched low and lay on the ground, pinning his ears back and listening.

Two familiar voices reached his ears, one that he wasn't surprised to hear, the other belonging to someone he thought dead.

Roach spoke again indistinctly and then a third voice rang out, this one chilling Anubis' blood in his veins. The voice itself was light and jovial, but the words that it held were filled with madness, cruelty and hatred.

"So, you found him then?"

Roach answered quietly, something like shame in her tone. "Yes. Yes, I found him, right where we expected. I found someone else, too."

"Really? And who is that? Who else on this pitiful world could interest me, besides The Hunter?"

This time Scott spoke, his voice too tinged with guilt and shame. "Anubis. The Hunter travels with Anubisarius the Fallen."

A sharp hiss stung the air as the third speaker breathed in quickly.

"Anubis? Anubis is dead. Isis reported his demise to me directly! You were there! Do not lie to me, Gegnan."

A moment passed and then Roach spoke once more.

"He doesn't lie. Anubis is now traveling with Silas. In fact, they seem to have bonded –"

Another hiss and a crash cut Roach off. "Silas? Silas what? Tell me his name! Is it Stone?"

Roach stuttered, feigning surprise by the third speaker's reaction.

"Y-y-yes. Silas Stone. How did you know that?"

The third voice laughed low in their throat, not appearing to notice that Ava was faking her emotions. "He and I are old friends. Old, old friends. He is the eldest son of Commander Stone, leader of the human forces, and he was my host's best friend in their human life. He almost killed me, once. Oh, the irony. Not only do I get to destroy The Hunter, I will finally have my revenge on that little brat. And then, I will make sure his severed head finds its way into the hands of his father. And there's another added bonus in slaying the infamous Anubisarius."

Anubis' eyes grew, realizing who the third speaker was, thinking to himself. *<Silas' best friend in his human life. Lucas. Ateneran. Shit. Of course, she knows that they know each other. Ava, what are you doing?>*

Roach's voice quavered as she spoke again. "Do you have to kill him? Why not just convert him?"

Ateneran laughed.

"Do you really think he could be converted? No. Your face says everything. He will fight to the death, no matter what is at stake. That's just who he is now, isn't it?" He trailed off, sounding somewhat wistful.

Scott spoke once more, addressing Ateneran. "Ateneran, Lord. What shall you have me do now? The colony in St. Louis thinks that I'm dead. Is there somewhere else I can be of use?"

Ateneran laughed. "Well, that's because you are dead, Gegnan! In answer to your question, no: I have no further use for you."

Roach squealed as several shots rang out in rapid succession and the telltale sound of blood splashing against a wall sounded.

Ateneran laughed again and then turned his attention back to Roach. "Now, dear Ava, come here."

Roach let out a small grunt as she stumbled across the floor. A wet smack was heard as a kiss was laid on someone, whether Ateneran kissed her, or she kissed him, Anubis couldn't tell. He assumed the former.

Ateneran's next words confirmed his suspicion.

"What, do I disgust you now? You realize what I've done for you, little girl, just to preserve your beauty? I've given you immortality, and you are still in control of yourself. That is more than I have ever allowed anyone. You were nothing more than a rat on the street when I found you. You would be dead or worse if it wasn't for me. Don't you dare pull away from my touch. I own you, bitch."

Another smack rang out, though this time it was the sound of someone being backhanded in the face. Roach whimpered and Ateneran snorted. "Come along now, we have to go."

Heavy footsteps began crossing the floor, but stopped after several seconds.

"Well, come on, don't just stand there... I said come on!"

Still no footsteps.

Ateneran grunted and Anubis heard the click of a weapon being cocked. Roach whimpered once more and began walking towards Ateneran, her footsteps heavy and dragging.

She whispered softly, barely enough for Anubis to hear.

"I know you're there, I know you followed me, I knew you were never asleep. I know you know everything. I am so sorry. Please, warn Silas. You can't let Ateneran kill him. Tell Silas that I love him. He has to know that I love him. Go now, while I distract this one."

"What was that?" Ateneran asked.

Roach snapped, shouting at him.

"I said, you're a worthless, disgusting piece of shit, and I wish you would have left me for dead in that street! If I knew what was in store for me, I would have holed up and starved to death, letting the cancer eat my guts from the inside rather than be stuck with you for eternity! You're a fucking monster!"

Anubis had already jumped to his feet and was tearing down the street by the time she'd finished, heading straight back for the school.

Ateneran laughed and patted Roach on the back. "I know darling, I know. Don't you just love it?"

****

Bullard

Ragger burst through the front doors of the school, shouting Silas' name both aloud and in his mind.

"SILAS! SILAS, WE HAVE TO GO NOW! SILAS, WHERE ARE YOU?"

His claws scrabbled against the slick tile as he tried to gain purchase and rubble fell to the floor as he jumped through corners, several lockers falling to the floor with a deafening clang.

Silas was already in the doorway of the amphitheatre when Ragger ran up, rubbing his eyes.

"Ragger? What's the deal? Where's Ava? What the hell is your issue, man?"

<We have to leave, now, she's betrayed us. She and Scott. They knew each other all along, they've told high command who and where we are. We have to leave now.>

"Wait, what?" Silas blinked, still half asleep. "Ava, betray us? Scott?" He laughed. "Scott's dead and Ava would never do that."

Ragger barked angrily, yelling. *<I don't have the time to explain, you idiot!>*

Enraged, he jumped at Silas, pinning him to the floor.

"She betrayed us, you fool. She fooled us both, and if we don't leave now, we're going to pay the ultimate price. In fifteen minutes, this building won't exist anymore. Ateneran knows who you are now; he won't stop at anything to find you."

Silas struggled and Ragger snarled, lunging down and biting him in the cheek, releasing a flow of images and memories.

<Anubis. The Hunter travels with Anubisarius the Fallen. – Lucas. Ateneran. This isn't good – Do you have to kill him? – That's just who he is now – I have no further use for you – I own you, bitch – Please, warn Silas. – Tell Silas I love him.>

Silas sat stunned, blue blood leaking from his already healing wound in his cheek. Ragger climbed off from the top of him, staring at him for several seconds before nudging him urgently.

<I'm sorry for that, but you wouldn't understand otherwise. We have to go. Now.>

Silas sat up slowly, touching his cheek and staring at the blood that came away with his hand. He looked at Ragger in an empty manner.

"Lucas? Luke?"

Ragger shook his head and grabbed Silas' hood in his teeth and yanked, pulling Silas further up. Jumping, he yanked Silas' to his feet.

<Come on. I'll explain who Ateneran is after we get away from here. We've wasted too much time as is. We have to go.>

He nipped at Silas' finger and then took off running, bolting out the door and down the hall, not waiting for Silas.

Silas stared around the room for a moment before running and grabbing his weapons and chasing after Ragger.

CHAPTER 26 – LOSING FAITH

They tore across the frozen desert, refusing to look back, Silas grinding his teeth together, Ragger trying not to let himself feel the pain of betrayal in his hearts.

A noise reached Ragger's ears and he threw himself to the ground, grimacing as Silas plowed into his back and face planted in the dirt.

<Don't move.> Ragger said.

They both lay perfectly still, listening as the whistling that had been filling the air from the moment they'd run, grew louder.

Suddenly, two *Klendeken* Class fighters blew across the landscape, headed directly for the school, several small missile pods detaching from their bottom as they curved and sped east. Silas covered his ears.

The resulting explosion was enormous, sucking all the sounds out of the air for a moment before blowing them back out in a massive rush of air and a sonic boom. Ragger whined as his eardrums blew out. <Alright, run!> He shouted.

They both jumped to their feet and took off once more, trying to outrun the resulting heat wave following the sonic boom.

They weren't fast enough.

Silas began to yell as his hoodie caught fire from the back, his hair torching and neck burning. Ragger's fur caught fire and his skin began to crisp. He howled in pain as he ran, triggering his transformation. Glancing to his left, he saw that Silas was already underway.

Growing with each stride, each stride growing by ten feet, they flew across the desert, trailing just ahead of the wall of fire.

After fifteen seconds or so, the heat at their backs began to subside as the flames slowed, the explosion losing its momentum. Still, they ran.

Bullard

Silas sat sullenly on the steps of an abandoned warehouse, staring out into the gray landscape that was now the mainstay of his world. He shivered, pulling his jacket closer around him and closing his eyes. One hand slowly crept towards his throat, fondling the talisman around his neck.

Ragger whined at Silas' feet, staring up at him, watching as miniscule tears slipped out from beneath the young man's lids. He whined once more and lay his head back down, allowing Silas a moment of silence. Humans felt pain on a level he'd never been able to understand. Neither understood, nor saw how they could bear. He couldn't imagine how overwhelmed Silas must feel.

After finding this place to rest and changing back, Ragger had disclosed his entire tale to a stony faced Silas, shown him what he had seen, let him hear what he heard, explained to him who and what Ateneran was. Ragger was worried, as almost no reaction had been elicited from Silas. He seemed empty, hollow. But Ragger knew better.

Several minutes passed, with no discernable movement from the two of them, other than Silas' fingers moving slowly up and down, worrying at the small metal piece.

Silas sighed and sat forward, setting his face in his hands, rubbing his eyes and upper cheeks, a single name on his lips.

"*Lucas...*"

A single tear fell from the tip of Silas' nose, falling the short distance to the ground and crashing to the pavement.

Ragger turned his head and looked away, unable to watch Silas' heart break softly there on the steps.

"*Ava...*"

Ragger could hear Silas' teeth grinding together and heard several teeth crack as he ground down.

Silas stood suddenly and stepped around Ragger and then stomped off, staring at the ground.

<Silas, don't do this to yourself.> Lin said.

<Lin... Please, don't. I don't want to hear anything right now. I don't want reason, or consolation, or sympathy. I should've known he

wasn't dead. I should've gone looking for him. A cracked skull? Of course he wasn't dead. I should've known. Should've known. There's no excusing this.>

<Yes, but ->

<Yes, exactly. Even you admit it. Yes, there's no excusing this.>

<That isn't what I meant, Silas, and you know it!>

<Please, just shut up...>

Lin began to worry for Silas. Several of the images flashing through Silas' mind were self-destructive and troublesome. He'd begun to wonder how he could end his own life, and even despaired at the thought that perhaps he couldn't.

Lin's mind raced, trying to figure out something that could stop the train of thought that he saw in Silas' mind.

<It isn't your fault. Ateneran could have fooled even us. You knew nothing about us, didn't know he wasn't dead and had no reason to believe otherwise.>

Silas shook his head. <I've been shot in the head and survived. I should have known that he wasn't dead! Why shouldn't I have had reason to believe otherwise once I knew how powerful the infected are?>

<Silas, you are Syarantil! You are completely different. And you wanted to believe that your friend was dead.>

<Which makes it my fault. If I'd been less blind, if I had been less eager to believe in my own invincibility, perhaps we wouldn't be in this mess.>

<If we hadn't gotten into this mess, we wouldn't have met Ava,>

Silas laughed. <Yeah, look how that turned out.>

Lin ignored him, pressing on. <And we would not have met Ragger. You would still be travelling from town to town, living off the underside of what remains of your society. Now, you have a purpose, a destiny!>

Silas snorted. <And if I don't want a destiny, don't want a purpose? What if I just want to die and go to Hell? Surely it can't be worse than this.>

<Do you really want to die, Silas? Do you want to kill yourself, and me? Do you wish to leave Ragger alone, your friend, Lucas, living in torment, and Ava in the arms of that monster? You heard what she said to Ragger. She loves you. She is a victim of circumstance. She

returned to him to get away from us, and to give us a chance to escape. Look, he knew exactly what town she was in. I have little doubt that he has some way to track her. I have little doubt that Ragger does as well. And that we probably do too. Likely anyone who has been in contact with her for a long period of time knows how to pick up on her particular brainwave. She left because otherwise, she would have led him to us.>

Silas sat silent for a moment, thinking.

<Yeah. I guess.>

<You know it's the truth. I know you do. Remember Silas... You and I are the same, now. And we always will be. You will never be alone, in any situation. And I will always be there to help you, if I can.>

Silas remained silent, though Lin saw the clear appreciation in his thoughts; he was still too overwhelmed to really feel any other emotion than deep sadness.

Lin felt bad for him. Here stood a being that should have achieved and accomplished absolutely anything he wanted, lived carefree and happy, but instead, he held the weight of a hundred worlds on his shoulders. Lin often wondered how the boy managed to keep from snapping, breaking into insanity. He'd seen exactly how close he had come before, but always, he managed to stave off madness.

Lin reflected on his own life. He was relatively young by his species, really, quite comparable to the age Silas was. But he knew in his hearts, if he were to face the same burden that Silas was forced to carry, he would turn away, shame himself, rather than endure such a curse. He couldn't think of any in his species that he'd ever heard of, besides perhaps Anubis, who would. They were a race of cowards, arrogant and proud.

He felt honored to know such a being, really. He knew Silas didn't think much of himself, but he was wrong. He was greater than any of their species, and he was capable of overcoming any single individual Yahntil.

Something unfamiliar flashed through Silas' thoughts, catching Lin's attention. He caught the thought in Silas' memory banks before it had time to dissipate and examined it quickly.

<Interesting,> he thought as he forwarded the information to Ragger. <Perhaps something may come of it. Who knows?>

Bullard

Silas' hand reached up and touched the necklace once more, his mind made up on a sudden impulse.

He turned and whistled back at Ragger, signaling him it was time to move.

Ragger hopped up and padded after him quickly, a quizzical look on his face as he spoke to Lin.

Silas turned once more and headed down the street, aiming for the church he had just caught sight of.

Adorned with broken colored windows, it was a decent sized cathedral, probably a hundred years old or more. A massive spire dominated the front of the building, soaring several stories upward before transforming into a large golden cross at its pinnacle.

As they approached, he could see two large oak doors at the top of its steps, one wide open, the other hanging from its hinges.

He slowed his walk, becoming cautious and drawing a gun. He hadn't detected any hostiles here, and neither had Ragger, but it didn't hurt to be vigilant.

He walked up the steps slowly, searching back and forth with the barrel of his gun, stretching out tendrils of thought, searching for any foreign brainwaves in the building. Sensing nothing but several starving rats, he withdrew back into his mind and holstered his weapon.

He stepped through the doorway and looked around. The pews were all turned over, bullet holes marked the walls, and several half rotted skeletons lay in rows along them. No plasma marks were anywhere to be seen. Silas frowned, realizing that this had been a battle between men, probably fighting over food and shelter. Little good had it done to anyone. They were all dead. Chances were that they had all been ambushed by the enemy during their own skirmish.

Silas shook his head and strolled up the still clear center aisle, heading for the altar at the front.

Many candles were missing, but of what still remained; Silas pulled a lighter from his pack and lit them before removing his necklace.

Bullard

Ragger sat silently in the doorway, watching Silas.

The stench of rotted flesh in the building was almost overpowering, but Silas didn't even seem to notice, walking slowly to the front of the building, where the altar sat. Looking up, Ragger saw that a giant wooden cross sat above and behind it, a giant man carved from wood hanging from it, a simple rag covering his loins and a bed of thorns adorning his head. Ragger frowned, staring. <Jesus?> They had the face all wrong.

Reaching the small wooden structure, Silas shouldered his pack to the ground and knelt, pulling a small object from within. From where he sat, Ragger couldn't see what it was.

Silas stood quickly and walked along the sides of the altar, touching candles as he passed, lighting them with the object in his hand. Ragger quickly realized what the object was.

Only about ten candles remained on either side of the altar, but Silas lit them all. Stopping before the altar once more, he shoved the lighter in his pocket and lowered his hood. Reaching up to the back of his neck, he fidgeted there for a moment before pulling his necklace and talisman off, holding it aloft the altar and staring at it.

Several seconds passed, and Silas stepped forward, kneeling before the altar and clasping the small cross between his hands and laying his elbows on the table.

His eyes turned upwards towards the caricature of Jesus on the cross and began to speak.

"I don't even believe in you, you know. I think you were a great man, a revolutionary who wanted to make the world a better place. But I don't believe in your father, not anymore. Not after all that I've seen. So I can't believe in you. If I don't believe in God, how can I believe in the Son of God?"

He laughed shortly and shook his head.

"I feel so stupid doing this. But I'm at the end of my rope; I don't know what else to do. I can't do this. I can't do this anymore. Everyone expects me to be something different, but in the end, they all expect me to save them. How can I do that? I'm nothing more than a kid. I've done my best, but what am I against an entire race? I'm just one man, I can't change anything."

He was silent for a moment before continuing. When he spoke, his voice was thick with tears.

"Like I said... I don't even believe that you're real. But my best friend did. He lived and died and swore his life by you. And I guess that will just have to be enough for me."

He choked and sniffed, trying to maintain his composure. Slowly, he bowed his head, laying the bridge of his nose across his clasped hands.

"If anyone is listening... God, Jesus, Allah, Mohammed, Yahweh... I don't know how to do this, but please, hear me. This world... My world, your world, is dying. And everyone expects me to save it. But I can't."

He choked again.

"I can't. Not by myself. And I can't stand another loss, another betrayal, another death. I don't know what to do, where to go. I'm just trying to survive from day to day, and I don't know what to do anymore. I just want to find a place to lie down and die... But I can't. It's just not possible. I know I have to get up tomorrow and do the same thing again, and again, until I'm killed."

Tears overflowed, spilling from his eyes.

"But I don't want to do it. I want to wake up when I open my eyes from this prayer, and find blue skies and green trees and clear water. But I know better. But please... Help me. Guide me. Show me what I have to do. Help us. If you're there... We are your people. Save us."

Several minutes passed in silence, Silas just laying his head into his hands, his fingers slowly rubbing the small silver cross contained there.

Ragger slowly padded up the aisle, staring at Silas, a strange feeling in his hearts.

Reaching Silas' side, he sat quietly, staring up at the cross.

Silas opened his eyes slowly and looked at Ragger, his eyes red.

<They got his appearance wrong, you know.> Ragger remarked.

<He had more of a squat nose, bigger eyebrows and boxier head. And he was dark skinned. This seems to portray him as an attractive white male. He wasn't. He was actually a very plain, dark skinned man. Very average looking. Homely, I believe is the word that he liked to use.>

Silas frowned.

Ragger turned his head to look at Silas, softening his tone.

Bullard

<But I knew him. I walked with him for many years. I was present at his death, and heard of his supposed resurrection, though I had already left the area by that time. He was a great man, regardless. And if he truly is who he claims to be and if there is an afterlife – which I believe there is. I have seen too many unexplainable things in my time, seen too many apparitions, heard too many stories; to believe otherwise – Then he is listening to you, Silas. And he will do as you ask. He was not one to abandon those whom he loved.>

Ragger stood slowly with the last of his words and turned again towards the door, walking out of the building.

Silas breathed deeply, a chill washing over him as he looked back up into the face of the carved Jesus.

He looked back down into his hands and the cross held there.

His eyebrows knit together momentarily and then, he opened his hands and let the cross fall to the altar.

Then he too turned and walked out of the church.

CHAPTER 27 – FROM THE OTHER SIDE

Ava stared sullenly out the membrane window of the freighter, examining the horizon for any sign of movement coming away from the obliterated, burning school. Several times, she started, thinking she had seen something, but forever fell back to her seat in despair. Eventually, the school faded into the distance, only a faint glow and the smear of smoke against the clear morning sky, the sun peeking under the clouds, the only sunlight the Earth ever saw anymore.

To her side, Lucas suddenly spoke. "He's dead, and you know it. They both are. Stop searching."

She scowled, tears welling up in her eyes and she pressed one hand to the clear material, leaning her forehead against it. A single tear transferred from her face and to the window, leaking slowly down and into the cornice. She sniffed and swallowed the lump of agony in her throat.

"I know," she whispered softly. "But I can always hope..."

This time, Lucas laughed. "Hope? Hope? Let me tell you something about hope: It's useless. Only iron hard determination and will, will get you anywhere. And I have the most powerful will and determination this universe has ever seen. I will take this world and crush it, before going onto crush every other world out there as well. With you by my side, dear Ava, I will rule everything this universe has to offer."

Ava had heard it all before, but before, she had heard it differently. It had sounded rich, glorious and magnificent. Now, she could hear the madness in the man's tone, the sheer insanity of what he thought he could accomplish. It was impossible. She turned towards him and examined him, drying her eyes.

He was a beautiful specimen of a man, really. Shoulder length curls of blond hair, bright, shining blue eyes, broad shoulders with a cut figure and a perfect smile; he never failed to take her breath away. He always had a smile on his face, slightly lopsided, eyes crinkled; he rarely looked angry or unfriendly.

But underneath it all lay a monster, she saw that now. She'd been so infatuated before, so in awe of all that he proclaimed himself to be, frightened by the way that the Yahntil forces readily bowed to him, that she had been blinded to it all. She had been dying and he offered her a way out, and she took it. She'd even forgiven him for the sadistic way in which he'd removed her parasite. After all, her Yahntil had been an enemy, conspiring against him. She had been honored, in a sick way, that she had been the tool of the traitor's demise. She had thought she loved him. After all, how lucky was she? She had complete immunity from any danger that could possibly be foreseen.

Had that really only been six weeks ago that she left his side to find the ultimate traitor?

Silas...

His name reverberated through the recesses of her mind, and she remembered the way his arms had wrapped around her, only hours before, the way he made her feel, the safety that enveloped her when she was near him. They were two completely different individuals, Silas and Lucas. Silas' life was a humble one, fraught with danger and moral tests. Lucas' was one of luxury and immoral ease.

Lucas stared back at her readily, unresponsive, merely watching her. She turned away, her skin beginning to crawl.

"What is wrong, Ava?" He asked as she looked back out the window. "Don't you love me anymore? Don't you believe in me?" He sounded genuinely hurt, but she couldn't believe that he actually felt anything anymore. Rage flaring in the pit of her stomach, she turned back to him, snarling.

"You just killed your best friend!" She shouted. "Killed him in cold blood, didn't even give him a chance!"

Fury flashed across the man's features, and Ava suddenly felt frightened. She had seen Lucas' wrath before, and it wasn't something she wanted to experience firsthand. Most of those who did didn't live through it. He stood slowly, towering over her in the confined space, his head brushing the blue-hued ceiling.

"You mean I killed him like he attempted to kill me! He drove that knife into my head while I was still conscious! Killed the parasite and then left me there to die! He could have saved me, found me help! He's the one that made me into what I am today! If you want to hate someone, hate him!"

Disgust filled Ava as she listened to his words and she jumped to her feet as well, jabbing a finger into his chest, no longer caring about what he might do to her.

"You had a *fucking* knife in your head, you idiot. Anyone would have thought you were dead. You showed me your memories. He thought you were dead, howled over your dead body, cradled you to his chest. He loved you, you were his best friend, and it destroyed him to do that. You haven't seen his eyes when he talks about you, or when he touches that god damn necklace of yours that he still wears!"

Lucas sat down hard, staring, wrapping a single hand about his own throat, rubbing. "Th-that he still wears? He has that? After all this time, he still holds onto that old thing?"

Ava stared at him, suddenly feeling sorry for him, but just as quickly pushing the emotion aside. "Yes. And whenever he's having a bad day, his hand is on it constantly. You think he left you to die? He would have rather died there on that pavement, if he thought it would have meant you would have lived."

Lucas said nothing, just rubbing at his neck, remembering.

Ava sat back down, looking out the window once more.

"You love him, don't you?"

She didn't reply, though tears welled up in her eyes once more.

"I asked you a question," he said, this time with more force.

She turned to look at him, staring him in the eyes, tears overflowing and leaking down her dirty features.

"Yes. But that doesn't matter now. You killed him, took from us the only person who still cared about either one of us."

"That's not true," he said. "I care about you."

She turned away again, ignoring him.

"I should have known that nobody could replace Emily..."

Neither one of them spoke for the remainder of the trip to the citadel, both lost in the memory of a good friend who no longer was, one fresh, the other peeling through the layers of his own hatred to find what was left of his humanity.

****

The freighter touched down softly, first dropping off the

massive machines that it carried in its underbelly: stolen human technology, hover tanks, giant walking battle suits, airfoil fighters and lithium armor.

Human governments were far more advanced than they had let their society believe, and many advanced weapons had come out of the woodwork, catching the Yahntil by surprise. They were still learning much about, and sometimes from the Human machinations. For example, they had created Titan Suits, modifications from a human battle suit which allowed Titans resistance to fire and massive firepower. The hover tank technology was priceless, and allowed for the creation of the surface drop freighters, hovering mere feet above the ground, the heavily armored freighters could drop entire squadrons of Snappers and Stalkers directly in the middle of enemy troops.

Ava stared at the ground, watched as a Titan in a suit lifted a damaged tank and set it into an elevator, taking it to a repair station.

Lucas tapped her on the arm and proffered his, gesturing for her to take it.

Reluctantly, she stood and gingerly put her arm through his.

Leading the way, he walked towards the front of the freighter, reaching out his right hand and pressing it into a fleshy looking portion of the hull, opening a door several feet ahead of them, a ramp extending to the ground.

As they walked down the ramp, he spoke softly to her.

"I'm sorry for hitting you. You know how I get sometimes. I shouldn't have done that. I love you, you know."

She snorted softly, though her heart softened. Part of the reason she had fallen for Lucas was that she felt sorry for him. His madness made sense, in some ways. He had lost everything in the course of a few hours. So had everyone else, but he had lost everything in a very personal way. He had watched the love of his life die, run through pools of her blood to try and escape the thing that was killing her. He'd never gotten over the guilt of it. Mere hours after, he himself had lost control of his body and hunted his best friend down against his will, attempted to kill him with his bare hands. In turn, he had almost been murdered by his best friend and then left to die in an alley, and almost had.

He was a product of his environment, she had told herself. She knew it was a lie, now. He chose to be this way, to escape from everything. She had no doubt that he could be like Silas, live like Silas, but he chose the easy life, chose by power, succumbed to the madness she occasionally saw in both their eyes.

Maybe they weren't so different, after all.

As they approached the citadel, her eyes drew upward, as they never failed to do. Massive metal archways lined the entrance to the spaceship, some with conveyor belts covered in metal scraps and parts of machinery, while others sported huge flights of stairs. The stairs were ornately carved, and two giant fountains of fire sat on either side. The size and beauty of the ancient structure never failed to inspire awe in her.

As they entered the building, the air thickened and warmed noticeably, and Ava sneezed, her lungs working to process the different chemicals in the air that Yahntil preferred to breathe.

Statues lined the walls, some new, others crumbling, some defaced. Most of those that were new were of the individual Raknila, their names emblazoned in a fiery glowing sigil upon their chest, but several of those that had been defaced were still vaguely recognizable as the Rakniran, the creators of the Yahntil race. At the end of the hall a mile away, two massive statues – originally Rakniran, now changed to look like Raknila – curved upward towards the ceiling, their arms stretched outward to touch one another's fingers at the pinnacle of the arched ceiling.

This is where they headed, towards the control deck and sleep quarters of Lucas and the ship's Raknila. Only five remained, and Raknila Darkoun had elected to stay at the ship nearest to Chicago, to keep a close eye on things.

Lucas, who was believed to be Ateneran by all other Yahntil, began to speak in his mind to Ava.

<Today is to be a day of days, love. Today, I make my ascension to the throne. We shall see how much of a dragon Darkoun really is.>

He released her arm and quickened his pace, waving behind him for her to follow. The Viral parted before him like a sea, not wanting to get in his way. Next to the Raknila, Lucas was the most feared creature on the ship. Not even Hulkens dared to defy him when he was in a mood. And with good reason.

As he walked, he began to grow, his stride lengthening, arms bulging. His hair fell in clumps to the floor where it vaporized against the floor filtration system. A master of his form, Lucas soon stood at his full form. Similar in form to Silas, large spikes running down his back and sitting upon his knees, he was slightly broader in the shoulders and chest, looking more like a football player in uniform than Silas' thin, whippy look.

Muscles rippled up and down his back and across his legs, which unlike Silas', faced forward. The spikes were absent from his shoulders, but several jutted backwards from his forearms, which allowed him to slice open his enemies from any angle, even when he couldn't reach them with his fearsome claws. Eight eyes opened in a row across his now flat, broad face and he snarled, breaking into a run.

Curious and fearful of what was about to happen, Ava followed suit, chasing after him down the hallway.

****

Lucas burst into the control room, startling several Changelings and Viral forms, who tossed themselves against the wall, pressing themselves there, recognizing the familiar rage in their second in command's eyes.

He veered left, heading for the huge, red ornate door which housed the living quarters of Judge Darkoun. Barreling towards it with one shoulder cocked to the side, he plowed into the door and took it off its hinges, skidding to a stop inside.

Raknila Darkoun stared at him expectantly, towering over him in its raised throne, his massive eyes taking in the scene before him, machinery whirring on his body. Lucas stared back, waiting for his moment.

The Raknila spoke slowly, its deep voice pounding in the skulls of all those who heard it. *<You had better have good reason to have destroyed my door like that, Ateneran. Is there an emergency?>*

Lucas snarled. *<My name is Lucas. Ateneran is dead. And yes, you could say that.>*

He jumped at the Raknila's face, who threw up an arm in sudden surprise.

****

From ahead of her, Ava heard a massive crack and boom, and a dozen Yahntil soldiers came flooding out, fear in their faces.

Bullard

She strained to hear the shouts from changelings that could be vaguely heard, as she was too far to hear the thoughts of those running.

"Ateneran has snapped! Run!"

"Oh shit," She muttered, putting on an extra bit of speed, allowing changes to overcome her as she ran.

* *

Lucas' claws raked against the Raknila's face, whose blood spilled on the floor, thick and viscous, the first time in millennia. Lucas rebounded off the chair and landed back on the ground, staring at the Judge.

The Raknila gurgled in surprise and then stood from its chair, wires snapping and cracking as they tore from the wall behind him, rising to tower at its full height of sixteen feet and leaping down to the floor.

<Show me why you chose the name Darkoun, ancient one.> Lucas taunted. <Can you truly live up to your name?>

Infuriated at the insolence of the commander, Darkoun watched as the little changeling leaped once more. Almost lazily, he swung a hand out, catching the creature in mid-air, batting him away.

Lucas flew through the air, smashing into a wall and electrocuting against a panel of wires before falling to the ground, winded.

Struggling to regain the ability to breathe, skin still crackling with electricity, he jumped to his feet quickly and dodging out of the way as Darkoun rushed him. Behind him, Darkoun crashed into the same wall and panel that Lucas had been smacked into. A scream rent the air as the Judge tasted the bite of the plasma that Lucas had been subjected to.

Turning to look, Lucas saw that the Raknila's claws had become jammed in a tangle of wires and optic fibers, sending a continuous current through him.

Lucas stepped forward to slash at the Judge, but hesitated. If he were to touch the creature, he would receive another shock, and if he did that, it may very well kill him.

The Judge yanked once, twice, and on the third time, yanked free.

Bullard

Hundreds of tiny lesions covered the Raknila's body, where the electricity had arced out of his body and back into the wires and floor. He stumbled, his hearts beating erratically, and fell to the floor. His last sight, rolling over to face his doom, was the massive clawed foot of his second in command plunging towards his face.

Ava skidded into the doorway, standing at her full form, ten feet tall, large claws on each hand, the hints of spikes coming out from her shoulders, a hideous grin of sorts on her twisted face, fangs bared. Slowly, she took in the sight that confronted her.

Lucas turned and looked at her, smiling.

<It's time. I wish to Cocoon with this creature, before its body dies.>

Ava mouthed wordlessly, slowly shrinking as she left Viral form.

Lucas held up a hand, signaling her to not change. <I need your help in dragging this to a secure space, where I may cocoon in peace.>

Sighing, Ava reversed the process.

<Where do you want it?> She asked, grabbing an arm and yanking the body towards the door.

Grabbing the other arm and dragging the body with ease, Lucas replied mysteriously, <I know just the place.>

****

In the underbelly of the ship, near an ancient and abandoned reactor system, Ava watched silently as Lucas pressed his now entirely naked human body against the strung up corpse of the Raknila. This was the perfect place, as nobody but Lucas even seemed to know it existed, and the entire ship was in an uproar, searching for the two of them.

As he gripped the body tightly and closed his eyes, Lucas' skin began to turn grey and exude a thick slime from the top of his head, carrying his hair down and out along the length of his body and the corpse. In response, the dead body also began to create the slime, mingling with Lucas' and slathering their entire form with a clear coat. After they were completely coated, the layer became thicker and thicker, until the two of them lay underneath six to eight inches of clear goo, which then began to rapidly harden, sealing the two of them away. A faint purple sheen could be seen around the two of them, as the fluid inside the hard coat began to work on dissolving the flesh of the creatures contained with it.

As Lucas' drifted to a hibernating sleep, he whispered softly in Ava's mind.

<I do this for us. After this, I will finally take my place among the rulers, and I shall be more powerful than any other before me.>

Ava stood for several minutes, contemplating waiting until they were beyond repair and cutting open the cocoon. And though she knew she should, she couldn't bear the thought of doing so.

She turned and ran, leaving the citadel, leaving the ship. After several hours of searching and hiding, she found an abandoned hover pod near the outskirts of the damaged weaponry yards that was still in working condition.

Mounting and starting it, she took off across the frozen landscape, headed for Chicago.

CHAPTER 28 – THE HERO RETURNS

Five days had passed; the giant orange shields that covered the city of Chicago were just barely visible on the early morning horizon, hiding among the vibrant pink and orange hues of the rising sun. They were less than ten hours away, and could probably reach the city by nightfall.

Silas was still nursing a broken heart and hadn't spoken out loud for the past two days, keeping to himself. Lin had been able to see his thoughts for the first few hours, bitter and cold, but soon Silas threw up an impenetrable wall of thought, refusing to let Lin in and refusing to speak to him unless absolutely necessary.

The last few days had been rough on all three of them. The weight of Ava's betrayal never left, and an ever constant reminder traveled with them: Her absence. She wasn't there anymore, a bubbly presence filling all of them with a tolerable amount of irritation and fun.

Silas sniffed, drawing a look from Ragger.

<Are you alright, Silas? You haven't said much these past few days.>

Silas sighed, looking down at the dog and rubbing him between the ears. *<I'm fine. Just having a hard time, you know? Didn't see that shit coming.>*

<Yes, I know. I didn't either.>

Silence lapsed once more.

After several minutes, Silas sighed. *<Looks like we'll be reaching Chicago soon. How's this going to work?>*

<What do you mean?> Ragger asked.

<How are you going to get in? I can bribe the guard with some of this alcohol.> He held up his pack. *<Will you just walk in with me? I guess that would work.>*

<Oh. I'd almost completely forgotten you'd picked that up. Haven't seen or smelled it. Not a drinker, I take it? And yes, that would

work.>

    Silas scrunched his face and shook his head. <E*h. No, not really. Not anymore, anyway. I used to drink almost daily...>*

    <*There was a time when I loved to drink, actually. When I was in Egypt, I would often have them bring me liquor, spending many languid, drunken hours out in the sun.>*

    Silas grinned, imagining a drunken Ragger staggering around the innards of pyramid, puking in various gold cups. It was the first time he'd smiled in days. A feeling of relief flowed through him as Lin relaxed. Silas' thoughts hadn't exactly been happy the past few days, and the parasite had been subjected to every single one that Silas hadn't actively hidden away. Silas wasn't surprised that Lin was relieved.

    <*Actually, Silas,>* Ragger continued, <*You probably won't be able to bribe your way into this city. It's not just another town filled with despairing, desperate people. There's bound to be more than one guard, more than one filter system. It's not going to be easy at all. I hadn't thought of that until just now.>*

    Silas stopped in his tracks, thinking. Ragger was right.

    "God damnit." He muttered angrily. "I never thought of that. Son of a bitch. All this way and we won't be able to get in?"

    <*Not quite,>* Ragger answered. <*There's always a way into a city. We just have to watch carefully.>*

    Silas frowned. <*What do you mean?>*

    <*I'll show you when we get there.>*

    ****

    <*Something is following us,>* Ragger said, not slowing his walk.

    Silas' eyes widened in surprise and he fought the urge to look around.

    <*Do you know what it is?>*

    <*No... The scent is familiar, but I can't put a finger on it. Figuratively.>*

    Silas smiled again.

    <*It isn't human. It's alien. But I don't believe it to mean us harm; it has been following us for five hours or so, sometime early this morning. It would have attacked by now.>*

    Silas strained to listen, not picking up anything unusual.

<How far from us is it?> He asked.

<About two miles.> Ragger replied

<Two miles? Hot damn. You can hear things from that far away?>

<Oh yes, easily. You can too, in Viral form. You just have to pay attention. I can't tell what size it is from here, just know that it's going in the same general direction.>

<Wow.> Silas whistled.

The jackal looked around, thinking. *<I think that perhaps we should wait here to see what it is. I'm tired, anyway. We've been walking for almost twenty hours. Would you care to rest?>*

Silas shrugged noncommittally. "Sure, I guess."

****

Silas came to his senses slowly, yawning and stretching, stiff from lying on the cold ground. Looking around, he located Ragger laying about fifteen from him, eyes still closed, though Silas knew his stretches were sure to have roused the dog.

Searching around him, Silas picked up a rock and chucked it softly upward twice, catching it. Cocking his arm he prepared to throw —

<Don't you even think about it! I'll bite you right in the ass.>

Ragger sat up slowly, arching his back and yawning, his ears pricking up and swiveling.

<Our little friend is nearby. Emphasis on the little... This creature is very small.>

Sudden irrational hope flitted through Silas, and it must have shown on his face, because Ragger shook his head.

<It isn't her. Even smaller. It could perhaps be a Leaper.>

Any animal smaller than a dog typically became a *Leaper*: Cats, raccoons, rats, they were usually infected by biting, and were directly linked to the Hive Mind.

Sometimes, the ones which were bitten grew enough to become burrowed into, and from there became *Leaper Generals,* able to see into the mind's of other *Leapers* and give them orders directly on the battlefield.

Regardless of size, they made formidable enemies, excellent spies, and were feisty fighters, fond of going for a target's eyes and throat. They were Silas' least favorite foe. His first fight against a *Leaper*, he had underestimated it and nearly lost.

Silas' shoulders tensed at the memory and he sighed in disappointment, letting the rock fall from his limp fingers. He sat up straight and looking around as faint scrabbling noises drifted to him and he frowned. If it was a *Leaper*, it was almost certainly newly infected.

He pulled himself to his knees and stood slowly from there, scanning the horizon, searching among the crumbling buildings. Ragger padded softly to his side and pushed his head into Silas' hand. Silas looked down, and smiled as he saw what Ragger was doing, and he slowly rubbed his fingers up and down along the dog's good ear.

<*I couldn't quite catch where the sound came from,*> Silas said. <*Though I think it came from this direction. Did you get a better bearing on it?*>

Ragger nodded, still pressing his head into Silas' hand. <*No, You're right, it was that way. Oh that feels good.*>

Silas laughed and scratched further down the dog's back, finding comfort in his friend's fur.

<*Do you think it's dangerous? I don't think it's a Leaper, it sounds too large for one and for two, it's awfully clumsy.*>

<*I agree,*> Ragger said, <*But I don't think we can rule out danger. We should go take a look, see what this creature is.*>

<*Alright,*> Silas nodded, relinquishing his fingers from Ragger's fur. <*That works.*>

He strode forward, Ragger close on his heels. He hadn't traveled more than ten feet when the sounds suddenly grew intensity, a shower of rocks falling and a cry of pain suddenly rent the air and tore through their minds.

<*AAAH! 'ELP ME!*>

The sounds had come directly from in front of Silas, and recognizing the voice in disbelief, he quickened his stride, breaking into a run.

After fifty feet or so, he came to a quick stop, staring, unbelieving.

Lying trapped waist high in a pile of rubble lay Saa, tears in his eyes. Blue blood lay in small puddles around the child's hands from where he'd cut himself trying to break his fall.

He looked up at Silas and whimpered, reaching his hands out

to him. <'Elp me!>

Silas closed his eyes and took in huge breath, letting it out slowly.

"Shit."

<Shit indeed,> Ragger emphasized, coming up behind Silas. <We can't haul a child around us, especially not one like that!>

Silas stepped forward towards the child, crouching down and grabbing it by its armpits.

<Still,> he replied. <He's just a kid. We can't leave him out here like this.>

<Never said we could. Just not sure what we're going to do. We can't take him into the city.>

"God damnit!" Silas cursed. "So many problems, one after another. For fate seeming so much in our favor before, it sure seems working against us now."

<You take the bad with the good. I guess in some ways, this somewhat makes things simpler. I can stay outside the walls with Saa.>

Silas had set Saa down and was looking at his hands, making sure they weren't seriously damaged. They seemed to have already healed. The child had inherited all the healing traits of his parent's race, apparently.

<I'm not sure that makes things simpler. What if I get in a spot of trouble in there, and don't have you to back me up?>

<Don't get in trouble.> Ragger replied shortly, looking around.

Silas laughed, scaring Saa momentarily. <Almost a million years old and those are the only sage words you can come up with?>

<Yup.>

Silas laughed again, this time not scaring the child so much.

"What are you doin' out here, little fella?"

Saa stuck a thumb in his mouth and stared at Silas with large, solemn eyes. <I runned. I runned from tuh fire.>

Silas' eyes widened.

<What fire?> he queried.

<Tuh fire, tuh fire that killed 'em all. Dey burneded the city down. Dey all gone... I follered your smell from the river.>

Silas fell over, landing on his backside, running a hand through his hair. The Renegade encampment had fallen. They had to take Saa with them, regardless. He turned his head and looked at Ragger, who shook his head.

<This is an unexpected turn of events. Ateneran must have killed them for sport, I have no doubt he knew they were there long before we were there. Or, perhaps he killed them to keep quiet about your existence. The last thing he wants or needs is an uprising.>

Silas snorted in semi-amusement. <Uprising? I don't think I would really make that much of an impact. There aren't that many Renegades...>

Ragger raised an eyebrow and Silas stared bemusedly at the expression, wondering how it was a possible for a canine to do that.

<Not that many Renegades? On Earth, there are probably three billion living Yahntil. Of them, there are probably five hundred million Renegade, and hundreds of millions more dissenters in the ranks.>

Silas drew a deep breath, picturing the numbers in his mind's eye, saying nothing. Ragger continued.

<If it were known that you lived, you would have close to one third of all the host of the forces of Earth drawn to your side and then perhaps, you could gain the trust of the human power centers and have them to your aid as well. And then if by some small chance you wrest this world from the grasp of the Judges and then there are a hundred thousand other worlds out there, some filled with nothing but entire civilizations of Renegade Soldiers. You would know this yourself, if you would take the time to speak to some of the Renegades we have encountered. You are no different than them now, Silas. It is time to stop acting like you are superior, that they are nothing but scum. You are both members of an intelligent species, and you need to grow up eventually.>

Silas was dumbfounded momentarily. He'd had no idea that the enemy had such trouble in its own ranks. He opened his mouth to speak when he was suddenly poked in the eye. Blinking rapidly, eyes watering, he turned to look back at Saa, who then spoke aloud in a very matter of fact manner: "Feed Me."

Silas stared at the child a moment longer, eyes still watering and then burst out laughing.

"Alright, alright," he said, pushing himself up with his hands. "Let's find you something to eat. There's got to be some sort of animals around here. Ragger, you heard anything else recently? I'm hungry too. We haven't eaten in a few days, now that I think of it."

Bullard

Several hours later Silas sat back, patting his stomach, having just gorged on the small herd of deer they had come across. They'd killed three bucks and let the fawns and does go, for next year's breeding season.

To his right, Ragger continued to gnaw on a large bone, attempting to crack it open and get at the marrow. To his left, Saa did much the same, sucking away at the end of a leg bone, occasionally smacking it on the ground, attempting to create a fracture.

A small fire crackled before them, small strips of meat still hanging from a stick suspended over the top.

The light was growing dimmer, the sun beginning to drop lower in the sky, the air growing chillier by the moment. The clouds began to dissipate as the crystalline atmosphere sparkled and shone above them. Crickets sang their sad song in the rocks around them, hunted by cockroaches.

Silas stared around, taking in the rocky, frosted and barren landscape, and he noted the slight tingle in his skin as his cells repaired the constant radioactivity damage. The government had permitted nuclear bombing of this area once the shields had been proven to be blast proof. Nothing was left of the sprawling suburbs that he'd once known. Here and there stood the burned out remains of a foundation, but truly... Nothing here was left.

Sadness washed across Silas as he suddenly thought of his friends. He knew he shouldn't think of either of them as such, but he couldn't help himself. He'd shared the better part of twelve years with Lucas, and Ava had wormed her way into his heart, even with her betrayal. They were, and always would be, his friends.

He closed his eyes and lay back, placing his arms beneath his head, a now seemingly ancient memory playing out in his mind.

"Howdy! Name's Lucas! What's yer name?"

The little blue eyed boy stared at him, awaiting a response. This would have been fine, but Silas wasn't sure how to respond.

Bullard

People didn't normally come up to him, especially here. They just stared at him sadly as they passed by. He was a bit of a loner by nature, and wasn't sure what this little boy was so interested in him for.

"Well, come on, what's yer name?" He had a slight southern accent, Silas noted. Not local, then.

"Silas," he replied. "Silas Stone."

"Ooh," said the little boy. "Stone, I like that. My las' name is Shorebringer. Hey, if we just went by our initials, we cud be brothers and nobody would know!"

Silas smiled. The boy was silly, but likeable.

"What are you in fer?" Lucas asked him.

Silas turned away, embarrassed, speaking to the wall.

"I'm here for leukemia. Something is wrong with my blood."

"Really? I'm here for the same dern thing."

Silas turned around, semi-excited.

"Really?"

"Yeh, I don't know why everyone makes such a big deal. I cut myself all the time; the blood looks fine tah me. Hey, does yer blood look funny?"

Lucas clambered up onto Silas' hospital bed, peering at him.

Silas pulled away, stuttering. "I-I-I, uh... No, it looks the same as everyone else's, I guess."

"Huh." The boy seemed disappointed. "So does mine. When they told me sometin' was wrong with my blood, I expected it to be green er chunky er sometin'. See here, I don't know what the big deal is. My momma cried when the doctor told 'er. Did yer momma cry?"

Silas shook his head, his eyes wide, slightly frightened by this strange, forward seeming boy.

"Huh. Oh well. Guess my momma is just a wuss. She told me I cud die. I told her I feel fine, 'cause I do! Darnit, I feel crappier since coming here. My hair is even startin' tah fall out!" He made a face, reaching up to touch the bandana that was wrapped around what could be seen of his blonde curls. "It's that shit they stick inta yer veins."

Silas' eyes widened at the curse word and his hands flew to his mouth.

"You shouldn't curse!" He exclaimed, pointing. "You'll get in trouble!"

"Pshaw," Lucas waved his hand. "If yer in here, ya can get away with anything ya like. See? Watch this!"

He suddenly flung his arm out to the side and threw Silas' lunch plate next to the bed off to the side, spattering ranch all across the wall and chicken nuggets skittered across the floor. He screamed, a long high note and then jumped off the bed and then started kicking the wall.

Silas just stared, eyes wide, pulling his knees up to his chest. The sound of running feet quickly sounded, and Lucas suddenly stopped and jumped back up on the bed, becoming quiet.

A nurse ran up quickly, looking flustered and staring at the two boys. "What's going on?" She asked, not unkindly.

Lucas pointed at Silas, whose eyes grew ever wider.

"He done threw his plate, and started screaming and kicking stuff. It's my fault, I'm sorry; I took some of his food. I thought he were finished!"

Silas' mouth opened slightly as he shook his head, staring at the nurse, who frowned at him before busying herself cleaning up the mess that Lucas had made.

"You know, Silas, I understand that you are stressed, but there are better ways to express your emotions! Now, would you like some more lunch? It doesn't look like you ate very much."

Silas nodded slowly, wondering why she wasn't swooping down on him with a belt, like his father would have done.

"Come on Silas, you have a voice, use it! Would you like some more lunch?" The nurse stood, tossing several ranch-sodden napkins onto his tray alongside the dirty nuggets.

"Yes," Silas said, nodding. "But I —"

The nurse didn't wait to hear what he said, sweeping off with the dirty dishes.

Silas turned back to Lucas, staring.

Lucas beamed, perfect little teeth showing. "See? Ya can get away with anything here. Nobody wants to be mean tah a sick kid. Anyway, I have to go! We should hang out again some time! I'm here for the next two weeks. How long you's gonna be here?"

Silas shrugged. "I just got here today, I don't know."

"Huh." Lucas jumped down. "Well, we'll see then, won't we?"

And with that, the little boy ran off.

Bullard

Junior year, Silas and Lucas were considered the two biggest trouble makers in the school. Silas was star of the hockey team; Lucas was quarterback on the football team, and they were both the best that the school district had seen in years. They were indispensable to the school's pride; therefore, they got away with anything they liked.

Lucas was always regarded as the more unruly one, constantly up to mischief and kicks, harassing girls in the hallways, smoking in the entrances, busted by the drug dog every year for pot in his locker. Occasionally, he would seem slightly cruel in his taunting of freshman, and sometimes went too far, even going so far as to pour acetone into one freshman's locker the day before midterm exams, destroying all the notes.

Silas was more reserved, though occasionally went along with Lucas in his destruction. However, he never really got in any more trouble than smoking on school grounds and sleeping with everyone's girlfriend but his own.

Lately though, Lucas had become slightly more tempered by this girl Emily that he had been seeing. He spent all his time with her, weekdays, weekends, and he'd even started going to church, which had become a strain on Silas' and Lucas' friendship.

One day after school, Silas had had enough and confronted Lucas.

"I'm tired of all this ditching me to go hang out with that bitch," Silas shouted, jabbing a finger at Luke.

"Don't call her that," Lucas muttered softly. "She ain't a bitch, and doesn't deserve to be called that."

"I'll call her whatever I damn well please, as long as she's taking my best friend from me. You know what though, you're right, she's not a bitch. She's a sweet girl. Exactly the opposite of the kind of girl that needs to be hanging around with the likes of you! Should I tell her what you used to do to cats? Prolly still do?" He stepped closer, sticking his face in Lucas', their noses almost touching.

Lucas' face reddened and he clenched his fists, saying nothing. Silas saw that he might have crossed a line and quickly lowered his voice, taking a small step back.

"This is bullshit, and you know it. What's so special about her, that you haven't made time to go blow some time off with me in the past four, five months, eh? Got yourself some ass, did you? Can't leave it alone for fear of losing it?"

Lucas looked to the side, towards the door, and Silas stepped in front of him, looking down at the slightly shorter young man. "You aren't leaving till this shit is settled, either through words or me kicking your ass."

"We aren't sleeping together. She's a virgin."

Silas' rolled his eyes and took a step back, throwing his hands up.

"Oh, forgive me. A virgin. Then what the hell is she worth staying with for, huh?"

"I love her, Silas... She makes me a better fella. But, you're right; I shouldn't have been blowing you off."

Silas froze, unsure of what he'd heard.

"You love her?"

"Yes, Silas. I love her. Now please, get out of my way. I promise I'll make some time for us to chill."

Without another word, unsure of what to say, Silas stepped to the side. Stepping around him, Lucas made his way down the hall towards the silhouette of Emily, standing by the doors.

Leaning silently against the lockers, Silas watched them go, angrily lighting a cigarette and chewing at the butt, something like regret filling him.

Maybe he'd been too hard on him. He was sure to be stressed now. Time to keep the animals inside for a few days.

"Fuckin' a."

****

By the time that college rolled around, Lucas had pulled his head out of Emily's ass, and Silas had gotten over his jealousy issues.

He still thought that Emily had turned Luke into a pansy. He had stopped taking part in Silas' mischief, and began going to church of his own accord. He even had started wearing a silver cross.

He told Silas that he had been saved by Emily and Jesus. Silas just shook his head every time he heard it.

Their time spent together had become a time of videogames and homework, nothing nearly as exciting or destructive as they had been doing.

Bullard

In light of all this, having lost his partner in crime, Silas too had mellowed out. He quit smoking and doing drugs in his senior year, graduated with decent grades, started trying dating steadily instead of just whoring around and quit trying to break a record for the most broken bones in a year. It had even been nearly a year since he'd gotten a speeding ticket.

In some ways, he was happy about the turn of events. He wasn't protected by his sports status anymore, and probably could have gotten in some trouble if he hadn't shaped up.

On the other hand, he was pretty bitter about Luke becoming the way he was. He was no longer as outgoing or mischievous and never really wanted to go out and do anything. He had quit drinking, even, something Silas hadn't thought would even happen. Lucas had been a borderline alcoholic. He'd really shaped up and turned his life around. He was nigh on *respectable.*

It irritated Silas to no end.

Lucas was a completely different boy than who Silas had grown up with.

At least, that's what Silas thought, until one day whilst smoking a joint; he had come across a skinned cat by the dumpster behind Lucas' apartment.

When confronted about it, Lucas had paled.

"Please, don't tell Emily. You know my condition, my anger issues. It's just... Please, please don't tell Emily. I hated that cat, I asked her to stop leaving it at my place."

Silas' eyes bugged momentarily. "This is *her* cat?!" He couldn't believe what he was hearing.

Lucas nodded slowly, attempting to explain. "It kept on shitting and pissing on everythin'! I couldn't stand it no more, and I've been feeling so anxious lately, with finals and all that stuff..." He trailed off. Silas knew all about the condition. It was the sickest, most effective of stress relievers for Lucas, killing something.

Silas shook his head, staring disapprovingly. "You killed your girlfriend's cat. I knew she was looking for it, but god damn. It didn't even cross my mind that you were back to doing this shit again. At least tell me you killed it first."

Lucas remained silent, and Silas shook his head once more.

"You're a sick fuck, Luke. I'm telling Emily —"

Lucas took a sharp breath and opened his mouth to protest.

"—unless you promise me you're going to get some help. Some god damn professional help."

Lucas stared, eyes smoldering with anger at having been caught and now cornered.

"Promise me, Luke! Or I'm telling Emily, and then by God, I swear, I'm never talking to you again!"

Lucas' lips tightened and he gave a small nod.

Silas sighed in relief, holding the cat up once more.

"What do you say we find a better place to dump this, eh? We wouldn't want her to find it…"

****

He had known Lucas was mad all along. Slightly insane, maybe even psychotic. He had an issue with his temper, and his past was something Silas had listened to exactly once, and wished he could forget.

But something attracted him to the young man, who not only possessed great charisma, but seemed to be able to get others to bend to his will, cover for him and hide his wrong doings for him. Silas knew the feeling well; he'd been subjected to it for years.

He opened his eyes and was greeted by the familiar grey sky. Morning already.

After that day, their relationship had never quite been as close as it once had been. But, Silas, being the loner at heart that he was, never made another friend that knew him anywhere near quite as well that Luke did.

Once Lucas and Emily moved into together and their first miscarriage, Lucas stopped spending all his waking moments with Emily, having her to come home to, and found more time to spend with Silas.

Things had almost gotten back to where they were when the invasion began. He hadn't seen Lucas since, hadn't even entertained the idea that he was alive. He wanted Lucas to be dead.

And now…

A single tear escaped the cornice of his eye. What had happened?

<Like I said Silas, there was no way you could have known.>

Silas ignored Lin, choosing to instead sit up and survey their surroundings. He must have fallen asleep during his daydreaming, as the sky was growing lighter and lighter, and a light wind was picking up, carrying the smell of stale death on it.

The sound reached Silas at the same time that Ragger sat up, staring around. A low pitched whine, coming from somewhere to the west.

Silas stood and quickly scuffed out the fire, kicking dirt at it and stamping on the smoldering cinders. Grabbing Saa, he threw them both to the ground, covering the child's mouth, staring at Ragger, who had yet to move, except to sniff vigorously at the air.

The whining grew louder, and suddenly Ragger crouched, whispering in his mind.

<Hover Pod!> It sounded like something else was playing around the edges of his thoughts, but he kept it to himself, and Silas didn't ask.

The whining passed them, heading towards the city, but none of them moved. Saa chewed on Silas' hand, trying to get him to let go, but Silas refused. He wouldn't let the child give away their position. Saa began to kick, struggling, not understanding why he was being held in such a manner.

Ragger tried to soothe him mentally. After a few moments, Saa relented, grasping that they were in danger. Silas sighed in relief and loosened his grip around the child, who grunted and rolled over, looking around with Silas.

Several more moments passed, and the whining noise came back towards them. Silas lay his head back on the ground, motioning for Saa to do the same.

As the whining grew closer and closer, another, different noise began to faintly reach his ears.

It was his name.

"Silas! Silas, I can smell you, I know you're there! Just come out... Let's talk!"

The whining grew closer and closer and Silas felt like his heart had stopped. He looked at Ragger, who shrugged.

Making up his mind and taking several deep breaths, Silas launched himself to his feet, scaring Saa, who threw himself to the side and cuddling up to Ragger.

The whining stopped and footsteps could be heard running as Ava made her way towards him.

Bullard

Ava sat on the ground by the new campfire, staring sullenly into the distance. Silas hadn't been as pleased to see her as she had been to see him. As she had run to him, he instead had turned away, tears streaming away and down his face. Silently, she had merely taken his hand in hers, and hugged him, his arms remaining limp at his sides.

He led her back to the fire pit and busied himself recreating the fire, not speaking. He and Ragger simply stared at her, refusing to say a word.

Finally Ava broke the silence.

"I left because I was scared. You don't know what he's like, Lucas."

Silas shook his head, his eyes angry.

"No, not Lucas. Ateneran."

Ava shook her head this time, slowly and sadly. Alarm filled Silas as the next words left her mouth.

"No… Not Ateneran. Ateneran is dead. You killed him, Silas. Lucas is acting of his own accord."

Silas suddenly felt like he was the one that had been punched in the face. He sat down hard, his hand going to his throat, but finding it empty.

"That's impossible," he almost shouted the words, anger coursing through him. "You lie!"

He stood with the last words, pointing in her face, finger trembling. "You lie!" He did shout this time. "You lie, you lie, you lie! You're nothing more than a backstabbing, lying bitch! Why should I believe you?"

"Because he is who made me who I am… There is no alien inside him. A madman, a monster, yes… But no alien. Not one that's living, anyway. And because I love you, Silas. And I love him, which is partially why I did what I did. Please, just believe me."

Silas' muscles sent small tremors racing across the surface of his skin as he fought to control his rage, fought to keep back the monstrous being that strained to burst forth out of him and rip the liar to pieces for all the pain and heartache that she had caused.

He sat down once more, heaving. He couldn't believe the

bullshit that was coming out of her mouth.

He pointed at her again. "How could Ateneran be dead, and Lucas alive? I stabbed him in the brain, there is no way that he survived and the damned little bug didn't."

She stared at him a moment in pity, realizing the heartache she was bringing him. Ragger too, stared at Silas, though he watched more warily, as if he expected Silas to lose his mind at any moment. Secretly, Linnerat fought to control the hateful and alarming thoughts that turreted through Silas' head, keeping back a thin membrane of madness that threatened to overcome the mind in which he resided.

"Do you remember how you stabbed him, Silas? Do you remember where the knife went in? Did it strike you as odd, how perfectly straight the knife went into his skull? Silas, the odds of what happened were… Astronomical. You stabbed him right along the canal of his brain, directly into the parasite at the back of his skull. The parasite died, while Lucas lived, although in a state of extreme shock."

Ragger started suddenly, staring now at Ava, having completely forgotten about Silas.

Silas moved to say something, but Ragger cut him off.

<Are you serious?> He asked, addressing Ava.

"Serious about what?"

<The host lived, while the parasite died, while still completely intact within the mind? Oh my…>

Silas glared at Ragger. "Is that even possible? Is there precedent?"

<Only one and they died long before my time. Silas, this could be the truth. I don't think even Ateneran could have known about something like this to lie to her about. It was something hushed, covered up. I only learned of it because it was still a concern among the Raknila when I rose to power. I'm sure that they have long forgotten it by now. Ateneran is relatively young, only a hundred to a hundred fifty thousand years old. He had only begun to make a name for himself when I left.>

"And?" Silas queried. "What happens?"

<I don't know all the details, however – You do remember me telling you that we are a species made almost completely of neuron tissue?> Silas nodded. <Well, whenever the parasite dies within a host mind, which should trigger a system shutdown within the host, so to ensure something like this doesn't occur… If that does not happen,

then the neuron tissue of the host combines with the dead body of the parasitic organism, imbuing that mind with the memories, personality traits and abilities of that dead organism. Lucas and Ateneran are essentially one, now. And it has probably driven him mad. Completely and utterly insane.>

Ava shook her head before Silas had time to absorb this information, drawing the attention back to her.

"I don't think so. Well, I do think it has driven him insane, but I don't think that he and that creature are the same person. He often fights within himself, withdraws for days at a time, seeming to have some sort of inner struggle between who he was, and who he has become. For example, when I told him that Silas still carries around that silver cross – which appears to not be true anymore – he sat down pretty damn hard, and stuttered to himself that it was impossible that you would still carry it around. Lucas is still in there... But he is fucking psychotic, and all the Viral forces believe him to be Ateneran." She paused, glancing at Ragger.

"Also, Ragger, I don't know if this is good news, considering what I have to say after..."

Dread grew in their stomachs as they listened to her next words intently.

"Lucas managed to kill Judge Darkoun."

<But...?> Ragger asked.

"He's planning to cocoon with the body. I'm not entirely sure what that implicates, but I'm guessing you might."

She hadn't even finished speaking when Ragger sat down, looking dazed.

<That-that can't happen,> he said, sounding frightened. *<He has all the strength and hate of Ateneran, the sheer insanity of a human mind lost to rationality, and now will have the ability to command any Viral force he sees fit. He will be the most powerful, most lethal creature my race has ever generated, in all our long history.>*

****

Several hours disappeared without a word spoken between any of them, Saa and Ava hungrily finishing off the rest of the meat, Ragger and Silas withdrawing into their own thoughts, Linnerat often conversing with both of them, trying to figure out the scope of the things that had been revealed.

Saa took to Ava quickly and began to follow her wherever she went, speaking of his mother, and how he was reminded of her by the way Ava moved, and by how her hair fell. Pangs of sorrow crossed Silas every time the child spoke about such things, but he didn't have time to consider anything else besides what he had been told.

Lucas was alive. Lucas was insane. Lucas had actively decided to try and murder him. In some small portion of Silas' heart, it didn't surprise him. Lucas had always been on the border of evil. With all that had happened to him, perhaps he had simply snapped, even without the alien tissue in his mind.

Perhaps he could be saved? Silas knew it was irrational, but he couldn't help it from crossing his mind.

Lucas chose his path a long time ago. But still, perhaps, he could be made to see the pain he was causing? No. It would never happen.

These sorts of thoughts bouncing through his mind at high speed, Silas grunted and lay back; staring at the now crystal clear skies and cursed the stars he could see. Stuffing his headphones into his ears and tapping on the Selenidi twice, he rolled over and tried to get some sleep.

****

The children followed close behind at his robes, tugging at the hem, begging for him to tell them a story. "Father! Father, please tell us about the Saint? Tell us how he saved you!"

"Ah, not that story again," one of the children complained. "Tell us how he saved Sister Theresa and Josh!"

Josh shook his head. "I don't like that story, I can't remember it and it scares me."

The old man kept walking slowly, a smile pulling at the sides of his mouth, but if one were to look, a deep sadness was in his countenance and pulled at the corners of his ancient eyes.

Reaching the front of the chapel, the old man turned and sat in his chair, staring at the children and playing with his beard. The children stared back in anticipation, quickly plopping themselves down on the floor in front of him.

Bullard

"Very well," Matthias said, "I shall tell you of the first time I saw him, the day he saved my skin from the Mayan."

The one child who had complained earlier let out a small groan, but kept his mouth shut, eyes focused on the old man before him.

Leaning back, Matthias settled into the chair and got comfortable and closed his eyes, beginning to speak.

"It was nearly two and half years past, now, and my bones were not quite so creaky... I had lived in fear for two months... Killed my wife and daughter to save my own skin from what they were becoming. I went from place to place, scavenging what I could, food and ammo, water... All were as precious as the other, then. It was not like here, behind these walls, where we have warmth and food every day, a factory which churns out a thousand bullets a day. Oh no, it was cold, and bitter, and desolate. Weapons were scarce, and something people would kill over. Many days, many hours I sat with the cold barrel of a gun in my mouth, trying to garner the courage to pull the trigger. But I never could. Something would never let me. And then, one fateful day, in a foolish fit of starvation, I had forgone all precautions and simply run into an old grocery store which I could see still had canned goods. Foolish, foolish indeed. But perhaps it was fortune? Who knows?"

****

Matthias crouched in the closet, a container of roasted peanuts clutched to his chest, his fingers scrabbling at it, trying to get it open, his eyes attached to the door, watching as it rattled, heart racing in fear. The top came off and clattered to the floor. The faint smell of mold reached his nose, layered under the smell of the peanuts. The can had been punctured, and the food inside was rotting slowly. His stomach growled, overriding his disgust.

He stuffed as many nuts as he could into his mouth and then stuffed the rest into his pockets, standing and backing away from the door. The growls were growing louder. They could smell him. His heart pounded in terror, his blood rushing in his ears. He had to find a way out.

Flicking on a small flashlight and pointing it upward, he examined the ceiling, several feet above him. It was a standard acoustic tile ceiling, and along the walls were several shelves, filled with cleaning supplies. If he were quick and quiet enough, he could get out of here alive.

Turning the flashlight off, he stuffed it back into his shirt pocket and reached up, grabbing at the shelving. Hauling himself up, remembering his training in the Marines, he stuck a leg across the space and braced it against the opposing shelf. Still chewing, he scuttled up the shelving and pushed up on the ceiling, removing a tile. Layers of dust fell, getting in his eyes and nose.

He sneezed.

A roar issued from across the store and he heard massive, pounding footsteps thundering towards the door. Panicking, he tried to throw himself up in the hole. The tiles around which he threw his weight snapped and crumbled, falling to the ground below, leaving Matthias hanging on a thin metal girder.

The door flew open and into the dark, tearing away from its hinges. A faint purple light shone about the room, and a terrifying grin crossed the monster's face.

Matthias screamed as it snatched his leg and yanked him down and backwards, before releasing him, flinging him backwards into the darkness of the store.

His scream was cut short as he slammed into a metal pole, knocking the wind out of him and sending him crashing to the ground. To his surprise, he couldn't feel anything, other than tightness in his chest, indicating that he couldn't breathe. Some vague part of his mind hoped that his neck had broken and he wouldn't feel anything after that. No such luck. Within a few seconds, pain screamed through him as his breath came whooshing back and his now broken ribcage cried out in agony.

He wheezed into the tile floor, drool and blood pooling out from his mouth. Trying to push himself to all fours, he struggled to crawl away. The claws found his leg once more, and another primal scream of fear erupted from him.

The creature laughed; a deep husky huffing noise from deep in its chest. It whirled him around and threw him once more, this time towards the doors. He hit the metal and glass with his shoulders and continued right on through it, landing on the cold ground. His left shoulder and arm shattered on impact, and he lay moaning in the dirt, his mind overcome with pain. Stepping out of the ruined doors, the

Mayan came up behind him and grabbed him around his middle. He struggled once, flailing his abdomen about and then gave up, lying in the monster's grip like a rag doll.

It laughed once more and turned back towards the store, walking back inside and tossing him against a wall and then began to walk among the aisles, piling things in the middle of the store, a companion coming forth from the darkness with a large cylindrical object and laying it with the materials.

Several minutes passed in what seemed like eternity, Matthias trying to focus on just not moving, because even the beating of his heart felt like agony. His legs had been broken when he had been thrown against the wall. He couldn't feel blood coming from anywhere, which surprised him in a small corner of his mind. With what he had just experienced, he should at least have sustained some cuts.

Instead, he felt like he had been tenderized, like a steak. A chill ran through him, and he focused on what the Mayan had been collecting.

Before him was a giant stone pot, surrounded by various herbs.

A scream began to build in his throat, but never had the chance to escape. He passed out.

****

Gunfire and a loud roar woke him. He attempted to leap up, an impossible feat with a broken arm and two broken legs. Pain ripped through him and he fell onto his good arm, the only results of his sudden jerking movement.

Flashes of light lit up the store, and another roar rent the air as several men went flying, cracking against a wall and moving no more. One of the men hit the ground near Matthias and a pistol slipped from the man's grasp, taunting Matthias.

Holding his breath and biting his cheek, he pushed himself up with his one good arm and shoved, pushing himself into an upright position and reached for the gun, which was barely out of reach. Gritting his teeth, he leaned and fell onto his broken arm, screaming and grabbing at the handle of the gun, his fingers closing around it.

Through the flashes of the light, he could see men with guns running towards the Mayan and its partner, guns blazing. With a hoarse yell, Matthias aimed high and squeezed off several shots before his strength ran out. One of the shots got lucky and hit the one which had grabbed him in one of its eyes and throat. It gurgled and clasped one hand to its throat. The soldiers focused their attention on it, now that it was wounded, opening fire, and it quickly fell.

With a scream of rage that chilled Matthias to the bone, the partner of the creature lowered its head and charged like a bull, flinging soldiers to the side and the rest scattering before it, running back towards the door. Huffing, the Mayan stood in the door and let out roar of defiance, which was cut off suddenly by the sound of a shotgun blast.

The creature stumbled back, the force of the buckshot hitting it in the chest throwing it off balance. It hissed, scraping one hand across its chest, smearing blue all across its hand. Several small bb's fell to the floor, the metal ringing against the ceramic tile. It hissed once more, taking several steps back, staring at something outside the door.

Straining to hear, Matthias could just barely hear the sound of light footsteps, crunching against the light February frost. Another blast rang out, this time catching the beast in the arm, twisting the creature around, loud snaps issuing from its spine as it popped with the force of the blow.

It screamed and took several more steps back before darting left into the darkness.

A young man armed to the teeth stepped through the doorway. He couldn't have been much older than eighteen years old, barely more than a boy; he carried himself like one he had seen far too much war. Matthias' mind flashed back to the first time he'd been out in the killing field for months at a time, and the look that had haunted his features for months afterward.

A shotgun in his hands, several handguns lined his legs, all the way down to his feet. Blades decorated empty spaces here and there, two machetes crossed on his back, several pairs of multicolored brass knuckles lined the first joint of his fingers, and taped to the back of each hand were two double ended knifes, open and honed to a perfect edge. On his head sat a pair of sophisticated looking goggles, no doubt to read heat and see in the dark.

The young man looked around with the goggles for several

seconds, searching for his enemy, finally settling on a particular corner of the store, smiling.

Satisfied, he reached up one hand and pushed the goggles back and then proceeded to walk along the wall, checking each of the damaged men, laying a hand against their neck, his expression alternating between relief and agony as he checked to see who had lived and who had died. Several times, he reached up and touched a small silver amulet around his neck, the design of which, Matthias could not see.

Finally the man reached Matthias, staring down. "Damn," he whispered. "How are you alive, old timer?" He crouched, assessing Matthias' wounds. He reached up and touched one ear. "Six dead, twelve wounded, three unconscious, and one tough old son of a bitch with a fractured skull, clavicle, shattered arm and one broken shinbone. Get the medical team in here, stat."

The young man stared down again, repeating his earlier question. "Like I said, how are you alive, old man?"

Matthias smiled through his pain, replying softly into the tile. "Semper Fi, mother fucker."

The young man laughed, but was cut short by a deafening roar. Looking up in surprise, the young man tried to bring his gun up, but was too late. The massive hand swatted him and the gun went flying in the opposite direction of the young man.

Both hit the ground hard, but the young man was back on his feet and rushing for his gun within an instant, a hand gun drawn and firing. The bullets slammed into the creature's flesh with several sickening thuds, and it stumbled back slightly, stepping on one of Matthias' legs, snapping it below the knee. A fresh howl of pain escaped him. The creature looked down at him, apparently not aware that there had been something alive beneath it.

Matthias raised his good hand with the gun and fired at it point blank, several times, emptying the chamber into its stomach. The creature lurched to the side, clasping a hand to its stomach, yowling and spitting in pain.

The young man ran up to the monster, yanking the trigger of the now recovered shotgun, but nothing happened. He stopped short, pulling the trigger several times again. Jammed.

Muttering, the youth threw the weapon to the side and leaped at the creature, tackling it and knocking it to the ground. A flurry of fists and claws followed, the young man sitting atop the beast, pummeling it with his metal laden hands, the bones cracking under the force of his blows. Every few seconds, he turned his hands at the last moment, causing the knives in his hands to leave deep grooves in the flesh of the creature.

The Mayan threw just as many swings, if not more, though it had a hard time bending its arms in a way to hit at the man. Several hits landed though, tearing through the man's clothing and renting his flesh, causing the youth to snarl ferociously each time.

Reaching under the man, the Mayan made to throw him off if its chest. But right before the shove erupted outward, the man punched downward with his hand open, grabbing at the creature's throat, digging his fingers in deep.

The Mayan had no time to respond, its arms already throwing outward.

The throat of the creature tore away with a wet, sickening sound, like a piece of old, wet moss being torn from the side of a pond.

The man went flying back into the darkness and landing hard on his back, where he lay stunned momentarily, his legs moving weakly.

Something hot and wet hit Matthias in the face, and turning his head back to look at the Mayan, he saw that it had attempted to struggle to its feet, barely making it to its knees, one hand clamped to its throat, copious amounts of blood spewing from between its fingers.

It tried to roar, staring at the fallen youth, but all that came out was a disgusting gurgle of sorts, and after a few moments, it fell to the ground, moaning, blood pooling beneath it. Several seconds later, a man carrying a medi-pak came up and put a full clip into the head of the beast as it lay on the ground. It twitched several times and then lay still.

Overcome with emotion, realizing that he had been saved, Matthias blacked out.

****

The children sat in awe, even the one who hadn't wanted to hear this tale again, their eyes lost in the fantastical images their mind's had conjured at the behest of the story Matthias told.

One child whispered softly, "He was a great man, wasn't he, Father Matthias?"

Matthias nodded, leaning forward and opening his eyes.

"He was indeed a great man. That is why he is our patron saint."

This time, Joshua looked up and spoke. "I remember the day he died."

Matthias looked at Josh in surprise. "Do you?"

"Yes." The little boy stared at him. "I remember Kendall crying. I remember you crying. Everyone was crying."

The little boy seemed lost in thought, his words soft and unsure. But then, with a tone like damnation from God himself, the little boy pointed at him with a frown and said, "You killed him."

Matthias sat back as all the younger children suddenly stared at him aghast, soft whispers moving through them. They hadn't been there, they couldn't understand. The older children remained quiet, however, remembering how they had all felt in that moment, remembering the reasons for which the deed had been committed.

"You killed him? Why did you kill Saint Silas, Father? Was he infected? Oh hush Josh; you don't know what you're talking about. I don't believe it. Father would never kill the Saint. You killed him? Why did you kill him?"

Matthias raised one weary hand, watching with mild interest at how badly it shook. He was getting old.

"I may have indeed killed the Saint. But, children, you must understand. It was under his own orders. We had a certain way we did things, and even he was not immune to them. We waited almost a full twenty five minutes to come out, when he had told us to wait only seven or eight. We did what we had to do, children. But yes. If he were not already dead, then I most likely killed him."

The children stared, unsure of what to say. Then the child, who had complained earlier about the story of choice, spoke up with an accusatory tone.

"So does that mean that ya wud kill us to, if ya had to?"

Matthias shook his head, alarmed at how the conversation was turning.

"No. No I wouldn't Cyrus. I would rather die than kill an innocent person again. I have seen too much death. And there is no such need for that sort of thing here, under the city domes. We are safe in this fortress. And if it came to it, I would die in your stead, if I could."

The children seemed to heave a sigh of relief. Cyrus, however, still stared accusingly at Matthias.

Cyrus was a different child. At only thirteen years old, he was one of the brightest minds Matthias had ever seen.

They had found the youth wandering the streets, half-starved and delirious with dehydration, a few weeks after Silas had passed from them. In the fashion of their group, they had taken the youth in and nursed him back to health.

The boy frightened Matthias. He was ruthless and cruel on occasion, but no one seemed to see it. Blond hair and blue eyes, he had the face of an angel, and knew it. He used it to feign innocence constantly, to get away with things that no other child could. Matthias himself had succumbed to the youth's wiles several times before. He did not believe the boy to be evil, but he was someone to be watched.

Matthias sighed, leaning even further back in his chair, letting the solid wood relieve the pressure in his spine. He waved his hand.

"That is a story for another day, children. One of sadness. If you truly wish to know the tale, please, go home and ask your parents. I do not have the strength to tell you tonight."

The children slowly filtered away, some still staring at Matthias with sadness and suspicion. Cyrus was the last to wander off, though his eyes occasionally turned back to Matthias and lingered upon him.

****

"Alright, so what's the plan?" Ava asked, crouching down around their group. Silas glared at her and she fell silent.

Ragger answered her question promptly, ignoring the tension in the air.

<Silas and I are going to enter the city via the waste entrance we observed yesterday morning. Once every six hours, a team of thirty or forty exit the compound and move through the weapon-deflector shield to dump what appears to massive amounts of food waste, along with barrels of raw sewage.>

Ava made a face.

Bullard

<During this time, only two guards are left at the door. The disposal team takes the waste about half a mile outside the city limits, presumably the furthest, safest distance they can manage to dump waste. We have about a seven minute window before they return. Chances are that they run a small patrol as well. There is a lot of Hive activity in this region, probably due to the ship-citadel near here.> He glanced at Ava, who looked away.

<Ava and Saa will stay here, out of sight and out of harm's way. If anything befalls us, it is your charge to take care of Saa, Ava. You know how to find Renegades. If we do not return in forty eight hours, then leave this place. You can still be instrumental in turning the tide of this war. Your brain has such potential; I haven't even begun to tell you my plans for you.>

Silas looked at the dog strangely, but said nothing, letting the beast continue.

<We will at three o clock today, when they take out their scheduled dumping.>

****

Silas stared intently, watching the men as they rounded the corner. As soon as their backs had disappeared, he and Ragger bolted from their hiding spot, tearing across the open space between them and the outer walls of the city.

<Hopefully they haven't modified this shield to shock parasitic organisms.> Linnerat said suddenly, almost startling Silas. The parasite had been silent for several days.

Silas' eyes widened. "They can do that?>

<Oh yes. It's our tech, remember? We used that feature to keep unauthorized personnel out of particular areas.>

<Why the hell didn't you say something before?>

<Not sure. Didn't think of it, I guess. You know how you suddenly think of all the things that could go wrong before you do something stupid.>

<Guess we'll find out. Brace yourself!>

Silas tensed all his muscles as he passed through the orange field. It was a strange feeling, like passing through a thin wall of Jell-O. At first, he met resistance, but within milliseconds, the field gave way to his organic tissue and he continued running.

Bullard

Ragger passed through just as easily, and no tingle passed through Silas' spine, indicating that it indeed had not been modified.

"Hey! Hey you! Stop!" The guards started running towards them, guns raised.

Silas threw his hands up and came to a stop, watching the guards as they drew near, and Ragger came to a stop and sat at Silas' side, panting.

They approached cautiously, guns at the ready. One of them stayed behind, looking around while the other continued forward, gun pointed at Silas' chest.

Silas peered at the guns, noting that they were military grade plasma tech. Not something seen very often. He'd heard that Chicago had been made the new capital, though, so perhaps not so rare in this area.

Reaching Silas and stepping forward, the guard prodded him with the gun. Ragger growled softly and the guard glanced down, staring. Ragger bared his teeth momentarily and then relaxed, staring at the guard.

The guard frowned and then looked back at Silas, jabbing the gun at him once more, but not quite touching his skin this time. Silas struggled to hide a grin. These men would run headlong into battle with an alien creature from outer space that would surely kill them, but they were still apprehensive of getting bit by a dog.

"Who are you? Where did you come from? What do you want?" As he spoke, he pulled a flashlight from a pocket and shined it in Silas' eyes.

Silas shook his head. "I don't want any trouble sir, that's for sure. This is the only entrance me n' Ragger here could find round this side of the city. We're tired and hungry, and kept hearing things further out, and didn't want to venture too far from our camp. We just want safe passage, sir. Please don't shoot me. I have an entire bag full of liquor, if you'll just let me go."

The guard thought about what Silas had said for a second and then nodded, seeming to accept it. He lowered the gun and clicked off the flashlight. "Can't be too careful. You could be one of them changelings. Dint mean to scare ya kid. And I don't drink, son, so that bribe wouldn't have worked anyway. Keaton will be pleased as punch to hear though."

Silas lowered his hands and rested them on his thighs,

nodding. "I understand. Trust me, I understand. Me n' Ragger here know what you're talkin' about. Don't we boy?" He rubbed Ragger's ears.

The guard glanced down at Ragger once more and then back up at Silas, smiling. "He friendly? Been awhile since I seen a dog!"

"Oh yeah!" Silas said. "He just thought you were threatening me. He figured out that you weren't though, else you'd be dead." He smiled and the guard's smile faltered as he stared at Silas. After a few seconds he seemed to overcome an internal struggle of sorts and turned, crouching down and looking Ragger in the face.

"Well, he sure is a purty one, ain't he?" He reached out and rubbed Ragger on his side. "What kinda dog is he? Looks like... Part German Shep and... Whippet, maybe?"

"You sure know your dogs, sir!" Silas replied.

The guard stood and stuck his hand out. "Names Nicholas, son. My friends call me Nick." He winked. "What's yer name?"

"Silas."

"Silas, eh? Like after Saint Silas?"

"Who?"

"Never mind. Course you ain't named after him. You'd still be in diapers." The guard laughed. He turned and waved to the other guard, yelling. "Hey Keaton! Get yer ass over here! This kid's alright, Says his name is Silas."

The guard jogged the thirty feet to them, and as he approached, a stir of recognition formed in Silas' stomach. It appeared that the guard began to recognize Silas as well, his jog slowing to a very slow walk as he came closer. Silas stared into the face of his friend, who was mouthing silently, unsure of what was happening.

"S-silas? Is that really you?" Keaton asked.

Nick looked back and forth between the two of them, confused. "Y'all know each other?"

Keaton ignored him, dropping his gun and reaching for Silas' shirt, grasping it up in his hands and yanking Silas towards him in a hug.

Nicholas was completely lost by this point.

Keaton pulled away from Silas and stared at him. "By God, it's really you." He peered into his face, staring intently. "You haven't aged a day. Hell, you look better than I remember!"

Silas shrugged. "Good livin' out here in the dirt, I guess."

Keaton laughed, tears forming in the corners of his eyes. "Really you."

"Alright, what the plumb hell is goin' on here?" Nick demanded.

Keaton turned to Nick and smiled. "It's him, Nick. It's the saint. It's Silas."

This time, it was Nick's turn to stare at Silas in awe. He fell to his knees and apologized profusely at Silas' feet.

"I am so sorry. So so so sorry. I hope I didn't bruise ya or nothin' with my gun."

Silas took a step back, staring, scrunching his face up in a confused look.

"What the hell is going on here? What's this saint business?"

Keaton looked back at him, eyes shining. "Come on. I'll show you. We're all here. You're our most famous resident here in the city, sir. The group you brought together? Well, we kept goin' sir, just like you would have wanted. And we kept doin' like you would have done sir, saving those that we could, searching out any survivors. By the time we reached Chicago, we had over six hundred people. And each and every one of them knows your name, know all your adventures by heart, how you saved all of us."

Silas swallowed. He was a celebrity? So much for low profile. He certainly never thought that his group would come back to bite him in the ass, but there it was.

Lin laughed in the back of his mind. <So much for low profile, indeed.>

"Come on!" Keaton exclaimed. "We have to tell the others!"

CHAPTER 29 — REUNION

Keaton left Nick at the gate to take Silas into the city, saying that he was sure command would forgive him for finding and bringing in a resource like Silas. "Patrols haven't reported any movements in the past two months anyway," he explained. "They're too busy in that damned ship of theirs. Cleaned up real nice from the rock that it was when it landed, or so I heard. Got all the architects in a tizzy a few weeks ago when we got phototelligence back. Pretty cool lookin' I guess."

Silas stared as they walked through the streets, marveling. The dome cleared a good sixty stories, so almost all the buildings in the inner city still rose as tall as they ever had, the tops of some simply sheared off by the nuclear blasts in the area. The dome kept out the radiation, so people could even live right underneath where the dome hadn't protected.

There were vendors in the street selling fruit and trinkets and all manner of electronics and weaponry. Silas was suddenly reminded of the Disney movie Aladdin, when the princess first walked the streets, but in a much more modern way.

There was color and life everywhere, children played in the streets, playing dodge ball and riding bikes and skateboards. The orange color of the dome filtered the light and made it almost seem like yellow sunlight basking everything, and the air was thick and warm. He shivered, realizing for the first time how cold he'd been for the past year. Not even the buildings in St. Louis had been very well heated, kept warm mostly by the body heat of the people living in them, and the machinery they operated.

His senses threatened to overwhelm him, and every few seconds he had to resist the urge to duck when a sudden noise rang out behind him, or to throw out a defensive punch whenever someone bumped into him or brushed against his arms. Lin kept his jerks in check, and every few moments, Ragger would comment from behind him, reassuring him that nothing was wrong.

Here and there, there were even working cars. He could hear Keaton talking to him in the background, but he simply couldn't focus. He hadn't ever imagined that there was anywhere left like this.

Looking down at his hands, Silas suddenly realized that he was absolutely filthy. In the orange light, he could suddenly see that his hands were coated in thick dirt, smudges covered every inch of visible skin. Passing by a store with a glass paned front, he looked at his face's reflection and saw that it too, was covered in dirt, his long hair was twisted and tangled and on the verge of falling into his eyes. He was amazed that Keaton had even recognized him.

As they walked, the people gradually began to thin out, and looking around, Silas saw that they were entering a residential area of sorts, with people sitting in doorways and eating their lunches, staring at him and whispering as he passed by.

"Don't mind them," Keaton suddenly elbowed Silas and he jumped. "We just don't get newbies around too much these days. Used to get them all the time... Now, though... You're the first soul we've seen in months, to tell the truth."

"Oh. That's kinda sad."

"Yeah, a little... Still, we have over two hundred thousand here."

"Only two hundred thousand?" Silas whispered "Chicago used to be four million..."

Keaton stopped short in his tracks for a second and then continued walking. "Yeah." He said shortly. "I guess when you put it like that, it sucks. But we're proud of it."

Keaton suddenly stopped and turned to look at Silas.

"Where have you been? How did you escape that blast?"

Silas sighed. "Please don't ask that."

Ragger spoke up from behind him. <You're *going to have to tell them eventually, Silas. Why not do it in front of everyone that trusts you?*>

<Are you nuts?! We are in the stronghold of what is left of humanity. They would kill me on sight.>

<Really?> Ragger asked. <Because he's been burning with that question since he first saw you, and you merely asked him not to ask that question... And he stopped. These people revere you, Silas. You are their savior, their shining beacon of hope. They will accept anything

*you tell them. So tell them the truth, instead of feeding a lie to the
people who love you the most.>*

Silas glanced at Keaton, who had indeed pursed his lips and
not asked again, but had begun rocking back and forth on the heels of
his feet.

Silas sighed once more and turned back to the man. "I will tell
everyone at the same time, Keaton. I think you all deserve to know the
truth."

Keaton glanced at him strangely, but blew out a long breath of
relief. "Alright," he said. "Then prepare yourself... We're here." He
gestured to the building behind Silas. Silas turned sharply and looked
at where Keaton had pointed. Two massive oak doors sat behind him,
the entrance to a massive stone church. Eyes traveling upward, Silas
could see that the top layers of the steeple had been sheared away by
the dome. It was an impressive building. But Silas didn't understand
why his group would be in a church.

"Why a church?" he asked as they walked up the steps.

"It's the biggest place for us. We are the biggest consolidated
group in the city besides the government. In fact, the government
consults with us before making any decisions... Matthias is on the
Head of the Council."

Silas laughed. "That old fart is still kicking?"

"Oh yeah. He leads us, now."

A sudden thought hit Silas and he stopped cold in his tracks,
teetering on the edge of a step. Ragger ran into the back of his knees
and a surge of irritation passed through the connection.

"What about... Is... Kendall?"

At this, Kendall sighed, and a ball of fear knotted in Silas'
stomach. "Oh, he's around. Him and your father."

Silas heart jumped, but he didn't ask, as he sensed Keaton
didn't want to talk about it.

Reaching the doors, Keaton pushed open the doors with both
hands, swinging them wide open.

Several people stared, hands shielding their eyes from the
light.

He turned to Silas and gestured him inside.

"Welcome home, Silas." His last word, his name, echoed up
the aisles and back to the door, and people turned to stare in disbelief.

Silas stepped past him, his eyes having found a hundred faces of those who meant a great deal to him. Hundreds of moments flashed before his eyes, memories attached to each face, from the moment they met, to the moment they passed from one another's lives. Later, hundreds of years down the road, as he visited the graves of each of them, this moment too, would appear before his eyes. The moment they reunited.

He walked slowly up the aisle, arms hanging loose at his sides, emotion coursing through him. Some people sat down where they stood, others cried. Children pointed and stared, and several ran up to him and touched him, while others pulled short, afraid that if they were to touch him, he would vanish forever.

After a long minute, Silas finally reached the front of the church, where an old man with a long white beard sat sleeping in a chair with a wool blanket pulled around him. Crouching down, Silas stared at the man for a long moment, the man who had been more like a father to him than his real father ever had been.

Sensing someone watching him, the old battle coon opened his eyes and smiled.

"Oh no… I'm dreaming again."

Silas smiled and shook his head. "No old man. Not a dream. I'm really here."

Matthias shook his head. "No, you're dead. I killed you. I remember."

"I survived, old man."

"No, no you didn't. Kendall saw your body. Saw it go out the back. Don't tease me again. I'm just going to wake up and find nothing here again."

He closed his eyes and pulled the blanket closer to him. "Just a dream. Just a dream."

Silas shook his head and laughed. "Matthias. Matthias. You stubborn old fart."

"Go away, dream." Matthias muttered.

"Matthias Mitchell Morrison."

"Just a dream, just a dream, just a dream…"

Silas sighed and smacked Matthias in the forehead with his fingertips.

Matthias eyes flew open, rather indignantly. "Who the hell did that? Who hit me? I'll kill 'em, I'll I'll I'll…" His voice trailed off, as he stared.

Bullard

"I did, old man!" Silas stood.

Slowly, Matthias rose from his chair, the blanket falling to the floor. He peered into Silas' face for several moments before sitting back down in his chair, hard.

"And now I'm seeing him when I'm awake... Dear Lord, I've finally gone senile."

Silas threw his head back and laughed, the deep booming noise filling the entire church. Matthias looked up with a strange look on his face.

"It's really you, isn't it?"

Crouching down once more, Silas reached out a hand and lay it on Matthias' knee before nodding.

A smile cracked across Matthias' face.

"I knew you'd find us."

Bullard

EPILOGUE

Bullard

Darkness. Head pounding. Constriction. Claustrophobia. Panic. Must get out!

I kicked, lashing my legs out, but for a moment, they felt so strange. Awkward. Too long.

Silas! I tried to yell, but only a muffled gurgle escaped my throat as a viscous slimed slid between my... pointed teeth? Something wasn't right. Images swam in my mind, memories that weren't my own.

Murder. Blood. Monsters. Silas, with a knife, Emily staring after me as I ran, terror and betrayal in her eyes. I pushed them away.

Emily. Where was Emily? Where was Silas? Why weren't they helping me? Bet he did this to me. I'd beat his overgrown ass when I got out of this mess.

I thrust my arms forward as hard as I could, moving through the slime that covered me. To my horror, they met resistance, like some sort of thick rubber, but it lasted only for a moment. Within seconds, my hands cooled as they touched air.

Without warning, I tumbled to the ground, landing on my head and back, knocking the wind from me. I lay there several moments, staring upward, at some disgustingly grisly cocoon which I seemed to have slid out of. I closed my eyes, but then realizing something, I opened them once more. My peripheral vision was far too wide. I shook my head and blinked a few times, but it was no use.

I could see out of the sides of my head. And yet another thing caught my attention and then – it was pitch black, but I could still see perfectly well, though everything was in shades of gray and blue.

What the fuck I tried to mutter, but only a harsh growl escaped my mouth.

Panic began to set in once more as I sat up and viewed my body. I was covered in slime from head to toe, but that did nothing to hide the awesome sight that lay before me. My skin had turned a deep black, and rippling muscle could be seen everywhere, twitching and twisting beneath the ebony flesh.

My legs ended in two massively clawed feet, with seven toes a piece, looking to my sides and raising my arms, I could see that I had grown two extra elbows, allowing my arms to twist any way they wished, in ways never seen before. My hands, too, were massive, the size of car tires. Seven clawed fingers, the length of a full-grown man's arms, extended and closed at my will.

Bullard

My eyes grew wide, and I gingerly raised my massive hands to my face. From the length of my legs, and the distance my hands had to go from the floor to my face, I must have been over sixteen feet tall.

With apprehension, I probed my clawed fingertips about my face. To my horror, I found nothing familiar. A flattened face, with slits for nostrils, I had six eyes, a high, broad forehead, and no ears... Just two thin membranes on the sides of my skull. Razor sharp teeth filled my mouth. All characteristics of a super predator. A predator not of this world, something whispered to me.

Clutching my hands to my temples, I shook my head in denial. "Noooo Noooo Noooo," I uttered, but the words coming from my mouth sounded deep, gravelly and just... evil.

I focused on a mirror in my mind, remembering my own, perfect image.

I'm Lucas Shorebringer, I told myself. I am Lucas Shorebringer! Six foot two, one hundred eighty pounds, star quarter back, loving fiancé, soon to be father!

It became a mantra in my skull, repeating over and over, until suddenly, I realized I could no longer feel claws against the top of my skull. That there was soft, curled hair laying against my fingers, and falling into my eyes.

Pulling my hands from my head, I opened my eyes, and all was darkness. I could still see some, though not nearly as well as I could before.

I ran my hands over my face, finding all the familiar features... But not quite. My broken nose was straight once more. The scar on my chin was missing as well. Something about that irked me, but my relief at finding two eyes and two ears more than overwhelmed that inkling of irritation.

Running my hands over my body, I realized that I was naked... And had far more muscle than I was accustomed to. I was taller, also.

Something like fear began to set in. What had happened? Had I finally lost it, like Silas had always said he might?

Silas. Where was he? I began to worry. We were never apart long. Whatever must have happened to me must have happened to him. I closed my eyes, rubbing my temples and thinking. What was the last thing I remember?

Silas came to my mind's eye once more. Dirty and streaked with blood, he held a large knife over me, tears in his eyes as he shook his head. His eyes pled with me, but I could not tell what ransom they asked for...

Without warning, my hand entered the picture, and struck a rock against Silas' skull. A tooth hit me in the face and then he leapt atop me once more, driving the knife towards me... and then darkness.

I opened my eyes. Confused. Why would...

Another memory came flooding back. Walls of water. Fire. The whole world, crumbling, crumbling. Blood, everywhere. Bodies, everywhere. Pain, everywhere. Overwhelming pain. It's on me. It's on my back, oh please, God get it off.

I fell to the side; pain building in my head as memory after memory came rushing back.

Emily I screamed! Emily! But then she turned, and her eyes were as gold, and fear knew me.

Running, tripping. Pain. Agony. Darkness

Silas! Help me!

Moving. Can't control my limbs. Chasing Silas. Don't hurt him, don't hurt him. *I will feed on his flesh.*

Silas. Knife. Pain. Agony. Darkness once more.

Waking amongst rubble. Ripping a knife from my skull. Darkness. Madness. Memories that weren't mine. Thousands of years of evil. Torment. Hatred.

They respect me. I can control them. Death. Murder. Torment. Pleasure.

A young woman. Cancer? The key. Kill her? No. Save her. Emily. Emily.

Roach? No, Ava. Silas. Syarantil? How *ironic*. Betrayal. I will feed on his flesh.

I knew not how long I lay there. But when I opened my eyes next, I knew. I knew the horrific truth.

Everyone I knew and loved was dead, or had betrayed me. Left me. Run from me. Been torn to shreds by me.

I would have revenge. I would have justice. Nothing could stop me anymore. Not now. Not with this body. Not with Syarantil dead. Not with Silas' corpse burning in that school.

Laughter echoed about the room as I looked down at my arm and beheld the changes coming over it. The laughter decreased in pitch as my bones snapped and rearranged, until only a deep, grating boom surrounded me, escaping between my serrated teeth.

Bullard

I stood at my full height, and peered down at my new body, appreciatively this time. And now, I could feel them, seething at the edges of my thoughts. It had worked. I was Raknila, and they would bow before me.

Was I insane? Perhaps. But that was of no consequence anymore.

In my human life, they knew me as Lucas Shorebringer. In my reign as God, they will know me only as *fear*.

I AM METUS, AND I WILL CLEANSE THIS WORLD.

END OF BOOK ONE
TO BE CONTINUED...

Bullard

Bullard

A round of special thank you's are in order:

Crystal Barr – Thanks for listening to my endless droning, and not strangling me for frequently interrupting our relationship for my relationship with my characters!

Hunter, my son – Thank you, for giving me the realization of responsibility and the scope of vision to imagine a world where heroes are born of necessity, to protect the ones they love. This one's for you.

Jake David – I aspire to write like you one day, even if you are a crazy son of a bitch. I look forward to seeing a compilation of your poetry. Truth be told, WMHF began as an attempt to outshine you. In that regard, I still feel that I've failed.

Melina Dina – Thank you for your invaluable grammar tips over the past two years! If anyone finds anything wrong, I'll point at you. Fair warning. After all, I failed English three times. There's a reason for that!

Kathryn Coates – Thank you, m'dear, for believing in my book, even when I didn't.

Jennifer Wendorf – You pointed out possibilities I hadn't thought of in the slightest. I'm rather upset our professional relationship was brought to such an abrupt halt. Hopefully everything resolves for you, as I'm looking forward to working with you on Book Two.

And last but not least – The fans of www.facebook.com/yo.dumbass Thank you so much for the years of support and entertainment. Much love to you all.

11859956R00176

Made in the USA
Charleston, SC
26 March 2012